Elizabeth Falcone ~~~~~~~~~~~~~~~~~ but lived for many years in East Africa. She now lives in Gloucestershire, and spends part of each year in the South of France.

Also by Elizabeth Falconer

THE GOLDEN YEAR

and published by Black Swan

The Love of Women

Elizabeth Falconer

BLACK SWAN

THE LOVE OF WOMEN
A BLACK SWAN BOOK : 0 552 99623 8

First publication in Great Britain

PRINTING HISTORY
Black Swan edition published 1996

Set in 11pt Linotype Melior by Kestrel Data, Exeter, Devon.

Black Swan Books are published by Transworld Publishers Ltd,
61–63 Uxbridge Road, London W5 5SA,
in Australia by Transworld Publishers (Australia) Pty Ltd,
15–25 Helles Avenue, Moorebank, NSW 2170
and in New Zealand by Transworld Publishers (NZ) Ltd,
3 William Pickering Drive, Albany, Auckland.

Reproduced, printed and bound in Great Britain by
Cox & Wyman Ltd, Reading, Berks.

To JF, NF, TF and Gabrieli

Alas! the love of women! it is known
To be a lovely and a fearful thing!

Byron, *Don Juan*

Chapter One

Nelly Turnbull walked briskly down the corridor of Ward Nine towards her office, trying to avoid catching anyone's eye and hoping to get a few minutes' peace and quiet to write up her morning's notes.

'Dr Turnbull?' Nelly turned and waited for the staff nurse to catch up with her. 'Could I have a word?'

'Of course,' said Nelly, 'come into my office.' She led the way into the small side-room and sat down at the desk, indicating the other seat. 'How can I help you?'

'It's Mr French, Doctor. I'm sorry to have to say this, but he's sexually harassing me.'

Nelly looked at the younger woman's plain, spotty face and lank greasy hair which protruded from the back of her cap in an untidy and rather meagre pony-tail, and suppressed the desire to laugh. Instead, she compressed her lips and frowned. 'What form does the harassment take?' she asked seriously.

'He pinches my behind when we're doing his rounds. It's not just me, Doctor. He does it to all the girls.'

'How stupid of him. Anything else?'

'Well, he says hands up all those not using Right Guard.'

'You mean hands down.'

'Do I? Whatever does he mean? Is it a contraceptive or something?' The staff nurse looked at Nelly, her face pink and shiny with embarrassment.

Oh dear, thought Nelly, poor girl, she does have a problem, you can't not notice it. She hesitated, then chickened out. 'I'll speak to Mr French,' she said. 'If you have any more trouble from him, let me know, of course.'

'Thank you, Doctor. I hope you don't think I'm making a silly fuss?'

'Of course not. You were quite right to report it. Don't worry, I'll sort him out.'

'Thank you.' The staff nurse stood up. 'I'd better get back on the ward.' She left the room, and Nelly opened her clip-board and wrote up her morning's notes without further interruptions. When she had finished she looked at her watch: twenty past one. I must get something to eat, she thought. On her way out, she paused at the nurses' station. 'Bleep me if I'm needed,' she said. 'I'll be in the canteen.'

In the canteen she got a cheese roll and a plastic cup of coffee and sat down at the nearest table. Her feet throbbed from pounding up and down the long corridors all morning, and she eased off her shoes under the table, flexing her toes. I hope my feet don't smell like Staff's armpits, she thought. Poor girl, what a rotten thing to suffer from, and not be aware of it.

'Are you keeping this seat for anyone?'

Nelly looked up at the tall, dark-haired consultant standing beside her and smiled. 'Andrew, the very man! Do sit down, I want a word with you.'

'Really?' Andrew French put his coffee on the table and sat down. 'How very delightful. Can it be that your resistance is crumbling at last?'

Hester Rodzianko came out of the *boulangerie*, her last port of call for her evening's shopping, and walked down the Rue St-Louis-en-l'Ile until she reached the little side street in which she lived. It had been a mild and tranquil day in late March and she could hear the bold song of a blackbird in a garden hidden behind a high, ivy-clad wall. She lifted her face to the evening sky and inhaled the fresh green smell of spring, cheered by the thought of the approaching summer. In a few minutes she arrived at a gated archway, originally the carriage entrance to a beautiful seventeenth-century mansion. Pushing open one of the massive carved wooden doors she went in, letting it swing shut behind her. A narrow, grey-painted door presented a secretive and unassertive face on the left-hand side of the *porte-cochère*. Hester set down her basket of shopping and after searching in her deep bag for the heavy iron key, unlocked the door.

The worn stone staircase that led up to her apartment rose steeply before her, and she put the basket carefully on the fourth step before standing on the bottom step and locking the door behind her. Turning round in the narrow stairwell, she picked up the basket and her bag in one hand and grasping the handrail of the delicate wrought-iron banisters with the other, she climbed the twisting stair to the small landing above. The walls of this space, only a little more than two metres high were limewashed a flaky, pale cream with darker patches where the damp of the stone walls was breaking through. The timbers of the low-beamed ceiling were painted white, though the colour had yellowed with age. A tiny leaded window stood open and let in light and air. The landing gave onto a dark narrow corridor with five panelled doors painted the same soft pale-grey as the entrance, with two doors to the right, two to the left and one in the middle, facing the top of the stairs. She took off her jacket and hung it on a hook, then pushed open the middle door and entered her kitchen.

Hester's apartment was, in fact, the former coachman's quarters of the mansion and occupied the *entresol*, a low storey sandwiched between the ground floor and the first floor. None of the rooms was higher than two metres twenty and a tall person had to duck to avoid colliding with the massive chamfered beams that stretched the full width of the apartment, supporting closely packed rough joists of irregular shape and thickness. In the kitchen, the beams retained their natural oak colour, a silvery grey-brown, which made the ceiling seem lower than it really was, but equally lent an atmosphere of warmth to the room.

She put down her basket on the round fruitwood table standing in the centre of the red-tiled floor, and unpacked her supper. She took the waxed paper wrapping off a pork chop and laid it on a green ivy leaf embossed plate, ground some black pepper and a trickle of olive oil over it, and covered the dish with a white net dome which she took from a meat hook hanging from a steel pole above her head. Pots and pans, bunches of dusty dried flowers, lavender and branches of bay, several willow baskets and a colander shared the pole, suspended above the sink and work-top and stretching along the length of one wall. She put the little pot of *crème fraîche* into the fridge, together with a small packet of butter. The wedge of Camembert she left on a plate on the table, then washed some salad leaves and dried them in a tea-cloth. She piled them into a Chinese bowl, glazed blueish-white, with a hungry-looking blue fish painted inside, and put it in the fridge to keep crisp. She washed two small yellow new potatoes and put them on the gas stove to boil. She laid the table with a knife and fork and a large white porcelain dinner-plate with a scalloped edge, together with a fat silver salt-cellar and the rather oily wooden pepper-mill. She left the fresh *baguette* on the bare wood of the table and set a tall heavy wineglass, cloudy with age, beside her plate. Then she checked the potatoes, turned down the flame, and then, taking a bottle from the fridge she poured herself a glass of wine. She went out onto the landing once more, opened the adjoining door and entered her sitting-room.

In this room, by far the largest in the apartment, the immense low beams were painted a soft matt ivory, reflecting the light which poured through the wide and deep windows overlooking the courtyard below. The room was also Hester's studio and her easel and work-table stood close to a window. She crossed the room and sat down in front of the easel, putting on her spectacles and looking critically at the half-finished icon before her. The bearded Byzantine face of St Mark, seated on a hard-looking chair and reading a manuscript, reminded her of George, her dead and still-mourned husband. She took a sip of her drink, her grey eyes travelling round the pale walls of the low room, resting on the sombre, unsaleable paintings that had been George's legacy to her. In his lifetime, his work had been unfashionable, though admired by the *cognoscenti* of Paris, but he had never made any serious money, and never on a regular basis. This had been partly on account of George's unwillingness to pander to the requirements of galleries, even more to his inability to meet deadlines. Nevertheless, he had been fortunate to acquire the lease of the *entresol* in the fifties, before the Ile St-Louis became fashionable, and he and Hester had lived there throughout their married life. The proceeds of one unusually successful exhibition had also enabled them to buy a very small house in Ramatuelle, a hill village near St Tropez, and here they had spent every summer with their small son Basil. The advent of Basil had been something of a surprise to Hester and George, a not altogether welcome one at the time. George had held the view that an English-woman's son should receive an English education, and they had somehow managed to send the nine-year-old Basil to Colet Court in London, and from there the obliging child had won a scholarship on to St Paul's School. There he had played bridge and billiards, and did just enough work to get himself to Cambridge.

Now that she was on her own, Hester let the little house at Ramatuelle during the Christmas holidays and for part of the summer, always keeping August and September for herself. She did this unwillingly, but realistically since it provided the money to cover the second lot of household bills and taxes, as well as her own travelling expenses. Basil, who now lived and worked in London, sometimes came with her to Ramatuelle, and they drove down in his elderly Riley.

Hester's eyes came back to her work-table of seventeenth-century blackened walnut. The top and sides were inlaid with ivory and blond wood in scrolls, urns and elaborate trails of leaves. The heavy piece was supported by four stout black corkscrew legs. Arranged on the table were the little screw-top jars containing her ground pigments and jugs holding her fine sable brushes, together with her gilding tips and burnishers. Beside the painting things stood a heavy gilt lamp, in the shape of a Corinthian column, bearing a white-lined, black-metal shade. Hester switched it on and its circle of bright light fell on old Russian silver photograph frames, ornately chased, displaying family mementoes: George as a small child, with his mother in traditional Russian dress, the little boy holding her hand and clutching a teddy-bear; Basil with Hester on the beach at Ramatuelle, squinting in the sunshine, revealing gaps in his front teeth; and Hester's own parents in the garden at home, unsmiling, preoccupied with dead-heading the huge Rambling Rector rose that scrambled appropriately up the wall of the vicarage which came with her father's living. Though both of them were long-since dead, Hester thought of them very often, and of her wartime childhood in that cold but beautiful house. Serious and dedicated to the parish, her parents' relationship to Hester had been friendly though remote. I suppose ours with Basil was a bit like that, she thought, rearranging the single white rose, her own small gift to herself, that shared a tall glass jar with a sprig of evergreen honeysuckle plucked surreptitiously as it hung over a garden wall. Hester glanced again at her new icon, and then at the others that hung in scattered groups, glowing red and gold among George's muted paintings. She would have liked very much to be able to paint them just to please herself, but the economic facts of life forced her to supply various shady dealers with fake antique icons. These were ostensibly for the tourist trade though Hester had a strong suspicion that quite a few of them had turned up in very grand sale-rooms from time to time. A knowledgeable little man searched skips in the older parts of Paris for her, and arrived at her door every few months with bits of ancient wooden panels, and cut-up floorboards, worm-holed and silver-grey with age. The same man spent hours searching through the stock of architectural reclamation establishments and occasionally came across small pieces of sixteenth-century panel, which he sold on to Hester at a small profit. Many of these boards and panels were now stacked against the walls of the room, waiting for her to transform them. Unfortunately, she was a meticulous and slow worker, so that although her dealers eagerly bought everything she offered them and paid her well, she was not able to earn a great deal: just enough to live on, nothing to spare for emergencies. She had sometimes considered the possibility of selling her house at Ramatuelle as a means of liberating herself from the necessity of painting the fakes, but had always rejected the idea. In the first place, it produced a proportion of her income, and in the second, the little house was so dear to her and so full of the memory of George that the very thought filled her with depression. In any case, if it could be managed, she intended that Basil should have it when she died. The lease of the *entresol* would expire on her death, and the house at Ramatuelle was the only thing she could leave him, apart from George's pictures and their furniture.

The light was beginning to fade, so Hester picked up her empty glass and crossed the room to the long, low divan that stood against the far wall, flanked by low, red-lacquer tables. The divan was covered by a large Shirazi rug, the colours of indigo and plum jam, and a pile of kilim-covered cushions formed a comfortable wedge at one end. On each table stood a tall lamp, converted from painted Russian church candlesticks, with rough natural linen shades. She switched them on, and the icons on the wall behind them sprang into life, as did the silvery Venetian mirror that reflected the two wide windows opposite, glimmering blue in the deepening twilight. She observed with a little lift of the spirits a pipistrelle bat flitting back and forth in front of the windows. Good, she thought, that's a real sign of spring. She went back to the kitchen, poured herself another glass of wine and turned on the grill for her chop.

* * *

Hugo Turnbull stood at the open window of the small back bedroom where he worked, unfurnished except for his desk, chair and bookcase, and stared down at the little brick-walled garden below. The narrow flowerbeds bordering the walls were empty, and their sour, cat-peed-on black earth discouraged any attempts at planting. The central paved area was also bare, except for a sooty-looking almond tree with diseased, peeling bark. A Victorian wrought-iron garden seat, painted white, stood beneath the tree with a child's blue bicycle propped against it. A pair of dirty orange roller-skates lay abandoned on the paving. A thin rain was falling softly, spreading its greasy film over the shabby garden.

Above Hugo's head, the thumps and heavy footsteps of his three young daughters Phyllida, Sophie and Gertrude, aged nine, seven and six, were making it extremely difficult for him to concentrate on his work, the first draft of a biography of Cardinal Richelieu. Suddenly, an almighty crash made Hugo leap out of his skin and brought a shower of plaster flakes down on his desk, covering his manuscript and reference books. There was a short stunned silence, then the shrill angry voices of little girls hurling abuse at each other, followed by another massive crash and a scream of pain.

'For Christ's sake, what now?' cried Hugo, wrenching open his door and rushing upstairs to the playroom. He flung open the door to find Phyllida, red-faced with rage and probably terror, desperately trying to lift the overturned table off the screaming Gertrude's trapped legs, while Sophie knelt beside her, loudly bawling but failing to help lift the table.

'Leave it, Phylly,' said Hugo as calmly as he could, 'and shut up Gertie, we'll have you out in a flash.' He lifted the heavy table, and as the pressure was released from Gertrude's legs and the circulation was restored, the little girl's screams rose to a frantic pitch of hysteria. Hugo knelt beside her and tried to assess the damage, gently touching the bruised and bloody shins.

'Don't touch! Don't touch!' she screeched. 'They're broken!'

'I don't think so, just a bit battered. Come on, get up.' He helped the howling child to her feet, sat her on his knee and held her in his arms, rocking her while her sobs slowly subsided. Sophie blubbed quietly at his knee, smearing her face with her hands, spreading an unattractive mixture of snot and tears over it. Hugo looked sternly at Phyllida, who stood on the other side of the table, arms crossed, looking extremely defiant. 'What the hell were you doing, Phylly?'

'It's her own bloody fault, I told her to get out of the way.'

'But what were you *doing*? And don't say bloody.'

'*You* do!'

'Don't answer back!'

'Well, you *do*. And fuck.'

'*Phyllida! What were you doing?*' Hugo roared, so that Gertrude gave a fresh wail of anguish.

'Sorry, darling,' said Hugo. 'Phyllida?'

'Ark.'

'What?'

'Making an ark,' mumbled Phyllida.

'And where's Mount Ararat, may one ask?' Hugo inquired sarcastically. 'On top of the wardrobe, I suppose?'

'Brilliant!' said Phyllida, brightening visibly and casting a speculative eye at the tall Victorian wardrobe.

'Don't even think of it,' said Hugo hastily, turning his attention to his youngest child. 'Now Gertie, let's see if you can stand, shall we?'

'I need a plaster,' whimpered Gertrude, nervously examining her damaged legs. 'Two plasters. Big ones.'

They repaired to the bathroom, washed the scraped legs and applied Elastoplast. Then they returned to the playroom and made some attempt at restoring order.

'Right, that's better,' said Hugo. 'Now, please pretend to be good will you, and play quietly?'

'Can we have the telly on?'

'OK, but keep the sound down.'

As he regained the comparative calm of his own room, the strains of the signature tune of *Neighbours* filtered down through the ceiling. He sighed, and looked at his watch: half-five. Still at least another hour to go before Nelly returned from the hospital. He opened his door again, went out onto the landing and leaned over the banisters. A radio was playing in the basement kitchen, and the smell of hot fresh bread wafted up the staircase. Inger must be baking he said to himself, that'll mean a cold supper; shit. The thought of the girls messing with their salad and making vomiting faces at each other to express their distaste did not hold any appeal for Hugo, and his spirits sank at the realization that the Easter holidays would be upon them in a few days. Inger, the *au pair*, had been informed of his need for quiet and was supposed to take the children out as much as she reasonably could between cleaning, shopping and cooking. They lived in a small square of tall, narrow houses with a private garden behind black iron railings in the centre. There the girls could run about, make a noise and generally let off steam in safety, and play with their friends.

They came out of school at half past three and Inger had been told to keep them out of the house until a quarter to six, when she had to start preparing supper. Today, as on so many days, she had failed to do this, and Hugo had been forced to endure the noise from their playroom since four o'clock. He went back into his room, shook the plaster dust from the papers on his desk and refilled his fountain pen. He shut the window, switched off his Anglepoise lamp and left the room, closing the door quietly behind him. He went silently down the bare pine stairs, taking care not to attract the attention of his children, and descended to the basement kitchen, where Inger was taking the loaves from the Aga. She was arranging them with great care on wire racks on the scrubbed pine table, so they looked like a spread from *Country Living*. Unimpressed by this display of domestic skill, Hugo took his Barbour coat from its hook on the back of the kitchen door and put it on.

'Didn't you hear all that racket from the girls?' he said coldly.

'No,' said Inger, taking the last loaf from the oven and deliberately not looking at him. 'I heard nothing.'

'They only managed to tip the table on top of Gertie. I can't believe you didn't hear the screaming?'

Inger stared at him challengingly with her huge blue eyes, as if daring him to call her a liar, but did not bother to reply.

'I'm going out for a few minutes,' he said, 'so please listen out for them.'

'Supper is at seven; it's my early night.'

'OK, I know.' Hugo smiled at her appeasingly, opened the door and ran up the area steps, avoiding the sordid black bins and the once-white Versailles boxes filled with variegated ivy and dead daffodils. He clanged the little iron gate at the top of the steps behind him, and walked quickly along the street in the direction of the pub, ducking his head in a vain attempt to prevent the rain from spotting the lenses of his spectacles. He really thought that he detested Inger, or maybe he was afraid of her, great louche sexy Swede. He was terrified that she might jump on him; the very idea horrified him. He would have much preferred that they got rid of her, but Nelly trusted her and would have laughed if he had voiced his fears concerning her. Inger was efficient and firm with the girls when she felt like it, and they liked her well enough. She was an adequate cook, in spite of the too-frequent salads and raw fish, but above all she made the wonderful bread that persuaded Nelly that theirs was a warm, loving home based on cosy, old-fashioned principles. Hugo knew that when she stepped through her front door and smelt the delicious warm smell, she could dismiss from her mind the worries he thought she sometimes felt about going back to work at the hospital and resuming her career.

He pushed open the swing door of the pub, with its ornate engraved-glass panel and brightly-polished brass fingerplates, and went in. At once, he saw Basil sitting on a stool at the bar in front of a glass of whisky and levered himself onto the stool next to him.

Basil turned and bestowed on Hugo his slow, pre-occupied smile. 'How's it going?' he said.

'Bloody awful,' said Hugo, and ordered whisky.

'Oh dear, what's up?' Basil looked at him, slightly concerned.

'Oh, the usual.' Hugo took off his frail, wire-rimmed glasses and wiped them carefully with his handkerchief. He replaced them, took a gulp of whisky and pursed his lips rather pettishly. 'I know I shouldn't whinge.'

'But you're going to anyway?'

'Yes, I bloody am.' Hugo laughed, in spite of his resentful mood. 'It's impossible to work at home, with the children roaring about and the indispensable *au pair* making her presence felt all day long, the great blonde cow.'

21

'Jesus,' said Basil, 'do you fancy her or something?'

'Certainly not!' Hugo looked startled. 'I think she may fancy me, though.'

'You *do* have problems,' said Basil, 'my heart bleeds for you.'

'Seriously, Baz, it *is* a problem.'

'Well, for God's sake, rent yourself a room to work in. There must be loads available if you look.'

'I would do exactly that. The fact is, I can't afford it.'

'Why ever not?' said Basil, with disbelief.

'Do you have any idea of how extremely little my books earn? They rarely make more than the advance, and that's microscopic in today's terms. Mostly, they earn rather less.'

'But your work is very well reviewed?'

'I know,' said Hugo. 'But it doesn't actually *sell* very well. Pathetic, isn't it?'

'Can't you explain to Nelly how difficult it is for you?'

'Yes, of course I could, and she would immediately rush out and take a lease on some splendid heated studio for me.'

'So? Isn't that what you need?'

Hugo looked at Basil, his oldest friend. They had been at school together, and then at Cambridge, where they had both become friends of Nelly Tanqueray. She was red-haired, clever and funny, and reading medicine. They had both been rather in love with her. In the end she had chosen Hugo, greatly to his surprise, and they were married soon after they graduated. It was only then that Hugo had discovered that Nelly owned a house in Holland Park, inherited from her father, and received an income from a family trust. He had known about the house previously, but had assumed that it belonged to her family and that she had the use of it for the time being. He had thought that the plan to begin their married life there was a temporary expedient and that they would find a place of their own, once Hugo was earning and Nelly had qualified. They had gone to Kenya for their honeymoon, spending a week on the coast, then staying with Hugo's parents on their isolated coffee plantation, some distance from Thika. It was there, while they were having breakfast on the verandah, that Hugo had asked Nelly why she had not told him earlier about her fortunate state of financial affairs.

'Why do you think? Knowing you, you would have immediately started questioning your motives, and would probably have backed off.'

In the event, they had settled happily in Nelly's house, while she continued her medical studies at a London teaching hospital and Hugo began to work on his first book, and did the shopping and cooking, a way of life that suited them both perfectly. In due course, his book was published and got excellent notices. Nelly went with him to various literary occasions, and was immensely proud of his achievements. Then she qualified, and got her first hospital job. Immediately, her salary was three times more than Hugo could earn, in spite of his doing occasional articles for glossy magazines, and some reviewing. It was hard for him not to feel rather a sense of injustice, though he did his best to conceal his resentment.

'Yes,' he said, 'a quiet place to work is exactly what I need, but can't have unless Nelly buys it for me. I do still have a small shred of pride left, Baz, though you probably think that rather stupid. As it is, Nelly pays for practically everything, including the dread Inger. And *au pairs* don't come cheap nowadays.'

'Don't they?' Basil laughed. 'I wouldn't know, thank God.'

Hugo glanced at the clock above the bar: twenty to seven. He stood up reluctantly. 'I'll have to go. Supper at seven, Inger's night off.' He looked at Basil. Poor old Baz, he thought, he looks a bit wan. 'Why don't you come and have pot luck with us, if you've nothing on? Though it'll only be fish salad and cheese, if you can bear it?'

'Thanks, I'd like to, if you're sure Nelly won't mind? It's ages since I saw her and the kids.'

They walked together down the street to the house, the wet pavements reflecting the white hissing gas-lamps illuminating the square. Hugo took out his latchkey and opened the front door, and they went into the warm, bread-scented hall. They hung up their coats, and Hugo led the way down to the kitchen, where supper had already begun. The three red-headed little girls were seated as far from each other as possible, and were all doing their best to avoid eating the herring salad, so carefully prepared by Inger. Instead, they were consuming vast quantities of the delicious fresh bread. Their mother, looking worn out, sat at the head of the table, keeping order, her hands cupped round a large gin and tonic. She was waiting for Hugo before starting her own supper. Inger had departed already, a fact thankfully observed by Hugo as he descended the stairs with Basil.

Nelly's face lit up when she saw them both. 'Baz! How lovely to see you.'

'Nelly, my dear. How are you?' Basil embraced her warmly.

'Baz! Baz!' shouted Sophie, banging her fork on the table and scattering bits of fish salad in the process.

'Look at my legs, Baz!' said Gertrude importantly, getting down to display her injured limbs. 'It was agony, they could of broke.'

'I bet,' said Basil, examining the legs. 'Golly, poor old you.'

'It was Phylly's fault,' said Sophie smugly. 'She dropped the table right on her, wasn't she *cruel*?'

'Hello, Baz,' said Phyllida, looking at him through her long ginger eyelashes. 'Been to the pub?'

'Don't be cheeky, puss,' said Hugo, bending to give her a conciliatory kiss.

She squirmed and pulled away, taking a mouthful of fish to discourage any further liberties. 'You smell of drink,' she said.

'And you smell of fish, I expect,' said Basil. 'How's my favourite godchild?'

'OK, s'pose,' said Phyllida, with her mouth full.

'Is there enough to spare for Baz?' Hugo kissed Nelly and sat down beside her.

'He can have mine,' said Sophie. 'It's disgusting.'

'Nonsense,' said Nelly, 'it's delicious. Get on, girls, do hurry up; it's time you were in bed. Yes, of course Baz, there's plenty. I'm so glad it won't all have to go in the bin.'

Hugo got up and took a bottle of wine from the fridge. Basil sat down on Nelly's other side, next to Phyllida, who looked gratified and smiled at him with some difficulty on account of her mouth being full of fish and bread, a tricky combination to swallow.

'I don't want any more,' said Sophie, 'I'm bursting. Please, Mum?' She turned large pleading hazel eyes on Nelly.

'Have you all had enough, really?' Nelly looked despairingly at their half-eaten plates.

'Yes,' said Sophie and Gertrude together.

Phyllida emptied the contents of her mouth into her hand, transferred it to her plate and covered it swiftly with a piece of bread. 'Me, too,' she said, wiping her hand on her skirt.

Nelly closed her eyes.

'Right,' said Hugo, decisively. 'Up you go at once, and no messing about, understand? I'll be up in ten minutes flat to bring your hot milk and read you a story. OK?'

'OK.' They got down from the table, Gertrude knocking over a glass of water, kissed their mother, said goodnight to Basil and thumped noisily up the stairs.

Nelly took a long pull at her drink, and began to get up from the table.

'Stay where you are,' said Hugo, 'you look completely knackered.'

Nelly smiled at him gratefully. 'I am a bit,' she said.

Hugo removed the debris from the table, wiped up the spilt water, rearranged the salad, set three proper places and poured some wine. 'It's only plonk, I'm afraid.'

'Can't even taste it, after whisky,' said Basil.

'Just as well,' said Nelly.

They ate the herring salad, which, though unprepossessing to look at, actually tasted very good, and then Hugo got some cheese from the fridge, and a partly consumed bunch of grapes. 'You two carry on,' he said, 'while I deal with the girls.' He put a pan of milk on the hob, and put three mugs on a tray. He put coffee into the percolator and lit the gas under it. 'Just talk quietly amongst yourselves,' he said, as he departed upstairs with the tray of mugs. 'I won't be long.'

'How're things with you, Baz?' said Nelly, after a pause.

'Same old routine,' he said quietly. 'The day-job's all right, for the moment, though life as an archivist has its *longeurs* after the first few years. Still, I'm slogging away at the translations in the evenings. That is, if I'm not too pissed by the time I get home.' He smiled at her, and took her hand. 'Hugo's a lucky chap to have you behind him, Nelly.'

'Oh, Baz, do you really think so?' Her eyes were clouded beneath the fringe of silky red hair that fell over her forehead. She pushed the hair out of her eyes, and leant her chin on her hand, frowning. 'As a matter of fact, I think he finds it all very difficult: the children, the noise, me going back to work, but mostly I think it's the money thing.'

'Well, one can understand that, but after all, he could always get a job, couldn't he?'

'Absolutely not, Baz. He's got a job; I think a very important one. He's a full-time writer, and a successful one, too.' Nelly's cheeks were flushed, her eyes bright.

'Sorry, sweetheart,' said Basil gently. 'You're quite right, of course.'

'Does it matter, *should* it matter, if my father's money pays some of the bills?'

'No, darling, it shouldn't. But it does, doesn't it?'

'There you are then. What to do?'

'You married the wrong man, old thing,' said Basil, and laughed. 'I wouldn't have minded.'

'Oh, *Baz*.' Nelly laughed too, then looked worried. 'Actually, it's no laughing matter. Next week, it's the Easter holidays, the girls will be at home for three weeks. It's going to drive Hugo up the wall. I would send them to my ma, in Florizel, but I'd be too scared to unless I were there with them. She's getting to be seriously old now.' She got up and went to the stove. She brought the coffee-pot to the table, and went to the dresser for cups.

Basil watched her thoughtfully. 'I wonder,' he said.

'What do you wonder?' Nelly put the cups on the table, and poured the coffee.

27

'Do you think he might like to spend a couple of weeks in Paris with Hester?'

'You mean with your mother?' She sounded doubtful.

'Yes. It's very quiet there, you might be in the country, and she's working all day herself.'

'But do you really think she'd have him to stay, just like that?'

'I'm fairly sure she would, if I explained the situation. I could ask her.'

'Well, I suppose it could be just what he needs. Poor Hugo, he works so hard, he deserves a bit of peace.'

'Well, that's settled then. I'll give Hester a ring, and sound her out, shall I?'

'Baz,' said Nelly, 'I think it would be best if this suggestion came from you, don't you? I wouldn't want Hugo to know that we'd cooked up this idea between us.'

'Point taken,' said Basil. 'I'll phone Hester tomorrow, and then give Hugo a ring here, in the daytime. You know nothing about it, OK?'

'You're a brick, Baz. I feel better already.'

'Good, that's the main thing, as far as I'm concerned.' He leaned over and kissed her lightly on the cheek. They heard Hugo's footsteps as he came down the stairs.

He came into the kitchen, grinning. 'Little monsters,' he said.

Nelly smiled, and poured his coffee.

Chapter Two

Una-Mary Tanqueray walked along the beach at low tide with her two King Charles spaniels, Wiggy and Pepys. Age and infirmity forced her to use a stick, but she still managed to descend the stony path which led through a tunnel of overhanging branches to the small cove below. She came down from *Les Romarins* every day, however forbidding the weather. Protected by her thick, rather dirty old Burberry and stout gumboots, with a woollen scarf tied firmly under her chin, she picked her way down the overgrown path, slashing at the brambles and nettles that threatened her on either side. Now she walked along the shining sand with the dogs as they pranced through the shallows, trying to drink the water and barking furiously at the gulls and terns that rode the small waves or stood in unconcerned attitudes on the sand, their yellow eyes insolent behind their ferocious, razor-sharp beaks.

She reached the jagged brown rocky outcrops on the far side of the cove and turned, looking back across the beach and out to sea. She could see Sark, misty and blue in the late afternoon, and faintly in the distance, Herm and Jethou as well as the uninhabited rocks uncovered at low tide. Wiggy and Pepys emerged from the sea, drenched and panting, and shook themselves vigorously, sending a shower of sand and sea-water over her coat.

'Sit,' said Una-Mary. 'Behave.' The dogs sat.

The smell of rotting seaweed from the uncovered rocks was carried towards them on the breeze blowing in from the sea, and the dogs sniffed the air hungrily. Her son Henry, a pompous man in his early forties, complained about the smell whenever he came to stay at *Les Romarins*. This was not a frequent occurrence, somewhat to Una-Mary's relief, since he spent a good deal of his time pointing out various items of family furniture, pictures and so on, to his wife. Jane was a sharp-faced woman in her late thirties, with an expensive pale blond haircut, and a discontented expression. Henry, in accordance with the laws of the island, would inherit *Les Romarins* when she died and this was a matter of some disappointment to Una-Mary, since she was perfectly well aware that he disliked the house intensely, and would doubtless sell it when the time came. She recollected that Henry had taken a very poor view of his father's leaving the Holland Park house to Nelly, though she could not actually remember him saying so, in so many words. One just knew.

She retraced her steps across the sand, followed by the exhausted dogs, and prepared to climb back up the tunnel to the cliff-top, and home. When they reached the top, the little company paused for a moment to regain their breath, and she turned and looked across the bay at the setting sun, which had slid down behind a bank of pearl-grey cloud, and now lit up the sea and the islands scattered between Florizel and Guernsey. It was a sight that never ceased to amaze her, and Una-Mary stood gazing from end to end of the horizon. Then she nodded to the dogs, and took the worn path through the sheep-grazed heather and gorse that led to the granite walls of *Les Romarins* and the small door to her garden. She went in, and walked round the side of the house to the kitchen door. The dogs flopped down on a ragged towel in front of the old black range. This was not very intelligent of them, since it was only lit when Nelly and her family came to stay. Nelly chose to cook on it, in preference to the modern electric cooker installed close by. Una-Mary did not often use even that, except to boil the kettle for tea or a hot-water bottle. Her lunch was brought in every day, kept warm between two plates, by Elsie, whose husband Alain now looked after the sheep for her, and tended the garden spasmodically. This was Una-Mary's only meal of the day, and if she felt hungry she made herself a cup of tea and ate a few biscuits. She also drank a good deal, usually gin. Her modest grocery orders were brought up from the village shop by Alain on the tractor. In one of her barns a four-wheeled cart was kept, and her elderly pony, Murphy, grew fat and lazy in his paddock. When Nelly came over she gave her girls riding lessons, and persuaded Murphy to back between the shafts of the cart, and drove the children and Una-Mary all over the island, and for a little while it was exactly like the old days.

She hung her coat on the kitchen door, poured herself a stiff gin, took a bottle of tonic from the crate on the kitchen floor, and went through the dining-room to the hall and into the drawing-room beyond, followed by the dogs. The room was large and beautiful, and filled with the shabby but comfortable chintz-covered sofas and chairs of her parents' time. The Georgian windows, installed in the late eighteenth century, had replaced the smaller ones of the original farmhouse. They faced westwards, looking out over the lawns and flowerbeds of the garden, and on fine summer evenings she took the dogs outside for a last walk round before bed. Now, however, she went straight to the fireplace

31

and put a match to the firelighter beneath the sticks and coal laid by Elsie earlier in the day. Then she switched on a lamp, took a swig of her gin and sat down in a low Victorian armchair beside the fire, and began to lay out the cards for a game of Patience on the small table in front of her. The dogs looked up at her with bright adoring eyes, then crashed down in front of the smoking fire, sighing gustily.

Hester had just finished putting away her shopping when the telephone rang in the sitting-room. I expect that'll be Baz, she thought, he's the only person who phones in the evening. She lifted the receiver and gave her number.

'Hi, it's me, Baz.'

'Hello, darling, I thought it was you.'

'You've been out.'

'I have. I've been to deliver some work to the evil Benoit this afternoon, and then I took a little promenade round the island. It's been a lovely day, almost like summer. It makes me regret that I don't have a bit of garden.'

'I hope he paid you, the crook?'

'Yes, he did.' Hester laughed. 'I always insist on cheque on delivery.'

'Well, good,' said Basil.

'Any particular reason for ringing? Are you planning a visit?'

'Not just yet, but I was wondering whether you could do a favour to my old chum Hugo?'

'What sort of favour?' said Hester.

Basil told her about his conversation with Hugo in the pub, and with Nelly subsequently. 'I was thinking that maybe you could have him to stay for a couple of weeks, so that he could get on with his work in peace? He'd pay for his board and lodging of course. I'm sure he'd be no trouble.'

'Would he be able to work in that tiny bedroom?' Hester sounded doubtful; she felt no inclination to share her own work space, at any rate not during the day. On the other hand, a bit of rent would be useful.

'I'm sure he would, he works in a very small dark room at home.'

'Well, all right. When would he want to come?'

'I'm not sure. Pretty soon; the kids' holidays start next week.'

'Well, let me know exact dates, Baz, won't you?'

'Yes, of course. Thanks a lot, darling. You're an angel. I'll ring you tomorrow, and let you know when he'll arrive.'

Hester said goodnight and put down the phone. She went thoughtfully back to the kitchen, mentally checking the contents of her airing cupboard. In fact, she knew that she had plenty of sheets and pillow-cases, and extra blankets. She poured herself a glass of wine, and sitting down at the kitchen table, began to snip the stalks off her beans.

Hugo sat at his desk trying to make sense of his much-corrected notes, and turn them into elegant but interesting and incisive prose. He felt slightly tense with acute awareness of the presence of his daughters in the house. They were not upstairs in their room, but down in the kitchen with Inger. An uneasy silence reigned, broken only occasionally by a distant scream or laugh from below. He stared at the wall, trying to think of a synonym for *hubris* but could not find a good word. He got up, went to the bookshelf and took down his Roget. *Arrogance*, that'll do he said to himself. Replacing the book on its shelf, he sat down again and picked up his pen. Down below, a door banged and heavy footsteps rushed up the wooden stairs. Hugo stiffened, praying that they would continue past his landing and up to the second floor. But his door burst open and a red-faced Sophie erupted into the room, followed closely by Phyllida.

'Phylly's a cheat, Papa! I hate her!'

'I am *not* a cheat!' shouted Phyllida, pushing her sister. 'She's just a rotten loser!'

'I am *not*, it's you that is! You change the rules all the time, so you win!' And Sophie, goaded beyond endurance, turned and hit her sister as hard as she could on the nose with her clenched fist. Phyllida yelped with pain and fell to the floor, clutching her bleeding nose and weeping noisily.

'Sophie!' shouted Hugo, leaping to his feet. 'What the hell do you think you're doing?'

Sophie folded her arms aggressively. 'I don't care. She hits me all the time. I hope it hurts. I hate her; I wish she was dead!'

At this, Phyllida turned up the volume of her sobs and drummed her heels on the floorboards.

'Get up at once,' said Hugo loudly, 'and stop this atrocious noise, both of you.' He picked Phyllida off the floor; she clutched him round the waist, still weeping, and bled all over his shirt-front. 'Here, use my hanky,' he said hastily, applying it to her swollen nose. He looked at Sophie, frowning. She stared back at him belligerently. 'I'm surprised at you, Sophie, I've never thought of you as a violent child.'

'A good thump is the only thing some people understand!' She glared at her sister, quite unrepentant. 'Especially *her*. And she *did* cheat!'

'I didn't!'

'Did!'

'Didn't!'

'Did!' Sophie's fist clenched again.

'Oh, for God's sake *shut up*, the pair of you! How on earth do you expect me to earn a living with this constant background of quarrelling and noise?'

The two girls looked at him, surprised, Phyllida holding the blood-stained handkerchief to her nose.

'But you don't have a proper job, do you Papa?' said Sophie. 'It's Mum who goes out to work, isn't it?'

Hugo considered trying to convince his daughters that he did work, but changed his mind; it would be a pointless exercise, he knew. Inside himself he felt put-down and a little sad. Who put that idea into their heads? he asked himself. Probably that bloody Inger. He looked at his watch: nearly half past four. 'Would you like to go out for half an hour?'

'With you?' said Phyllida, her voice muffled.

'Yes, with me.'

They went downstairs to the kitchen. Inger was ironing placidly and Gertrude sat at the table. She was vandalizing a first edition of *Winnie the Pooh*, handed down to them by Hugo's mother. She was colouring the black-and-white drawings with felt pens. Hugo opened his mouth to protest, and then closed it again. It was too late anyway.

'Hello, Papa,' she said. 'I'm being good, aren't I?'

'Yes, darling, you are. Very good. Come on, we're going out for a bit.'

'Do we have to put on coats? It's quite warm to-day.'

'No, I don't think so. We'll have a sack-race, shall we? That'll keep you warm.'

'Oh, good,' said Sophie, 'I expect I'll win.'

'It's not fair,' Gertrude wailed. 'I never win. It's not my fault I'm the littlest.'

'Do shut up,' said Hugo. 'We'll have a handicap.'

'What's a handicap?' they said together.

'You'll see. Now, bin-liners.' He looked in the cupboard under the sink, found a roll and tore off half a dozen. 'Right, up you go.'

He followed his daughters up the area steps to the pavement, and they crossed the street to the gate that led into the square's private garden. As he unlocked the gate, Hugo heard the telephone ringing through the open kitchen window. He hesitated, and thought of going back. The phone stopped ringing. Oh well, Inger will take a message, he thought, and going into the garden with his children, began to explain to them the principles of handicapping.

Nelly drove out of the staff exit of the hospital just after six. She had been on duty since six o'clock that morning. She felt very tired indeed, and had a headache. She longed for a hot, deep, scented bath, and a drink. It's awful, she thought, I'm only thirty-three years old but sometimes I feel about a hundred. I suppose it's a combination of work and having babies. Whatever happened to my youth? She stared through the windscreen as the car crawled down Hammersmith Road. Every single traffic light was red, and the rush-hour traffic was even heavier than usual. She thought of their happy times together in Cambridge, she and Hugo and Baz. She remembered the lazy summer afternoons in a punt on the river, pretending to work, with a bottle of wine hung over the side, keeping cool in the water. She remembered the intoxication of her first real taste of freedom, doing exactly what she felt like in a dream-world of grown-ups, with no rules. Baz and Hugo had, so to speak, been on their own since they were quite small boys, since both their parents lived abroad, but she had had to endure the confines of an English convent school. She had been in any case a serious and obliging child, without any real urge to rebel. The holidays from school had been spent in Florizel, with her mother and her much older brother, Henry. Nelly had always loved both her mother and the island, and was happy to return there often, but at the age of fifteen she had realized that the last thing she wanted was to spend the whole of her life in that small, close-knit community. She was not surprised that her father preferred his little London house, close to his clubs and old Foreign Office cronies. She had looked to university as the obvious escape route, and had worked single-mindedly to get there. A place at Cambridge had been an achievement that had exceeded all her expectations, and her time there had been years of absolute happiness.

Nelly smiled, remembering the last May Ball, the noise of the bands, the coloured lights, the explosions of dancing, the lobster salad, the champagne. But most of all she remembered lying in Hugo's arms, in a punt tied to a tree on the riverbank, both of them slightly drunk.

'Is there any chance', Hugo had said, 'that you'd consider marrying me one day?'

'Are you proposing to me, Hugo?'

'Yes, I suppose I am.'

Nelly had put her arms round his neck and kissed him. 'If you still want to in the morning,' she had said, 'ask me again.'

'And what will your answer be?'

'Probably yes.'

Then Baz had appeared with another bottle of champagne, and Nelly had stepped out of her frock and gone swimming in her knickers, and Baz had immediately stripped off all his clothes and jumped in after her, followed by Hugo, all of them happier than they had ever been, or would ever be again. I suppose it can't all have been quite as wonderful as I think it was, Nelly thought; it must have rained sometimes.

The last set of lights turned green. She released the handbrake and drove slowly home. She parked in her resident's parking space, took out her briefcase and bag, and locked the car. Sounds of laughter and little girls' chattering voices came up the area steps from the kitchen window, clear in the warm evening air. Nelly drew a long breath of fresh air, went up the three steps to the front door, painted a cheerful yellow, and let herself in with her latchkey. She hung up her jacket, dumped her bags at the foot of the staircase, and went down to the kitchen. The girls were having their supper, fish fingers and pasta with tomato ketchup. This was a popular meal, and Inger was not having any difficulty in getting the children to eat it.

'Hello, Mum,' said Phyllida, her mouth stained with ketchup, her nose still swollen.

'What happened to your nose?'

Phyllida pointed at Sophie. 'She bashed me. She's a cow; I hate her.'

'Well, she's a cheat,' snarled Sophie. 'She cheats all the time; she even cheated in the sack-race, when Gertie was winning. She pushed her over.'

'I DID NOT!'

'YOU DID!'

'That's enough, girls,' said Nelly. She poured herself a gin, and Inger looked away, pretending not to notice.

'Is Papa still working?'

'Yes,' said Gertrude. 'He played at sack-races with us, and he helped me win, so he's got to do overtime.'

'Aha,' said Nelly, smiling. 'I'll go up and see him.'

'There is a casserole in the oven, for your dinner,' said Inger, 'and potatoes in the pan, ready to go on. I've done the ironing.'

'Thanks, Inger, you're an angel.'

Inger shrugged. 'It's my job.'

'It's your job, it's your job!' said Sophie loudly, bits of pasta trailing from her mouth.

'Mucky pig,' said Phyllida.

Inger stood up, looking tall. 'So if it's OK with you, Nelly, I'll be going out after I've got the girls ready for bed.'

'Yes, of course, fine.' Nelly left the kitchen hastily, and went upstairs to Hugo's room, trying not to spill her drink. Slipping through the door quietly, she saw at once that he was on the phone and hesitated, not wishing to seem to be listening in. He turned in his chair and beckoned with his free arm, smiling. She came in and perched on his desk, sipping her drink. I wonder if that's Baz, she said to herself.

'Well, Baz, that sounds marvellous, are you really sure she won't mind?'

Nelly could just hear Baz's voice at the other end, but could not make out what he was saying.

'Yes, fine,' said Hugo, 'but I'll have to talk to Nelly about it. I'll ring you back in a few minutes, OK?' He put the phone down and swung his chair round to face Nelly. 'That was Baz.'

'I guessed that, darling.' Nelly smiled.

Hugo got up, put his arm round her and kissed her ear. 'The thing is, I was having a bit of a whinge to him the other night about how hard it is to work when the children are at home. Very disloyal of me, wasn't it?'

'Not at all, it's the truth.'

'So he suggested that I might go and spend a couple of weeks in Paris. Stay with his mother on the Ile St-Louis. He says it's very quiet, and near some of the locations I need to check for the book. What do you think?'

'I think, terrific idea. You must go, of course.'

'You wouldn't mind?'

'Of course not, why should I? As a matter of fact, it would be a weight off my mind if you went. It worries me that the girls are getting on your nerves when I'm at work.'

'It's not just the girls,' said Hugo. 'It's that bloody Inger too. She spooks me, stupid creature.'

'Ah, well,' said Nelly, and laughed. 'You're too sensitive, my love.' She stood up, put her arms round Hugo and gave him a hug. 'You'll go, of course?'

'Well, yes, if you really think I should. I'll have to pay some rent, for food and so on.' He looked at her through his glasses, his blue eyes apprehensive.

Nelly resisted the urge to shake him. 'Well, I expect we'll manage that,' she said lightly. She picked up her drink and went to the door. 'I'm going to have a quick bath, I stink of hospital, and then I'll settle the girls and get supper on the table. Inger's going out.'

'Thank God for that.'

'You'll ring Baz now, then?'

'Yes, I will,' said Hugo. Nelly opened the door. 'Nelly?'

'Mm?' She paused in the doorway.

'You don't stink.'

She smiled and closed the door behind her. She went to their bedroom, and turned on the taps in their bathroom, pouring an extravagant amount of Penhaligon's *Bluebell* into the running water.

'Yes,' said Basil, 'that's right. He'll be with you around seven on Friday evening, is that OK? Good, fine. Yes, this coming Friday. That's not too short notice? Good, that's settled then. OK. Take care. Talk to you soon.'

He put down the phone, and sat for a moment, looking at his notes and the reference books scattered on his work-table. A cloud of boredom and tiredness crept over him. At the end of yet another boring day in the archives of the museum he found it almost impossible to work up the necessary motivation to get on with his own private work in the evening, translating contemporary Russian poetry into English. He spoke the language fluently, his father having taught him during the school holidays, not wishing his son to lose touch with his heritage completely, but Basil did not write it as well as he spoke it, and constantly had to check both grammar and spelling. Now, he had the horrible feeling that his dreary mood was becoming reflected in his writing.

He got up and went to the window of his dingy sitting-room, with its brown paint and blocked-up fireplace, and second-hand, broken-springed sofa. He had done nothing to improve the room, except to fill the bookshelves, the legacy of a previous tenant, and hang one of his father's small early paintings over the mantelpiece. He opened the window and leaned on the sill, and watched the people and cars in the street below. The evening air was warm, and smelt of car-exhaust and faintly of lime-blossom. Two grey pigeons perched close together on the parapet on the other side of the street, and from time to time the male strutted back and forth in an agitated manner.

'What's on your mind, mate?' said Basil. He turned back to his work, feeling restless and unsettled. 'Sod, it,' he said crossly, 'I wish *I* were going to Paris.' He got up and went to his little kitchen, more a cupboard than a room, and took a bottle of vodka from the fridge. He put ice into a glass and poured a generous slosh of vodka over it. Then he returned to his room and sat down at the table in a resolute manner. Presently, the phone rang. It was Nelly.

'Thank you, Baz,' she said. 'You really are a huge friend. He's thrilled to be going.'

'Anything for you, my love,' said Basil lightly. 'Where is he now?'

'Gone up to the pub for some cigarettes. He'll be back in a few minutes. Come and see me when he's away, I'm going to be jolly lonely.'

'Certainly will.'

'Well, thanks again. See you soon.'

' 'Bye. Thanks for calling.' Basil replaced the phone, and sat for a moment drinking his vodka, imagining Nelly in her kitchen, preparing supper, the little girls in bed, Hugo on his way back from the pub. That's what ails you, Basil old lad, he said to himself. You wish you were in Hugo's shoes, don't you? Nothing's changed, nothing at all.

Basil had been stunned when Nelly had chosen to marry Hugo. At the time he had been quite unaware that marriage was on anyone's agenda, and the realization that his sexual relationship with Nelly was at an end was scarcely less painful to him than the virtual loss of his closest friend. They had been inseparable at school and it had been Basil's self-appointed task to protect the rather frail, bespectacled Hugo from the bullying that is often the lot of such children. It had seemed a natural thing to share rooms at Cambridge and the advent of Nelly into their lives had been a huge excitement for them both. She had seemed to love them both equally, and they had not minded sharing her at all; or so it had seemed to Basil at the time. Now, he thought that perhaps he had actually rather hated her, for subtly taking to herself the charge of looking after Hugo, at the same time giving him the things which Basil himself longed for: a stable family life, children, a home.

Of course, he had eventually come to terms with the marriage, and did his best to feel pleased for them and to share in their happiness. He found a flat quite close to them, although he was aware that this was probably a mistake, but his continued attraction to Nelly, as well as his love for Hugo conspired to keep him hanging around the fringes of their lives. Over the years he had had the occasional casual relationship with other women, but these rather half-hearted affairs seemed always to wither away. A couple of years previously, partly out of curiosity and partly driven by sheer loneliness and the need to talk to someone, he had had quite a long-standing liaison with a much older man. Herbert was a quiet and fatherly man, a senior official at the museum, who had shown him sympathy and kindness in his sadness and lack of purpose. Though no longer lovers, they still remained on friendly terms, and occasionally lunched together, or went to the opera. Basil had never mentioned this attachment either to Hugo or to Nelly. Hugo was far too self-absorbed to be interested, and Nelly seemed quite happy to assume that Basil would always be there for her, a convenient private fan-club. God, I'm pathetic, useless, he said to himself.

He finished his drink, got up from the table and put on his jacket. Then he went downstairs to buy his supper from the Indian take-away in the street below.

Chapter Three

Hester looked round the spare bedroom to check that everything was ready for Hugo; that she had not forgotten anything. The small square room was painted ivory, which made the low-beamed ceiling seem less oppressive, and the deep uncurtained window overlooking the courtyard below admitted quite a lot of light and air. The wide window-seat provided a space for books and writing materials, and in front of the window Hester had put a small Russian writing table of ebony inlaid with mother-of-pearl, and a sturdy country chair, painted blue, rather chipped and worn, with a rush seat. She had furnished the table with a tortoiseshell desk-set, and a brass student's-lamp with an adjustable green-glass shade. She had bought a bottle of ink – black – which she considered appropriate for a biography of Richelieu. Opposite the window, the bed, high, hard and narrow, was covered in a blue-patterned Provençal quilt, and had three large square white pillows piled at the head. The bed was flanked on one side by the door, and on the other by a pretty old rosewood chest of drawers, with brass handles and escutcheons. On the top was another reading-lamp, the twin of the desk light, as well as a tumbler and a bottle of mineral water. If he needs books, she thought, he can take what he wants from the sitting-room.

On the wall above the chest, and close to the ceiling, was fixed a set of delicate Gothic mahogany shelves, with fretwork sides and a pair of miniature drawers under the bottom shelf. The shelves held a collection of English Dinky toys, model motor cars, for this had been Basil's room as a boy, and Hester felt no wish to remove them. Indeed, under the bed was concealed a school trunk containing all the paraphernalia of his childhood: books, a cricket bat, boxes of shells and fossils and much more, including some of his school clothes. His black blazer with its little silver scholar's fish, and his games things were all in there, smelling of Lifebuoy soap and mothballs.

On the wall, sandwiched between the shelves and the chest, was a group of miniature paintings in narrow silver frames, portraits of Rodzianko forebears, poker-faced men in Cossack uniforms and frail-looking women in high-bosomed gauzy white dresses, their hair in corkscrew curls. Beside the miniatures hung an old silver icon, elaborately moulded, chased and incised, with the painted faces and hands of the Virgin and Child visible through the holes cut in the silver for that purpose. Before the icon hung a small silver oil lamp with a purple glass to shield its flame, suspended from the ceiling by three fine silver chains. The room was otherwise unfurnished, except for a narrow wardrobe built into one side wall, facing two unframed paintings of George's on the bare wall opposite.

Hester opened the window to air the room, and then went to the bathroom to get towels from the airing cupboard. She hung them on the wooden rail fixed to the back of the door in Hugo's room, then returned to the sitting-room and her work. She looked at her watch: nearly half past two. She had five hours left before the visitor's arrival, plenty of time to transfer the cartoon of her new icon to its gessoed panel, now waiting on her work-table. She took the cartoon, this time a nativity in the Novgorod style of the late fifteenth century, and taped it to the surface of the panel. The Novgorod period was a favourite one of Hester's, the icons often being larger than usual, and the image containing a lot of pure vermilion, a colour she loved for its exuberant brilliance. She was intending to gild the Virgin's halo and the background, which would make the icon look satisfyingly sumptuous, even if it cost her rather a lot for the books of precious gold leaf. She selected a darning needle from the pot on the table and began to punch holes through the pencil line of the cartoon drawing, piercing the surface of the gesso below at the same time.

At half past five, Hester put away her tools and went through to the kitchen. She put the kettle on to make a cup of tea, then went back to the sitting-room and put the icon on the easel, ready to begin the painting proper the next day. She tidied the work-table, returned to the kitchen to make the tea and sat down at the table to drink it. She felt tired, after several hours of intense concentration, and slightly nervous. She had been on her own for so long now, nearly five years, that she had become quite reclusive and made no effort to see people. She and George had never been particularly sociable, in any case, and had been perfectly happy in each other's company. In fact, the only person who had been in the apartment at all since George's death had been Basil, and then only for flying visits. If he came with her to Ramatuelle in the summer he stayed longer, sometimes as long as a fortnight. Now, she felt a small twinge of anxiety, a reluctance to admit an unknown quantity into her ordered and tranquil existence.

Hester washed her cup and looked at her watch: five

to six. She did not want to start work again, she felt too tired and restless. Should she lie down and have a short rest? No, she said to herself, I'll go and walk by the river for a while, then do the shopping and be back in good time before he arrives. She put on her jacket, picked up her bag and her basket and went downstairs to the street.

Hugo's plane landed at Charles de Gaulle Airport just after five-thirty, and he followed the rest of the passengers through passport control, and then to the arrivals to wait for his luggage. His suitcase was extremely heavy, containing mostly books and manuscript paper, and he armed himself with a trolley. He had only brought a couple of extra shirts, pants and socks, assuming that there would be a convenient laundromat somewhere in the neighbourhood. Surprisingly, his flight number came up on the monitor screen almost at once, and soon the bags appeared on the carousel, his own among the first. He lugged it off as it trundled past, and heaved it onto the trolley. Good, he thought, I am being amazingly efficient. Here I am, without Nelly, and I have actually managed not to get lost so far. Wimp, he said to himself under his breath and began to push the trolley towards the customs. The officers looked remarkably uninterested and Hugo walked straight through, trying not to look nervous or guilty as he did so. He headed for the exit, following other more confident-looking people and joined a queue of passengers waiting for the Air France bus into Paris. In a few minutes a coach arrived, and Hugo and his fellow-travellers got on. The bus sped off and in a little over half an hour arrived at Porte Maillot. As the vehicle slowed to a stop he noted, thankfully, the line of waiting taxis. He got himself and his bag off the coach and into a cab as swiftly as he could, and soon found himself speeding down the Avenue de la Grande Armée towards the Etoile and the Arc de Triomphe.

The evening traffic was incredibly heavy and amazingly aggressive, but the taxi driver, totally undaunted and perfectly relaxed, tore down the Champs Elysées and round the Place de la Concorde. In a few minutes Hugo found himself cruising along the *quais*, passing the Ile de la Cité across an arm of the river to his right. My God, he thought, we're here already. He looked at his watch: ten to seven. Shit, he said to himself, I'm going to be frightfully early. The taxi crossed the Pont Louis-Philippe, drove down the Rue Jean-du-Bellay and turned into the Rue St-Louis-en-l'Ile. The driver asked Hugo what address he wanted, and he gave the name of the street.

'*Quel numéro?*' said the driver, turning into the side street.

'*Il faut s'arrêter ici,*' said Hugo, panicking at the thought of his early arrival. He got out, struggling with the heavy bag. He paid the driver, who thanked him and drove away. Hugo stood on the pavement and tried to collect his wits. Should he go back into the main street again, buy a paper and kill time in a café? But the thought of lugging the suitcase around any more than was absolutely necessary appalled him. He heard a church clock strike seven. I'll find the place, he thought, and just wait till half-past before I ring the bell. He located the big wooden gates of the carriageway to Hester's courtyard without difficulty, following Basil's instructions. One heavy leaf of the double doors stood half-open. He entered the *porte-cochère* and saw Hester's discreet door in the wall on the left-hand side.

Putting down his bag close to the wall, he sat down on it, glad to have a rest and compose himself.

Hester, turning into the porch ten minutes later with her basket of shopping, saw at once the slight, dejected figure of a sandy-haired, bespectacled man sitting on a suitcase beside her door.

He looked up as she approached, and got hastily to his feet. 'Is it? Can you be . . . ?' he stammered shyly.

'I am Hester Rodzianko and you must be Hugo,' said Hester, perfectly at ease, now that he was actually here, and evidently feeling even more nervous than she had been herself. She held out her hand and Hugo took it, with a little inclination of his head.

'The key.' Hester began her usual hunt through her bag. 'Here we are.' She unlocked the door and turned to Hugo. 'You'd better go up first, with that cumbersome-looking bag,' she said. 'I'll lock the door and follow you up.'

Half an hour later Hugo had unpacked his books and clothes, and had a wash. He had taken off his jacket and put on a sweater; the apartment felt warm and balmy compared with London. Then he left his room, closing the door quietly, tapped on the kitchen door and went in. Hester was sitting at the table chopping parsley and capers with a *demi-lune* knife. She had a glass of wine in front of her, beside an open bottle.

'Come in,' she said. 'Pour yourself a drink. There's wine, or vodka if you prefer. Get a glass from the shelf.'

'I'd love a glass of wine, thank you.' He got a glass, sat down at the table and poured some wine from the open bottle.

'It's nice to be in Baz's room,' he said. 'It's an extraordinary feeling, his Dinkies make it seem like yesterday. He used to cart those cars round in his pocket, and make vroom noises under his breath during prep.'

'Did he really?' Hester smiled. 'He always seemed very grown-up to us; I can't remember him playing, except at the beach. He used to lie on his bed and read, or go to the cinema. He liked the theatre too, he used to go out early and queue for the Comédie Française.'

'Is it far?'

'No, it's just across the river, behind the Louvre. It's part of the Palais Royal.'

'Richelieu's Palais Royal?' Hugo took a sip of wine. 'I want to see it.'

'Unfortunately, it's not open to the public; it's occupied by the Council of State. Though you can walk in the courtyard, and sit under the trees and watch the children playing round the pond and the fountain.'

'Sounds lovely,' said Hugo.

'It is.'

'Can I do anything to help?'

'I hope you like fish?'

'Certainly.'

'There were some nice-looking skate-wings in the market, so I got two. They're in the fridge. Perhaps you could give them a rinse under the tap for me?'

Hugo got up, found the package of fish, took out the triangular skate-wings and washed them carefully. 'What now?' he asked.

'Put them in that flat pan, and cover them with cold water. I don't think we'll fry them, they do make rather a powerful smell, don't they?'

'I don't know,' said Hugo. 'I've never actually eaten them before.'

'Ah,' said Hester. 'A lot of people do consider it a weird-looking fish, with too many bones.'

51

'Anything else?'

'Give the potatoes a prod, will you?'

Hugo found a pointed knife and tested the potatoes. He was beginning to feel hungry and was glad to see that there were six potatoes in the pan.

'They're done, I think,' he said.

'Good; could you drain them?'

Hester lit the flame under the fish, and added salt and vinegar to the water. She put salad and bread on the table, and set two places. Then she put a lump of butter on the potatoes and a good grinding of pepper. She took two large yellow dinner-plates from the oven, and refilled their glasses. She watched the simmering pan carefully, then tested the skate, drained the water off, skinned the fish and slid them onto the warm plates. She sprinkled the chopped parsley and capers over them, with salt and pepper. She put butter into a small pan and heated it until it was brown and bubbling, and poured it foaming over the fish. Then she deglazed the pan with a little vinegar, and added the reduction as a final flourish to the dish.

'God,' said Hugo, 'it smells wonderful.'

'Sit down,' said Hester. 'Let's eat it while it's hot.'

They ate the fish slowly and carefully; it came away from the bones very easily, to Hugo's relief, and tasted delicious, sharpened by the buttery caper-and-vinegar sauce. The potatoes were yellow and earth-tasting; encouraged by Hester, he ate four of them.

'I'm not usually as greedy as this,' he said, 'but it's so good, and I didn't have any lunch. I was afraid I'd miss the plane; one has to check in so early these days.'

'Salad?' said Hester, pleased that he had enjoyed the skate.

'Thanks,' said Hugo, 'after you.'

After supper, he washed the dishes and stacked them

in the wooden draining rack, while Hester made coffee and took the tray to the sitting-room. Hugo rinsed out the sink carefully, and hung up the dish-cloth. He dried his hands on the tea-towel, an English one he noted with 'linen cloth' written across it, and followed Hester through to the other room. She had switched on the lamps and the place glowed in the pools of light, reflected in the big silvery mirror, the gilded icons shimmering, seeming to float against the white walls of the room, above the sofa.

Hugo caught his breath, surprised by the size and beauty of the room. Since he measured only one metre seventy himself, the ceiling did not seem to him oppressively low, and he looked about him, captivated. 'What a wonderful room,' he said softly.

'It is, isn't it?' said Hester. 'Come and have your coffee.'

Hugo crossed the room and sat down on a low chair, beside the sofa, where she had installed herself against her pile of cushions.

'Would you like a cognac?' she asked.

'I'd love one, but only if you let me get it. You look so comfortable, tucked in there.'

'It's in the kitchen cupboard, with the glasses.'

Hugo found the cognac and the glasses and came back, putting them down on the red lacquer table at Hester's side. 'Shall I pour some?'

'Please.'

He filled the two small glasses, handed one to Hester and sat down.

'Baz was a lucky chap,' he said. 'Imagine coming home here every holiday.'

'What about you, Hugo? Where was your home?'

'Kenya,' said Hugo. 'I flew out there for the long summer holidays. For the others I went to aunts, one in

53

Scotland, one in Winchester. My father could only afford one air-fare every year.'

'You must have missed your parents, when you went away to school?'

'I suppose I did. What I really missed, most of all, was the place itself. The house was a bit tatty, I realize that now, with a corrugated-iron roof and rusty mosquito-gauze in the windows. But there was a marvellous big covered verandah right round the house, with bougainvillaea growing over the roof, and moonflowers climbing up the brick pillars. At night the scent was unbelievable, almost overpowering. The garden was wonderful too, acres of lawn and trees, or so it seemed to me as a child. It was impossible to know where the garden ended and the forest began. At the back of the house was the camp, and the stables and the coffee factory, and beyond that the coffee.'

'What was the camp?'

'Oh, that's where the huts were, the *rondavels*, where the Kikuyu families lived. There was a wooden school building with a thatched roof, where my mother taught the *totos* English and arithmetic, and a little clinic where she dispensed basic medicines, and bound up cuts and stuff. Anything serious meant a thirty-mile ride in the Landrover to the nearest proper settlement.'

'Are they still there, your parents?'

'Yes, but only just. They only have a few acres of coffee now, and a handful of their remaining Kikuyu to help them. The school doesn't operate any more, or the clinic. It's all a bit sad, but they'll never leave, at least not willingly.'

'What a shame,' said Hester. 'Don't you miss it? All that space, and the sunshine, so much freedom?'

'I used to. Not now though. It all seems unreal to me, like a dream. Nelly and I went to visit my parents on our honeymoon, and of course Nelly adored it and longed to live there, run the farm, and set up a medical centre after she had qualified, but I talked her out of it. It's crazy to believe there's a future for white people there now. And really, that's as it should be, if one is honest about it.'

'I suppose so,' said Hester. 'One can't help wondering what will happen to places like your farm in the end.'

'They'll all be divided into smallholdings, it's already started, long ago. Most of my father's coffee has gone that way.'

'Don't you ever see them now?'

'Hardly at all,' said Hugo. 'We did take the children out one Christmas to see them, and my mother came to London for a couple of weeks, two years ago. Every time we part I have the awful feeling I'll never see them again.' He finished his coffee, and sipped the little glass of cognac, suddenly feeling tired.

'It's sad about children and parents,' said Hester. 'It was a bit the same with mine. They lived in the Lake District, and once I'd settled here with George, it might just as well have been Timbuktu. They had no spare cash for travelling, and neither did I. Though it has to be said, we did manage to go to Ramatuelle every year; I still do.'

'Well', said Hugo, 'if I had had to choose between England and the south of France, I know what I would have done.'

'You're right,' said Hester. 'Ultimately, you do what you really want to do, don't you?'

Nelly lay in her big double bed, unable to sleep, feeling lonely and restless without Hugo beside her. It was the first time since their marriage that they had been deliberately apart, and she was surprised at how much she missed him. He had not telephoned; she imagined because he had not wished to ask Hester if he might, or maybe it simply hadn't occurred to him. Although she would have liked to talk to him, to hear his voice, she felt unwilling to appear to be keeping tabs on him and had promised herself that she would not contact him unless a really urgent reason for doing so presented itself.

Hugo had been gone for three days now. During the day, when she was at work, she was too busy to think about him much, but the evenings seemed unnaturally long and strange without him. The children, too, seemed to sense a certain unease and were quiet and rather subdued, as though their father's absence were their fault; as if they realized that their noisy presence had been the reason for his departure. Nelly was rather thankful to have been on duty at the hospital during this first weekend without Hugo, despite having to endure Inger's resentment of the fact that she, too, had had to be on duty.

Tomorrow, Monday, she would have a day off and so would Inger. What shall we do? she asked herself. Where shall I take them? Suddenly, she passionately wished that they were at *Les Romarins*, that she could drive out with them with Murphy and the old four-wheeler, or go down to the cove and build sandcastles or look for shells in the rock-pools. She wished that she were a million miles from Holland Park, from the hospital, and most of all from her underlying nagging suspicion that in spite of all her efforts to make sure that her household ran smoothly while she was at the hospital, things were not working out quite as well as she had expected. Deep down she acknowledged that if they had been hard-up and badly needing two incomes to survive, like so many couples, Hugo would have accepted much more readily her return to work, and the intrusion of an *au pair* into their lives. But equally strongly Nelly felt that she had a right, as well as a duty to use her brains and training in a way she knew to be useful, to others as well as herself. There you are then, she said to herself, it's back to square one again. She sighed, and turned over. Oh dear, she thought miserably, if only Hugo were as uncomplicated and relaxed as Baz; maybe I did marry the wrong man? But she thought of her three red-headed daughters, asleep in their room above hers, and knew she had not.

This is stupid, she thought, I must get some sleep. She got out of bed, went to the bathroom and got a sleeping pill from the locked cabinet. She took the pill, relocked the cabinet and put back the key on its high shelf. Then she shook up her pillows, and got back into bed. She put out the light and closed her eyes, willing herself to relax and go to sleep. But her head remained obstinately full of squirreling thoughts, and sleep still eluded her, so she turned on her radio to the World Service, very softly to avoid waking the children. She listened to a harrowing account of some terrible famine in Africa. As she listened, the pill began to work and she fell asleep. She began to dream, and her dreams became confused with the radio voice still insistently piercing her consciousness. She dreamed that she was in Kenya at the farm, that the house was on fire and she was running through the forest with her three little girls, all of them bleeding and dirty. They ran and ran, but she could not find Hugo, and though she tried to call his name, no sound came from her mouth. The children were all crying and falling down, and she turned to pick them up. As she gathered them to her, she saw a huge circle of flames soaring high above the trees, and heard a great roaring sound. She woke, sweating, her heart pounding, and heard a strange, low-pitched growling noise. She lay for a moment, frowning, wondering what it was, and then realized that the radio was still switched on. She stretched out her hand to turn it off, closed her eyes and slept again, heavily.

She was awakened by the sound of footsteps overhead, and a moment later Gertrude appeared in the doorway. 'Can I come into bed with you, Mummy?' she asked rather wistfully.

'Come on then.' Nelly turned back the duvet. Gertrude ran across the carpet and leapt into the bed, and Nelly put her arms round her and held her tightly.

'It's sad without Papa, isn't it?'

'It is a bit, yes. But we must do something jolly today. What can you think of? A really nice treat?'

'Don't know, really. Go to Pizza Express for lunch?'

They heard more footsteps and then the other sisters appeared, bleary-eyed and cross.

'It's not fair, Mum,' said Phyllida, 'she always gets into bed with you.'

'Get in, there's plenty of room,' said Nelly, and they scrambled in on either side, Sophie dislodging Gertrude from her mother's hug, and tucking herself firmly into her place. Nelly stretched out her arm to encircle the ousted Gertrude and gave her shoulder a reassuring squeeze. Gertrude turned her large, adoring eyes on her mother, and smiled the confident smile of the special youngest child.

After breakfast, and Inger's departure, came the serious business of deciding how to spend the day ahead. The weather did not look particularly promising, so Nelly thought that it would have to be something under cover. 'Tell you what,' she said, 'how about going to the BM, and maybe we'll see Baz there? We could take him out to lunch if he's not too busy.'

'Can we see the mummies?' asked Sophie. She was rather a ghoulish child, with a marked preference for the macabre.

'Of course; they won't have gone anywhere,' said Nelly, to the intense amusement of the two older girls.

'Why not?' said Gertrude, mystified; this was to be her first visit to the museum.

'Because they're *dead*, dumbo,' said Phyllida, in a superior tone.

'The mummies are dead?' Gertrude's voice trembled.

'They're dead, they're dead,' said Sophie in a hoarse whisper.

'Dead as mutton,' added Phyllida, gleefully.

'In their coffins!' shouted Sophie, and the older sisters broke into mocking laughter and clutched each other. Two fat tears rolled down Gertrude's cheeks.

'That's enough, girls,' said Nelly firmly, and began to explain about the mummies to Gertrude, who listened carefully, and then decided that it might be all right, after all.

She looked at her sisters without rancour. 'You are rotten,' she said.

'Yes, you are, sometimes,' said Nelly. 'Now, go and make your beds, while I phone Baz and see if he's free.'

The two older girls stuck out their tongues at Gertrude, as soon as Nelly turned her back, and Gertrude stuck hers out at them, crossing her eyes at the same time, then they all thundered upstairs to make their beds.

Nelly put the phone down. Good, she thought, it'll be much more fun for them with Baz there. She stacked the breakfast things in the dishwasher, and put the empty milk bottles on the area step. Or perhaps I really

59

mean much more fun for me? she thought, with a twinge of guilt. For heaven's sake Nelly, don't be so ridiculous; do grow up. You've a perfect right to have a bit of fun, you're not a bloody nun. She ran upstairs to the hall, calling to the girls to hurry up. The mail was lying in a heap on the doormat, and she picked it up. Among the bills and mailshots was a card from Hugo, with a picture of Notre Dame on it. On the back was written in his minute, scholarly script an enthusiastic account of a visit to the Conciergerie, where Marie-Antoinette and many thousands of victims had been imprisoned before meeting their death on the guillotine.

'The most touching thing is M-A's cell; poor woman, it's heart-breaking. I only wish you were here to share it.'

Oh, darling, thought Nelly, as she re-read the card, do you really? It's so stupid, we could all be there together. I could easily have rented a flat for a couple of weeks. 'God, it's too difficult,' she said aloud, then shouted up the stairs again to the children to get a move on. No, that wouldn't have been the answer, she thought. The fact is, he needed to get away from us, from me, to be on his own. And that's exactly what he's done. And I couldn't have taken time off from the hospital just like that, anyway.

The girls clattered down the stairs, and they all put on their coats and went out to the waiting car.

Chapter Four

After his first visit to the Palais Royal, Hugo walked back to the Ile de la Cité and ate his lunch under the trees in the little garden at the tip of the island. He had discovered the garden down some steps, behind the statue of Henry IV in the middle of the Pont Neuf. He carefully read all the guides and leaflets with which he had equipped himself, laboriously translating all the words he did not recognize with the aid of a pocket dictionary. He began to realize that he had missed quite a lot of interesting things, and decided to go back the following morning. It was astonishing, he reflected, that in view of his long friendship with Basil, he had never before visited Paris nor met either of his parents. Always went straight to Kenya, I suppose. And Hester never came to Cambridge, not even for Baz's graduation. Too broke I guess, he thought, same as Mum and Dad. All around him, the river flowed silently, the warm sun sparkling on the water and flashing on the windscreens of the cars which crowded the *quais* opposite. The *bateaux-lavoirs* cruised past, their engines throbbing, the sound bouncing over the water, lending a carnival atmosphere to the scene. The leaves on the trees were growing thicker each day; they trembled in the gentle breeze and cast dappled shadows on the ground. Hugo crumpled the cellophane wrapping of his ham roll and put it in his pocket. Then he gathered up his notebooks and files, and began to walk back to the Ile St-Louis. He followed the Quai des Orfèvres as far as the Pont St-Michel, then turned left into the Boulevard du Palais, intending to visit the Ste-Chapelle and see the medieval stained-glass. But when he got there he found a long, slow-moving queue of people waiting to get in. He looked at his watch: nearly three o'clock. I should be working, he thought. I'll come another time.

He walked slowly back to Hester's apartment, through the Place du Parvis, stopping to gaze up at the three great portals of Notre Dame. He shook his head in wonder and disbelief, and continued his walk round the cathedral walls, saluting the statue of Charlemagne as he passed. At the eastern tip of the island, he crossed the Pont St-Louis to the smaller island and made his way home.

Hugo really did feel at home in Paris. He felt happy and relaxed, and full of energy and eagerness to get on with his book. He loved working in Basil's little room, at the funny little inlaid desk in front of the open window, with the courtyard below and the blue spring sky above. He felt totally private and alone there, and somehow safe, and was beginning to realize how much he had been needing such solitude. What a selfish shit I am, he thought. Nelly bends over backwards to make things easy for me; why am I so difficult?

Hester was, by the very nature of her own self-contained way of life, the ideal companion of their evenings. She did not ask about his work, or show the slightest interest in it, neither did she talk about her own. In the evening, after supper, when they sat in the sitting-room with their coffee, Hugo noticed that the easel was turned to face the window and all the pots and brushes had been washed and left neatly on the work-table, ready for the next day. The room was always beautiful, immaculate, and extraordinarily restful, glowing in the soft lamplight. Sometimes Hester turned on the television and they watched the news, sometimes they listened to Haydn or Mozart on the record player, mostly they did neither of these things and just talked.

Hugo found himself remembering things concerning his childhood in Africa that he had completely forgotten. He told Hester about his friend Gabrieli, a boy two years his senior, whose job it had been to look after the ponies. The two boys had been great friends and used to ride together every day, sometimes round the coffee *shambas*, sometimes in the forest and sometimes out on the plain, where herds of buffalo and gazelle grazed. In the dry season other game often came to the water-holes; then Hugo and Gabrieli took care to stay upwind of them, hidden in the trees, silent, just looking. When Hugo went away to school in England, Gabrieli came to Nairobi with his parents to see him off, and just before Hugo departed with the air hostess through the embarkation gate, Gabrieli had put out his hand and pulled a hair from Hugo's head and put it in his shirt pocket.

'*Kwa heri, bwana kidogo*,' he had said.

'*Kwa heri, Gabrieli*,' Hugo had replied, making an enormous effort not to cry.

It was strange, he told Hester, he had found it much harder to part with Gabrieli than with his mother and father.

'And what happened when you came home again? Was it all just the same?'

'At first it was. For a year or two. But then Gabrieli had to work full-time. We could only ride out in the evenings, and Dad usually came with us. He said he needed the exercise, but really it was because of the gangs holed up in the forest. One of our neighbours had been murdered, it made everyone rather twitchy.'

'Did your father carry a gun?'

'Oh, yes. Always. So did Mum.'

'Real Wild West stuff?' Hester smiled.

'Sounds bizarre, doesn't it?' He smiled too. 'I don't know why I'm telling you all this; I haven't even thought about it myself for years, much less spoken about it. I don't dare to, or Nelly would have us all packed up and going out to carry on the farm. It's the sort of thing that seems hugely adventurous to her, and appeals to her sense of duty, too. She's never forgiven me for not doing VSO.'

'You don't feel any philanthropic urges yourself?'

'No, I don't. All I feel equipped to do in that respect is to try to look after my daughters, and Nelly, though that's not really necessary. She's more than capable of looking after herself.' Hugo felt himself to be hovering on the edge of disloyalty. 'What I really mean is that I'm a selfish prat,' he went on quickly. 'All I ever want to do is live in my ivory tower and write about the things that I think are interesting and important.'

'Don't let it worry you,' said Hester. 'All artists are like that, hadn't you noticed?'

'Not really. I don't know any, except Baz, and you.'

'Oh, me. I don't count, I'm just a hack.'

'Balls,' said Hugo, and Hester laughed.

'Let's have a nightcap, shall we?' she said.

The next day Hugo returned to the Palais Royal. He sat down on a bench and re-read his notes: 'In 1624 Richelieu, who had recently been made prime minister, bought a property and some land near the Louvre, and in 1632 he commissioned the construction of a huge set of buildings, comprising eight courts and a theatre complex. This great edifice was to become the Palais Cardinal, and the Comédie Française. On his death Richelieu bequeathed the palace to Louis XIII, but the king very soon followed Richelieu to the grave. The king's widow moved in with her son, the boy king Louis XIV, then aged four. The palace was known from then on as the Palais Royal.'

Hugo had been to see the Comédie Française the day before, and had gone up to the first floor gallery to look at the chair in which Molière had collapsed during a performance of *Le Malade Imaginaire* in 1673, dying shortly afterwards. He had also stared up at the beautiful balcony of number 6, Rue de Valois, where Richelieu had held the first meetings of the Académie Française in 1638. In spite of the fact that the major part of the palace was closed to the general public, Hugo realized that he could explore the courtyards and gardens and look into the curious assortment of shops, restaurants, and what appeared to be betting establishments built around the inner gardens. This amazing piece of real-estate development had been commissioned by Louis-Philippe d'Orléans in 1780, as a speculative venture. Always short of cash, he built elegant town houses round three sides of the garden, and let out the ground floors as boutiques, cafés and restaurants. Hugo was fascinated by the discovery of the little shop where Charlotte Corday bought the knife with which she stabbed Marat. Then he spent a nostalgic half-hour in a gallery that had a special little room devoted to Colette, full of old photographs, charming furniture and bowls of fresh flowers. He saw the windows of her apartment overlooking the gardens, and imagined the grizzle-haired old lady tucked up in her bed, crippled with arthritis but still writing, watching the world through her windows, observing the seasons changing, looked after by her husband, her cats curled on the bed beside her. He peered through the windows of the *Grand Véfour*, nearly next door, full of eighteenth-century gilded mirrors and painted silk wall-hangings. Colette had often dined there he discovered, as had another Palais Royal resident, Cocteau.

Hugo sighed, and turned back into the garden. He could not think of any place in London so dedicated to the cosseting and nurturing of its literary giants. In England, such people tended to live in the country and rarely met each other. In France it seemed to be quite the reverse. The country was for holidays; Paris was for work and café life, talking, seeing friends, serious eating, more talking. As he walked back along a gravelled path towards the entrance he noticed a small column supporting a little toy cannon. He discovered to his intense joy that this dear little gun had thundered at noon every day from 1786 to 1914, when the midday sun activated a detonator positioned under a glass lens, and had recently been restored to working order. Suddenly, he felt a pang of home-sickness and wished that Nelly and his daughters had been there to see it with him and hear the little explosion, but he knew that this was just a fleeting feeling. None the less, he went back to the galleries and bought some cards to send to them, and a copy of *Belles Saisons*, ostensibly for Nelly, but really for himself, he knew.

Nelly parked her car outside the house, put on the handbrake and switched off the engine.

'No point in suggesting a quickie in the pub?' said Basil.

Nelly looked in the rear mirror at the three silent, tired little faces in the back, smiled and shook her head. 'No, they're pooped. I must get them straight to bed. You can come and help me, if you like.'

'Why not?' said Basil cheerfully. 'Come on girls, one last effort.'

The girls looked owlishly at Basil, as if he had said something remarkably silly, but they got out of the car and stomped up the steps obediently, followed by Nelly and Basil.

'You organize them into their dressing-gowns, and I'll get their supper on the table,' said Nelly, unlocking the door.

'Right.'

Basil unpeeled Gertrude from her coat, and shepherded them all upstairs. Nelly went down to the kitchen, opened the fridge door and took out milk, butter and bacon. She emptied a large can of baked beans into a baking-dish, arranged three slices of bacon on top of the beans and put the dish into the oven. She put plates in the lower oven to get hot, and cut three thick slices of wholemeal bread to make toast. She poured milk into a pan, and set three places at the table. Then she went to the cold, brick-floored cupboard where they kept their better wine, and chose a bottle of Côtes du Rhône. She opened the bottle and poured herself a glass. Then she looked in the oven. The beans were bubbling and the bacon, sizzling, was making an appetizing smell. She closed the door and made the toast.

The children, lured by the aromas of bacon and toast stealing up the stairs, came down into the kitchen and sat in their places, followed by Basil. Nelly put the food in front of them, and they began to eat, docilely, without comment. Basil looked over their heads at their mother, his eyebrows raised in query.

'Tired,' she mouthed silently. 'What about a drink?' she said aloud.

'Thanks, I'd love one. I feel pretty knackered myself, it was a long day.'

Nelly poured him a glass of wine, and they sat down at the table.

'I'm not really dreadfully tired,' said Gertrude, 'it's just my legs are.'

'Do you want a hotty, darling?' asked Nelly.

'Of course she doesn't,' said Phyllida. 'Don't be such a dreary little baby, Gertie.'

Gertrude looked mutinous. 'They do so hurt,' she said plaintively, 'they're *agony*.'

'Right,' said Basil. 'A hotty it is.' He got up and put on the kettle.

After she had settled the girls, Nelly came down to the kitchen again and sat down at the table, feeling as if her legs, too, were about to give way.

'Poof,' she said, 'what a day. You forget what a strain it is, answering three sets of questions simultaneously. It's as if they're hooked up to an information drip, and you're the pack.' She poured another glass of wine for them both.

'They're excellent children, you know it really?'

'Yes, of course,' said Nelly. She took a slow sip of wine, and relaxed, gently stretching her stiff neck.

Basil looked at the kitchen clock. 'I'd better be off.'

'Why? Do you have to? Can't you stay and have some supper with me?'

'I really ought to do some work; I'm terribly behind my schedule.'

Nelly looked at him, her hazel eyes soft, and smiled. 'Whatever you like, love.'

'I'd like to stay, please,' said Basil, weakening.

'Good.' Nelly got up. 'I wonder what M and S can offer?' She opened the freezer door and took out half a dozen packets. 'Let's see. How about snails in garlic butter, followed by chicken with wild mushrooms and a *gratin dauphinois*?'

'Sounds fantastic,' said Basil, thinking of the take-away he would otherwise be having.

Nelly put the surplus packets back in the freezer, took the wrapping off the chicken and the potatoes, and put the foil trays in the oven. She peeled the film off the tray of snails and stood the shells up carefully so that the butter would not run out. 'They only need ten minutes,' she said, reading the instructions and setting the timer to go off in twenty minutes. 'Let's go out in the garden, it's really quite warm still.'

Basil picked up the glasses and followed Nelly through the glazed door at the end of the kitchen, into the narrow, concrete, pot-lined passage and up the little curved flight of steps leading to the garden. Nelly paused in front of the closed French windows to the sitting-room. 'It's funny,' she said, 'we hardly use that room at all. It's just like an old-fashioned parlour. I don't know why Hugo doesn't use it as his work-room, it'd be a lot quieter for him there.' She led the way to the seat under the almond tree. They sat down and she looked around her with a dull despair. 'What an ugly, boring dump this is. I'd like to get one of those garden people in to make something pleasant and green of it, but I don't dare to. You know how Hugo is?'

Basil looked thoughtfully at Nelly and took a mouthful of wine. 'Are you asking for my opinion on the subject?' he said quietly.

'Yes, Baz, I am.'

'Well, since you ask, I don't quite see the logic of your not enjoying either the fruits of your own labours, or your good fortune, merely to protect Hugo's tender ego.'

'Don't you?'

'I can see perfectly *why* you do it, but I think you're wrong. It's time Hugo faced the fact that it's quite unlikely that he'll ever be able to compete financially with you, or your family. He should learn to compromise and get on with what he's incredibly good at, and thank his lucky stars he's got you. Not to speak of those adorable little red-headed things upstairs.'

He leant over and kissed her on the cheek. She turned her face towards him and he kissed her softly on the mouth.

'It's not as easy as all that, Baz,' she said, returning his kiss. The timer rang in the kitchen, and she disengaged herself reluctantly and got up.

'It could be, Nelly,' said Basil, following her back into the house, 'it could be.'

'Hester,' said Hugo, a few days later, 'please would you allow me to take you out to dinner?'

'What a nice idea, Hugo. Thank you, I'd love to, as long as we don't go anywhere too far to walk, or too grand.'

'Well,' he said, 'I was thinking of the *Grand Véfour*, naturally, but since you insist, what about *Au Gourmet de l'Isle*? I was looking at the menu the other day; I don't think it will break the bank, do you?'

Hester laughed, and agreed that the *Gourmet* would be perfect. 'Let's go now, then,' she said. 'We can have a walk and a drink somewhere before dinner. There's an interesting house I want to show you in the Rue

Chanoinesse; it's the oldest surviving part of the Cité.'

'Good. We can book a table at the *Gourmet* on the way there.'

They descended to the street and walked round the corner into the Rue St-Louis-en-l'Ile. At number 42 they stopped and Hugo booked the table for eight-thirty. A marvellous smell of real country cooking was already drifting through the restaurant, and his nose twitched in anticipation of the good meal to come. 'It's a funny thing,' he said, as they walked towards the Pont St-Louis and Notre Dame, 'at home, I don't really think about food very much. Here, I find myself thinking about it quite a lot.'

Hester smiled. 'It's true, one does. Not surprising really, when every little shop and market and bistro makes such an art of every aspect of food and drink. To the French, it's just as important as sex, maybe more so.'

'Really? How very intelligent of them. I imagine that sex could often be a disappointment in one's life, or cease to exist for some reason or other, but there's always the comfort of food and drink, isn't there?'

'You're absolutely right,' said Hester. 'After George died, I could very easily have gone completely to pieces. But I kept on working all day as usual, and every evening I went out and did my shopping, and cooked dinner exactly as I always had done for us both, and set the table properly and that sort of thing.'

'Did you find it hard to do that?'

'No, it made him feel much nearer, as if he were still around.'

'You must miss him terribly.'

'Yes,' said Hester, 'I do.'

They crossed the Pont St-Louis and walked along the Rue du Cloître-Notre-Dame and into the Rue

Chanoinesse. At number ten, Hester stopped in front of a high, closed gateway. 'It was here in the precincts of the cathedral', she said in a scholarly tone of voice, 'that the canons of the eleventh and twelfth centuries took in as boarders the pupils of the ecclesiastical schools which grew up around charismatic young lecturers like Bonaventure and Abélard. They formed a modern break-away group as a reaction to the Establishment, and used to give open-air lectures on the Left Bank. Pierre Abélard in particular very soon attracted scholars from all over the world, and the influence of their disciples gave rise eventually to the founding of the Sorbonne, a century later.'

'And Richelieu had the buildings rehashed, and a new church built in the seventeenth century, didn't he?' said Hugo. 'Isn't his tomb there?'

'Hugo, why didn't you stop me? You know all this stuff already, don't you?'

'Absolutely not. I only really know about Richelieu. Go on telling me about Abélard, please.'

Hester looked at him severely. 'You really don't know?'

'I really don't know.' Hugo tried not to laugh. He was in fact aware that Abélard had founded the Conceptualist school, the forerunner of the Sorbonne, but obviously there was more.

'Well, all right.' Hester pointed to the gateway. 'This is supposed to be the site of the house of Canon Fulbert, one of the clerics who took lodgers. Quite by chance Pierre Abélard, then thirty-six years old, came to board in his house. Do you know about this, Hugo?'

'No, I don't,' said Hugo, truthfully.

'Well, also living in the house was the old man's niece, Héloïse, then aged seventeen. Fulbert was too mean to pay for tuition for his niece, an exceptionally bright and very beautiful girl, and part of the deal he struck with Abélard required that he give free lessons to Héloïse. He even gave him permission to beat her if she didn't pay attention.'

'Rotten old sod,' said Hugo.

'He was.' Hester walked on, and turned into the Rue de la Colombe. 'Am I boring you?'

'Certainly not.' Hugo followed her down the narrow street towards the river. 'Please go on.' They sat down on a bench on the quay.

'Well,' she continued, 'not surprisingly, the two very soon became lovers. Héloïse became pregnant, and they ran away together to Pierre's sister. They were secretly married, and in due course a baby boy was born. They called the poor child Astrolabe. Weird name, isn't it?'

'Very. What happened next?'

'They returned to Paris together, but when the awful old canon found out about the marriage he flew into a fury, and hired some thugs to kidnap Abélard and castrate him.'

'Jesus!' Hugo winced. 'How simply frightful.'

'Not very nice, was it?' said Hester. 'As you can imagine, this horrific event rather put paid to his ecclesiastical career, as well as wrecking his sex life.' She looked at her watch. 'We'd better start walking back; I'm beginning to feel like a drink, aren't you?' They walked along the Quai aux Fleurs, crossed the bridge to the Ile St-Louis and stopped at one of the small cafés with tables on the pavement.

'And was that the end of their relationship?'

'Not at all. He became a monk, and lived in a sort of cell, but being the kind of chap he was, it soon developed into a monastic school, in spite of the fact that his teachings had been declared heretical by a church synod. Héloïse had become a nun herself, but she continued to write passionate daily letters to Abélard, poor girl. The years went on, she became abbess of her convent, and eventually her nuns took over Abélard's school. He went to Brittany and became an abbot, but later returned to Paris and started lecturing again; he was a perennial thorn in the side of the established church. He died on his way to Rome, where he was going to defend his doctrines against charges of heresy. His body was brought back to Paris, and Héloïse had him buried at their monastic school. Twenty-four years later, she herself was laid to rest beside him. An incredible miracle was widely reported, and believed at the time. When they opened the coffin, Abélard is supposed to have stretched out his skeletal arms to embrace his faithful lover.'

'What a touching story,' said Hugo. 'At least, they were reunited in death.'

'Not quite,' said Hester. 'A bit later on, a prudish old mother superior had them dug up and reburied in separate coffins.'

'You're joking?'

'I'm not. But six centuries later they were dug up yet again, and taken to Père-Lachaise, where they were buried together in a single grave.'

'Can one see the grave now?'

'Yes, of course. They've got a very posh tomb, very Gothic; I believe it's one of the most visited of all the famous tombs in the cemetery, and always has flowers on it.'

They finished their drinks, and walked down the Rue St-Louis-en-l'Ile to the *Gourmet*, where Hester was greeted as an old friend, and they enjoyed a delicious and protracted dinner. Hugo boldly decided to try *andouillettes*, in spite of Hester's warning that they were made from chitterlings. He found them robust and delicious and needing the powerful red wine recommended by their waiter.

As they walked slowly home afterwards, enjoying the cool night air and the starriness of the sky above, Hugo reflected that he had rarely felt as comfortable in his own skin as he did at that moment.

It was Easter Monday, and Nelly was on duty at the hospital. She had finished her round of the women's surgical ward and now sat quietly beside Mrs Norris's bed, writing up her notes. When she looked up, she saw that the patient had woken up and was gazing at her with faded-blue, rheumy eyes.

'Ah,' said Nelly, 'there you are.'

'Back from the dead?' whispered the old lady. 'Bit of a waste of time, all this, isn't it?' Her eyes wandered to the tubes and drips festooned around her.

Nelly stood up and sat on the side of the bed, taking care not to jog the bandaged hand stuck full of the tubes that were keeping Mrs Norris alive. 'How are you feeling?'

'Awful, thanks.'

'Is the pain very severe? Do you need more morphine?'

The old woman coughed, and flinched. 'Will it hurry things up, if I have more?'

'What do you mean, Mrs Norris?' said Nelly, knowing perfectly well what she meant.

'Will I pop off a bit quicker?'

'Mrs Norris.' Nelly sounded kind but firm. 'You seem very determined to die this morning. By tomorrow morning, you'll be feeling a great deal better, and glad to be alive.'

'No, I won't.'

'Won't what?'

'Be glad to be alive.'

'Why not?'

'Because I don't want to, there's no point.' Mrs Norris raised her eyes to Nelly's and they were full of pain and anxiety. 'If I do get better,' she went on tiredly, 'they'll put me in a home.'

'Would that be so bad?' said Nelly gently.

'Yes.'

The old woman closed her eyes. A tear formed in the corner of her eye and rolled down the worn furrows of her cheek.

Nelly stood up, unable to think of any more words of comfort. 'Have a sleep now,' she said. 'I'll come back and see you in a little while.' Mrs Norris said nothing, but another tear slid down her cheek. Nelly checked the drips, adjusted the curtains which gave the patient a small amount of privacy, and left.

'Keep an eye on Mrs Norris,' she said to the staff nurse, 'she may be on the way out.'

'OK,' said the staff nurse, without much interest. It was nearly time for her coffee break.

As Nelly walked down the corridor to the men's surgical, she was stopped by one of the younger nurses. 'Dr Turnbull?'

'Yes?'

'I wonder if you'd have a word with a patient's wife for me? She's giving me a hard time.'

'What's the problem?'

'Well, it's Mr Simons. He came in last night with suspected appendicitis, he'll probably go down to surgery this afternoon. She's kicking up hell because the private wing is closed for Easter, so he's having to rough it with us here.' She raised her eyes to the ceiling, with feeling.

'I see,' said Nelly, without expression. 'Bring her to the office, will you?' She went to her office and sat down behind her desk. The nurse showed Mrs Simons into the room, and Nelly indicated a chair. 'Do sit down, Mrs Simons.' Mrs Simons sat, looking pink and agitated. 'I'm sorry the Lingford Wing is closed, it always is at Christmas, Easter and Bank Holiday weekends. It's hospital policy, I'm afraid.'

'What's the point of paying out for insurance if you can't get private treatment when you need it?' Mrs Simons looked round the dreary little office with distaste, and gave Nelly a sharp look.

'I can assure you that your husband will receive excellent care.' Nelly spoke quietly. 'The surgical facilities of the hospital are exactly the same for all patients, whether paying or otherwise. The only difference for private patients is the luxury of a private room, and rather nicer food.'

'And when will the private wing be open again?' inquired Mrs Simons, realizing that she was on a losing wicket.

'On Wednesday.'

'I see. So he can be moved to the private then, if he's still here?'

'Yes, of course. I'll make a note of it.' Nelly stood up, terminating the interview. 'I'm sure your husband will be fine; we have a first-class team on the ward.'

'Oh,' said Mrs Simons, determined to have the last word, 'I don't doubt that; I'm not bothered about *him*. It's just not getting what I've paid for that irritates me.'

'Well,' said Nelly mildly, going to the door, 'that's very understandable.'

In the afternoon she supervised the changing of blood-transfusion packs on a patient just back from emergency surgery, then went to men's surgical to help a relatively inexperienced young nurse dress the stumps of a double-amputee, the victim of a motor-cycle crash. The nurse looked pretty green as she peeled off the dressings, and Nelly looked at her sympathetically. 'Luckily, we don't get too many of these,' she said quietly.

The young man, with crew-cut hair and tattooed arms, lay on his pillows staring at the ceiling, stoically enduring everything they did to him. His mate had been killed in the accident and it had been Nelly's sad task to tell him this, when he asked for news of his friend. Their eyes met briefly, and she smiled, but he did not respond and looked away.

'You OK now?' she said to the nurse, as they finished taping up the dressing on the second leg.

'Yes, I'm fine. Thanks very much, Doctor.'

'Right, I'll get on then.' She went to her office, drank the cold cup of tea waiting on her desk, and wrote up her notes. Then she returned to the women's ward and spent another ten minutes with Mrs Norris. She woke once and smiled faintly at Nelly.

'Still here then?' she whispered.

'We'll bring you some tea later on,' said Nelly cheerfully, though she did not think that this would be possible. As she left the ward, she spoke to the staff nurse. 'Hasn't anyone come to visit Mrs Norris?'

'No, I don't think so. I don't think she's got any family. If she has, they haven't been here.'

'I see,' said Nelly.

At six o'clock a young woman was admitted. Mrs Stephens was on the next day's list, though it was not yet possible to tell her exactly when her operation would take place because her consultant was away for the holiday. Nelly took the patient's blood pressure, listened to her chest and went through the consent form

with her. At seven, the anaesthetist came in and repeated the process. Nelly checked the identity bracelet
on Mrs Stephens's wrist, and was surprised to learn that
she was only thirty-two. Bit young for a carcinoma of
the colon, she thought.

'Right,' she said. 'You're all ready for Mr Williams. It
may be tomorrow, or maybe the day after. We'll know
more later.'

'OK,' said the young woman laconically. 'Thanks,
nurse.' She picked up her *Cosmopolitan* dismis-
sively.

Nelly was extremely tempted to put her down. Instead, she walked down the ward to Mrs Norris's bed
and sat beside her until she died, without waking up,
just after eight o'clock.

It was a quarter past nine when Nelly drove into the
square, and stopped outside her house. It was a fine
evening, and the sliding roof of her car was open. Up
the steps of the area came the sound of loud pop music.
She got out of the car and looked over the railings.
Through the open kitchen window the music blared
and she could see her three daughters chasing each
other round the table, screaming with excitement. She
could also see Inger, her finger stuck in her ear, talking
on the telephone.

Nelly got back into her car, drove round the square
and stopped. I can't cope with this, she thought. If I go
in there now, I shall lose my temper with that bloody
Inger. Then she'll give notice, and then what? More
problems. Oh Hugo, she thought, why aren't you here,
you selfish brute? 'Sod it,' she said, 'I'll go round to
Basil's.' She drove out of the square and round to Basil's
street, a couple of blocks away. She locked the car and

rang Basil's bell. An upstairs window flew open, and Basil's head poked out.

'Nelly!' he sounded alarmed. 'What's up? Anything wrong?'

'Yes,' she replied. 'I'm having a nervous breakdown.'

His head disappeared and a few moments later she heard his footsteps on the stairs, and the door opened.

'Come in.'

They went up to his flat and Nelly sat down on the sofa, and explained why she had come. 'I'll telephone from here, and say I'm delayed at the hospital. May I use your phone?'

'Of course, help yourself.'

She had to dial the number three times before she could get through. At last she got the ringing tone. Inger answered the phone, and gave the number. Nelly could hear the music blaring in the background.

'Inger?'

'Yes, this is Inger.'

'Inger, it's me, Nelly. I'm afraid I'm delayed at work, an emergency, so I'll be a bit late tonight.'

'That's OK, I will be here, of course.'

'Yes. Thanks.' Nelly felt as if Inger were doing her a favour. 'What's that music? Are you having a party or something?'

'Oh, no. It's just the radio.'

'Are the children in bed?'

'Er, yes. They are just going now.'

'Good,' said Nelly, 'it's pretty late. Goodbye, I'll see you later.' She hung up, afraid that she might say more. Then she turned to Basil and burst into tears.

He took her in his arms and held her tightly against him. 'What you need is a stiff drink.'

Nelly sat on the sofa, mopped up her tears and blew

her nose, while Basil poured vodka and brought it to her. 'Drink it all in one go,' he ordered.

She did as she was told. The alcohol hit her stomach like a bomb, and she gasped and blinked. Then she gave a wobbly laugh. 'Jesus, Baz,' she said, 'you'll get me pissed.'

'Have you eaten today?'

'Not really.'

He made her a hefty cheese sandwich and stood over her while she ate it. Then he poured two more vodkas and sat down beside her on the sofa, putting his arm round her shoulder. She leaned against him and told him about her day, from start to finish, with all the tragic and repellent details.

'How can you stand it?' he said, when she finally stopped talking.

'I do sometimes wonder. But something makes me go on with it, and it isn't always so foul. Sometimes people get better, mostly in fact, and then I feel that I'm doing something positive for the human race.'

'Well, it's your life, but to me it seems a bit perverse. You're young, beautiful. You have three lovely children, and a brilliant husband, as well as money. Isn't that enough for you? Why must you spend so much of your life in that chamber of horrors?'

Nelly laughed, and turned towards him. 'Do you really think I'm beautiful?'

'You know I do, Nelly.'

'Do you still love me?'

'I still love you.'

'Would you like to prove it?'

'Oh, darling, are you pissing me around?'

'I'm perfectly serious.' Nelly put her arms round his neck and kissed him.

'Nelly, my dearest girl,' said Basil, trying to prevent

himself from responding, 'you're married to my best friend, remember?'

'So, does that necessarily prohibit my loving you, too?'

'It's the vodka talking.'

'Don't treat me like a child, Baz.' She undid his tie, and began to unbutton his shirt.

'What, here?' said Basil, faintly.

'Why not?' said Nelly.

At eleven-twenty Nelly let herself into her dark and silent house, stole upstairs, undressed and got into bed. She lay in the dark, her eyes closed, smiling. Then she slept like a child until morning.

Chapter Five

Reluctantly, Hugo returned to London and his usual routine. The children had gone back to school, so he was able to have long stretches of relative quiet in which to work. The heavy presence of Inger still made him nervous and that, coupled with the old stifling atmosphere conspired to make his task laborious and slow once again. In his absence, Nelly had had his desk and books moved down into the sitting-room, which she said would be much nicer and quieter for him, as well as having doors into the garden. He had thanked her, but secretly rather wished that she had consulted him first. As it was, the little garden had a stack of fat yellow plastic bags containing compost piled under the tree. A young man, in designer jeans and a Fair Isle sweater, was in the process of enriching the impoverished soil of the flowerbeds, and filling them with bedding plants, and this activity was proving to be somewhat distracting.

Hugo sighed and wrote a letter to Hester, expressing his gratitude for her hospitality and kindness, and offering to be her lodger any time. He wrote this as a joke, but in fact he meant it. He sealed the letter, stamped it and went out at once to post it.

*   *   *

When Hester received Hugo's letter she was rather touched. She read it twice, put it carefully back in its envelope, and propped it against the photograph of George and his mother in the silver frame on her work-table.

As she worked at her icon, skilfully floating gold leaf onto the background already coated with red bole, she thought about Hugo and his visit. She realized with some surprise that she was missing him, and that the last three weeks had been the first really happy time for her since George's death. She stroked the gilded surface with featherlight dabs of a dry sable brush to eliminate wrinkles, frowning with concentration. Then she put down the brush, took off her spectacles and stared through the open window into the pale-green translucent leaves of the lime-tree, unfurling in the warm spring sunshine which filled the courtyard. It was just the fact of someone being in the place, she thought. It was so nice having him working away so unobtrusively in Baz's room. And it was pleasant shopping together and sharing a meal together. He was so kind, and intelligent, and undemanding; so careful not to take over my space, and George's.

Often when Basil came on a visit, Hester was quite thankful to see him go again in spite of the pleasure of his company. He was so tall and bearded and big, he seemed to dwarf the rooms of the *entresol* and somehow managed to lessen the beauty of the place in her eyes. Hugo, on the other hand, small and slight, with his bespectacled diffident air seemed perfectly designed to fit the space. Maybe he would have been a little coachman himself in former times, she thought, smiling at the idea. Then she took a sheet of writing paper from a drawer in the table and wrote a note to Hugo, offering to rent the apartment to him in August when she would be in Ramatuelle. She did not send the letter at once, in case she regretted her action in a day or two. But she did not change her mind, and on Friday she dropped the letter in the post on her way to do the evening shopping, and felt a strange contentment at having done so; the feeling lasted throughout the evening.

Nelly had no wish to threaten the stability of her marriage in any way, and she made it plain to Basil that their brief reunion, however satisfying at the time, was not to be repeated. He drank with Hugo in the pub as usual and had a meal with them sometimes, especially now that the weather was warmer and Nelly's new garden had become quite inviting, full of pale, country flowers and pots of lavender and thyme. She had also bought three more white-painted iron chairs and a table so that they could eat outside sometimes.

'Don't mention the gardener, Baz,' she said one evening as they sat on the seat under the almond tree, now in full leaf. 'Hugo hasn't mentioned it, and neither will I.'

'Whatever you say, my love. You're the boss.'

'Am I?' Nelly swallowed half a glass of wine.

'Yes, of course you are.'

'How do you mean?'

'Well, it's a sort of circus, isn't it? You're the ring-master, and everyone else trots obediently round while you crack the whip. Hugo, the little girls, Inger, me. I expect you've got them all knocked into shape at the hospital, too.' He stopped, slightly surprised at what he had just said.

'Is that what you really think?' Nelly spoke quietly.

'I suppose I must.' He turned his sad grey eyes to meet her cool hazel stare.

'Not just sour grapes?'

'Probably,' he replied miserably, as Hugo came out of the house to join them, carrying a bowl of black olives and the wine bottle. He did not mention to either of them that he had received a letter from Hester. The post had arrived that morning after Nelly's departure to the hospital and Hugo had picked it up from the doormat. Among the usual bills and prize-draw circulars was a welcome albeit belated royalty cheque, and a letter to him with a Paris postmark. Hugo's heart had missed a beat when he saw the letter and had filled with a glorious joy when he read it. For some reason, obscure even to himself, he decided not to mention either the cheque or the letter to Nelly. He put the letter in a drawer in his desk and locked it, hiding the key in an envelope in one of his filing trays. What on earth are you up to, Hugo? he said to himself, and laughed guiltily as he went down to the kitchen to make himself some coffee. Neither Inger nor the gardener could dispel his mood of elation and he worked well all day, almost recapturing the tranquil, monastic ambience that had brought him so much happiness in Paris.

Basil stayed for supper as usual, despite his earlier firm decision to go back to his flat and work. 'How was Paris, Hugo?' he asked, as they ate cold chicken, a salad of broad beans sprinkled with chives and fresh thyme from Nelly's pots, and baked potatoes.

'Heaven,' said Hugo. 'Utter heaven. I wish I lived there, Baz. You're so lucky to have a place there, to go to whenever you want to.'

'Yes, it is lovely, though I do tend to keep hitting my head on the beams.'

Hugo laughed. 'I can imagine,' he said. 'More beans?'

Nelly ate her supper silently, feeling slightly excluded, and not a little irritated as the two men talked about their special places in Paris, and made rather coarse reference to the shattering mutilation of Pierre Abélard.

'Did you go to Père-Lachaise and see their tomb?' asked Basil.

'No, I didn't seem to get the time.'

'Next time, you must go. It's one of my absolutely favourite places.'

'Next time, I will,' said Hugo quietly, his eyes shining behind his spectacles.

Later that night, Nelly lay beside the sleeping Hugo, and found herself tense and unable to sleep. She was beginning to regret that she had seduced Basil, even though she had been enormously comforted and reassured by the episode at the time. It had seemed to give her back a sense of her own power and worth. Now that Hugo was back a reaction of doubt and unease was setting in, robbing her of her new-found confidence. It's very unfair of Baz, she thought. He was always encouraging me to challenge Hugo, to spend money if I wanted to, to do my own thing and not be so scrupulous about his sensitivities. And now that I have done exactly that, and gone to bed with him to boot, he doesn't want to know. In fact, he's ganging up with Hugo, I can tell. He's a shit, I hate him. She felt her cheeks reddening with mortification and turned over fretfully, thumping her pillow. After a few moments she stretched out a hand and touched Hugo's back, tentatively.

'Darling? Are you asleep?'

Hugo gave a slight snore and slept on.

*   *   *

Basil, for his part, worked late into the night, making a huge effort to get back into the rhythm of his work, to find the English words that reflected exactly the Russian meaning of the original. He did his best to put Nelly out of his mind. After her marriage to Hugo he had tried very hard to accept the loss of Nelly as a lover, and had thought that he had partially succeeded in doing so, but he never forgot how terrific sex had been with her, and often wondered whether it was as good between her and Hugo. Now he found himself constantly re-enacting their recent night together. He felt guilty at the betrayal of Hugo, and torn apart with longing to be with Nelly again.

He looked at his watch: nearly three o'clock. He re-read the poem in front of him, the Russian one in the beautiful Cyrillic script, and his own English version. Now that he had forced himself to get on with his private work again Basil felt a release from tension, a pleasurable tiredness, a kind of catharsis. He got up from the desk, and put on the kettle. He opened the window of his room and leaned out, taking deep breaths of fresh air, and watching a late taxi cruising by below. He closed the window, made some tea, black Russian tea with sugar, and went to bed. He leant against his pillows and drank his tea. He thought of his long friendship with Hugo and of his love for him. He knew that Hugo was infinitely dearer to him than Nelly could ever be. I suppose that's why I'm being shitty to her now, he thought. It's just a sex thing with her, that's all. Hugo will always mean much more to me. I must get away from them both for a time. Maybe I can take a long sabbatical from the museum; go to Paris, or Ramatuelle, really work. Get her out of my system, and get things back on a civilized footing. I'll ask for leave tomorrow, I don't suppose there'll be the slightest difficulty; they won't even miss me.

At the beginning of July, Inger gave notice, saying that she wished to return to Sweden and spend the summer with her family. Nelly could see that Inger probably did not intend to come back to them, so she telephoned the agency and asked them to find her a new *au pair* to start in September. She was due four weeks holiday herself, and informed the hospital that she would be away for the whole of August.

At supper that night, she spoke to Hugo. 'You'll be glad to know that Inger is leaving us.' She poured him another glass of some rather nice Barolo.

'Good.' Hugo looked up, his mouth full of Marks and Spencer's *fritto misto*. 'When?'

'At the end of the month.'

'Can't be soon enough for me. Have you got someone else lined up?'

'Not yet; the agency's working on it.'

'What about the school holidays? You'll need someone then?'

Nelly put down her fork and took a sip of her wine. She smiled at Hugo kindly. 'I thought that maybe we could have a month in Tuscany, take a villa with a pool. Would that be nice?'

'Um, yes.' Hugo looked into his glass. 'Very nice, darling.' He hesitated. 'The only thing is, I'm planning to go to Paris for August. Hester offered to rent her apartment to me while she's at her summer place.'

'Did she indeed?' Nelly flushed angrily. 'How very thoughtful of her. And how very considerate of you, Hugo, to consult me before you accepted the offer. Which presumably you have?'

'Yes,' he replied quietly. 'I have.'

'I see.' Nelly tried to remain calm. 'OK, forget Tuscany. I'll take the girls to bloody Florizel as usual, I suppose.'

'Why not take them to Tuscany? I'm sure they'd love it.'

'Hugo, the idea was for us all to have a family holiday together, don't you understand that?'

'I'm sorry,' said Hugo without looking up, 'but I can't bear the idea of a family holiday with noisy, quarrelling children, particularly when my book is at a critical stage, and I need peace and quiet to sort it out, if I'm going to deliver it on time.'

Nelly stared at him with disbelief. 'Are you telling me that you don't care about the girls any more; that you don't want to be with them, or with me?'

'I do care about them, and you. But the book is my immediate priority at the moment, and I can't afford to be distracted from it.'

'You can't afford anything much, can you?' said Nelly spitefully.

'Precisely.'

'Sorry,' said Nelly quietly.

'That's OK.' He looked at her then, his blue eyes steady behind the steel-rimmed spectacles, a tuft of his short, sandy hair sticking up on the crown of his head.

'So you'll go to Paris?'

'Yes.'

'For the whole of August?'

'Yes. Sorry, Nelly, but I'm going, I'm afraid.'

Basil parked his car in the first free space in Hester's street, and walked back to her entrance, carrying his bag. Like Hugo before him, the case contained mostly manuscripts and reference books and was heavy. It was the third week in July, and Paris was hot and dusty. Basil intended to do as much work as he could before he and Hester left for Ramatuelle at the beginning of August. They could not leave Paris before then, as the holiday let did not finish until the last day of July, and the *femme de ménage* would need a couple of days to get the house ready for them. At Hester's door, he put down his bag and rang the bell. They had often discussed the question of whether or not to modernize the door and have latchkeys, but neither he nor Hester liked the idea of vandalizing the seventeenth-century door in such a way, so Hester's ancient, heavy key remained the only means of getting in and out of the apartment. There was a spare key, but it was rather big for carrying in a pocket, and usually hung on a hook in the kitchen.

'There you are, darling,' said Hester, opening the door and stepping down into the porch. Basil put his arms round his mother and hugged her. She felt rather thin, and her dark hair appeared to be more streaked with grey than he remembered, but her calm grey eyes were shining and her face and arms were tanned by the sun.

'You look as though you've been on holiday already,' he said, releasing her.

'I know. The weather's been quite perfect for the last month. I go and sit on one of the *quais* most lunchtimes. The sun has been wonderfully hot, it's got rid of all my arthritic creaks.'

'Good.' Basil went ahead of Hester up the steep winding stair. 'You'll be even better once we get south, and so will I.'

'I can't wait.' She closed the door and followed him upstairs, and into the kitchen.

Basil unzipped the pocket of his bag, and produced a bottle of vodka. 'Got this at the duty-free on the boat. Actually, I think it's a rip-off. It's probably cheaper in the supermarkets here.'

Hester got glasses from the shelf, and took ice and a jar of olives from the fridge. They sat at the table, and Basil poured two generous drinks.

'Hugo sent you his love,' he said, passing a glass to Hester. 'He's looking forward to coming back here.'

'He's a dear, I really enjoyed having him.'

'How will we manage the key, if we're leaving before he gets here?'

'I'll leave the spare with Mme Corot; I've already sent him a card about it.'

'Oh, good, well done.' Basil took a swallow of his drink and topped up his glass. 'What time's supper?'

Hester looked at her watch: 'Half eight?'

'Great.'

'Well, go and get your things unpacked, have a bath if you like, and I'll get started on the food.'

Basil departed with his drink and his bag, and Hester went to the fridge and got out the plate of steak, already coated with oil, pepper, chopped herbs and garlic, and put it on the dresser to come to room temperature. She put some soft goat's cheese into a bowl and broke it up, then beat in some *fromage frais* until she had a semi-liquid cream. She added chopped cucumber and fresh mint, and poured the mixture into shallow bowls, decorating them with thin slices of cucumber and mint leaves. Then she drizzled a little runny black honey round each bowl, and put them in the fridge to chill. Hester loved making this dish, it had been a great favourite of George's; she thought it had reminded him of Russian food, his mother's food probably. It *is* lovely having Baz here, she thought. He's so like George, the same dark curly beard, the same voice, the same self-contained, secretive manner.

She took a bulb of fennel and two large, ripe tomatoes from the fridge. Then she roughly chopped a big onion and put it in a frying-pan with olive oil and garlic, and cubes of bacon. She fried the onion gently for a few minutes, and then added the fennel, cut in quarters, stirring it around the pan to take colour. Then she added the sliced tomatoes, a glass of white wine, some bay leaves, salt and a good grinding of pepper. The most delectable smell began to fill the little kitchen, and she covered the pan, leaving it to simmer while she made a salad and set the table. She put fresh bread, fruit and some Roquefort cheese on the table, set two places with the old Rodzianko silver and china, and opened the bottle of *Moulin-à-Vent* she had bought as a treat. She had considered a *Musigny*, but decided against it as she had guessed, rightly, that Basil would drink a good deal of vodka before dinner, so that a less illustrious wine would be more appropriate. She poured herself a glass, and went through to the sitting-room. She put a cassette in the recorder, Glenn Gould playing the Goldberg Variations, and switched it on. Then she sat down in front of her easel for a moment, looking thoughtfully at her day's work and enjoying the cool, leaf-scented air drifting in through the open window, and the crisp purity of the music floating on the still evening air.

Hugo drove Nelly and the three girls to Heathrow for their flight to Guernsey. From Guernsey Airport they would take a taxi to St Peter Port and travel by launch to Florizel, a trip of about fifty minutes. The children were excited about going to their grandmother's house but disappointed that Hugo would not be going with

93

them this time. They sat rather silently in the back of the car as they drove along the M4, conscious of the tension between their parents.

Nelly stared straight ahead, her face expressionless though her jaw was tight. Hugo glanced at her nervously from time to time, but did not break the uneasy silence. They arrived at the airport and he stopped at the departures entrance to drop them and their luggage, then got back into the driver's seat. 'I'll park in the short-stay car park,' he said. 'I'll be with you in five minutes.'

'Don't bother,' said Nelly through the open window, 'I can manage perfectly well on my own.'

'I'm sure you can,' said Hugo, 'but I'll come and say goodbye, Nelly.'

'Whatever you like.' Nelly turned her back on him and began helping the children load the bags onto a trolley. Hugo sighed and drove round to the car park. He felt unhappy and confused, but deep down he knew that if Nelly was determined to make a trial of strength out of their present *impasse*, then it was important that he should make a stand. After all, he thought, she's been making some pretty firm declarations of independence of her own lately, now it's my turn.

He parked the car – Nelly's car – and walked quickly back to the departure lounge. She had already registered the baggage and was sitting on a plush banquette with her daughters, who were examining their boarding-passes with interest. He approached his family, walking carefully on the slippery marble floor, and thought how attractive they looked, with their identical shining coppery heads and freckled creamy skin. They all wore blue jeans and trainers, and white T-shirts, and Hugo knew that they had heavy Guernsey sweaters in their hand-luggage, for the sea trip. He was going to miss them and asked himself whether he was being foolish and stubborn. As he reached Nelly's side, she did not make room for him on the seat, so he pretended not to notice this and turned his attention to his children.

'What about some comics and stuff for the journey?' he said cheerfully. Three pairs of eyes stared at him, considering this suggestion.

'Yes, please,' said Phyllida, getting up. The two younger ones got up too, and Hugo took them to the shopping area and bought them comics, puzzle books and tubes of fruit gums. He also bought several newspapers for Nelly, and the latest *Gardens Illustrated* magazine, as a silent acknowledgement of her transformation of the London garden. Only connect, he thought rather sadly. That's the trouble with us just now – we don't.

Nelly accepted his presents without comment, other than a simple 'Thanks', and refused Hugo's offer to get her a coffee. 'I hope you haven't lost your boarding-passes?' she said, eyeing the children severely. The cards were produced from jeans pockets, Gertrude's with some difficulty, as a result of which it finally appeared in a slightly mangled condition. 'You'd better let me carry them for you.'

The flight to Guernsey was announced at that moment, somewhat to Hugo's relief, for he saw the expression of mutiny on Sophie's face and her fist closing tightly round the pass. The cards were handed over without fuss, then they kissed Hugo sedately on the cheek, and formed a tight little group behind their mother. Nelly turned to Hugo and gave him a quick kiss on the side of his mouth.

'Phone me tonight, won't you?' he said, his blue eyes bright behind his spectacles.

They needed cleaning, Nelly observed. 'Or you phone me?' she said.

'Right.'

'Well, goodbye. Look after yourself.'

'You too, darling,' said Hugo quietly.

'Goodbye Papa,' said Gertrude.

'Goodbye,' said the other two.

'Take care of Mummy,' said Hugo.

'Come on, we'll miss the plane,' said Nelly firmly, and they walked quickly away, Gertrude running, and disappeared into the group of passengers travelling to Guernsey and Jersey.

Hugo made his way to the car park, and drove slowly back to London. He felt sad and rather low, but at the same time he knew that he had taken an important decision, and had had the guts to stick to it.

Hester had left the little Russian desk in Basil's room, and now he too was greatly enjoying working there. After a day or two he realized that his previous visits to the Ile St-Louis, even as a boy, had always been holidays. He could never remember actually settling down to do any real work; to live, so to speak, rather than merely pass the time. He recognized how perfectly George and Hester had organized their existence and how well Hester was continuing to do so on her own. She seemed quite detached and self-absorbed during the long working morning. She was awake hours before he was and had made coffee and begun working by the time he got up. It was such a contrast to the noise and dirt of London, to sit looking out on that sunlit leafy courtyard and hear only the twittering of sparrows in the trees, and the occasional hoot of a barge on the river. No wonder the work flowed well and the right words formed themselves as if by a kind of osmosis. At lunchtime, they walked up to one of the little cafés near the Pont St-Louis and had a glass of wine and a sandwich.

'Hugo was telling me about your showing him awful old Fulbert's house,' said Basil. 'He thought it a wonderful story, if a bit horrific.'

'I know,' said Hester. 'It is rather nasty, isn't it? Poor Abélard, and poor Héloïse.'

'I might go out and see their tomb this afternoon. It would be nice to walk under the trees and visit the dead. Why don't you take the afternoon off and come with me?'

'No,' said Hester. 'I really can't spare the time. I must deliver this job by Friday afternoon, and then I can relax and prepare for a good long break.'

'You deserve it; you work very hard. Too hard, really.'

'Nonsense.' Hester turned her face to the sun. 'I love it, I'd die of boredom if I didn't do it.' And loneliness, she added silently to herself. She smiled at Basil. 'You go, you'll enjoy it; it must be years since you last went?' She did not say what was in her mind, that cemeteries continued to upset her very much and had the power of diminishing the vibrant presence of George that still remained with her, both here on the island and at Ramatuelle.

Basil emerged from the *métro* at Père-Lachaise and walked down the Boulevard de Menilmontant to the main entrance to the cemetery. He bought a plan at the porter's lodge, and after consulting it he made his way to the old Jewish cemetery and found the elaborate Gothic tomb of the medieval lovers close by. He stood for quite a long time, staring at the tomb and thinking of the brilliant, handsome priest and his love for the beautiful seventeen-year-old Héloïse. They were lucky, he thought. It ended tragically from a sexual point of view, but they never lost the true essence of their love or forgot each other. He did not find the idea of Abélard's holding out his skeletal arms to welcome Héloïse to the grave at all unlikely. He smiled and turning on his heel retraced his steps along the hilly, tree-shaded avenues lined with their extraordinary tombs built like tall miniature houses, complete with entrances, windows and roofs. He would not have been at all surprised to see smoke issuing from the chimneys. Reaching the Avenue Principale, he turned right and presently arrived at the tomb of Alfred de Musset, who was resting under a weeping willow-tree, this having evidently been his wish. The tree looked like a fairly young specimen. They must replant it from time to time said Basil to himself. He sat down at the foot of a tree, not wishing to show disrespect by leaning against a tomb, and studied his plan. He decided to pay a visit to Marcel Proust. His tomb was on the other side of the cemetery, behind the Columbarium, and Basil enjoyed the walk in the warm sunshine along the leafy avenues. This must be the least sad cemetery in the entire world, he thought, though I daresay it's a bit grimmer in the winter, when the leaves have fallen and it's raining.

He found Proust, and then noticed on the plan that the tomb of Oscar Wilde was quite near. Oh, good, he thought, I've always wanted to see the Epstein sculpture. He walked round the Columbarium and followed the Avenue Transversale and turned left into the Avenue Carette. As he approached the tomb, its winged-sphinx relief sculpture standing out among the formal 'house' tombs, Basil observed that two people were already there, a man and a girl. The girl was sweeping dust and leaves from the tomb with a small brush and dustpan, and the man held open a plastic supermarket bag into which she was tipping the rubbish. When she had finished, she put the brush and pan into the bag, and the man placed a small bunch of roses on the conveniently-sited flat shelf beneath the stone torso of the winged male figure. Then they stood together, looking at the tomb and talking quietly. The man was tall, with greying curly hair cut extremely short and close to the skull. He wore a black linen suit and a white collarless shirt. Basil noticed that he wore no socks, his feet were bare in his well-polished black leather loafers. He seemed to be in his middle forties, though his slender build gave him a rather more youthful appearance. The girl, who stood with her arm linked in the man's, was very much younger than he, around nineteen or twenty Basil guessed. Her pale-blond frizzy hair was very long and rippled abundantly over her shoulders and down her back, confined only by a piece of scarlet silk tied round her forehead and knotted at the back. She wore a long, rather ragged, embroidered antique Indian coat over faded-blue jeans, and on her feet were soft red-leather slippers. Even before she turned round, Basil knew that her face would be beautiful.

He walked quietly up, and stood just behind them, not on the narrow pavement in front of the tombs but in the cobbled road. Suddenly, he realized that they were speaking English. On an impulse, he came forward and stood beside the girl. 'I couldn't help overhearing you speaking English,' he said. 'What a nice idea, to tidy up Oscar's tomb.'

The girl turned and looked at him, without surprise. Her eyes, heavily ringed in dark-grey kohl, were a brilliant, translucent aquamarine under the red silk bandana and shone in her pale narrow face. 'Someone has to,' she said. 'If the tombs are neglected, they're in danger of being removed to make way for someone else.'

'What an awful thing to happen,' said Basil.

'Indeed,' said the girl.

Basil held out his hand. 'My name is Basil Rodzianko.'

The girl took his hand and pressed it gently. 'Olivia Wickham, and this is my uncle, Giò Hamilton.'

'How do you do?' said the older man, shaking hands. 'Are you Russian? You speak excellent English.'

'I rarely get the chance to speak Russian, I'm afraid. My mother is English, I went to school in England.'

They started to walk back towards the main entrance together.

'Are you by any chance related to the painter, George Rodzianko?' asked Olivia.

'He was my father.' Basil smiled at her.

'How amazing! I admire his work enormously, he's one of the greats, in my view. It's tragic that his output was so small.'

'My mother has quite a lot of his paintings and drawings, here in Paris.'

Olivia looked at Basil, her eyes shining. 'Really?' she said. 'I'd absolutely love to see them sometime, if your mother wouldn't mind?'

'Honestly, Olly,' said Giò. 'You are pushy.'

Basil laughed. 'Not at all,' he said. 'I'm sure she'd be delighted to show them to you.'

They walked to the *métro* together.

'We're getting off at St-Michel,' said Giò. 'What about you?'

'That'll suit me very well,' said Basil. 'I'm staying on the Ile St-Louis.'

'In that case, why don't we go on to St-Germain-des Prés and have a drink at the *Flore*? It's rather nice, now that it's no longer the buzz place.'

'Why not?' said Basil.

They found a free table on the pavement at the *Flore* and Giò ordered a carafe of wine.

'Are you a painter, too?' Olivia lit a cigarette. 'Like your father?'

'No,' said Basil. 'I wish I were, but I have no talent. My mother paints icons, and I translate Russian poetry into English. That's about the nearest to Russia that we get, now.'

'I suppose there must be quite a lot of interest in Russian poetry, now that the cold war is over?' said Giò.

'Curiously enough, there was much more when most of the poets were dissidents.' Basil drank some wine. 'In any case, I work terribly slowly. The poems, when they finally appear, come in very slim volumes, to coin a phrase. I make very little out of them, financially, nor do my long-suffering publishers.'

'Poor you,' said Olivia, 'how do you manage? Do you have a job?'

'I do.' Basil was amused at Olivia's directness. 'I have a day-job in the British Museum; I'm an archivist.'

'Is that interesting, or just a stop-gap?' asked Giò. 'You don't look much like an archivist.'

Basil laughed. 'To tell you the truth I don't feel very much like one, but I haven't got the bottle to chuck it. Maybe I will, when I've had time to think out what I really want to do. In the meantime, it pays the rent.'

He looked at Olivia, who gazed at him attentively, her brilliant blue eyes half-closed behind a drift of cigarette smoke. 'And you?' he said. 'What do you do?'

'I'm in my second year at the Beaux-Arts. I have a

particular interest in print-making, especially etching. Like you, I'll probably find it difficult to make a living.'

They continued to discuss the problems of making a full-time career in the arts, and Giò sat quietly, listening to their conversation, drinking his wine, saying little. He thought Basil interesting and attractive and would have liked to talk to him alone, to get to know him better, but found the presence of Olivia inhibiting. In a few days she would be leaving Paris, and going down to her little house in Souliac for the summer. Perhaps Basil would be staying in Paris for a while, and they could arrange to meet?

'Are you staying long in the Ile St-Louis?' He spoke casually, glancing in Basil's direction.

'No, I'm going to Ramatuelle for a couple of weeks. My parents have had a village house down there for years; I'm driving my mother down next Tuesday. I'm going to lie in the sun for a bit, and do some house-maintenance for her.'

'Oh,' said Olivia, 'so am I. Well, not to Ramatuelle, to Souliac. It's a village near Uzès. My grandparents live there, and I have a tiny cottage of my own there.'

'Lucky girl,' said Basil.

'Yes,' said Olivia. 'In Paris, I'm still living in my parents' apartment, which is OK, but down there I can do exactly as I please, work, eat, talk all night if I want to; it's amazing.'

'It must be.' Basil smiled at her enthusiasm.

'Why don't you make a little detour, and come and stay with me on your way back? I've got a spare room, I can easily put you up.'

God, thought Giò, she doesn't waste time, does she?

'Well, I might well do that, Olivia. Thank you; I'd like to see Uzès again. Are you on the telephone?'

'No,' said Olivia, 'but my grandmother is.' She wrote

the number on a page of her pocket-book. 'Leave a message with her, and I'll ring you back, OK?'

'OK.' Basil put the note in his pocket. 'I'll look forward to it.'

'Basil,' said Giò, sensing that his chances were slipping away, and that Basil was being totally hi-jacked by Olivia. 'Does your mother ever sell her icons?'

'All the time; she needs the money.'

'I was wondering whether perhaps I could meet her? It might well be that I could sell some of her work in my antiques shop in the Place des Vosges.'

'I'm sure she'd be very interested. Maybe you could meet in September, after the holidays?'

'Yes, why not?' said Giò. 'In the meantime, here's my card. She might like to come and have a look at the shop, and perhaps have lunch with me. You too, of course, if you're in Paris.'

'How kind of you, I'd love to. So would Hester, I'm sure.'

'Well, good. Will you ask her to phone me?'

'I'll do that,' said Basil.

Later, as he walked back to the islands he smiled rather complacently to himself. It seems I'm not quite losing my pulling power he thought smugly, perfectly well aware that both Giò and Olivia seemed to fancy him, and greatly cheered by the fact.

Chapter Six

Basil drove into the Place de l'Ormeau just after six and parked the car by the church wall, as close as possible to the archway that led into the maze of narrow streets encircled within the stone ramparts of the village. From here, it was necessary to unload the luggage and carry it all to the house, piece by piece. The car had then to be driven round to the car park. Since the hill-villages around St Tropez had become fashionable in the sixties, the traffic had become an increasing problem, and during August a *gendarme* was almost always on duty to prevent parking in the centre of the village.

They got out of the car, and Basil unloaded the bags and stacked them in a heap by Hester's side. She gave him the key to the house, and he picked up two bags and disappeared under the archway while she leaned against the car, guarding the luggage, savouring the evening air and the smell of thyme-grilled *brochettes* issuing from the bistro across the square. She felt tired after the long hot journey, but overjoyed to be back in the place where she and George had spent some of the happiest weeks of their life together.

Basil did two more trips and then came back, red-faced and sweating. 'Any more?'

'I can carry this.' Hester picked up the grip containing

all her pigments and brushes, and two panels, already gessoed.

'Right, I'll just park the car then,' said Basil. 'See you in a couple of minutes.'

'You look hot. Why don't you have a beer in the café when you've dumped the car? I'll get things sorted out at home.'

'Well, if you're sure you can manage?'

'I'm sure.'

Hester walked under the archway and turned left, following the narrow stone-paved alley, shaded by the tall buildings on either side. She passed under another deep archway, formed by massive horizontal chestnut-beams, the colour of roasting coffee. These were overlaid with wide planks, and supported an upstairs room connecting both sides of the narrow street. A shuttered window lit this room, and a pink-and-orange bougainvillaea fell in a strident shower down the sun-bleached, pock-marked stone wall of the house on the left. She climbed a short flight of rough stone steps under yet another archway, stone-vaulted and rather badly repaired with concrete by the owner, and turned right at the top. Straight ahead stood her little house, squeezed in at the end of the alley. The house was in fact two ancient, poky dwellings knocked into one. The part facing her was in the shape of a tower, its curved walls covered in a vigorous ivy. Three steps led up to a door, set in the deeply recessed half-metre-thick wall of the tower, with a white-shuttered window beside it. There was an identical window, its casements open, immediately above and the rose-pink, Roman-tiled semi-circular roof that capped the tower rested on the top of the window like a heavy eyebrow, protecting the half-dozen swallows' nests built under the eaves. Hester's heart gave a little leap of joy when she heard the shrill scream of the swallows as they pursued each other, swooping along the alleyways over her head and alighting with practised ease on their nests. Beyond the door, another shallow step led to a short narrow passage giving access to the larger, three-storey rear part of the house. A glazed door formed a right angle with the tower, and marked the end of the alley.

From the roof terrace of the adjoining house on the left-hand side, a large white oleander spilled out of a terracotta amphora and tumbled over the iron railing into the void below. It was so thick and luxuriant that it completely obscured Hester's bedroom window, situated above the glazed door. I shall have to do a bit of gentle cutting back, she thought; I must have a word with Claude. Rising above the offending oleander she could see the top floor of her house, with the open windows of Basil's attic room, and the intense deep-blue sky arching over everything. Hester put down her grip at the door to the tower, unlocked it and went into her kitchen. She crossed the room to the sink and opened the window over it, pushing back the shutters at the same time. She leaned against the sink for a moment, gazing down the alleyway. She checked out all the dear remembered things, the heavy old street lamp, green with verdigris, suspended from a scrolled iron bracket on a house wall; the pots of scarlet geraniums and bright-green basil on window ledges and in doorways; the lean skulking cats that haunted the alleys. She sighed with pleasure. Everything was exactly as it had always been, shabby and beautiful. The smell of hot charcoal, seared meat, thyme and rosemary drifted through open kitchen windows, as evening meals were prepared, and mingled with the particular everyday village-smell of garlic, cats, heat and drains that brought tears to the eyes of sentimental lovers of the place like Hester, and was the despair of the more fastidious.

She washed her hands under the kitchen tap, a large old-fashioned affair of corroded chrome that dripped permanently into the deep stone sink, and was pleased to find that her tenant had left a large, square hunk of olive-oil soap in the dish. She looked in the fridge and found that Louise had got in milk, butter, eggs, mineral water and two bottles of the local *rosé*. In the cupboard she found tea, coffee and potatoes, also left by the tenant, pots of jam and honey, and half a litre of olive oil. She would need to go to the butcher for meat, and get bread and vegetables in the village. She thought that they had plenty of red wine in the cupboard under the stairs, and went to check. There were two cases, and she brought a bottle back to the kitchen and poured herself a glass, to fortify herself before carrying the bags upstairs. Then she picked up her grip, went through to the sitting-room, where Basil had dumped all the luggage, took hold of her heavy suitcase and climbed the worn, spiral stairs that led to the first floor, and her bedroom. Thankfully, she put the suitcase down on the bench at the foot of her high, wide bed. I'm getting a bit past humping heavy bags, she thought, Baz can carry his own. She glanced briefly and affectionately round the small white room, and opened the window from which under normal circumstances one could see the life of the little street below. A heavy scent of oleander flooded the darkened room. She opened her suitcase and took out her photo of George, and stood it on the night table. Then she picked up her grip and came out onto the narrow landing again, passing the latched cupboard door concealing the steep stair that led up to Basil's room, and went into the circular tower-room over the kitchen. This had been

George's summer studio, and was now her own.

If Hester ever doubted George's continued existence, it was in this room that she felt most strongly his undiminished presence. His easel and stool, now hers, stood in their customary place by the window, and Hester could almost see his broad, blue-shirted shoulders and brown neck, beneath the thick, grey-brown hair, and his freckled, blue-veined hand holding the brush poised, while he considered the next precise stroke on the painting before him, with its pared-down, almost minimal palette and taut, spare composition. The greys, taupes, indigos and broken-whites of his colours were those of an intellectual of the far north rather than a lover of the south and the sun. Hester imagined that the one made a kind of counterpoint to the other, and had brought George's essential Russianness into sharper focus for him. Several of his smaller still lifes hung on the white-washed walls, with some framed drawings, as well as two small icons of her own, which had been birthday presents to George, long ago. To the left of the window that looked down the alley hung George's most treasured possession, a Morandi etching of a group of bottles. This painter had been much admired by George, who had felt that he and Morandi had been barking, so to speak, up the same metaphysical tree.

Beside the door was a framed sketch, a Bakst costume design for *Petrouchka*, given to them by Baz when he was still a schoolboy and Hester loved its brilliant colours and bold confident drawing. Books filled the shelves lining the walls, and a round wooden table, battered and scarred, and stained with paint and turpentine, stood in the centre of the room and carried jars of brushes, a tape-recorder, sketchbooks and a black adjustable lamp of a pre-war Bauhaus design. Hester put her grip on the table and crossed the room to the window, brushing the easel gently with her fingers as she passed, and stood for a moment looking out, inhaling the familiar, comfortable evening smells. Then she left the room, and went down to the sitting-room below, with its wide stone fireplace, big decrepit sofa covered in a ragged blue Provençal quilt, and red-tiled floor. The glazed door led to the street, another to the kitchen, and French windows opened onto a small, rather dank and dark back courtyard. This cramped little space boasted a rather sad-looking bay tree, which really should have been removed long ago, since it cut off even more light than the high walls surrounding it, leaving only a small square of sky at the top. A door in the courtyard wall revealed a lavatory and a primitive shower, the only form of bathroom in the house. The one tremendous advantage of this unappealing place was its permanent state of coolness, even in the hottest part of the year, and by leaving the French windows open a cool draught acted as a natural air-conditioner and made the whole house comfortable, however high the temperature rose.

Hester went into the kitchen, finished her glass of wine, took down a basket from a hook in the ceiling, picked up her handbag and went out to do her evening shopping. The butcher lived in another alley close by, and she went there first. She bought two thick lamb chops, cut from the loin, quick and easy to grill. The lamb was from Sisteron, M. Monti told her, 'the best', so she knew that it had been reared on high pastures filled with mountain herbs, and would taste delicious. She also bought a rather scrawny-looking yellow chicken, and some pork belly. She exchanged news for a moment with M. Monti, an old friend, and then hurried to the Place de l'Ormeau to do the rest of the shopping. In the *bar-tabac* she could see Basil propping up the counter, engaged in an arm-waving conversation with some of the regulars, most of whom he had known all his life. She smiled, and turning into the Rue Clemenceau continued to the *alimentation*. She shook hands with Clementine, ensconced behind a modern check-out machine, and asked after her baby and her mother, from whom Clementine had taken over the business. But a short queue of clients awaited her attention impatiently, so Hester continued round the cool little mini-market and selected salad, cheese, fruit, tomatoes, some lemons and a pot of basil. Then she filled a plastic bag with black olives from a big round earthenware bowl, eating a couple as she did so.

She carried her basket to the check-out, paid, wished Clementine *bonne soirée* and hurried back to the Place de l'Ormeau. Facing her, as she passed under the archway on her way back to the inner village, stood the *boulangerie*, and Hester went in, through the beaded fly-screen that hung in the doorway. She exchanged brief greetings, and bought a freshly-baked, still-warm *baguette* and a *pain de campagne*. On her way home she reflected on how much things had unavoidably changed since she and George had bought their little house, so long ago. Most of the local shops were now run by the children of the original proprietors, and unlike their parents they conducted their business rapidly, without unnecessary fuss. Hester could remember very well a time when it would have been considered extremely rude not to exchange all your family news, requiring a chat of at least five minutes before the transaction could politely take place. She supposed that it was natural that the new generation should be ambitious and efficient, and take full advantage of the tourists and summer visitors who came in their hordes during July and August. God knows thought Hester, the season's awfully short, they need to provide for the quiet months during the rest of the year, poor things. None the less, she couldn't help regretting the slower pace of earlier times, and was not convinced that inflated house prices and queues of cars full of hot and irritable people really added much to the sum of happiness of the permanent inhabitants of Ramatuelle. Well, maybe I'm wrong, she thought, and it does actually please them enormously. In any case, I expect it was people like George and me that started the rot, so I shouldn't complain.

Stepping over a cat, unknown to her, she opened her kitchen door and entered her house once more. She put away her shopping, and set about preparing dinner for herself and Basil, happy to be there, and secure in the knowledge that her summer place, snug inside the fortifications of the ancient hill-top village was mercifully unchanged, and likely to remain so.

Basil drove to the beach early every morning, usually before nine-thirty, and stayed there till about noon, when it began to fill up with holiday makers from St Tropez and family parties from nearby villas, and became noisy and crowded. Then he would go home, have a drink in the café, lunch with Hester, and then work in the afternoon, in the cool and quiet of the courtyard. Around five o'clock, knowing that the sun-burnt crowds would have retreated once more, he would again drive down to the beach for a quiet, solitary swim. Sometimes Hester went with him; usually he went alone.

On the first morning he decided to go to the beach they called *Cabane Bambou*, because one passed such a cabin on the way. He followed the dusty minor road that led through the vineyards, past the sun-smitten *domaines* protected by tall clumps of aromatic umbrella pines, and finally arriving at the sea through the screens of rustling bamboos that grew behind the dunes. At the entrance to the sandy track that led to the beach, Basil paid his ten francs, and the young Algerian gate-keeper raised the barrier and he drove into the makeshift car park, where scaffolding pipes supporting woven mats provided an area of shade. He parked the car and walked to the beach through the soft, pock-marked sand, flecked with dry, wispy shreds of bleached and withered seaweed. A wooden hut, a beach café with a terrace, furnished with half a dozen plastic tables and chairs, stood on a slight eminence. In front of the café, on the beach, the proprietor had erected a series of open-sided shelters with bamboo ceilings, the sand neatly raked and with enough space in each for several mattresses to be spread without crowding. As usual so early in the day the beach was empty, and Basil climbed the short flight of wooden steps to the café and hired a mattress from the bronzed young man who was yawning behind the bar, drinking coffee. He chose one of the shelters closest to the water and spread out his mattress and his books, kicked off his espadrilles, took off his shorts and waded into the sea.

The sand sloped sharply away, the water became deep almost immediately, and he dived beneath the surface, enjoying the cool, sensual caress of the green, pellucid water. He swam for about thirty metres, then broke the surface and turned towards the beach, treading water. He looked up and down the long, familiar stretch of sand, curiously flat-looking from the sea, with the blue mountains of the Maures clearly visible in the distance, as well as the closer, tree-clad hills of

Ramatuelle and Gassin. To his right he could see the Cap du Pinet, to his left Cap Camaret, its rocky headland marking the end of Pampelonne beach. Hidden beyond that headland, and reached on foot by a goat-track, was another beach, L'Escalet, a deeply indented bay of sharp red rocks interspersed with long natural pools of clear emerald water, shimmering over hard white sand between the rocks. This beach, too, became crowded during the day, but was often practically empty in the early evening and from time to time Hester liked to go there for a swim with Basil. She much preferred L'Escalet and hardly ever went to Pampelonne.

Basil swam back to the shore, dried himself on his towel and put on his shorts. He had found some Ambre Solaire in a rather gritty old bottle at the house, and now put some on his neck, shoulders and thighs, and also on his feet which always seemed to get badly burned. Then he spread the towel on his mattress and stretched out, his head supported by a small triangular wooden prop, which went under the top end of the mattress to form a kind of pillow, and was very comfortable. As well as making it possible to read, this arrangement also enabled one to keep an eye on the other visitors to the beach and watch the occasional windsurfer or yacht passing by. Basil, unlike his mother, was not averse to a bit of voyeurism.

He read for a while, and then put the book down and closed his eyes, allowing his mind to drift, almost falling asleep. His thoughts wandered back to Paris, and to his meeting with Olivia and Giò at Père-Lachaise. What an attractive creature she is, he thought, it might be amusing to see her again. Maybe I *will* take her up on her invitation; what was the name of the village? Souliac, that's it.

He read another chapter of his book, then walked up to the café and bought a bottle of water. Quite a few people had arrived on the beach by now and it wouldn't be too long before he would take himself home. He sat in the sun and drank his water, watching what appeared to be a Scandinavian family, blond and tanned with two little boys, playing on the edge of the water, affectionate and well-mannered, enjoying each other's company. Basil remembered similar happy times of long ago, with his father and Hester. I wish I'd had Hugo to play with, he thought, but of course he always went to Kenya.

A topless girl and a man walked by with a large unruly black Alsatian dog on a chain, kicking up sand as they passed. Time to go, he thought. He had another swim, then packed up his things, told the bartender that he had finished with the mattress and made his way back to the car.

As he drove through the vineyards, his skin tingling after its first exposure to the sun, and his old car toiled up the steep winding hill through the olive groves and cork-oaks of the slopes below Ramatuelle, Basil reflected on how fortunate he was to have this enchanted landscape so deeply embedded in his blood and how dearly he loved it, in spite of the satin shorts and Wally Waggons of the tourist hordes.

The Assyrian came down like the wolf on the fold, And his cohorts were gleaming in purple and gold. Too bloody right, Byron you old sod, he said to himself as he drove round the battered outer walls of the ramparts and up into the village, drowsy and peaceful in the noonday sun.

Nelly was having some difficulty in catching Murphy, who seemed reluctant to surrender his long freedom and allow himself to be harnessed to the four-wheeler in order to transport Nelly, her mother and her three little girls to the village store. The girls sat on the gate of the paddock, watching with interest as their mother approached the pony, shaking the bucket of oats she had brought to tempt him. As soon as he had his head in the bucket she grabbed his luxuriant piebald mane, but each time he jerked his head away and broke loose, galloping away with remarkable speed for such a fat and elderly animal. Every time this happened the three girls dissolved into delighted giggles, which they tried but failed to conceal.

'Right,' said Nelly crossly, handing the halter to Phyllida, 'you try.' She sat on the gate herself, red-faced with irritation, and Phyllida took the halter, picked up the bucket and set off across the field. Her sisters sat on the gate with Nelly, holding their hands over their mouths, trying to contain their laughter. 'Don't be silly,' said Nelly, frowning at them, 'it's not particularly funny.'

Phyllida walked slowly across the field, calling 'Murphy! Murphy!' She put the bucket down on the grass and Murphy lifted his head and looked at her, then at the bucket. Phyllida held the halter in her left hand, concealed behind her back, and went on calling in a quiet voice. After a moment he came up to Phyllida and she held her free hand under his nose for him to smell, then gently stroked his face. After a moment he lowered his head into the bucket and they could all hear the crunching noise of him feeding. Very slowly, Phyllida slid the halter round his neck and stood quietly while he finished his snack. He lifted his head and Phyllida, still talking to him, slipped the nose-band over the pony's face and ears and calmly led him back to the gate. Nelly sat on the gate, open-mouthed with surprise, and Sophie and Gertrude clapped their hands in spontaneous applause.

'There you are, Mum,' said Phyllida, grinning.

'Well done,' said Nelly, drily. 'Do you want to lead him back to the stable?'

'OK.' Phyllida, looking smug, led Murphy along the path beside the orchard and round the back of the house to the stable.

Alain had swept out the dirt and cobwebs from the four-wheeler and dusted the seats, so all that needed to be done was to put the harness on Murphy and back him between the shafts. When this operation had been completed Nelly took the long reins and climbed into the driver's seat, the girls got up behind her and she drove round to the front door of *Les Romarins.*

'Run in and tell Granny we're ready,' said Nelly, and Sophie jumped down and ran into the house. 'I expect Granny would rather sit in the back with two of you. You can sit beside me, Phylly. Since you're such a clever-clogs, I'd better start teaching you to drive. What do you think?'

'Great.' Phyllida scrambled with alacrity onto the bench beside Nelly.

Una-Mary and Sophie came out of the house together. The old lady was wearing a flowered Liberty-lawn frock to the ankles, a man's grey cardigan, and a battered straw hat with a stuffed seagull on it. She carried a cream linen parasol which, when opened, would reveal a dark-green lining. It had a blond wooden handle with a cream silk tassel. Sophie thought it the most desirable umbrella she had ever seen.

'Had it in India,' said Una-Mary laconically, in answer to Sophie's query as to its provenance. 'And the frock.'

'Not the cardy though?'

'No darling. That was Grandpapa's, his favourite.'

116

Nelly and Phyllida got down, and Phyllida held the pony's head while Nelly helped her mother into the carriage, she not having quite enough spring left in her legs to get up without a bit of a push from below. At last they were all settled and ready to go. Wiggy and Pepys stood on the steps of the house looking beseechingly at Una-Mary.

'Can they come?' asked Gertrude.

'Will they run behind, and behave?' said Nelly.

'I expect so.' Una-Mary put up her parasol and gave it a twirl, to Sophie's joy.

'OK. Come on, dogs,' said Nelly.

The dogs fell in behind the carriage and trotted sedately along, as Murphy ambled through the gateway and into the lane, and began the fifteen-minute drive to the village shop. It's really sad, Nelly said to herself, as she gently flicked the long reins on Murphy's fat rump to encourage him, the girls are always as good as gold here. They have so much to occupy them and so much freedom to run about on their own. Hugo could have had all the solitude he needs here. The house is big enough, heaven knows; it would have been perfect for him.

In the afternoon, Una-Mary retired to her bedroom for a nap. When Nelly was staying with her she liked to have dinner with her at night, after the girls had gone to bed, so that a rest during the afternoon was essential. The dogs were getting far more than their usual exercise anyway, so she could dispense with the obligatory walk to the cove.

Murphy was given a good brushing and taken back to his paddock, and then Nelly and the children headed for the beach, accompanied by Wiggy and Pepys. Even in the height of summer the little bay below *Les Romarins* was usually empty, presumably on account

117

of the difficulty of getting to it, and the steepness of the climb back up again. Nelly sat on a slab of rock, watching her daughters as they played in the shallows with the two dogs. She was so busy at *Les Romarins*, cooking, washing clothes, or organizing some trip or other that she had very little time to herself. By bedtime she was so tired and so full of sun and fresh air, that she could hardly stay awake long enough to clean her teeth, much less try to think about her problems. She was finding full-time child-care far more exhausting than her long hospital days, and in some respects far less interesting. The days here seemed interminable, she admitted to herself. Of course, she loved her children dearly and had wanted them all badly at the time. Becoming a mother had seemed a natural expression of her love for Hugo, and the logical outcome of their marriage. Now, she recognized that the image of the perfect family life she had originally visualized and longed for had been a naïve pipe dream: that young children are not docile, sweet and affectionate, but frequently violent, noisy and assertive. She had soon become aware of how much she longed to escape from them, for some of the time anyway, and how thankfully she had resumed her career. She had told herself that once the girls were all at school, it was her duty to use the skills of her training and qualifications and return to work. Deep down, she was an ambitious young woman, and saw no reason why she should not rise very high in her profession. She knew she had the brains to succeed, and the capacity for hard work. She was more than happy to be back at work again, and sure that her decision was the right one. So, she thought, as she watched a pair of speckled juvenile gulls fighting over some rotting mollusc, why do I have to keep on convincing myself? Why don't I just get on with it, and not allow other people's opinions to get to me? Why?

'Because I love Hugo, and he thinks I'm short-changing the children and him, and he's distancing himself from me somehow,' she said aloud. Unexpectedly, tears filled her eyes and spilled down her cheeks, splashing onto her bare knees as she sat hunched on her rock. Self-pity will get you nowhere, she said to herself. Stupid woman, stop it at once.

Sophie came running up and clambered onto the rock beside Nelly, sticking her skinny brown legs out in front of her. She looked up at her mother and saw the streaks on her face. 'Mummy, are you crying?' she asked, and put her arms round Nelly.

'No, darling, it's just the wind in my eyes.' Nelly hugged her daughter. 'Just the wind. Can you taste the salt on your lips?'

The tip of Sophie's pink tongue passed over her mouth. 'Yes, I can,' she said, in a surprised voice.

After the heat of the day it felt quite cool in the drawing-room and Nelly lit the fire in there most evenings. Somehow, it made her feel more cheerful and she could tell that her mother was glad of it, too. Poor old thing, thought Nelly, her circulation's a bit sluggish, I expect. Every evening she made a special effort to cook something delicious, and they ate a lot of wonderfully fresh fish, and the fruit and vegetables from their own garden. Milk, cream and eggs arrived daily with Elsie, and Nelly made bread every other day. She enjoyed doing this and found kneading the dough a satisfying and relaxing task. The old black range was not quite as reliable as her Aga in London, which was gas-fired and hassle-free, and it needed a good deal of cosseting and expert fiddling with dampers to get it to co-operate. I'm completely off my trolley, she thought, as she riddled out the grate and carried the ash-box out to the metal bin beside the coal-shed. But somehow the horrible old range was part of *Les Romarins* and she knew that she would never willingly use the electric cooker, though it was sometimes useful as a back-up.

After dinner, she washed and dried the dishes, hung the tea-towel on the range, picked up the coffee tray and went to join her mother in the drawing-room. Una-Mary sat beside the fire, a dog on either side of her, feeding them doggy-chocs while she waited for Nelly. She had already laid out the Scrabble board on the low table by her side and drawn up a cane-bottomed nursing-chair for Nelly, who poured the coffee and took a cup to her mother. She was surprised that Una-Mary could drink coffee in the evening but made no comment, since she felt that her mother probably knew better than anyone what suited her best.

'Thank you darling.' Una-Mary took the cup. 'Lovely dinner, I never get tired of lobster.'

'Me neither,' said Nelly, laughing.

'What about a little cognac?'

'Why not?' Nelly went to the library table where her mother kept a supply of bottles and glasses, on a heavy silver tray. They drank their coffee and the cognac, and then settled down to their game.

'What's the score so far?' asked Una-Mary.

'Eighteen to you, three to me.'

'Goodness, is it really?'

Nelly smiled. She knows what the score is, she thought, she just wants to hear it said. They played three games, of which Una-Mary won two. The clock struck half past ten.

'Shall I turn on *Newsnight*?'

'Do you want to watch it, darling?' Una-Mary sounded bored.

'Well, I do, quite.'

'Turn it on then, of course.'

Nelly curled up on the old velvet Knole settee, with the end let down so that she could see the television, and watched the news with the volume turned low, while her mother played a game of Patience. After ten minutes, Nelly switched off the set. 'There's no news, really,' she said.

'Thank heavens,' said her mother, picking up the queen of hearts and placing her below the knave of spades.

'Ma, you're cheating,' said Nelly, and laughed.

'Oh,' said Una-Mary, 'so I am. I really ought to wear my specs.'

Nelly sat down on her nursing-chair and watched her mother finish the game, without cheating.

'Nelly, my darling,' said Una-Mary as she gathered up the cards, 'why don't you ring him up?'

'Ring who up?' Nelly swallowed hard on the lump that had mysteriously formed in her throat.

'Hugo, of course. Who else?' Una-Mary looked at her daughter, her faded-blue eyes tender and full of compassion in her wrinkled face, wispy white curls escaped from the solid tortoiseshell combs that restrained her hair. 'You're having problems, aren't you?' she said gently. 'That's why he's not here?'

'Well,' said Nelly, 'a bit, I suppose. It's not serious, just a difference of priorities really.'

'I thought so. I had quite a lot of trouble with your father, when he wanted me to be with him in Istanbul, and I felt I should be here, with you and Henry.' Una-Mary sighed. 'Poor old Henry, he was such a difficult, unhappy little boy. He must have been so

121

lonely here, when I was abroad with your father. When you came along so much later, I put my foot down and insisted on staying here with you both. But by that time it was too late, and I think he loved Nanny more than me, poor child. It wasn't an easy time, with your father accusing me of failing in my duty to him, so whatever I did was wrong.'

'Really? I never guessed. I thought you were the happiest couple I knew; I was quite jealous sometimes.' She looked at her mother, thoughtfully. 'The odd thing is,' she went on, 'with Hugo and me, it's the other way round. It's me who wants to be in Istanbul, and Hugo who wants me to be at home.'

'You're not thinking of going abroad are you, darling?' Una-Mary looked startled.

'No, no. I just meant that Hugo hates me being back at work, having an *au pair* for the girls. He thinks it perverse of me, when we don't need the money.'

Una-Mary stacked the cards and put them in their box. She looked serious.

'Do you think he's right?' said Nelly, quietly.

'No,' said Una-Mary, 'I don't.'

'Well, what to do? Tell him to grow up?'

'No, I don't think that would help. The important thing is, darling, do you still love him?'

'Yes,' said Nelly. 'I do, very much.'

'And he loves you?'

'I don't know. I think so. I hope so.'

'Well, good, that's the main thing.'

'Perhaps I will ring him, just to say hello?'

'Well, it's a good idea to keep in touch, isn't it?' said her mother, mildly.

Nelly went out to the hall, where the big, old-fashioned telephone crouched blackly on the marble-topped console table, with the phone book beside a glass vase filled with blue hydrangeas. She had written Hester Rodzianko's number in her Filofax, which was in her bag upstairs, but she remembered both the code and the number perfectly and picked up the phone. The long ringing tone seemed to go on interminably. He must be out, she thought, and was about to replace the receiver, when there was a click.

'Hello?'

'Hugo?'

'Oh, Nelly. Hello, is anything wrong?'

'No, nothing's wrong. I just wanted to say hello.'

There was a slight, perceptible pause, as though he were trying to think of something to say. 'How are the girls? Are they being good?'

'They're fine. I'm teaching Phylly to drive.'

'Isn't she a bit young for that? I thought cars weren't allowed on the island?'

'They're not. I'm teaching her to drive Murphy.'

'Oh, yes, of course, Murphy. I'd forgotten about him.' Another pause.

'How's the work going?' asked Nelly.

'Pretty well. I've got to chapter eight.'

'Oh, good. Well done.'

'How's your mother?'

'She's fine. We had lobster for dinner.'

'Lucky you,' said Hugo. 'I had a piece of ham from the *charcuterie* and quite a few glasses of wine; I'll have to watch it.'

'That's nothing.' Nelly lowered her voice. 'Ma gets through at least a bottle a day, plus her gins and cognacs.'

Hugo laughed. 'Good on her, it's obviously a recipe for a healthy old age.'

'Well,' said Nelly, 'I'm glad you're all right, darling.'

'You too. Give my love to the girls, and your mother. Talk to you soon.'

'Yes,' said Nelly, 'talk to you soon.'

She replaced the receiver in its cradle, straightening the fat beige plaited cord, and looked at her reflection in the large gilded mirror that hung behind the table. Under the heavy copper-coloured fringe her hazel eyes stared uncertainly back at her, concerned and rather sad. She sighed. She did not feel that her olive-branch had elicited a particularly keen response from Hugo. My hair needs cutting, she thought irrelevantly, and went to the kitchen to make some hot milk for her mother, glad that another day was almost over.

Chapter Seven

It was true that Hugo was enjoying his solitary life in Hester's apartment and was working very well. He followed exactly the pattern of Hester's days and shopped daily for his supper in the Rue St-Louis-en-l'Ile, taking a walk round the islands at the same time. To save money he did not always go to a café for lunch, but had the rest of his breakfast baguette, a piece of cheese and a glass of wine in the kitchen. In the evenings he cooked his supper, then permitted himself to go into Hester's sitting-room and lie on her sofa, reading or watching the TV. He did not think much of the programmes, but found that watching and listening improved his French. Sometimes he felt rather lonely and began to realize that the feeling of the place wasn't quite the same without Hester's presence. What he had so much enjoyed during his first visit had been not only the solitude and peace, enabling long, unbroken hours of work, but the evenings with Hester. He remembered their walks together, the food-shopping, their quiet delicious dinners. He remembered the calm, relaxed, undemanding atmosphere around her: the kindness and the listening. Looking back, he realized that he had told her an awful lot about himself, practically the story of his life. How strange, he thought, I've told her things I've never even told Nelly. About Gabrieli, and Mum and Dad, and how I worry about them but don't do anything, things I'm really rather ashamed of. I suppose the difference is that Hester understands and accepts things as they are, without making judgements, whereas Nelly, good woman that she is, always feels that she has to rush in and put things right; take charge. I suppose she's a natural empire-builder, he said to himself, like her father. Perhaps it would have been better if she'd done her empire-building before we were married, and got it out of her system. Or else gone on with it, and not married and had children at all. The same goes for me, he thought sadly, I hadn't found out who I really was either. I certainly hadn't learnt how to stand on my own two feet without Nelly to organize everything; and pay for nearly everything, too. Now I know that what I really want, all I'll ever really want is the freedom to write without cluttering my life with cars and houses, pension funds and school fees, accountants and bloody *au pairs*. The trouble is, it's impossible to have children without all that, or so it seems. A life like this, simple, hard-working, without pressure would suit me perfectly, though I don't doubt that it's ungrateful and egocentric of me to feel that way, as well as a bit late in the day. I wonder if Nelly assumes that I ought to feel grateful and toe the line, because of all the possessions? I wonder if it's right that I have the nagging feeling that I *should* feel grateful? God, he thought, I'm muddling myself.

He got up and went over to the window and leaned on the sill, looking down through the leafy branches of the trees to the courtyard below, cool in the evening air. A young couple, chattering and laughing, holding the hands of a small boy, walked across the paved court and disappeared through a magnificently carved door-way on the other side. Graceful, tall windows flanked the doorway and Hugo watched as lights sprang on in one of the ground-floor rooms. Then the heavy curtains were drawn, leaving Hugo feeling ridiculously excluded and lonely. He sighed; he was missing his own children, he knew. He closed the window, went back to the kitchen and poured himself a cognac. He went back to Baz's room, sat down at the little desk, re-read his day's work and made a few corrections. Then he undressed and got into bed, and was asleep before eleven.

Giò Hamilton sat alone at a table outside his usual café in the Place des Vosges, smoking a *Gitane* as he drank his coffee after dinner. It was the third week of August, most of his acquaintance had departed to the country or the sea, and business in his shop was fairly quiet. His sister Anna, her husband Patrick and their little boy had gone to Normandy, and Olivia was in Souliac. I suppose I'd better go over to Grands-Augustins and check out the apartment for them he thought, anyone could break in up there and no-one would know. I could do with the walk anyway, and it's a lovely evening. Glad of something to do, he signalled to the waiter, paid the bill and set off across the *place* towards the Rue de Birague, heading towards the river through a maze of side streets. He crossed the Pont de Sully to the Ile St-Louis, and followed the left bank of the island along the Quai de Béthune and the Quai d'Orléans, crossing the Pont St-Louis to the Ile de la Cité. He rested for a few minutes in the garden near the Deportation Memorial, watching the brightly-lit *bateaux-lavoirs* filled with tourists passing by, with the occasional heavily-laden, throbbing old working barge, slow-moving and low in the water. He continued his walk, past Notre Dame, leaving the Cité by the Pont St-Michel and walking up the Quai des Grands-Augustins and through the narrow, almost invisible entrance that led to Anna's staircase. He decided to go up in the rickety old lift, crossing himself superstitiously as he closed the gilded-wire gate and pressed the button. The antique contraption ground its way up, stopping with a jerk at the top. He got out, closing the gate carefully behind him, and felt in his jacket pocket for his keys. He walked the few metres to Anna's door, glad to see that there was no sign of intruders.

Inside the apartment everything looked perfectly in order. He crossed to the windows overlooking the river and opened them wide to air the rooms, which felt hot and airless. That's the trouble with these old attics he thought, the roofs get as hot as hell in summer and there's no proper insulation. Still, it makes up in atmosphere what it lacks in construction. It really is a nice place; I'm not surprised they go on living here. He went to the small kitchen and got himself a bottle of water from the fridge, and sat down on the big sofa to drink it. It was covered in a coarse natural-linen for the summer and felt cool and comfortable. He looked around the big room, sparsely furnished but with its walls lined with shelves, filled with books, video-tapes and CDs. Many paintings and drawings, all in beautifully gilded frames, together with some small pieces of carved and gilded wood were hung or mounted in spaces deliberately left between the books. The whole feeling of the room was intensely personal to Anna and Patrick, but Giò did not feel that he was an intruder in their home. On the contrary, he felt comfortable and welcome there and curiously safe. He considered having a cigarette, but decided against it; he knew that Anna was paranoid about anyone smoking up there. It was true, the place really was a fire-trap. He shuddered at the very idea and stood up. He closed the windows, looking across the river to the Cité as he did so. Doesn't that chap Rodzianko's mother live on the Ile St-Louis? he asked himself. He went over to the telephone and looked for the number in the directory. Yes, here it is: Rodzianko. It must be her, it's not a common name. He wrote down the address and telephone number in his pocket-book, feeling like a sleuth. I'll take a little look on my way home, he thought, just to amuse myself. He locked the apartment carefully, took a quick look into Olivia's room across the landing and then ran down the stairs to the street.

In fifteen minutes he reached the Ile St-Louis, walked along the Rue St-Louis-en-l'Ile and found Hester's side street. He walked through her gate and found her door, with a card marked 'Rodzianko' beside the bell, written in faded black ink, and slipped into a small brass frame screwed to the stone wall. He looked through the *porte-cochère* into the beautiful seventeenth-century courtyard, lined with trees, luminously green in the evening light. A few windows, tall and narrow, elegant in their carved stone frames, glowed with soft lights, but most were dark. Everyone is away, he thought. He walked into the courtyard and turned round, looking upwards to see whether he could identify the Rodzianko apartment. Two of the *entresol* windows were lit and a man, in his thirties Giò guessed, was leaning out of one of them, resting his elbows on the sill. Giò did not think that he had been observed, obscured as he was by the trees, until the man spoke.

'*Cherchez-vous quelqu'un, monsieur?*'

Giò was startled and took a step backwards. 'Are you English, by any chance?' he said, and smiled.

'Is it so obvious?'

'I'm afraid so.'

'Well, sorry if I seemed rude, I just thought you might be looking for someone,' said Hugo.

'Well, I was, actually. I was looking for Mme Rodzianko, is this her apartment?' He knew, of course, that Hester was on holiday but did not wish to appear to be snooping.

'Yes, this is her place, but she's away at her house in Ramatuelle; she'll be there until September. I'm house-sitting for her.'

'So Basil's not staying here, then?'

'No, he's down there too, lucky chap. It must be marvellous in this weather.'

'Oh, well, good,' said Giò. 'If you speak to them, say I called, will you?'

'I will, certainly. Who shall I say?'

'Of course, sorry. My name's Giò Hamilton.'

'Joe Hamilton,' repeated Hugo. 'OK, I'll tell them.'

'Thanks very much,' said Giò. 'Goodbye.' He raised his hand briefly and disappeared below the *porte-cochère*.

Hugo had been half-inclined to invite the stranger in for a drink but had dismissed the idea immediately, thinking that it would be a kind of betrayal of trust to ask anyone into Hester's place in her absence. Still, it would have been a pleasant change to talk to someone in English and this Joe Hamilton seemed like a nice chap. He very nearly ran after him to suggest having a drink at a café together, and then thought better of it. Instead, he put a tape on the cassette-player and wandered round Hester's room, studying George's paintings minutely, admiring their subtle, ascetic restraint. Hester's icons, so brilliantly alive, vivid with vermilion and gold seemed to illuminate the spaces between the sombre work of her husband. Like a blood transfusion

130

for someone suffering from anaemia he thought. Perhaps that's what made them so happy together; their life wasn't a competition, they complemented each other perfectly. Poor Hester, he thought, she must miss him dreadfully. She doesn't seem to have any friends here. No-one ever telephones. There are no letters, except bills. I've been here two weeks now, and the only person who's phoned has been Nelly.

At that moment the telephone rang and Hugo went to answer it. I expect that's her now, he thought. But it wasn't Nelly, it was Basil.

'Baz!' said Hugo, delighted to hear him. 'How are you?'

'Fine, how are you getting on?'

'OK. I've got a hell of a lot of work done, it's been great.'

'That's good,' said Basil. 'Because Hester was wondering whether you'd like to spend a few days down here? Change places with me? I'd like a week in Paris before I go back to the dreary old BM. What do you think?'

'Terrific, I'd love it. But are you really sure that Hester wants me to come?'

'Well, it was her idea, she suggested it.'

'I suppose I'll have to ask Nelly,' said Hugo.

'Why? Do you really have to clear everything with her?'

'Well, I'll have to tell her where I am,' said Hugo.

'Certainly,' said Basil crisply. 'But you don't have to have her *permission*, Hugo. You're not a child.'

'No,' said Hugo mildly, 'you're quite right, thanks. How will I get there, and when will Hester expect me?'

'Come on the Friday night Nice train, and get off at St Raphaël. Hester will meet you there in my old banger on Saturday morning. I'm going to spend a day or two with someone near Uzès. I'll go by train, and go on to Paris on the TGV, I've always wanted to travel on it. Then you can drive Hester back home at the end of the month. How does that sound?'

'It sounds wonderful Baz, I look forward to it. By the way, a chap called Hamilton came round this evening, looking for Hester.'

'Oh, really?' said Basil, smiling to himself. 'What did *he* want?'

'He was looking for Hester, or was it you? He seemed a nice chap.'

'He is. As a matter of fact, it's his niece I'm going to visit. She's a knockout.'

'Really?' said Hugo drily. 'Lucky old you.'

Basil laughed. 'Saturday morning at St Raphaël, then?' he said.

'Saturday morning. Tell Hester thank-you, and I look forward to seeing her.'

'Will do.'

'Enjoy yourself, you old lecher.'

'I live in hope,' said Basil. ''Bye.'

' 'Bye.' Hugo replaced the phone. I won't speak to Nelly now, he thought, I'll wait till nearer the time. She might try to talk me out of going, or make me feel guilty. He felt tremendously excited at the idea of going to Ramatuelle and happy that he would be seeing Hester again. What a good friend Baz is to me he said to himself, as he ran water into the bathtub. I always had the feeling that he still lusted after Nelly, but he seems to have his knife into her lately; I wonder why?

Olivia happened to be in her grandparents' house in Souliac, putting her laundry in their washing-machine when Basil telephoned. Robert, her grandfather, who was upstairs in the *salon* trying to sort out her grandmother's chaotic filing-system, answered the telephone and shouted down the stairs: 'Olly, it's for you.'

Olivia closed the door of the washing-machine and turned it on. She ran up to the *salon* and picked up the phone. '*Oui?*'

'Olivia? This is Basil Rodzianko, remember me?'

'I certainly do.' Olivia smiled to herself. 'How are you?'

'Fine. I was wondering, would it still be convenient for me to cadge a bed off you for a couple of nights?'

'Why not? I've no-one staying, it's pretty quiet here as a matter of fact, only me and my grandparents just now. I'd be quite glad of some company.'

'Can you meet me? I won't have a car, I'll have to take the train.'

'That's OK, I'll pick you up,' said Olivia.

'Which is the better station for you, Nîmes or Avignon?'

'Nîmes is nearer, but I prefer Avignon, given the choice.'

'Avignon it is, then.'

'When will you come?' she asked.

'Is Saturday OK?'

'Fine.'

'Good. About noon, outside the station?'

'OK, I'll be there.' She put down the phone, and gave a little hop of satisfaction.

Robert looked at her affectionately over the top of his horn-rimmed spectacles. 'You look pleased with yourself, puss.'

'Oh,' said Olivia, 'not specially. It's just a friend. You'll like him, he works in the British Museum.'

'I say,' said Robert, 'how impressive.'

'I suppose I'll have to find some sheets for him. I'd better ask Grandma.' She departed silently on bare feet, cool on the tiled floor. In the doorway she turned and gave Robert a long, blue stare, as if debating whether or not to say more. Then she grinned, her teeth white in her sunburnt face, her pale frizzy hair pulled into a thick plait hanging down her back. 'Actually,' she said, 'he's an older man, Grandpa. At least thirty, I'd say.'

'Thanks a lot, sweetheart,' said Robert. 'That makes me feel really good.'

Olivia laughed and ran downstairs to the courtyard garden to consult her grandmother.

Hester sat in the old Riley with the hood down, waiting for the arrival of the train from Paris. It was very early in the morning and Basil had left an hour earlier for Avignon. It was going to be yet another beautiful day and a flawless sky arched overhead like a huge, shimmering, inverted blue bowl. At this hour it was still cool and a gentle breeze blew off the sea. While she waited for the train Hester was reading *Var-Matin*, bought at the *bar-tabac* where she and Basil had had a coffee on the way to the station at St Raphaël.

One of the nicest things about St Tropez and all the surrounding hill-villages was their inaccessibility. There was no station, and no airport. Coming by car down the Paris-Nice *autoroute*, you left the A8 at Le Luc and drove along the slow, vertiginous and narrow mountain road with its many hairpin bends, climbing up to the summit at the village of La Garde-Freinet, then plunging down to Grimaud and St Tropez. To reach Ramatuelle one left the road just before reaching St Tropez and drove through vineyards, then climbed the wooded hills to the high *villages perchés* beyond. At least the difficulty of access did discourage a lot of visitors though needless to say, the rich and famous arrived in the harbour by yacht, or by helicopter from Nice Airport. The whole area, mountainous and heavily wooded, had always been difficult for would-be invaders. The Saracens had managed to get in from the sea in AD 884 and had set up a base at La Garde-Freinet, sending out plundering parties all over the area. Ramatuelle had the distinction of having foiled the Saracens, helped by a fortuitously-swarming cloud of bees that had attacked the intruders as they tried to scale the ramparts of the village, stinging them so mercilessly that they were forced to flee. In the old days there had been a delightful naïve painting depicting this thrilling event hanging on the wall of Chez Tony, a family-run *bar-restaurant* in the Rue Clemenceau. Hester had not been there for some years, and didn't know whether the painting was still there. She hoped very much that it was, and that the place still functioned. I must check it out she thought; Hugo and I might have supper there one night; it used to be a good place.

A loud roaring and hissing announced the arrival of the train and in a few minutes Hugo emerged from the barrier, holding a small canvas hold-all and a bulging briefcase. He looked around him myopically, trying to locate the car. Hester gave a little toot on the horn and waved. At once, Hugo looked towards her, smiled and came hurrying over. She got out of the car to greet him.

'I nearly failed to get off,' he said. 'I didn't understand the announcement and I missed the signs, what a panic!'

Hester laughed, and touched his cheek, red with haste and agitation. 'Goodness, you *are* hot,' she said. 'Take off your jacket and tie, Hugo, and put them in the boot with your bags. Then we'll go and get you a cold drink before we drive home. It's nice to see you,' she added.

Hugo bent and kissed her cheek. 'It's lovely to be here; sorry to be so sweaty.'

Hester drove into St Raphaël, and they sat under an umbrella at a café table while Hugo slowly drank most of a litre of cold Evian water, and Hester had another coffee.

'I feel dreadfully dehydrated,' said Hugo, 'after a night on that boiling top bunk with all the windows tightly shut; it was hell.'

'It can be. Didn't you take anything with you, water for example?'

'No, more fool me. It never occurred to me. I have to be the most incompetent and moronic traveller that ever was, left to myself.' He smiled ruefully at Hester, who resisted the temptation to laugh.

'Better now?' she said.

'Much.'

'Let's get on then, before it gets really hot.'

Hugo paid and bought another bottle of water, then they walked slowly back to the car, parked across the road.

'We could go home by the coast road,' said Hester, 'but it's terribly built-up. It's hideous, I hate it. So I'm going to show you a much more interesting way.'

'How do you mean, interesting?'

'You'll see.'

She drove out of the town and on to the N7. She drove fast to Vidauban and then turned into a minor road, with a faded signpost saying 'La Garde-Freinet'. She followed the road through scrubby woodlands of ever-green-oaks and umbrella-pines, with rock-roses, myrtle and sparse clumps of spiky lavender growing out of the hard, sun-baked earth beneath the trees. As they drove, the sharp aromatic scents of the *garrigue* filled Hugo's nose as if he had sniffed it from a bottle, and he sneezed.

'Is it too much?' Hester glanced at him. 'Shall we put up the hood?'

'No, it's wonderful, it's clearing my head of the train smell.' He sneezed again, and laughed.

As the sun rose higher in the sky and grew hotter, the air was filled with the strange, percussive music of cicadas, and Hugo felt himself dragged backwards down the wrong end of a mental telescope to a landscape of wide yellow plains, shimmering in the heat-haze, dotted with thorn-trees, sheltering herds of gazelle, their short tails flicking, their heads alert, bright-eyed, looking for danger. 'It sounds just like home,' he said. 'Like Africa.'

From time to time, they passed concealed driveways marked *Proprieté Privée*, though the actual houses were usually hidden behind the trees.

'I wouldn't like to live up here,' said Hester. 'I'd be too worried about forest fires.'

'Do they happen often?'

'Far too often, it's a terrible problem. Some people think that the fires are sometimes started deliberately, to clear the land for the vile property developers.'

'Really? How ghastly, in such wonderful country.'

'Well, you know how it is. There are always greedy men itching to throw up whole new villages of concrete villas masquerading as traditional Provençal houses. You should see the coastal area. Or rather, you shouldn't, it's too depressing.'

'It's the same everywhere, I suppose, isn't it? When it comes to the crunch, the conservation lobby has few teeth.'

'You're right,' said Hester. 'But at least in Ramatuelle, the *commune* is extremely strict, they really do preserve the village. Long may it last.'

The road began to climb, twisting and turning round

hairpin bends with stomach-churning drops on the right-hand side of the road, their side.

'I see what you mean by an interesting drive,' said Hugo, fighting a strong impulse to grip the dash-board.

'Look at the view, Hugo.' Hester, smiling, kept her own eyes firmly on the road. 'It's worth it, I promise.'

Hugo looked, and saw the great dark-green curving sweep of the tree-clad mountain as it rose sharply up on their left, and then fell away down into the valley, hundreds of feet below on their right. High in the sky, buzzards circled, riding the thermals. 'Wonderful,' he said faintly.

'It's not as bad as it looks; you soon get used to it.' She drove on, steering carefully round the hairpins, slowing to a crawl when a descending vehicle appeared round a bend, usually hogging the middle of the narrow road, to Hugo's anguish. At last she drove into La Garde-Freinet. The village straggled along the summit, lazy in the sunshine, with flea-bitten dogs lying basking in the dust and swallows wheeling overhead, dodging the electricity cables slung haphazardly across the street.

'The worst is over,' said Hester. 'It's downhill all the way now, and not nearly as alarming.'

'I can't say I'm sorry to hear it.'

They started the descent towards the coast and Hugo began to relax. It was true, the landscape was unbelievably beautiful; he looked around him, trying to freeze the images in his memory.

'The best time to be here is really May,' said Hester. 'It's not so hot, and the forest is covered in flowers; it's magical.'

'It's pretty perfect now, isn't it?'

'I'm glad you think so.'

As they rounded a bend and drove down a comparatively straight section of the road towards Grimaud, Hugo caught a glimpse of the sea, blue as the sky, the Gulf of St Tropez. He felt as thrilled as a child. 'It never fails, does it?' he said.

'The sight of the sea? No, it never does. I hope it never will.'

They drove through Grimaud, pretty enough but full of the signs of wealthy summer visitors whose preferred form of transport appeared to be either a stretched-Mercedes or huge glitzy super-jeeps, full of bronzed blonde bimbos. Hugo's heart sank. Hester drove fast along the coast road, passing petrol stations with extravagant car-washes, hot-dog and *frites* stalls, as well as large roadside signs promoting visits to local potteries and *caves co-operatives*.

'Horrendous, isn't it?' she said. 'Don't worry, we'll soon be out of it.'

Before reaching the outskirts of St Tropez she turned right. There was a sign low on the road marked 'Gassin-Ramatuelle', but Hugo would never have noticed it on his own. Almost at once they were in another country, or so it seemed to him. They had entered a gentle, pastoral landscape of vineyards surrounding small farmhouses, with faded shutters and soft, apricot-coloured Roman-tiled roofs, shaded by clumps of tall umbrella-pines. At the entrance to many of these small *domaines*, a home-made sign said 'Chambres d'hôtes'. They drove through the vines for several kilometres and then the narrow road began to climb upwards, winding round a wooded hillside to the village above, just visible on its summit. Hester drove round the outer road to the car park, and they left the car and walked down into the Place de l'Ormeau, where the Saturday morning market was still in full swing.

The fish-merchant had every kind of fresh local fish arranged on large slabs of ice in his van, its let-down side-panel opened to display the day's selection.

'What do you think, Hugo? Would you like grilled sardines for supper?'

'Sounds good,' said Hugo, who was beginning to feel hungry.

Hester bought a kilo of sardines and asked the fish-man to remove the backbones. Hugo watched, fascinated, as he slit each fish down the belly and gutted it, taking off the head simultaneously. Then he flattened out the fish, skin-side uppermost, pressed firmly along the spine with his thumb-nail, and flicked out the backbone with swift, practised skill. He dealt with the entire kilo of fish in a couple of minutes.

'Marvellous, isn't it?' Hester paid the man and picked up the small plastic carrier bag. 'It would take me a good half-hour to do that at home; it makes one go off the whole idea.' They bought peaches and tomatoes, and then bread at the *boulangerie*.

'That briefcase looks awfully heavy,' said Hester, as they emerged from the hot little shop, and turned right along the alleyway towards her house.

'It is, it's full of books. It weighs a ton.'

'Never mind, we're nearly there.'

The midday sun sent dazzling shafts of light into the narrow chasms between the houses, making the shadows under the deep archways almost black, and intensifying the flaming brilliance of the bougainvillaea as it fell down its wall like a river of fire. Hugo had an amazed sense of *déjà-vu* as he saw it – just such a bougainvillaea climbed vigorously over the corrugated-iron roof of the verandah of his parents' house in Kenya; he quite expected to see a moon-flower round the next corner. Then they climbed the short flight of steps under another archway, and turned right at the top.

'That's it,' said Hester, 'straight ahead.'

Hugo put down his bags and looked at the little house, so snugly tucked in at the end of the alley. He thought it utterly enchanting, and said so. Inside the house, it was cool and dark after the brightness of the sunlight. Hester tipped the bag of fish into a bowl, covered it and put it in the fridge.

'I expect you'd like to go to the beach for a swim,' she said, 'but it's really too crowded to be pleasant until after five o'clock. So what about having some lunch now, and then a siesta?'

'Sounds absolutely perfect, Hester. I'm dying to go out and explore the village too, but I must admit that I still feel pretty shattered. I hardly slept at all on the train.'

'Good, that's what we'll do then. You go on up with your stuff and unpack, and I'll get on with the lunch.' She explained the geography of the house to him, and Hugo picked up his bags and went up the stairs to the attic room.

Like Basil's room in Paris, it was simple to the point of austerity. The spaces between the rafters supporting the tiled roof had been lined with heavy insulation-boards, and lime-washed like the rough walls of the room. In the rear wall was a very small open window, its single shutter closed against the heat of the sun. Beneath it stood a low divan bed, covered in a plain white cotton counterpane, with three square white pillows. Beside the bed was a small wooden table, a reading-lamp with a simple parchment shade and a pile of books. On the opposite side of the room was a bigger window, also shuttered, and Hugo put down his bags, crossed the bare, dusty, pink-tiled floor and threw open

141

the shutters. As he had hoped, the high window had a spectacular view over the Roman-tiled roofs of the lower neighbouring houses, with their variously-shaped chimneys and forest of television aerials, to an incredibly lovely landscape of vineyards and olive groves that fell gently away to the blue sea, he guessed about seven kilometres distant.

'What a place,' he said, leaning on the sill, rejoicing in the sun and the small breeze that flowed past him into the room. Guiltily, he thought of Nelly and the little girls, probably enduring rain and cold in Florizel, when they could all have been together in Tuscany, in a place very like this. He had chickened out of telephoning her and had sent a card, giving Hester's phone number in Ramatuelle. He had considered giving Basil's return to Paris as his reason for going to Ramatuelle, but decided against it in the end. He thought that if he was going to make a proper stand with Nelly about making his own choices, then it was probably wiser not to make any excuses at all for his actions. None the less, he knew that she would be extremely angry with him, and rather quailed at the prospect of the row that would doubtless ensue. Oh well, he thought, I'm here now, so I might as well enjoy it.

He closed the shutters, leaving them slightly ajar but held together by the heavy iron latch. He unpacked his hold-all and changed into khaki cotton trousers and a T-shirt, hanging his hot, crumpled clothes on the hooks behind the door. His brown shoes looked unsuitably citified and he frowned at them impatiently. I expect I can get espadrilles locally, he thought, taking off his socks. There was a table, with a rather nicely shaped rush-seated chair standing beside the big window, and Hugo unpacked his manuscript and reference books and arranged them neatly, ready to continue with the work.

He went downstairs to the kitchen, where Hester had already put plates on the table and had prepared a large platter of sliced tomatoes in a rich, garlicky dressing, scattered with glossy black olives and roughly chopped basil. She had hard-boiled eggs cooling under the slowly-running cold tap, and as he came into the room she took the eggs from their bowl, shelled and halved them, and arranged them on the tomatoes. She cut the baguette into fat slices, took a bottle of *rosé* from the fridge, and they sat down.

Hugo inhaled the wonderful, almost intoxicating smell of basil and garlic, and took a deep drink of the chilled wine Hester poured for him. 'You know, Hester,' he said, dipping his egg into the fragrant, oily dressing and then into the glass bowl of coarse sea-salt, following her example, 'I could easily become seriously greedy when I'm with you.'

'What's wrong with that?'

'Nothing.' He smiled at her. 'It's lovely.'

In the early evening Hugo drove them to Hester's favourite beach, L'Escalet. They left the car at the top of the cliff and descended the goat-track – narrow, slippery and the colour of red-ochre. It was bordered on either side by gorse-bushes and coarse grey spiky plants, smelling of curry after the heat of the day. The cove lay below them, the sandy bottom clearly visible through the deep inlets of water that flowed between long flat outcrops of rock, worn smooth by winter storms and age. At either end of the little bay, jagged red rocks fell abruptly into the water, looking ferociously hostile and razor-sharp, though extremely picturesque. One or two late sun-worshippers were lying naked on the high rocks, catching the last rays of the sun, and a few more were on the flat rocks at the water's edge, or swimming in the long natural pools. Most were young, and had brown and on the whole rather beautiful bodies, but one or two were distinctly sagging and wrinkled, though their owners did not seem to feel at all inhibited by this depressing state of affairs.

'I'm afraid I'm too vain to expose my ageing body any longer,' said Hester, taking off her cotton robe and revealing a sensible grey-cotton swimsuit, faded and elderly. She laughed, and slid into the water. 'I expect I make myself far more conspicuous by my coy behaviour,' she said. 'It's my Protestant upbringing, no doubt.'

'You don't mind if I do?' Hugo pulled off his T-shirt.

'Of course not. If I were your age, I would myself. I always used to, I loved it.'

Hugo took off his clothes, folded them neatly, putting his spectacles carefully into a trouser pocket, and followed Hester into the sea. It was refreshingly cool and he felt soothed and relaxed as the water flowed over his body. He opened his eyes as he swam under the water, watching out for sharp rocks. On the sandy bottom he saw some smooth round boulders, rather slippery with seaweed, and he knelt on one of them carefully and studied the underwater life. He saw shoals of small silvery fish, a sea-cucumber and colonies of spiny black sea-urchins. Better watch out for *them*, he thought, the little sods. He swam slowly back to Hester, who had already got out of the water and was sitting on her rock, gazing out to sea. Hugo pulled himself onto the rock and wrapped his towel round himself.

'What do you think?' said Hester, smiling at him.

He put on his glasses, and smiled back. He did not say what he thought, that she looked rather beautiful with her grey eyes brilliant in her lined, deeply-tanned face, her dark, grey-streaked hair wet on her forehead, her strong, blue-veined brown hands clasped round her knees.

'Total, utter bliss,' he said. 'Thank you so much for asking me.'

'My dear boy,' said Hester 'it's such a pleasure to have you here.'

Chapter Eight

Basil had arrived in Avignon soon after ten so he killed time by walking to the nearby Palais des Papes, to see an exhibition of medieval illuminated manuscripts. At half past eleven he walked back to the station and saw Olivia sitting in a battered-looking pea-green *Deux Chevaux* with the hood down, reading a magazine. She wore a black baseball cap, dark glasses and a white singlet, and her long fair hair was tied back in a single plait. It took Basil a moment to recognize her, she looked so completely different to the fantastic creature he remembered in Paris, and much younger. He stood beside the car for a few moments before she looked up and saw him.

'Oh,' she said, 'there you are!' She got out of the car, revealing long brown legs below khaki shorts. 'I went into the station, but there you weren't.'

'No,' said Basil. 'I got an early train and arrived here much sooner than I expected. I went to see the exhibition in the Palais.'

'Was it good?'

'Very. But rather hot and crowded, unfortunately.'

'Put your bag in the boot,' said Olivia. 'Do you want to see any more of Avignon, or shall we head for Uzès?'

'What about lunch? Would you like to go somewhere here, or somewhere on the way? I'm getting pretty hungry, myself.'

'Can you wait half an hour? Or forty minutes, really?'

'I think so, yes. Why?'

She pointed to the rear seat and Basil saw that she had brought a large cold-box with her. 'Lunch,' she said. 'I thought a picnic on the river would be nice, and a swim.'

'Great,' said Basil. 'It's roasting here, isn't it? Hotter than the coast.'

'Always is, I think.' Olivia got back into the driver's seat. 'And colder in the winter, too. It's a tough climate.' She drove over the Rhône and took the road to Nîmes, rattling along towards Rémoulins, where she turned off and followed the signs to Pont du Gard and Uzès.

'Oh,' said Basil, 'the Pont du Gard. Do we pass it?'

'I won't take you there now Basil, it'll be stiff with Japanese tourists, whirring away with their camcorders. We'll come in the evening, it's quiet and beautiful then, OK?'

'Fine, I'll look forward to it.'

She drove on for a few more minutes and then turned left down a dirt track, leaving a plume of white dust behind them. They passed a crumbling domaine, half-hidden by a clump of evergreen-oaks, the surrounding vines growing right up to the buildings, and then followed the track through willow-trees and more oaks. Olivia pulled over into a small passing-place, and stopped the car. 'Now we must walk,' she said.

They got out of the car and took out the cold-box and Olivia's bag, and she checked that the boot was locked, then put the keys in her pocket. Basil picked up the cold-box and followed her down the steep narrow wooded track, emerging in a couple of minutes into a small clearing on the river-bank. A minute shingly beach about four metres wide with two large flat grey rocks beneath the shade of a willow, lay as if awaiting their arrival.

'There,' said Olivia. 'Will that do?'

'Brilliant.' Basil put down the cold-box in the shade of the tree. 'And not a moment too soon.'

Olivia pulled a towel from her bag. 'I think I'll have a swim before lunch,' she said. 'Can you wait five minutes?'

'It's so hot, I'd love a swim myself.'

She stripped off her clothes and walked into the shallow water. She was evenly brown all over, Basil observed as he took off his clothes and followed her into the river, which was unexpectedly cold.

'My God, it's freezing,' he said, almost changing his mind about the swim.

'It's lovely after a few minutes, you'll see. It comes from underground springs somewhere; this part of the Gardon never dries up even in the hottest summer.' She turned onto her back and floated downstream on the current. Basil lowered himself carefully into the water and swam a few metres, gasping with shock at the coldness of the water. After a few minutes his body adjusted to the temperature as Olivia had said it would, and the river felt cool and refreshing. He caught up with her and they floated side by side, squinting up at the golden ball of the blazing sun through the canopy of willow-leaves quivering in the light breeze over their heads.

'Race you back!' She suddenly turned like a fish in the water and swam swiftly back to their beach, her powerful crawl leaving Basil labouring in her wake, spitting out water as he fought against the current with his inefficient breast-stroke. She sat on one of the flat rocks, water running in rivulets down her body, already unpacking the lunch as he swam slowly up.

'Swimming's not really my thing,' he said, wading ashore.

'I can see.' She laughed and handed him a bottle of *rosé*. 'Put that in the water to keep cool, Baz.' He took the bottle and wedged it between three large stones. Then he sat down on his rock and Olivia handed him mineral water and a glass.

'Thanks,' he said, 'I need it badly.' He took a long cold drink, thinking how good water tastes when you are really thirsty.

Olivia spread a towel on the shingle, and laid out bread, tomatoes, ham, hard-boiled eggs, a covered plastic bowl containing salad and a jar of olives *à la grecque*. She had brought two mustard-coloured plates, knives, forks and salt. ' "I must have things daintily served," ' she observed primly.

Basil laughed and piled ham onto his plate. 'I'm glad to hear that you haven't totally rejected your English side.'

'I couldn't if I wanted to,' she replied, 'which I don't anyway. My brother sees to that. Mind you, he's as bad as I am, for opting out of his native land. He's working in Prague now.'

'Really? What does he do?'

'Architect.' Olivia spoke indistinctly, her mouth full of egg.

'Does he like it there?'

'Yes, I think so. He's very keen on conservation, like Grandpa, and there's a hell of a lot of it needing doing in Prague, or so it seems.'

'What a worthwhile and interesting thing to be doing.'

'Yes, it is. The old stone buildings are crumbling from decades of neglect, Josh says, but at least they're still there to be saved, which is something, isn't it?'

'Indeed.'

149

Basil spat an olive pit into the water and piled ham, tomato and egg onto a piece of bread. 'How come there are no flies or wasps here, Olivia? It's extraordinary.'

'It's the breeze. There's always a wind blowing on the river, even on the hottest day. There's shade and there are no flies, ever. That's why I love coming here, it's my special place. Are you ready for some wine?'

'Thanks,' said Basil, 'I'll get the bottle.' He retrieved the wine from the water, uncorked it and filled the two glasses she held out to him.

'*Salut*,' said Olivia, lifting her glass.

'*Salut*,' Basil responded. 'And thanks for bringing me here, it's a lovely place.'

When they had finished eating they packed everything carefully back in the box, then lay on their rocks chatting lazily of this and that. Basil told her about his job, and how basically dull it was, though just well-paid enough to discourage his leaving for the time being. He described his dreary flat, and his evenings there, flogging away at the poetry translation.

'Why on earth don't you chuck it, and come and live in Paris?' Olivia turned her head and looked at him seriously with her startling blue eyes.

'Too chicken, I suppose,' said Basil. 'And what would I do for money? I'd have to have a job, part-time anyway.' He did not mention his other reason for staying in London: his involvement with Hugo and Nelly.

'I should have thought that someone with fluent Russian, as well as French and English, would have plenty of opportunities. What about the media? Telly, newspapers, radio?'

'You mean foreign-language broadcasting?' Such an idea had never occurred to Basil, presumably because he had been offered the job at the BM immediately after graduating, and a combination of habit, laziness and his closeness to the Turnbulls had kept him there.

'That, or there must be loads of other things.' Olivia spoke with the easy confidence of youth. 'I could ask my stepfather, if you like. He works in the telly in Paris; you'd like him.'

'Is he English?'

'No, no, he's French. He's a dish, actually. My mother divorced my father to marry him.'

'And how did that affect you?'

'Only too thankful, my dear,' said Olivia, and laughed. 'It meant going to live in Paris; the *Lycée* was much more fun than my single-sex school in London, and now I'm at the Beaux-Arts, it's bliss.'

'You're very lucky.' Basil smiled at her.

'I know I am,' Olivia said seriously, 'very lucky.'

They swam again, and then Olivia took her watch out of her bag, and looked at it. 'Nearly half-five,' she said. 'It'll be less crowded at Pont du Gard, if you still want to go. What do you think?'

'To tell you the truth,' said Basil, 'I feel remarkably lazy, full of food and sun and river.'

Olivia smiled. 'OK, let's go home. We can have a drink at the café; it's the focus of social life in Souliac. You can watch the local talent playing *boules*, have a go yourself if you like.'

'Sounds fun, but is there somewhere I can take you out to dinner?'

'Well, there are quite a few places in Uzès, but my current favourite is *La Cigale* in the next village. It's only a little bistro, but the food's very good, it's not crowded and it's not far to drive. In fact, we could easily walk.'

'Shall we go there, then? Would you like that?'

151

'I'd love to, Basil; thank you,' said Olivia, and led the way back to the car.

At *Les Romarins*, Nelly read and re-read Hugo's card with disbelief followed by anger. How could he be such a shit? she asked herself; what the hell is going on? She put the card in her pocket and went into the garden, in spite of the fact that a thin rain was falling and a grey fog covered the island like a blanket. Far out to sea, she could hear the fog-horn's intermittent mournful sound. Like a cow in labour, her father used to say. She walked across the sodden lawn in front of the drawing-room windows to the crumbling summer-house where the croquet things were kept. She pushed open the glazed door, its frame cracked and peeling and badly in need of a coat of paint, and went in, closing it behind her. She sat down on a dusty wicker chair and taking the card from her pocket, read it again. An experience completely new to Nelly, a sensation of absolute helplessness came over her. Her mouth felt dry, she had a pain at the back of her eyes and she felt a stab of fear. She slumped in the chair, closing her eyes. What is happening? she asked herself. Is Hugo leaving me? Is he having an affair with this woman? Impossible she thought, he can't be. She's Baz's mother, she's an old woman, isn't she? Not as old as Ma I suppose, but she must be about sixty. Surely it's out of the question? Doubt, and a deep feeling of humiliation and misery engulfed her and tears filled her eyes. She gave a choking sob and the hot salty rivulets ran down her face, unchecked. She felt in her pocket for a handkerchief and, realizing that she did not have one, wiped her face and then blew her nose on the hem of her skirt.

'Disgusting,' she said aloud, and sniffed. She tried to compose her thoughts, to think logically. What have I done to deserve this? she asked herself. Am I really so unbearable? So insensitive and domineering? Are the children so awful that they deserve this, either? No, they're not. It's Hugo, he's a big-headed, selfish little shit. She realized that she had got back to square one again and gave a small, painful laugh. She looked at the card again. All it said, actually, was: 'Gone to Ramatuelle for a few days, see you soon, love to all. H.' He had written Hester's phone number at the bottom of the card.

Nelly sighed. Perhaps she was over-reacting a bit? Deep down she recognized that hurt pride was the problem – not Hugo's but her own. Slowly she admitted to herself that she had not expected Hugo to challenge her in this way, ever. But what am I to do? she thought. What? I simply don't know how to handle this any more. She wiped her nose with the back of her hand like a child and got up, shaking out her sodden, crumpled skirt. Perhaps I should do absolutely nothing? I'll give it a day or two, and think about it again. Or maybe talk to Ma? But I don't really want to do that, not yet anyway. In any case, I must get on, and help Elsie with the beds.

She left the summer-house and ran back to the house through the rain, the eerie moan of the fog-horn sending an apprehensive shiver down her spine. Henry and Jane were expected this evening, but would probably be delayed in Guernsey by the fog. She could imagine her brother's irritation at having his plans disrupted, and the tight-lipped silent coolness of her sister-in-law. She sighed and went to look for Elsie. Nelly was not looking forward to her brother's visit. Neither, come to that, was her mother, she was pretty sure. Why the hell didn't I

153

take the girls to Tuscany, she thought, and tell Hugo to get knotted? Why not indeed?

Olivia drove under the arch and into the Place de l'Eglise at Souliac. She parked outside her own door and they got out of the car. Basil looked round the beautiful, though crumbling little eighteenth-century square, drowsy in the evening light under the shade of its plane trees, its moss-covered fountain gently dripping water into the carved stone basin beneath. Facing Olivia's house stood the squat-towered church, flanked by village houses. The *Mairie*, the *boulangerie*, the café and the *alimentation* were on one side of the square, while the *Poste* and the Presbytery dominated the other. A few middle-aged men were engaged in a game of *boules* under the trees, and the muffled sounds of the juke-box and the fruit-machine came from the café. The doors of the houses stood open, some protected by fly-screens, and the smell of cooking, powerfully scented with herbs and garlic, issued from them.

'Lovely place,' said Basil.

'It is, isn't it?'

They took the cold-box and Basil's bag out of the boot of the car and Olivia unlocked her door. Leaving it open to let in the evening air, they entered the narrow hallway. At the far end was a narrow, steep stairway to the upper floor. Immediately to their right was an archway leading to the small square kitchen.

Olivia went in and put the cold-box down on the stone floor, beside the pearwood table. 'Poof,' she said, 'it's hot in here.' She flung open the shutters of the deep window overlooking the square. Immediately, a cool breeze blew into the little room. The church bell struck seven and she turned to Basil. 'What about a drink?'

'Thanks, I'd love one.'

She went to the dilapidated old fridge and took out a bottle of cold mineral water. 'Take a seat,' she said, seating herself at the table. She filled two tall glasses and handed one to Basil.

'Thanks.' He took a thirsty swig. 'The trouble with boozing in the afternoon is, you get so dehydrated, don't you?'

Olivia laughed. 'Too true. One does seem to drink rather a lot, down here.'

'Road to ruin; what a way to die.' He looked round the kitchen, with its black range and cracked old sink. An open fireplace filled one wall, its massive carved oak mantel hung with a frill of sooty-looking Provençal fabric, in a blue-and-yellow lozenge pattern. Above the frill was a shelf with a row of yellow scalloped plates, rimmed with brown, and two blue fish-shaped *pastis* jugs, holding stiff fronds of pampas grass. Some copper pans hung from hooks hidden behind the frill, as well as a smoke-blackened ham and two dried sausages in nets. In the hearth, heavy old iron firedogs supported an elaborate system of pulleys and chains, that had once worked the rusty spit suspended over the mound of ash below. A wooden armchair, its rush seat covered by a blue cushion, waited by the fireplace. A small oak dresser stood at a right angle between the fireplace and the kitchen window, its shelves displaying more plates and some jars of preserves. A fat beige salt-glazed jar held a bunch of wild flowers; a pot of basil and a glass tumbler containing parsley stood beside it. On the other side of the window, a tall long-case clock reached to the ceiling, its friendly face telling the time in black Roman numerals, its brass pendulum visible through a circular glass window, as it swung slowly from side to side. Facing the window was the shabby fridge, a small bottled-gas cooker, and a closed door of carved and moulded chestnut, like all the doors of the house. The heavy beams overhead, supporting the wide bare floor-boards of the room upstairs, were equally of chestnut. On the lime-washed walls hung several pictures in heavy black frames. One was a daguerreotype of the 'Last Supper', and the others sepia photographs of rather stiffly-posed people, a middle-aged man and woman, and a younger man. Basil felt sure that they were all long dead. He looked at Olivia and smiled. 'This is a total time-warp. Obviously, you haven't altered it in any way, have you?'

'No, not in here,' said Olivia. 'But I have through there.' She pointed to the closed door. 'That's my work-room. Sadly, I had to get rid of the copper and the mangle that Honorine used for her laundry, to make room for my press.'

'Honorine?'

'Ah, darling Honorine. She helped my grandmother bring up my mother and Giò, then me and my brother Josh. She died in an accident, and she left her house and her vineyard to me. Wasn't it sad, she had no family of her own left?' Olivia pointed to the pictures on the wall. 'Those two are her parents, and the other one is poor Jacques, her fiancé. He was shot by the Nazis, in the war.'

'Poor things, how tragic.'

'It was, yes. But she loved us all, and we loved her, we were her family, really. I miss her still, every time I come down to Souliac.' She looked at the clock. 'If we're going to walk to *La Cigale*, we'd better get a move on. You'd like to wash and change, wouldn't you?'

'Yes, I would, thanks.'

They finished their drinks, and Olivia led the way

upstairs and opened the door to the guest-room. 'In here,' she said. She opened another door, revealing a minute bathroom. She flicked a switch beside the door. 'That's the immersion heater, but the hot water takes a bit of time to come through, OK?'

'Great, thanks.'

Olivia opened the third door at the end of the little landing and went into her room, closing the door behind her. Basil went into his room and put down his bag. He crossed the room and pushed open the shutters, leaning out of the window to look at the little back-yard below. It was about four metres square and was furnished with a small faded rattan table and two chairs. Terracotta pots full of scarlet pelargoniums, basil, thyme and lavender were grouped in clumps around the stone walls. A blue-painted door in the rear wall led into a dusty lane which appeared to run along the backs of the village houses. Vines were planted right up to the far side of the lane; they stretched away in neat, green-gold lines, and Basil could see the heavy bunches of purple grapes beneath their protective covering of blue-speckled leaves. Beyond the vineyards, he could see the rolling *garrigue* country, and beyond that the blue hazy outline of distant mountains. I must look at the map again he said to himself, as he pulled off his shirt and opened his bag.

Olivia came back from the bathroom and opened the door of her *armoire*. She stood for a moment considering her wardrobe, then chose a long, navy-blue chiffon wrap-around skirt, and took a long white skinny T-shirt dress from the pile on a shelf. She put on the dress, the deep scooped neck revealing the soft curve of her small breasts. Then she sat down in front of her dressing-table and undid her plait of hair, shaking it out over her shoulders. With her wide-toothed comb, she worked her way carefully through the dense wavy mass, until it rippled in a golden shining river down her back. Then she took the long piece of scarlet silk that hung from a hinge of the looking-glass, and wound it round her forehead, tying it in a knot at the back. She wiped her face with skin tonic, then applied silvery eyeshadow and dark-grey kohl round her eyes, so that they seemed twice their usual size, much wider apart and brilliantly blue.

Olivia enjoyed the process of re-inventing herself with make-up and clothes, and she looked at her reflection in the mirror with an air of complicity as she applied lip-gloss. Then she wrapped the chiffon skirt around her waist, and thrust her feet into transparent plastic 'jelly' sandals, fastening the velcro clips. Finally she took her soft black leather bomber-jacket from the *armoire*, unzipped one of the pockets and put in the lip-gloss, a comb, a slim phial of scent and her car keys. She hung the jacket on the back of a chair while she removed the white counterpane from her bed, carefully folding it and putting it on a shelf in the *armoire*. She took out two fat white square pillows and put them on the bolster. She turned back the sheet, plugged in the anti-mosquito burner and closed the shutters of her windows. Then she picked up her jacket and went downstairs. Basil was already in the kitchen, sitting in the armchair reading a paper; he was wearing clean blue jeans, a white T-shirt and a black leather bomber-jacket like her own.

'Snap!' said Olivia as she entered the room, and laughed.

Basil put down the paper and looked at her. 'Olivia,' he said. 'You look absolutely ravishing.' He crossed the room, put his hands on her shoulders and kissed her. 'I hope you don't mind?'

'No, I don't mind,' said Olivia. She put her arms round his waist and looked up at him, smiling. He kissed her again, and she returned his kiss.

Basil closed the shutters to the kitchen window and they left the little house, locking the door with the heavy iron key.

'Could you carry it for me, please? I haven't got my bag, and it's a bit big for my pocket.' She looked up at the church clock: nearly half past eight. 'What do you think? It's getting rather late for walking, shall we drive?'

'Why not?'

She took out her car keys and handed them to him. 'You drive, and I'll tell you where to go.' They got into the car and drove under the archway, and took the road through the vines to the next village.

The bistro was in fact very busy, but the proprietor's wife found room for them in a corner of the terrace, and wiped down the white plastic table with a damp cloth. She put a carafe of red wine on the table, two glasses, a bowl of shiny black olives and the menu.

'I am *incredibly* hungry.' Olivia studied the menu with great concentration. 'I'm going to have *Soupe de Poissons* and the *Lapin Provençal*. How about you?'

'Um, hang on a minute, I haven't read it all yet. OK, I'll have the *Moules au Basilic* and the *Risotto* with *Pistou* and pine-nuts; sounds terrific. Now what about the wine? Is this OK, do you think, or should we have something a bit grander?'

'This is fine for me; I love country wines.'

Basil gave the order, and then filled the glasses. Olivia bit into an olive and took a sip of wine. 'Have you ever noticed how wonderful they taste together?' she said, spitting the pit into her hand.

'Can't say I have.' Basil ate an olive and drank some wine. 'You're right, the combination is delicious.'

The lights from the little restaurant shone onto the narrow terrace and the village street was lit by strings of bright, white lights stretched across the road between the buildings. The *Fête Votive* had taken place during July and the festive lights had still not been taken down. Basil observed that suspended in the centre of several of the strings of lights were large motifs, apparently depicting the heads of cows with long sharp horns.

'Why the fierce-looking cows?' he asked, looking at them with interest.

'*Bulls*, Basil. They're *bulls*!' said Olivia, laughing.

'And?'

'They run them through the streets twice a day during the *Fête*. They bring them up from Arles and Nîmes, with the *gardiens* on their ponies from the Camargue. It's like a sort of mini-Pamplona, and all the young bloods run with them and everyone pretends to be terrified, it's great.'

'No-one gets hurt?'

'Not often. Occasionally one hears that a bull has made a bog, and gone into a café, or climbed a flight of steps and got stuck. It's all part of the fun.'

The first course arrived and they ate in silence for a few minutes. Olivia finished her fish soup quickly. She put down her spoon with a small sigh of pleasure. 'Wonderful, I love it,' she said. She watched, her elbows on the table as Basil carefully extracted each mussel from its shell and tipped the sauce into his mouth, slowly savouring each aromatic swallow. She smiled. 'Is it good?'

'Marvellous. I love basil, don't you? Raw, or in *pistou*, or with garlic and tomato and olive oil, like this. It's the true taste of the south, of summer, isn't it?'

'It is.' Olivia looked at Basil, noticing the whiteness of his teeth, normally rather hidden behind the soft, brown wavy beard that covered the lower part of his face. He ate the last mussel, wiped his mouth and fingers with his napkin and took a sip of wine.

'At this moment,' he said, 'I feel extraordinarily happy.'

Olivia looked into his eyes, grey, rather sad and fringed with straight black lashes. Is this a rather crude pass? she asked herself. And if I know that it is, why are my insides melting down? Or am I being stupid and taking everything far too seriously? Does he behave like this to every woman he meets, as a reflex action? Perhaps I should call his bluff and ask him? What then? The evening will be spoiled, I will have acted like a child, it will all end in tears. Instead she smiled at Basil and took a sip of wine. 'Curiously enough,' she said, coolly, 'so do I. It must be the atmosphere, the food and the wine.'

He smiled at her. 'Do you really think so?'

She did not reply, but stretched out her hand and took hold of his beard, giving it a little tug. 'Have you always had this? Or do you sometimes shave it off?'

'Well, not often,' said Basil, 'on account of its covering my receding chin, you see.'

Olivia withdrew her hand as though she had been stung. 'Oh, sorry,' she said. 'I didn't mean—'

'Gotcher!' said Basil, and burst out laughing.

'You rotten swine!' Olivia laughed too, and threw a piece of bread at him.

Their plates were removed and the main courses brought to the table. The *lapin provençal* turned out to be a large red sweet-pepper filled with pieces of *sautéed* rabbit, baked in the oven and served on a mound of buttery noodles sprinkled with delicate young thyme leaves. It looked and smelt delicious but Basil's *risotto* was a true masterpiece. A large, blue-rimmed thick white earthenware soup-dish contained the fragrant, tenderly melting creamy golden rice with its pool of brilliant-green *pistou*, the whole sprinkled with toasted pine-nuts. Olivia looked at it with envy, wishing she had chosen it herself. '*Pistou* with everything, Baz?' she mocked.

'Absolutely,' said Basil. 'Do you want a taste?'

'Yes, please.'

He passed the dish to her and she dug in her fork and took some rice and a little of the sauce.

'It's delicious,' she said. She picked up her knife and split her pepper in half, and the rabbit pieces with the liver and baby onions spilled out onto the plate, the sauce running into the noodles.

After some goats' cheese and figs they sat at their table drinking coffee and watching people coming and going, amused by the activity in the kitchen, visible through a small hatch in a wall.

'How does he produce such excellent food, for so many tables, in that tiny space?'

'It must be terribly hot in there, poor chap,' said Olivia. 'No wonder he yells at his wife all the time.'

'She seems quite cheerful, all the same, doesn't she?'

'I suppose she must quite like him?'

'Perhaps she does,' agreed Basil. 'Would you like an Armagnac?'

'Who's driving home?'

'I will, if you like. We haven't had all that much to drink, and a colossal amount of food.'

'True,' said Olivia. 'OK, an Armagnac would be lovely, thanks.'

They drank the Armagnac and some more coffee

and suddenly they were the only people left in the restaurant.

'I have the feeling they want to pack up, don't you?' Basil got up, went into the bar and paid the bill. They wandered down the street to the car and drove slowly back to Souliac through the silent vineyards. Overhead, the sky was velvety black and the stars seemed immensely far away, tiny points of distant light.

Basil parked the car outside the house, switched off the engine and turned to Olivia. 'Thank you for a lovely day,' he said.

'Thank *you*, Basil, for taking me out. It was very kind of you; it was fun.'

They got out of the car and Basil took the house key from his pocket.

Olivia hesitated for a moment. 'It's such a beautiful night,' she said, 'shall we take a walk round the square?'

'Why not?'

He took her hand and they walked under the trees and listened to the golden orioles that had nested there that year. The extraordinarily clear bell-like notes, one very close at hand, the other somewhere in the trees in the back lane, echoed across the little square, the haunting song emphasizing the lonely stillness of the night. They sat on the rim of the fountain, saying little, until the church clock struck one.

'Is that the half-hour,' said Basil, 'or is it really one o'clock?' He peered at his watch. 'It's one o'clock.'

'Time to go to bed.' Olivia stood up and put her arms round Basil's neck.

'Really go to bed?' he said, gently covering her breasts with his hands.

'I think so, Basil. Don't you want to?'

'Of course I do,' Basil said, and kissed her. 'I just don't

want to ruin everything, or take advantage of you in any way.'

'You won't be.'

'You're sure?'

'Yes, quite sure. There's only one thing . . .'

'What's that?'

'I'm not on the pill, so do you have a *preservatif*?'

Basil tried not to laugh, but failed. 'Yes,' he said, 'I have. Pink, blue or *eau-de-nil*?'

They dissolved into silent giggles and then walked back across the square to her house, their arms round each other. As they drew near, Olivia put her finger to her lips. 'Shh,' she whispered, 'we mustn't wake the neighbours.'

Chapter Nine

Una-Mary lay in her high old bed on a soft pile of lacy pillows, her arthritic hands with their old-fashioned diamond-and-sapphire rings holding a small leather-bound copy of the poems of Tennyson. She was not actually reading the book, and her spectacles had slid down and were resting on the end of her nose. Her eyes were closed but she was not asleep. She was thinking about Nelly and also about her son Henry, who had now been in the house for three days and nights with his dreary silent wife. Was it really my neglect of him as a child that made him such a discontented and awkward boy? she asked herself sadly. Middle-aged man now of course, he's well into his forties. It's such a pity he seems to get so little pleasure from life, and Jane doesn't seem to amuse him very much, either. Birds of a feather I suppose.

The door opened and Phyllida came into the room, carefully carrying a breakfast tray.

'Good morning darling, how kind of you.' Una-Mary closed her book and heaved herself to a sitting position against her pillows.

Phyllida put the tray down on her grandmother's knees. 'Is that all right, Granny?' She looked anxious. 'Shall I put the tea-pot on the bedside table?'

'Good idea, it is a bit wobbly, isn't it?'

Phyllida moved the little tea-pot and its cork mat to

the table. 'Shall I pour you a cup while I'm here?'

'Thank you, that would be lovely.'

The little girl, her silky red hair flopping over her sunburnt face, poured the tea with great care, not spilling any. She replaced the pot, then sat down gingerly on the foot of the bed.

Una-Mary took a sip of tea. 'Have you had your breakfast, Phylly?'

'Yes, ages ago.'

'What's happening today?'

'If it doesn't rain, we're going to the beach. Anything to get away from Uncle Henry, Mum says.'

'Oh dear, is it as bad as that?'

'He's a real pain-in-the-bum, Mum says,' said Phyllida, emboldened by her grandmother's mild tone, 'always whingeing and complaining. Aunt Jane's not much better.'

Her voice sounded so like Nelly's that Una-Mary choked on her toast and had to have a gulp of tea to get her breath back. She wiped her eyes on her napkin, laughing. Phyllida laughed too, pleased that she had amused her grandmother.

'I'm sorry to say that your mother is quite right. Never mind, maybe they'll get fed-up with the weather and go back to the mainland, who knows?'

'Wouldn't you be sad?'

'To tell you the truth, I wouldn't. But please don't say I said so, will you darling?'

'Certainly not.' Phyllida stood up, preparing to depart. 'What do you take me for, a baby?'

'Never that, darling,' said Una-Mary. She looked at her grand-daughter with gentle faded eyes, and thought how extraordinarily like Nelly she was. She smiled tenderly at her as she walked to the door. You were born wise, like your mother, she thought. I only hope you won't have as many problems as she does. Though I expect you will, we all do. And if we haven't got any we invent them.

Phyllida went down to the kitchen where she found Henry and Jane at the table, silently drinking coffee and pointedly not eating the blackened toast so laboriously made by Sophie on the kitchen range. Nelly was stuffing clothes into the washing-machine, a very old top-loader, and looking grim.

'Can I help you, Mummy?' asked Phyllida, giving her impersonation of the perfect and obliging child for the benefit of Henry and Jane. Even to herself she sounded nauseating, and she squirmed with embarrassment as she stood beside her mother.

Nelly looked up at her and grinned. 'How kind of you to offer, darling. It's OK, I've nearly finished.'

Phyllida looked nervously at the pile of dishes in the sink. 'What about the washing-up?'

'Henry and Jane will do that I'm sure, when they've finished their breakfast,' said Nelly, and switched on the machine. 'We must get down to the beach quickly before it starts raining again. Go and round up the others, Phylly. And the dogs.'

Phyllida disappeared thankfully through the door to the kitchen yard. Henry banged his heavy breakfast cup into its saucer. It was one of an old Quimper set decorated with stiff-looking Breton men and women, and Nelly flinched at the thought of him breaking one of them. Bad-tempered pig, she thought.

'Doesn't Elsie do the washing-up?' he demanded loudly, red-faced and sweating in his too-tight Guernsey sweater.

'It's her day off, I'm afraid.' Nelly spoke quietly. 'I'll just run up and see if Ma's all right. You two can keep an eye on her while we're at the beach, can't you? I'll be back to do the lunch, don't worry.' She left the room before Henry could think of a good enough reason to refuse, and ran up the stairs to her mother's room. She relieved Una-Mary of her tray and sat down on the bed. 'Bloody man,' she said crossly, 'he'll drive me round the bend.'

'Oh, dear,' said Una-Mary. 'I'm afraid he's become a pompous old bore.'

'I don't know why he bothers to come here at all, everything seems to get on his nerves, doesn't it?'

'I know. What saddens me most is that the house will have to come to him eventually, and he doesn't even like it, does he? Much less, the island?'

Nelly looked at her mother and sighed. 'It makes me sad too, and angry really. At the end of the day he'll sell it, I expect.'

'Yes, he probably will.'

'Well, I could always buy it from him, couldn't I? I could if I sold the London house.'

'Oh darling, do be careful. What about Hugo?' She put on her spectacles and looked anxiously at her much-loved daughter. 'You've got enough problems to cope with already without adding to them, haven't you? And your career, darling, you must think of that. After all, it's only a house, isn't it, on a rather inconvenient little island?'

'No, it isn't,' said Nelly. 'It's your home, your parents' home and mine too. I won't let it go that easily, I promise you.' She leaned over and hugged her mother. The old woman felt bony and frail in her arms, and the skin of her cheek was dry and papery, and smelt of Pear's soap. 'Darling Ma,' she said.

'Darling Nelly,' replied her mother. 'Nothing you might do would surprise me, and you're quite right, he is a pain-in-the-bum.'

'Did I say that?'

'Well, Phylly did.'

'Oh.' Nelly laughed. She picked up the tray and went to the door. 'If I were you, I'd take it easy this morning. I'm taking the children to the beach now, but I'll be back to do the lunch, and then maybe we'll go for a drive this afternoon. What do you think?'

'Lovely,' said her mother, 'I look forward to it.'

Basil opened his eyes and stared at the unfamiliar rectangle of the open window facing him, framing leafy green foliage topped with a band of blue sky, criss-crossed with the black lines of electricity cables. The smell of freshly-baked bread drifted into the room. The shrill screams of house-martins broke the cool early silence as they pursued each other over the rooftops. He turned his head on the pillow and looked at Olivia lying naked beside him, brown and beautiful, with her extraordinary fair hair spread over the pillow. She was fast asleep, her lips slightly parted like a child's. Her hand lay lightly on Basil's stomach. He smiled, then lifting it gently, he laid it on the sheet beside her. She sighed and stirred in her sleep but did not wake. He waited for a moment then got quietly out of bed, taking care not to disturb her. He picked up his clothes from the floor and silently left the room.

He washed, then went to his own room, put on a pair of shorts and went downstairs to the kitchen, his bare feet noiseless on the worn stone stairs. He opened the shutters, then unlocked the front door and walked across the square to the *boulangerie* to buy bread for breakfast. He felt wonderfully relaxed, carefree and glad to be alive. He could not remember when he had last spent an entire night in a shared bed. He supposed he must have done so with Nelly at some stage, but at this moment his previous life seemed unreal, a very long time ago, unimportant. He pushed his way through the fly-screen of the *boulangerie* and bought a *gros-pain*, crisp, golden and fragrant.

'*Merci, monsieur. Bonne journée.*' The dark-eyed girl behind the counter smiled at him as she gave his change, and wrapped the loaf in a sheet of tissue paper.

'*Vous-même,*' Basil replied, smiling back. '*Au voir.*'

He went back to the house, carrying the still-warm loaf under his arm. In the kitchen he put the bread on the table, filled the black kettle and put it on the gas hob, then looked around for coffee. He found it in the fridge, as well as butter and apricot *conserve*. It's hot in here with the stove on, he thought, and opened the door between the fridge and the cooker to see whether he could make a current of air flow through to the back-yard. Olivia's studio was bare and white, with a solid-looking table lit by a small window on one side, and the etching press on the other. Facing him was another door, presumably leading to the courtyard at the back. It was bolted, and he undid the bolts and opened the door. At once, a cool breeze fanned his bare skin, and he stepped out into the little garden, full of the early-morning scents of herbs from the flourishing pots. It would be nice to have breakfast here he thought, I'll bring the things out. He went back into the studio and noticed for the first time the set of prints clipped to a wire stretched over the table close to the ceiling, and looking like laundry pegged to a clothes-line. Carefully, touching only the edges, he turned the pieces of hand-made paper in order to examine the printed images. Each tiny etching was deeply pressed into the centre of the paper, the sooty black impression marooned in a virgin sea of white. Basil was astonished, both by the technical ability displayed, and the maturity of the artist's vision. It was difficult to believe that it was the work of a second-year student.

'What do you think?'

Basil turned and saw Olivia standing in the doorway. 'Does it matter what I think?'

'No, it doesn't, but I'd like to know, anyway.'

He crossed the room, took her face in his hands and kissed her, rather chastely. 'I think they're pretty amazing; like you, Olivia, my dearest child.'

She wound her slender brown arms round his neck and smiled at him, remembering. 'But I'm not a child, Basil, am I?' she said quietly.

'No, darling, you're not.'

On Monday morning Olivia drove Basil to Avignon to catch the Paris train. She waited with him on the platform until the train arrived. 'When do you go back to London?'

'End of this week. Hugo will be driving my mother back on Thursday, and we'll return to England Friday or Saturday I imagine.'

'I won't see you again.'

'Why not?'

'Well, you'll be in London, won't you?'

Basil took her hand. 'We'll have to work something out, won't we? Maybe I *will* come and live in Paris, if I can find a job.'

The train roared into the station, doors opened and people hurried past all around them. Olivia turned towards Basil and he put down his bag, folded her in his arms and held her tightly. She looked up at him and smiled, trying not to show how desolate she felt at his going. 'I hope you will; come to Paris I mean.'

'I hope so too.'

'Hurry, they'll be closing the doors.'

'Don't wait, I hate goodbyes,' said Basil.

'So do I.'

He jumped onto the train, and Olivia watched him through the window as he found a seat and stowed his bag. The train began to move slowly along the platform, and she resisted the impulse to run along beside it. Basil looked through the window and waved, smiling. She raised her hand briefly, then turned and walked quickly out of the station.

Olivia drove back to Souliac, reliving the entire weekend in her head. She felt tired and wound-up, slightly anxious. As she drove, her body ached with a painful longing to be in bed with Basil, every instinct telling her that in him she had probably found what could very well prove to be the love of her life. On the other hand, her egocentric, cool and independent other-self was not at all sure that she wanted to go down that road. She was well aware that for a woman with serious career plans, a permanent relationship could very easily become a situation of diminishing returns. Well she thought, it really doesn't matter, does it? Neither of us has made any sort of commitment; there's no need to get heavy about it, is there?

She put a Django Reinhardt tape in the cassette-player. The track was *I can't give you anything but love, Baby*. She listened, feeling unaccountably sad, amazed at the song's capacity to move her.

Hugo rewrote the last sentence of his second draft of *Richelieu*, numbered the page and carefully put it in the box file. He closed the spring-clip and put the file into his briefcase. It was a tight fit, although the case was quite wide. His manuscript was now ready for transference to his word processor, which had long been lying idle in London, under its grey plastic cover. Hugo quite liked working on the word processor. Its printed pages made the work seem more real, more professional in a sense, and he was able to do a lot of editing as he went along. He packed away the rest of his papers, the notes and reference material, almost filling his grip, leaving a little space at the top for his few spare clothes and his shaving things.

He went to the window and gazed out over the rooftops towards the sea, shimmering in the midday heat, trying to retain an indelible image in his memory. It was the last day of his stay in Ramatuelle. Tomorrow he and Hester would start the drive to Paris at five in the morning, to get as far north as possible before noon and avoid the worst of the heat. His eyes wandered over the distant vineyards marching in straight lines to the sea, and back up through the olive groves and wooded hillside to the jumble of Roman-tiled roofs beneath him, lichen-blotched and glowing, a soft golden faded rose-pink. He sighed. He had been so happy in this place and had worked so well, that the thought of it all ending and his resuming the old London pattern of life filled him with gloom. He had missed his daughters and Nelly too, and had thought of them often. But deep down he knew that he would have to find a legitimate way of maintaining his new-found freedom, on a part-time basis at any rate. He had tried quite hard to analyse his motives and reached the conclusion that after twelve years of being a part, albeit a major one, of Nelly's master plan, he had come to have a serious need for a certain independence, to belong more to himself.

Then there was Hester. He thought that she too had enjoyed their quiet uninvolved life together. She had been an example to him, if he needed such a thing, of how to live and work in a solitary state. He knew how important it had been for her to learn to be dependent on herself alone, and he was beginning to believe that he, too, could achieve this desirable mental freedom for himself. None the less, in her strange, calm fashion she had become important to Hugo and he did not want their friendship to fade away after his return to London.

He closed the shutters and went quietly down to Hester's studio. He tapped on the door and went in. 'Am I being a pain? Are you busy?'

'Well, yes, I am Hugo, but as it's our last day, I suppose I'll have to stop.'

'Sorry,' said Hugo, feeling guilty.

Hester laughed. 'Don't worry, I think we both deserve a bit of a break. What shall we do?'

'I was wondering whether you'd like to have lunch at the bistro, maybe?'

'Good idea.' She washed her brushes. 'Especially as it's fish-day, so they'll probably have *moules*.'

They walked slowly through the narrow streets to the Place de l'Ormeau, drowsy and deserted in the lunch hour.

'Later on, when it's cooler,' she said, 'we could go for a drive and have a last swim at L'Escalet, what do you think?'

'That would be perfect. And while we're at it, we could get the tyre pressures checked and fill up with petrol, ready for tomorrow, couldn't we?'

'How practical you are, Hugo. We'll do that, it'll save time in the morning.'

They sat down at a table on the shady terrace, next to a fat man drinking a *pastis*. A bowl piled with steaming *moules* was placed before him with a basket of freshly sliced bread, then the *patronne* came to take their order.

'*Bonjour, Emilie*,' said Hester. '*On va prendre des moules?*'

'*Bien sûr, madame.*'

Basil lay in his narrow bed in Paris, lazily contemplating the day ahead. He felt happy, restored, full of energy and confidence. He did not even dread, particularly, the return to London and the museum. He felt quite sure that he had crossed a crucial bridge, and that it would be perfectly possible to work out a much more amusing, creative and civilized way of life for himself. The forces of inertia, he thought, those are the destructive elements. I must take good care not to drift, ever again.

He thought of Olivia lying cool and golden next to him in her bed in Souliac, and smiled, congratulating himself on what he regarded as a very successful weekend, which had been a tremendous boost to his self-esteem. Then he thought of Nelly, and decided that lovely as Olivia was, she could never be a real substitute for his lost love. Still, it had certainly been a step in the right direction, and he thought of her with gratitude and affection.

He got out of bed and went to the kitchen to make tea, and began to plan his remaining three or four days in Paris. I'll go and see the exhibition at the Grand Palais this morning he said to himself, then I'll go and suss out Giò Hamilton's shop. It's ages since I saw the Place des Vosges, and I'd really rather like to see this Giò chap again, anyway. I'm pretty sure he fancies me; it would be amusing to explore a bit in that area, just for fun.

He laughed and took his mug of tea into the sitting-room and sat down at Hester's work-table. He looked at the photographs of his parents and grandparents, and of himself too, as a small boy. His eyes wandered round the beautiful low room, so full of his parents' work and personality. It's a lucky thing that Hester has this place he said to himself. I could easily live here for a bit, while I look for a job and an apartment. And maybe Olivia's stepfather *might* help me find work, she seemed pretty confident that he could; we'll just have to see. He felt as though he was at the beginning of an exciting new period of his life, where anything could happen, and most probably would. 'I should have done this years ago, more fool me,' he said aloud to the empty room, and went to have his shower.

The shadows were beginning to lengthen as he walked across the gardens of the Place des Vosges and passed under the pleached lime-trees which surrounded the arcades running round all four sides of the exquisite seventeenth-century square. Under the arcades were many small antiques shops selling furniture, rare books and prints, a few galleries and some smart boutiques selling designer clothes. There were also plenty of restaurants and cafés with tables and chairs spilling out across the pavement under the arcades, in the traditional summer manner. In spite of all this activity, the beautiful square retained all its calm elegance and self-possession. Basil walked along the arcade, looking for *Le Patrimoine*, which he remembered was the name of Giò's shop. He very nearly walked past it, since it was extremely small and two people looking into the shop were partially obscuring the gold letters proclaiming the name on the plate-glass window. The door stood open and he walked in. The delightful little establishment was in fact a series of three inter-communicating rooms, running from the front to the rear of the building. All the connecting double-doors stood open revealing the entire *enfilade*, and Basil saw Giò in the second room, talking to a client. He caught his eye and Giò smiled and raised his hand in greeting, but politely continued to give his full attention to his customer. Basil sat down rather carefully on a low, cane-seated chair, looking about him with interest. He noted the subtlety of the lighting which appeared to come from real candles in the many silver-backed sconces crowding the walls, interspersed with beautiful mirrors and eighteenth-century French and English engravings in gilded frames. The candles, he realized with amusement, were actually electrified but had a convincing flicker built into the mechanism. Personally, he thought that Hester's icons would look pretty good in that ambience, but rather wondered what she would think herself. Probably she would consider the place, like Giò, too chic for her taste. Equally, she might well be delighted at the idea. After all, anything would be an improvement on some of the tacky people she deals with now, he thought, I'm sure she'd agree.

Giò took his client to a small desk, sat down and wrote something on a note-pad, then processed the man's credit card. There was a brief pause while the machine went through the verification process then burst into life, disgorging its slip of paper for signature. The man duly signed and Giò gave him his receipt slips and card, then accompanied him to the door.

'*Vers la fin de la semaine, croyez-vous?*'

'*C'est ça,*' Giò replied. '*Au revoir, et merci bien.*' The customer left the shop and Giò turned to Basil. 'Hello, Basil. How nice to see you.'

Basil stood up, smiling. 'Very good to see you again, Giò. How are you?'

'Hot,' said Giò. 'How was Ramatuelle?'

'Hot, too, but wonderful as usual.'

'Did you get to Souliac?'

'I did. I stayed with Olivia. What a nice village it is; and the Presbytery too – what a beautiful house.'

'Yes, it is,' said Giò. 'Except that I have nightmares about finishing up there, a bad-tempered, rheumaticky old bastard with a cat, bored out of my mind.' He laughed, and Basil laughed too, amused by this half-serious piece of self-analysis.

'In the meantime, you seem very busy and successful here? What a stunning shop; presumably it's all your doing, you don't have a stylist or anything to arrange it?'

'Perish the thought,' said Giò, looking gratified. 'So, what do you think? Would your mother's stuff look OK here?'

'I'm sure it would. But of course, you'd have to come to her place first and see the icons. At the end of the day, *you* might not like *them*, it's quite possible.'

'I suppose you're right,' said Giò. 'Is she back in Paris yet?'

'No, she'll be returning at the end of the week.'

'I see. Well, I'll telephone her when she gets home.' He looked at his watch. 'Nearly seven, let's close the shop and go and have a drink, shall we?'

'Good idea, I'm dying for a long, really cold beer.'

Giò locked up the shop, and they walked down the arcade and found a free table outside a café which had a long list of famous wines inscribed on its window. They sat down.

'Do you think they'll have a humble beer here?' Basil sounded doubtful.

'Of course they will. You can get almost anything you feel like in a place like this, even a boiled egg.'

'Just a beer, thanks.'

Giò ordered the drinks and a pack of *Gitanes*, and took off his linen jacket, hanging it over the back of his chair. He sat down, pushing up his shirt sleeves.

'Lucky chap, you're properly dressed for the weather,' he said. 'The shop's air-conditioned, so I'm alternately frozen or boiled, it's a bore. I'd really prefer to be warm all the time, wouldn't you?'

'Absolutely. You should thank your lucky stars you live in Paris. In London, it pisses with rain nearly all the time, or so it seems to me. It's really depressing.'

The waiter arrived with the drinks and put them on the table, with Giò's cigarettes and a bowl of salted almonds. Giò took a handful and pushed the bowl towards Basil.

'I wish they wouldn't do this; I can never resist. It just makes one even more thirsty, and one drinks too fast and too much.'

'I expect that's the idea.' Basil helped himself to the almonds and took a long pull at his beer, wiping his beard with the back of his hand. Giò poured iced water into his wine and drank half the glass. He leaned back in his seat and looked at the younger man.

'Tell me about yourself, Basil,' he said. 'How's the poetry going?'

'In a word, slowly. I've done nothing at all since I've been on holiday. Well, that's not strictly true, I did quite a bit before I went to Ramatuelle, but once I hit the beach, the resolve rather faded, I have to admit.'

Giò smiled. 'That's very understandable, isn't it? Do you have a deadline to meet?'

'Not really. I think my publishers rather pray that I'll run out of steam altogether, and let them off the hook. They don't sell very many of my books; in fact I'm pretty sure they lose money.'

'It doesn't sound as though you're really enjoying life very much, does it?'

Basil drank some more beer and looked at Giò seriously. 'You're dead right. I've been in a ridiculous rut for years. So I am planning to do something about it without delay.'

'And what's that?'

'Well, I shall quit my boring job, get rid of my dreary flat and move to Paris, for a start.'

'Bravo,' said Giò 'sounds like a good idea.' He spoke casually, but inside him a small bubble of excitement began to fizz, like Alka-Seltzer in a glass of water.

'I can't think why I didn't do it years ago,' Basil went on, though he knew the reason perfectly well. 'I'll have to be my mother's lodger till I get a job and find a place of my own. I quite fancy the idea of an attic in Montmartre, or something like that.'

'Do you have anything in mind, job-wise?'

'Olivia thinks that my Russian could be the key to that, she suggested working in radio or telly. Foreign correspondent, something along those lines. She thinks I might perhaps talk to her stepfather about it.'

'Patrick?' said Giò. 'Of course. He's a marvellous man, tremendously nice too, he's my brother-in-law.'

'What does he do, exactly?'

'He makes documentaries for television. I'm quite sure he'd put in a word for you in the right quarter, if he thought you a suitable candidate.'

Basil began to feel as if he had moved to Paris already, and made a daily habit of drinking in a pavement café with someone like Giò. At that moment, a slim black cat came running along the pavement and leapt onto Giò's lap, purring ferociously.

'Hullo, you old bugger,' said Giò, stroking the cat, 'where did you spring from?'

'Is this the cat you're going to finish up with in Souliac, a pair of old crocks together?'

Giò laughed. 'Certainly is. Unless of course Mr Right comes along, then we'd be two old crocks together with a cat, wouldn't we?'

Basil looked at Giò as he sat stroking his little cat, which crouched on his knee, eyes tightly closed, purring ecstatically. Then Giò raised his head and looked straight at Basil, and the signal from his dark eyes was unmistakable. 'Are you free tonight, Basil? What about dinner, and maybe go to a club afterwards?'

'Sounds fun,' said Basil, though unaccountably he suddenly felt extremely nervous and for two pins would have made an excuse and left. Don't be idiotic he said to himself; stay cool, you can handle this.

They dined at a small restaurant further down the arcade, Giò opting for a table inside rather than one on the pavement. The dinner was excellent, the service unobtrusive, and Giò chose a Montrachet to accompany their Dover sole. Soothed by the exquisite food and wine, and the charm of his host, Basil began to relax and enjoy himself. Encouraged by Giò, he told him about his dreary job in London, and his even more dreary flat.

'Well,' said Giò, smiling, 'don't be too impressed by *my* lifestyle. It has more than its share of *longeurs*, I can tell you.'

'But at least you live in a marvellous place, and deal with beautiful objects all the time.'

'I suppose so.'

After dinner, they walked together under the trees,

enjoying the cool night air after the heat of the day. Then without warning, Giò hailed a cab and they left the Place des Vosges and drove through quiet, dimly-lit streets in an area unknown to Basil. The taxi stopped beside a shabby nondescript door, bare except for a small hole at eye-level. Giò pressed a button on the entry-phone in the wall and gave his name, and presently the door opened with a small click and they entered a narrow hallway. The door closed behind them with a dull sigh and Giò led the way to the end of the dark hall. The muffled throb of pop music rose from below, and a flight of steps led down, presumably to a cellar. At the bottom of the steps was a heavy, dark-red curtain trimmed with Victorian bobble-braid. Giò pulled it aside, and the full roar of the music broke over them like a wave. The cellar was packed with dancers, bopping away in the tropical heat of the badly-ventilated room, under the strobe lights which circled the space, flashing on and off in time to the music. As they fought their way through the crush to the bar, a young man flicked his long hair back from his face and a shower of malodorous sweat landed on Basil, drenching his face and shirt-front. Revolted, he followed Giò to the bar, and propped himself against it, looking at the crowd. Slowly, he became aware that everyone in the room was a man.

'Whisky?' said Giò.

'Thanks.'

Stunned by the heat and the noise, Basil drank his whisky, realizing with increasing alarm that he was totally out of his depth. Fleetingly, he thought of his gentle affair with Herbert, and was appalled at his own naïvety and ignorance in the face of the frenetic scene taking place around him. Turning to Giò, he saw that his glass was already empty. He put a two-hundred franc note on the counter. The barman refilled their glasses and took the money; he did not offer any change.

'Do you want to dance?' said Giò.

'Why not?' agreed Basil, though it was the last thing he wished to do. They attached themselves to the fringe of the crush and Basil did his best to appear to be enjoying himself, keeping his eyes on Giò as the end-lessly swirling coloured lights lit up his smiling face. The dancing seemed to go on and on, and the music boomed away, seamlessly moving from one half-remembered rock-and-roll hit to another. Basil's legs were beginning to weaken, his head throbbed and his lungs were bursting, but a stubborn pride prevented him from being the first to admit defeat. As for Giò, he danced like a man inspired, radiant, laughing, until suddenly he stopped, took Basil by the arm and pushed his way back to the bar.

'God, it's hot!' he said. 'What'll you have, a cold beer?'

'Thanks,' said Basil. 'Good idea, I'm dead.'

They drank the beer, still breathing heavily, leaning against the bar and watching the dancers. Without warning, a wave of nausea hit Basil and he felt as though he were going to throw up. He turned to Giò. 'Is there a loo?'

'I don't think so, no.'

'I need to get out of here.'

Giò shot him a worried glance and they pushed their way out, up the stairs and into the street, where Basil vomited violently into the gutter. Then he sat down on the pavement, leaning against the wall, white-faced and trembling. After a few minutes he stood up, but his legs gave way and he sat down again, heavily.

'Christ,' he said, 'I'm pissed.'

Giò laughed, took him by the wrist and hauled him to his feet. They staggered along the pavement to the corner of the street. A cab cruised past and Giò shouted

'Taxi!' The cab stopped and Giò bundled Basil into the back. 'Place des Vosges,' he said to the driver.

The next morning, Basil woke to find himself lying on a big red sofa, with a ferocious headache, still fully-clothed and stinking of vomit. He closed his eyes again. 'My God, what happened?' he croaked. 'What have I done?'

'You haven't done anything,' replied a cross voice, 'unless you count getting paralytic and throwing up all over a taxi and my bathroom.'

Basil opened his eyes and focused with some difficulty on Giò, standing at the foot of the sofa with a cup of coffee in his hand.

'Jesus, did I really? How awful, I'm terribly sorry.'

'Here,' said Giò, slightly less crossly, 'drink this.'

Basil sat up and drank the coffee. His hands shook uncontrollably as he did so, and the smell of his own vomit threatened to overwhelm him again. He handed the cup back to Giò, and stood up unsteadily with as much dignity as he could manage. 'I must go home and sort myself out,' he said. At the door, he turned to Giò. 'I'm really very sorry, Giò; I've made a complete fool of myself, I'm an idiot.'

'Don't worry about it. It's not the end of the world, is it? There'll be other times.'

Basil walked back to the Ile St-Louis, feeling incredibly fragile as well as humiliated and extremely foolish, but greatly relieved to have escaped from a situation in which he had so rashly got himself involved.

Nelly and her daughters, with Wiggy and Pepys, toiled up the stony path from the beach, their arms full of heavy wet towels and in Nelly's case, the picnic basket. The beach had been hot and humid, and the air in the green tunnel formed by the overhanging branches arching across the track seemed cool and refreshing by comparison. Nevertheless the little dogs were panting, their sides heaving, their pink tongues hanging out. God, thought Nelly, I hope they don't pop their clogs before Ma, she'd be shattered. They had remained on the beach as long as possible, but it was now nearly six o'clock and preparations for dinner had to be started. Fortunately, Henry and Jane had been invited to a drinks party at the *Manoir* so they would have a couple of hours' respite from them. This would give Nelly and the children time to have a quiet drink with her mother without the unwelcome, heavy and argumentative presence of Henry.

They reached the top of the steep cliff-path, and stepped out of the tunnel onto the gorse-studded, sheep-cropped turf.

'Oof!' said Gertrude, red-faced with exertion, 'I'm knackered.' She sat down heavily on the short spiky grass.

'*Not* a nice word in the mouth of a child, Gertie,' said Nelly, automatically but without any great conviction, as they all flopped down together, the dogs lying flat on their stomachs to cool off. Nelly lay on her back and gazed at the sky, now a pearly blue after the recent days of rain and fog. She had spent several wakeful nights agonizing about Hugo, and trying to analyse what it was that had cast such a shadow over their marriage. It can't just have been my fault, going back to work and all that, she reasoned in her logical way. There has to be something else. The thing is, what? The horrible thought that Basil might have told him about their fleeting affair did cross her mind briefly, but she dismissed it as really quite unlikely; Baz would never betray her, she was

185

sure. The advent of Henry had provided a welcome counter-irritant in a curious way, and his presence had tended to diminish the impact of Hugo's uncharacteristic behaviour.

Nelly sighed and sat up. 'Come on, girls, the last lap,' she said, standing up and pulling the reluctant Gertrude to an upright position. They staggered across the field to the garden gate of *Les Romarins*, and trailed tiredly round the side of the house to the kitchen. 'Hang the towels on the line, darlings. Phylly, you're in charge.'

Nelly was opening the fridge door to get some ice, when she heard the telephone ringing. She waited a second in case Henry answered it, then ran through to the hall and lifted the heavy old receiver.

'Hello?'

'Dr Turnbull?'

'Speaking.'

'Could you hold a second please, Dr Turnbull? I have a call for you from Mr Vaughan-Thomas.' Vaughan-Thomas, thought Nelly, who the hell is that?

'Nelly, this is James, from Uppingham Press.'

'James!' exclaimed Nelly, realization dawning. He was Hugo's publisher.

'I've had quite a job tracking you down, my dear; through the hospital eventually. I'm afraid I have some terrible news.'

Nelly's heart stopped; her blood froze. 'Is it Hugo?'

'No, no. It's his parents, my dear. I had a call from the High Commission in Nairobi, they couldn't reach Hugo or you.'

'What is it, James?' Nelly sounded calm, but faint.

'It's his mother and father, I'm afraid. They've been murdered in their beds by armed robbers, and the house ransacked.'

'Guns?' said Nelly.

'No, machetes or whatever they're called. You know.'

'Pangas,' said Nelly. 'Oh, God, how frightful, poor old things.'

'I am so very sorry; I feel awful having to tell you.'

'I know.' Nelly collected her wits, and swallowed hard. 'Thank you, James, you're a real friend. I'll phone Hugo right away, he's in France.'

'Let me know if there's anything at all I can do, won't you?'

'Thanks, I will.'

'Goodbye, my dear. Take care.'

'Goodbye, James. Thanks again.' She replaced the receiver and went back to the kitchen, taking several deep breaths to steady herself. Should she ring Hugo immediately, or have a stiff drink first? She decided that a small drink would be a good idea, while she tried to think of the least painful way of telling Hugo the appalling news. She poured herself a whisky, and sat quietly at the table drinking it. The girls came in from the garden and she asked them to go and check that Murphy had had his supper and that his haynet was full. Phyllida shot her a worried look and then shepherded the other two away without any questions; Nelly supposed she must look pale or sick.

Henry came into the kitchen and opened the fridge door, looking for ice. 'Where's the bloody ice? Have you taken it all?'

'No, Henry. It's on the bloody draining board. And you can take your bloody shitty self, and your bloody boring wife and jump in the bloody lake!'

Henry stared at Nelly, astonished. 'What the hell's eating *you*?'

'Fuck off, Henry.'

He went. Tears rose, stinging her eyes and blocking her nose. Not now, she thought. Not *now*, Nelly, *please*;

time for that later. She swallowed the rest of the whisky, blew her nose and went back to the telephone, taking Hugo's card from the back pocket of her jeans. She dialled the code for France and then Hester's number in Ramatuelle. The elongated high-pitched ringing tone seemed to go on for ever. Then she heard a click.

'*Oui?*'

'*Mme Rodzianko?*'

'*Oui.*'

'This is Nelly Turnbull, Hugo's wife.'

'Oh, hello Nelly. You want to speak to Hugo?'

'Yes, please.'

'Hold on, I'll call him.'

In a few moments Hugo came to the phone. 'Hello, darling.'

'Hugo, I'm afraid something terrible has happened.'

'Nelly, what is it? Is it one of the girls?'

'No, darling, it's your mum and dad.' She told him everything that James Vaughan-Thomas had told her, as calmly and sensibly as she could. When she had finished there was a long pause. 'Hugo?'

'I'm still here; I'm trying to think what to do, Nelly.'

'When are you coming back to Paris?'

'Tomorrow.'

'Could you start back tonight, do you think?'

'I'll have a word with Hester.' Nelly waited; she could hear Hugo's voice and Hester's, sounding very far away.

'Hester says of course, we'll start at once, we'll be in Paris by three in the morning.'

'So I'll book you on a flight to London first thing, and then we can catch the plane to Nairobi tomorrow night, will that be OK?'

'Thank you, darling.'

'I'll make the bookings now, and then I'll ring you

back to confirm. You'll be there for a couple of hours, you'll have to eat and pack before you leave, won't you?'

'Yes, all right.' Hugo's voice shook. 'Bless you, darling. What would I do without you?'

'When you get to London, go straight home. With any luck, I'll get an early plane from Guernsey, so I'll probably be there before you. I'll hang up now, and ring the airport, then I'll ring you straight back.'

'OK.'

'Hugo?'

'Yes?'

'I'm so terribly sorry.'

'Thank you.'

Nelly replaced the receiver and went sorrowfully to the drawing-room, where she found Una-Mary playing a game of Patience. Very quietly she told her mother what had happened, and asked her advice about what to tell the girls at this juncture. Una-Mary looked at her daughter with admiration and compassion.

'Nothing, just yet,' she said. 'Let them stay here with me, and Elsie can stay in the house in case of accidents. Go and book your flights at once, darling, and ring Hugo back. And when you speak to him, give him my love.'

'I will,' said Nelly, getting up. 'I'll get Phylly to bring you a drink, shall I?'

'Please, darling. Where's Henry?'

'Gone to his drinks party, I hope. I told him to fuck off.'

'Did you darling? Quite right, too. I should have told him that myself, long ago.'

Chapter Ten

The plane touched down at Nairobi twenty minutes late and taxied slowly to a stop. Hugo undid his safety-belt and looked at Nelly, sitting quietly beside him. She smiled, trying to conceal the anxiety she felt for him. She touched his hand briefly. 'OK?'

'OK.' Hugo got up and Nelly followed him as they shuffled through the aircraft with the rest of the passengers. As they descended the waiting steps the heat hit them like a blast from a furnace door. After they had passed through immigration a slim young man stepped forward and addressed Hugo.

'Mr Turnbull?'

'Yes.'

'My name is Colin Sitwell; I'm from the High Commission, sir. I'm here to assist in any way I can. I have transport to take you to your parents' farm; the police are in charge there, of course. May I say how very sorry we all are, sir?'

'Thank you,' said Hugo. 'You're very kind.'

'Do you have luggage to collect?'

'Yes,' said Nelly. 'One suitcase.'

They went to the baggage delivery area and joined the small waiting crowd. Hugo turned to Colin Sitwell. 'Where are my parents now?'

'In the hospital mortuary, sir. I expect you remember Colonel Tanner? He has already identified the bodies.

You don't have to go through that again, sir, unless of course you wish to do it yourself?'

Hugo looked at Nelly, and she nodded. 'We'd like to see them.'

'Of course.'

The luggage arrived and they left the airport building. An official car with a driver drove up to the kerb as they came through the doors, and they got in.

'We'll go to the Commission first, so that we can fill you in with all the details, tell you about the inquest, the funeral arrangements, and anything else you might wish to discuss.'

'Thank you,' said Hugo, suddenly feeling very sick.

'Then I thought you might like to go to the Muthaiga Country Club, have a wash and some lunch before we go out to the farm.'

'I'm not a member,' said Hugo.

'But your father was, and I am. I have already spoken to them, and they are very happy to help in any way they can.'

'How kind.' Nelly smiled at young Mr Sitwell. 'You've thought of everything.'

'I thought the club would be quieter than a hotel, you can be more private.'

'When will we go to the hospital?' asked Hugo.

'Whenever you feel you're ready, sir.'

Hugo looked at Nelly.

'Let's go there now, and get the worst part over, darling,' she said quietly.

'Yes, let's. Is that OK?'

'Of course,' said Colin Sitwell and told the driver to go straight to the hospital.

At the hospital they followed the young Kenyan doctor to the mortuary. Hugo had never been in such a place before. He felt cold, slightly unreal and nauseated by the smell of formaldehyde. Nelly was, of course, perfectly familiar with the surroundings and she took Hugo's arm and held it tightly while the long sliding drawers were pulled out one by one, revealing the frozen, horribly lacerated corpses of his parents, the heavy bandages round their heads stained with dark congealed blood. Hugo stared at the pinched, purple-bruised, disfigured faces of his mother and father with horror and with pity.

'They might as well be meat,' he said, his voice sounding dull and detached. He looked at the doctor, his eyes stones behind his spectacles, and nodded. 'Yes,' he said. 'It's them.' The doctor closed the drawers.

They left the mortuary and the car took them to the High Commission, where a senior officer saw them. He was polite and business-like. 'The police are doing everything they can to find the gang,' he said, 'but it's like trying to find a needle in a haystack up there, with so much forest. There's little chance of bringing them to justice, I'm afraid.'

Hugo nodded, and smiled faintly. 'I know that,' he said.

'Sitwell and the car are at your disposal. He'll do everything possible to make things as easy as he can for you. The inquest is tomorrow, and the funeral can take place whenever you wish after that. I imagine that you will want to bury your parents in the Anglican church?'

'I suppose so,' said Hugo distantly.

'I'll cope with all that, sir,' said Colin Sitwell quickly.

'Thank you.' Nelly glanced at Hugo and stood up.

'Well, that's about all,' said the senior officer, standing too. 'If there's anything else, please let us know.'

'We will. Thank you very much indeed for your help.' Nelly took Hugo firmly by the arm and led him out of the room, followed by Colin Sitwell, looking worried.

They left the Commission and got back into the car.

'Muthaiga Country Club,' said Colin Sitwell to the driver.

'Sir.' The car moved off silently.

'Lunch,' said Nelly.

'I'm not hungry.' Hugo sounded petulant, like a child.

'Hugo, you're going to have a huge gin and then lunch. We all are, OK?'

'OK,' whispered Hugo and began to cry, long, hard, racking sobs. Nelly put her arms round him and hugged him close to her.

'My poor love,' she said, holding his head and biting hard on the insides of her cheeks to stop herself from breaking down too.

After lunch they drove out to the farm. In former times the trip would have taken about two hours, depending on the weather. But now the road surface was so poor and so full of potholes that it was difficult to maintain any kind of speed. About a mile from the farm, a dirt track led them through forest until they emerged at last into a wide clearing. The rambling, shabby house with its corrugated-iron roof, surrounded by its wide brick-pillared verandah stood silently in the centre of a large sun-bleached lawn, encircled by the tall trees of the uncleared woodland. It was not difficult to imagine what a short time it would probably take for the forest to claim it all back again. The rudimentary drive, rutted and weed-infested, led straight to the front of the house and the High Commission Mercedes drew up as elegantly as it could beside the short flight of steps up to the verandah. Hugo and Nelly got out of the car, followed by Colin Sitwell.

At a little distance, seated on the grass in a silent

semi-circle was a small band of Kikuyu, mostly old women and children, watching and waiting. A skinny old man wearing a bush-hat, a brown-tweed jacket, patched khaki trousers and black patent-leather shoes detached himself from the group and advanced slowly towards them, leaning on a stick.

Hugo turned and then went quickly towards him, holding out his hands. '*Kinanjui! Jambo; habari?*'

'*Jambo, bwana.*' Kinanjui seized Hugo's hands. '*Habari mbaia, bwana. Mbaia sana, sana.*' His voice shook and his rheumy old eyes were full of tears.

Hugo, with an enormous effort, asked Kinanjui whether he remembered Nelly.

The old man turned to Nelly and took her hand. '*Ndyo, bwana; sabu Nelly. Jambo, memsabu.*'

'*Jambo, Kinanjui.*' Nelly shook his calloused hand, and suddenly the whole meaning of the lives of the two dead old people was made plain to her. She realized that their long years in that beautiful but vulnerable place had not only been concerned with forging a livelihood for themselves, but had made an important contribution to the lives of several dozen families. No doubt, as Hugo had so often said, the fundamental concept of colonialism, however paternalistic, kind and caring was wrong, but the demeanour of the affectionate and gentle old man told her another, equally valid story.

Colin Sitwell asked Kinanjui where the police were, and Kinanjui said that they had gone back to Thika, but a patrol would return at night. He unlocked the door and they went into the house. The verandah doors led straight into the big light sitting-room, with its cedar-planked ceiling and white-washed walls. What had been a simple but beautiful room was now a shambles, with books, pictures and ornaments lying broken and scattered on the wood-block floor, some even lying in the ashes in the wide stone fireplace. The furniture, including some very nice old English pieces, had been hurled around and some of them had obviously been deliberately kicked to pieces. The Persian rugs, lovingly collected over the years during the Turnbulls' rare visits to Mombasa or Malindi, had vanished and were doubtless even now on their way back to the coast for resale.

It was Nelly's turn to feel sick. She turned away and walked quietly out onto the verandah, and sat down on one of the collapsing wicker chairs that had stood out there since before Hugo's birth. She put her head down between her knees, in an effort to regain her strength and control. As she waited for the roaring noise in her ears to fade she heard the sound of a motor, and straightened up. A green Landrover drew up behind the Mercedes and a tall handsome Kenyan got out of the driver's seat and came up the steps. Nelly stood up and went to meet him. She thought that maybe he was from the police, though he was not in uniform but wore khaki shorts and a safari-jacket.

'Mrs Turnbull?'

'Yes.'

'Is Mr Hugo here, ma'am?'

Suddenly Nelly recognized Gabrieli, and held out her hand. 'I'm so sorry, I didn't realize it was you, Gabrieli. Yes, Hugo's in the house, do come in.'

At that moment Hugo came out onto the verandah, and Gabrieli took a step towards him. '*Bwana kidogo?*' he said.

'Gabrieli!' Hugo almost threw himself at his friend and the two men hugged each other, and once again Hugo began to weep as though his heart would break.

Nelly hesitated for a moment, and then spoke loudly

and clearly. 'Hugo, I'm going to go with Kinanjui to the kitchen and make some tea. You come and help us will you, Mr Sitwell?'

While Kinanjui got the stove going in the kitchen and put the kettle on to boil, Nelly and Colin Sitwell went to the Turnbulls' bedroom. As she had feared, the horror and the chaos were unspeakable, and she made up her mind at once. 'I can't bear the thought of Hugo having to cope with this nightmare,' she said. 'Could we please bundle these dreadful sheets and things up in a pillow-case, and hide them where he won't see them? We'll lock them in this cupboard; you take the key. If the police need them for any reason, you can explain. Is that all right?'

'Yes, of course. Look, you go and take out the tea, and I'll tidy everything away here, and then come and join you. How would that be?'

'Brilliant, you're an angel. Thank you.' Nelly returned to the kitchen, where she found Kinanjui feeding the fire with little bits of stick to encourage the kettle. The sweet, acrid smell of woodsmoke and charcoal filled the soot-blackened little kitchen and conjured up for Nelly the whole essence of the way of life of her parents-in-law. A thin jet of steam issued from the spout of the kettle and Nelly took the aluminium tea-pot from its shelf, and spooned tea into it from the tin caddy beside it. She put flowered cups and saucers on a tray and looked in the fridge for milk. There was none. Well, doesn't matter, she thought.

Kinanjui hobbled swiftly to the back door. '*Ngoja kidogo, sabu.*' He disappeared through the door. Nelly, who had not understood, made the tea. The old man reappeared with a large enamel mug. He took a china jug from a hook, poured milk from the mug into it and put it on the tray.

'Wonderful,' she said, and tried to remember her few scraps of Swahili. '*Sante sana, Kinanjui.*'

As she picked her way through the sitting-room to the verandah Colin Sitwell caught up with her and held open the fly-screen for her. 'All done,' he said, quietly.

Nelly smiled at him with relief and gratitude. 'Thank you, Colin, you've been marvellous.' She put the tray down on a wicker table and poured tea for Colin, Kinanjui and herself. The old man was standing rather hesitantly near the steps leaning on his stick, looking as if he might take himself off, but Nelly took him a cup of tea, and he sat down on the low brick wall of the verandah, firmly rejecting a chair.

Hugo and Gabrieli were walking slowly up and down along the far edge of the lawn, where the flowering shrubs gave way to the forest trees. Gabrieli's arm was round Hugo's shoulder and he bent his head towards Hugo's as they talked. At last they came across the lawn to the verandah and Nelly poured tea for them. She looked vaguely round to see where the Commission driver had got to, but could not see him. She looked at Colin.

'Would the driver like tea, do you think?'

'Don't worry, he'll have fixed himself up in the quarters, I'm sure.'

'Oh, I see,' said Nelly, though she did not.

A car horn sounded in the woods and a battered old pick-up rattled across the lawn and stopped beside them.

'It's Colonel Tanner.' Hugo got up and went to meet his father's old friend and neighbour.

'My dear boy,' said the grey-haired elderly man, grasping Hugo's hand, 'this is a ghastly business. Ghastly.' He shook Nelly's hand. 'I'm so sorry, so very sorry.'

'It's dreadful for you too,' said Nelly. 'They were your friends.'

'Indeed.'

'Would you like some tea?'

'No thank you, my dear. Hugo, my dear boy, we must talk.'

'Of course,' said Hugo. 'Come into the study, that's if there's anything left to sit on. You come too, Gabrieli.'

The three men went into the house. Kinanjui picked up the tray and took it away to the kitchen. Nelly and Colin sat without speaking, watching as the sun dropped slowly down into the trees and the blue dome of the sky began to lose its colour. Nelly felt numb with fatigue.

'It'll be dark in an hour,' said Colin. 'We ought to start back fairly soon, I'll go and round up the driver.'

It was late by the time they got back to Nairobi, and Colin took them into the club, carrying their bag for them and arranging for dinner to be brought to their room. 'I'll telephone you in the morning and you can tell me what you wish to do,' he said.

'Won't you stay for a drink?' said Nelly.

'No, thanks all the same, my wife will be worrying. Goodnight. I hope you both get some sleep.'

'Goodnight Colin, and thank you for everything.'

'Glad to be able to help.' He turned and walked quickly away to the waiting car.

Nelly and Hugo followed the steward to their room, and Hugo asked him to bring a bottle of whisky, ice and mineral water.

'I'm going to run you a bath, darling,' said Nelly, 'and while you're having it, I'm going to phone Ma, and check that the girls are OK.'

Hugo stared at her blankly. Then he realized that he had completely forgotten about the existence of his children and Una-Mary in Florizel, of London, of Hester in Paris. How weird, he thought. Am I going out of my mind?

'Good idea,' he said. 'Give them my love.'

In the bath, Hugo lay with his eyes closed thinking about his parents. He tried to visualize his childhood, with his mother and father as the key figures of his early life, but other, much more vivid pictures rose in his mind. He saw himself and Gabrieli riding in the woods, the sweat dark on the ponies' necks, Gabrieli's strong black legs with his hard bare feet in the stirrups, the long, stinging swish of the ponies' tails flicking from side to side as they tried to rid themselves of the ubiquitous black flies. He saw the Kikuyu women bringing the loads of coffee from the fields, their deep heavy woven-sisal baskets slung round their shaven heads on leather straps, their ears hung with many wire hoops threaded with small coloured beads. He saw these same women making their way home to the camp behind the house every evening, bent double beneath enormous, towering loads of firewood held in position by the same leather head-straps. As a child, it had seemed to Hugo that the older and more frail the woman, the bigger the load of wood she carried. He had often wondered what would happen if the strap slipped off the forehead and caught the old woman round the neck. Would she be garrotted? Perhaps some had been, though he could not remember such a thing actually happening. In his mind's eye, those load-bearing old women passed in procession, blackly silhouetted against the reddening sky as they approached their huts, where smoke was already seeping through the pointed thatched roofs and a scented blue haze drifted on the evening air. Inside the huts, other women had already scoured the smoke-blackened aluminium cooking pots to brightness on the insides, and were steaming maize-meal on charcoal fires for their supper. Suddenly, Hugo did remember his parents quite clearly, sitting with him at their candle-lit dining-table, attended by the much younger Kinanjui and Njomo the cook. Then he remembered lying on the rug in front of the blazing cedar-wood fire, resin-scented and inclined to fire sparks into the room, while his mother read aloud to him. His father smoked his pipe and did the three-week-old *Times* crossword puzzle, and outside in the dark star-sprinkled night, the drums throbbed without menace. The tears rose again at the memory. Resolutely, Hugo sat up in the bath and took a sachet of shampoo from the well-stocked basket provided by the club and washed his hair. He could hear Nelly's voice in the bedroom, talking to her mother. Presently she came into the bathroom, carrying two whiskies.

She sat down on the stool and gave Hugo his drink. 'All's well,' she said, taking a sip of her own. 'Supper will be here in about fifteen minutes, the chap said. After you with the bath, darling.'

'Sorry, I'll get out at once. I've been lying here selfishly, indulging in nostalgia.'

'If it helps, good.'

'I think perhaps it does, a bit.' Hugo sighed, took a swig of his drink and got out of the bath. He knelt beside Nelly, wrapped his wet arms round her, burying his head in her lap. 'I don't think I could have handled this without you, darling Nelly.'

To her surprise, several sharp rejoinders occurred to Nelly as she sat on the stool with Hugo's wet hair soaking her skirt. Instead, she put her hand tenderly on his cheek. 'I'm glad that I could be of some use,' she said very quietly, without irony.

Hugo released her, and wound one of the large white towels round his waist like a *kikoi*. Nelly smiled and took off her clothes. 'You look like a beach-boy at Malindi,' she said.

'I quite wish I was one, sometimes.' He sat on the stool slowly sipping his drink while Nelly, with the hot tap running, soaked away the stiffness of the last forty-eight hours. They had slept very little on the plane and she felt exhausted, mentally as well as physically. She sensed that Hugo was extremely tense, fighting against his anguish, determined not to go to pieces.

'Colonel Tanner told me that the bank was about to foreclose on Dad,' he said, without preamble.

'Hugo! How absolutely awful! Why?' Nelly stared at him, appalled. 'Why didn't he tell us, let us help him?'

'God knows. Pride, I suppose.'

'Poor Dad, how humiliating for him, and how dreadful for your mother.'

'He probably thought the next harvest would straighten things out, you know how optimistic he always was?'

'Poor man, in a place like this I imagine you have to be.'

Hugo picked up their glasses and went to the bedroom to refill them. He sat down on the stool again. 'There's more,' he said. 'Worse, really. It seems that selling the farm, the house and what's left of the contents, would be unlikely to raise enough money to pay off the loan. It's a mess.'

Nelly said nothing, but looked thoughtful. She sipped her drink and waited.

'The sadness is, that Gabrieli would like to take over the farm and live there. He could sell his place and get loans from the development funds, but old man Tanner doesn't think he could raise enough to square the bank. They're not particularly helpful these days; it's understandable I suppose.'

'Do you think Gabrieli would make a go of it? You don't think it would be a millstone round his neck, too?'

'If anyone could, he could,' said Hugo. 'He has rather ambitious ideas. He's thinking of having paying-guests, tourists, and taking them on safari to see the game. That way, he wouldn't be totally dependent on the coffee, unlike poor old Dad.'

'It's a good idea. What about his wife? Is he married?'

'Yes. She's an accountant, very highly qualified. She works for a firm in Nairobi.'

'Bully for her,' said Nelly, surprised. 'Does she commute every day?'

'No, shares a flat in town and comes home every weekend.'

'No children, then?'

'No, not yet.'

'Her salary must make a difference?' Nelly glanced at Hugo, with a faint smile.

Hugo looked back at her, his eyes obscure behind his steamed-up spectacles. 'Yes,' he said, 'I'm quite sure it does.'

There was a light knock on the door to the bedroom and Hugo got up and opened it to admit the steward with their dinner. Swiftly and efficiently he set the table by the window, gave Hugo the chit to sign, and took himself off as silently as he had come.

Later, as they lay side by side in bed, exhausted and sad, Nelly stared at the ceiling, her hands clasped behind her head.

'Hugo?'

'Mm?'

'Would I be interfering and insensitive if I suggested

that we fly down to the coast for a couple of days? Just to be quiet, have a rest on the beach?'

Hugo was silent, and she turned her head to look at him. He lay on his side, his eyes big without his glasses. He looked puzzled, and rather worried. 'How could we?' he said, wearily. 'There's so much to deal with, here and at the farm.'

'I realize that. But after the inquest, and the funeral, and the lawyers, we will almost certainly be completely shattered. I just thought that a short break before we fly home might be a good idea?'

Hugo managed a tight little smile. 'Is that your professional advice?'

Nelly laughed and put a hand on his cheek. 'Yes, it is. Please think about it, darling, won't you?'

' "Man that is born of a woman hath but a short time to live, and is full of misery." ' Too bloody true thought Hugo bleakly, standing beside Nelly in the little church. The two coffins rested on their trestles in front of them, a posy of flowers from the garden on each lid. Candles burned on the altar, covered with a plain cloth and unadorned except for the simple silver-gilt cross. The priest seemed nervous and ill-at-ease, sweating profusely as he fumbled his way through the burial service, dropping his bookmarks and losing his place. Perhaps it's the first time he's done one, thought Nelly. He certainly looks young enough, poor guy.

At last the first part of the service was concluded and the pall-bearers, dressed in their best, advanced to the front of the church and led by Hugo and Gabrieli lifted the two coffins onto their shoulders and processed down the narrow aisle and out into the sunshine of the churchyard. Slowly and carefully they lowered the coffins into the prepared grave, one on top of the other. Then the young priest came out of the church, with Nelly, the Tanners, Colin Sitwell and Gabrieli's wife Margaret, followed by Kinanjui and his quiet, subdued band of Kikuyu women in their best robes, necklaces and ear-hoops, the copper wire binding their arms glinting in the sunshine. The little company of mourners straggled across the dusty, uneven grass of the churchyard and surrounded the open grave.

' "We therefore commit their bodies to the ground," ' intoned the priest. ' "Earth to earth, ashes to ashes, dust to dust, in sure and certain hope of the Resurrection to eternal life." ' Hugo picked up a handful of dirt and threw it onto his mother's coffin, and Nelly did the same, followed by Gabrieli. Margaret threw a red hibiscus flower and Kinanjui and the women scattered small twigs of eucalyptus, their leaves silvery-green and resin-scented in the sun. The priest pronounced the blessing, and everyone stood around uncertainly, as if waiting for something more. Nelly took Hugo's arm and they turned away, and walked slowly through the churchyard to the waiting cars. Nelly looked for Gabrieli; he was just behind her, with Margaret.

'Gabrieli, do you think you could ask everyone to come back to the farm for some tea?'

'Are you sure?' Gabrieli looked anxiously at Hugo, who stood staring towards the grave, where the soil was already being shovelled back into the hole, each spadeful of dirt thudding on the lid of the coffin.

'Quite sure. It's all organized, and the house is tidy now. Hugo wishes it, please.'

'Of course,' said Gabrieli. 'You go on, and I'll sort out the transport and follow you in ten minutes.'

'Excellent, thank you.' She turned to Margaret, who

stood looking calm and elegant in a plain white cotton frock, a black ribbon round her neat, curly head. 'Margaret, could you be very kind and come and help me with the tea?'

'Of course, I'd be glad to. Shall I come with you now?'

'Could you? I'd be so grateful if you would.' The two women smiled at each other, in sympathy and understanding.

Colin Sitwell opened the door to the High Commission car and the advance party got in and drove away.

'Oh, God,' said Hugo forlornly, 'I forgot to thank the priest.'

'It's all right,' said Colin, 'I did; and dealt with the rest of it.'

'Thank you,' said Hugo, feeling useless.

At the farm, Mrs Tanner was already in charge in the kitchen, boiling kettles for the tea, and checking the cups she had borrowed from her women's group. The day before, she had brought over her own staff to help Kinanjui put the house to rights as much as possible, after the departure of the police. Her steward was now immaculate in his best white uniform, and looked tall and impressive in his dark-red fez, as he stood behind the long dining-table. This had been covered with a white cloth, and carried an assortment of sandwiches, cakes and biscuits protected from flies by muslin cloths. In the event, there was very little for Nelly and Margaret to do, so they walked in the garden for a few minutes, while Hugo and Colin disappeared into the study.

'We are so very sorry about Hugo's parents, especially Gabrieli,' said Margaret. 'I'm sure you know that?'

'Yes, I know,' said Nelly, 'thank you.' She felt shy, rather awkward and unsure of herself. She stopped, and bent to smell a large, creamy-white, pink-flushed rose.

' "Peace," ' said Margaret.

'What?'

' "Peace"; it's the name of that rose.'

'Oh, is it? How appropriate. I do so hope it's true for them.'

'I'm sure it is,' said Margaret. 'They were good people.'

Nelly hesitated, began to speak, then changed her mind. I must not interfere, she reminded herself. They walked back across the grass together, as the first cars began to arrive.

When everyone had got a cup of tea, and Mrs Tanner's steward was circulating with the plates of food, Colin came and sat on the brick wall of the verandah beside Nelly. 'How are you, Nelly? Nearly over now, you must be thankful?'

'I am, very. There's just the will, the lawyers, all that. Hugo's told you what the form is?'

'Yes, he has. I'm afraid it happens quite a lot these days.'

'*Shauri ya Mungu*, isn't that what they say here?' Nelly smiled wearily.

'The will of God? Do you really think that?'

'No, of course I don't.' Nelly sighed. 'I'm afraid I don't know the answers, Colin.'

'Who does, my dear?'

'The appointment with the lawyers is on Thursday, in Nairobi. I am trying to persuade Hugo to take a couple of days at the coast before then, a short break. He needs it, we both do.'

'What a sensible idea. Have you thought of Lamu? You could fly there easily. I have a friend who has a house on the beach, an Italian. He only uses it for a few weeks of the year; I rent it to suitable tenants for him.

It's very comfortable and cool, and his staff are always in residence.'

'Oh, Colin, it sounds perfect. Are you serious?'

'I'm perfectly serious. I could telephone his steward this evening; you could fly there in the morning. He would meet you, do the shopping and cooking for you, and all that.'

Nelly stared at him in disbelief. 'Do people really still live like that?'

'Some do,' said Colin, with a wry smile.

'Golly,' said Nelly. 'Well, yes please. Thanks.'

'You don't want to discuss it with Hugo?'

'Sometimes it's better to take a unilateral decision, and I'm taking it.'

'Right. I'll arrange it for you.'

Suddenly, the events of the past few days seemed to grow into a huge black cloud, pressing down on Nelly's spirit, threatening to crush her. The idea of a vast, empty, clean white beach, fringed with palm trees and lapped by the crystal-clear green waters of the Indian Ocean seemed unbelievably appealing, an escape from the present misery. She felt incredibly tired and weak, a painful lump rose in her throat and tears pricked behind her eyelids. Not now, she thought, not yet. But when I get into that beautiful water, I will.

Colin touched her hand, briefly. 'You're a brave woman, Nelly Turnbull; I admire you.'

'Do you really, Colin?'

'Yes, I do.'

Nelly looked at him for a moment, her hazel eyes red-rimmed beneath the fringe of copper-coloured hair, then she glanced towards Hugo. 'Trouble is,' she said, 'I'd rather be loved.'

'I'm quite sure you are.'

'Take no notice,' said Nelly, turning away

impatiently. 'That was just a stupid moment of weakness. I'm talking nonsense, forgive me.'

'There's nothing to forgive,' said Colin briskly. 'You're completely exhausted, that's all there is to it. It's our turn to look after *you*, my dear girl. I shall begin this evening.'

Chapter Eleven

'Poor Hugo, he was completely shattered,' said Hester, chopping onions and herbs to make a stuffing for the guinea-fowl. 'He hardly spoke a word all the way back to Paris, just drove rather fast; it was quite alarming.'

'Hardly surprising,' said Basil. 'It was a ghastly thing to happen, wasn't it?'

'Horrible, I can hardly bear to think about it. Poor man; poor Nelly too. I imagine they're having a rough time just now, with inquests, the funeral and all that.'

'I suppose so. Poor things, I hope they're all right.'

'One has to be, darling,' said Hester quietly. Basil leaned across the table and kissed his mother on the cheek.

'I know,' he said. 'Now, what can I do to help?' It was the last night of his stay and he did not want things to get too emotional. For that matter, neither did Hester.

'Well, you can beat this egg in a cup, while I sweat the onions.'

'OK.' He had just finished beating the egg when the phone began to ring in the sitting-room.

'Answer it will you, Baz? My hands are all oniony.'

Basil put down his fork, went through to the sitting-room and picked up the phone. 'Hello?'

'Basil?'

'Giò! Hi, how are you? I must apologize about the

209

other night, I really did behave rather badly. I meant to call you; it's been on my mind.'

'Forget it, Baz. It didn't matter at all. I was wondering, as it's your last night, could we have supper together, or a drink?'

'Afraid not, my mum's cooking.' He hesitated, then, not wanting to seem rude, went on: 'Actually, hold on a minute, Giò. I'll have a word with her.' He put down the phone and went to the kitchen. 'That's Giò Hamilton on the phone. He sounds as though he's at a loose end. Do you think the food will stretch to three?'

'Why not? Good idea.'

'Thanks, I'll ask him.'

Hester packed the stuffing into the cavity of the guinea-fowl, then anointed the bird with olive oil and put it in the oven. She was quite pleased not to be spending the evening alone with Basil, this Giò person would make it more amusing for him and take the pressure off her.

'Eight-fifteen, OK?' said Basil, coming back into the kitchen.

'Fine. You'd better run out and get another loaf and some more fruit.'

'Any particular kind?'

'You choose, darling.'

She heard Basil clump down the stairs and slam the street door. More flakes of limewash on the stairs to sweep up, she thought. Oh, well, doesn't matter. She peeled potatoes and put them to boil on a low flame. Then she made a salad, and looked at her watch: ten to eight. She checked the guinea-fowl and basted it, pouring a glass of wine over it. It smelt very good, a gamey, rich, slightly spicy smell; the scent of autumn. I need a drink she thought, and untypically, poured herself a stiff vodka. The idea of a stranger, a guest for dinner suddenly seemed rather formidable. She took her drink and went to the sitting-room to turn on the lights and check that everything was in order. From her work-table the kind bearded face of George looked at her benignly. She could almost see him shake his head, and hear his voice: 'Don't work yourself up, sweetheart, it's of no importance. Nothing ever is, at the end of the day.' Then she heard Basil's step on the stair, swallowed the rest of the vodka and went back to the kitchen to set the table.

Giò arrived five minutes early, and they went into the sitting-room for a drink before dinner. 'Do you mind if I look at the pictures?' he asked after a short pause, during which his eyes had swiftly assessed the contents of the room.

'By all means,' said Hester. She left them and went to the kitchen to turn down the oven and cover the bird with foil. It had produced a gratifying amount of delicious-smelling sauce on its own, so there would be no need to make more. She tested the potatoes, then dressed the salad and put it on the table. She poured another vodka, picked up a bowl of olives and went back to the sitting-room. Basil and Giò stood side by side looking at one of George's paintings. Giò's hand rested on Basil's shoulder.

'They're beautiful, Baz,' he was saying. 'I'm not surprised that Olivia admires your father's work. You must be very proud of him.'

'I am.' Basil turned and led the way to the sofa, where Hester sat quietly in her usual place. Fortified by the vodka, she felt better now, less tired and more in control. She offered the bowl of olives to Giò. He took two, and had a sip of his drink. He looked covertly at Hester. He thought that she was very cool, detached and proud, and realized that he must handle her carefully.

211

He decided not to beat about the bush. 'I think your work is fantastic,' he said, 'and if you do decide to allow me to sell your icons, I should be honoured to do so, on any terms you choose.'

'Good heavens!' said Hester, and laughed. 'How surprising. But they're not in the same league as my husband's work, you must know that?'

'They're a totally different *genre*, aren't they?'

'I suppose so.'

'One is not better than the other; they're two completely different things. Nevertheless, they do look wonderful hung together, whatever you say.'

'Well, thank you.' Hester's response was a little grudging. 'I'm glad you think so.'

All sorts of ideas were taking shape in Giò's mind. He thought he might steal a march on Olivia and bring his brother-in-law to see the Rodzianko paintings; it could very well be that Patrick would wish to make a short film about him for one of his programmes. One step at a time, he thought. I mustn't alarm the old dear. But what a splendid excuse for making sure that Baz comes back to Paris, and then, who knows?

'Time to eat, don't you think?' Hester got up a little stiffly from the sofa and led the way to the kitchen.

The dinner was delicious, the wine perfect, and the candles guttered in the evening air blowing through the open window. Giò, as he could be when he chose, was delightful and amusing, and Basil seemed to enjoy his company. Hester could see that he was pleased that Giò was impressed with his father's work, but she was a cautious woman and did not allow herself to fall entirely under Giò's spell. Why is he so anxious for us to like him? she asked herself.

After dinner Basil made coffee while Hester took Giò back to the sitting-room. They walked round the room together looking at George's paintings, one by one.

'Are these all there are, Hester?'

'No. I have about fifteen or so in Ramatuelle, and quite a lot more in store with a friend.'

'Do you ever think of exhibiting them?'

'No, I haven't planned to do that.'

'But would you, perhaps?'

'I'd have to think about it. They're very precious and personal to me, I'd hate them to be mauled by the critics, as they were when he was alive.'

'It doesn't necessarily follow that they would be now, does it?'

'I don't know,' said Hester. 'I suppose not.'

'Well,' said Giò, 'think about it, won't you, please?'

Basil brought the coffee and the cognac, and they smoked and talked a little longer. At eleven Giò rose to his feet and said it was late, he must go.

'Yes,' said Basil, getting up. 'It's an early start tomorrow. I'll see you out.'

Giò thanked Hester for the dinner, and Basil led the way down to the *porte-cochère*.

'Walk with me a little way?' suggested Giò.

'No, better not. I must get to bed, it's a long drive tomorrow.'

'Oh well, another time. I look forward to your coming to Paris, Baz.'

'Me, too,' said Basil. 'Goodnight.'

The aircraft flew low over the islands of the Lamu Archipelago, circling above the clear green waters of the Indian Ocean as it approached the airstrip on Manda Island. As the plane banked, dipping its wing, Nelly could see the long white palm-fringed beaches through her small oval window and told herself that

213

they had not made a mistake in coming here. Hugo sat silently beside her, preoccupied with his own thoughts. It was impossible to know what he was thinking. The plane straightened itself, losing height as it flew slowly towards the airstrip. It hit the ground with a series of bumps and taxied to a stop. They undid their safety-belts and stood up, stretching their legs as they waited with the half-dozen other passengers for the steps to be wheeled to the aircraft. The door was opened and they descended into a crowd of clamorous touts, each one determined to obtain their custom for the hotel he represented. Through the crowd appeared a tall handsome Arab, wearing a snowy turban wound round his head, an equally immaculate white *kanzu* to the ground and a plain grey waistcoat. He pushed his way through the noisy importunate touts and halted in front of Hugo.

'*Bwana* Turnbull?'

'Yes,' said Hugo.

'My name is Farah, *bwana*. I am *Bwana* Galigani's steward. I am here to welcome you and the *memsahib*, and take you to the house.'

'Thank you,' said Hugo, relieved not to have to cope with the crowd. 'We are very glad to see you, Farah.'

'You have luggage, *bwana*?'

'Yes, one bag.'

Farah led the way to the stack of bags which had already been off-loaded from the plane and Nelly pulled their case from the pile. Farah took it from her and they made their way towards the jetty where the Lamu ferry was waiting. But Farah took them to another mooring, where the Galigani launch was tied up. A boy of about twelve years sat waiting in the stern, wearing a kikoi, the coastal sarong of red-white-and-yellow-checked cotton. At their approach, he stood up politely.

'*Jambo, bwana. Jambo, memsahib.*'

'*Jambo,*' said Hugo and Nelly together.

'This boy is called Mahommed,' said Farah.

'Mahommed,' said Nelly. What a big name for a little boy she thought, and smiled at him.

'*Sabu,*' replied the child, grinning. His teeth were huge and brilliantly white in his smooth-skinned black face.

Farah handed them into the launch and they sat together on one side, with Farah on the other with their bag. With practised ease the boy cast off, pulled the string of the outboard motor, sat down at the tiller and shot across the waters of the channel towards Lamu Island, making waves as he went. Farah looked at him severely, frowning. '*Pole-pole,*' he said and Mahommed slowed down. The waters of the channel between the two islands were glassy calm and the coastline of Lamu Island beckoned. Halfway across, the domes of the mosques of Lamu town became visible, glinting in the sun above the waving palms. Mahommed pushed over the tiller and swinging to the left followed the shoreline to Shela, a village a mile or two further south. Mahommed slowed right down, then stalled the engine, throwing a small anchor over the side into the shallow water.

Farah stood up and hitched up his kanzu, tucking it elegantly into the waistband of the khaki shorts he wore underneath. He vaulted nimbly over the side of the launch into two feet of water, then held out his hand to Nelly.

'Now you must get wet.'

Nelly took off her sandals, rolled up her cotton trousers and taking Farah's hand, slid over the side into the water. 'Thank you,' she said, 'I can manage now.' She waded the few yards to the beach, her bare legs caressed and soothed by the warm crystal-clear water. She stood on the sand and looked at the beautiful old Arab house immediately in front of her, shaded and protected by the thick groves of tall graceful palm-trees that stretched right along the beach on either side. The façade of the house was square and built of blocks of coral, dazzling white against the green palm fronds. The arched main entrance had massive double doors of intricately carved wood, dark with oil and standing wide open to catch the breeze. Smaller arches and narrow slits formed windows facing the sea. These appeared not to have glass in them; instead they had delicate wrought-iron grilles to allow the free passage of air.

Carrying their bag, Farah led the way up the terrace steps and into the house, and at once Nelly noticed the astonishing coolness of the interior after the heat of the sun. They entered a high white room, the walls punctuated by many small niches, like a medieval dovecote. In each niche stood a piece of porcelain, a vase, a bowl or a small oil-lamp. There were no books or pictures and very little furniture. A long divan covered in striped ticking stood in the centre of the room, with several large cushions made from camel bags. The polished stone floor was strewn with fine Persian rugs, and more fat cushions were thrown down beside a low, modern Italian glass coffee-table. The whole effect was extremely sumptuous, but simple. There were no doors inside the house and graceful archways allowed the breeze to blow right through the building.

Farah took them upstairs and showed them the spacious, airy white bedroom, the fine white mosquito-net like a tent, suspended on its mahogany frame above the big low bed. The windows overlooking the sea stood open and had wooden-slatted shutters opening inwards. An archway led to the small immaculate modern bathroom, already prepared for them with towels, as well as a basket of bath-essence, soap and a large natural sponge.

'I hope you will be comforted,' said Farah. 'Lunch will be at one o'clock. You will eat fish, *memsahib*?'

'Lovely,' said Nelly, sitting down in a cane chair, feeling rather overcome by the comfort and kindness.

Farah left the room on silent bare feet and Nelly got up and crossed to the window where Hugo stood staring at the sea. 'Are you glad we came?' she asked quietly.

'Yes, I am, very. It reminds me of our holidays here when I was little, and they were much younger. Mum and Dad I mean. There must be some photos somewhere.'

'I'll ask Gabrieli to find them for you, darling. All of them.'

'Yes, thanks. That would be good of you.' He sounded strange and distant, and somehow rather formal, as if they hardly knew each other.

'What about a swim before lunch?' she said gently.

'Good idea.' He looked at her then, his blue eyes full of pain behind his spectacles. 'Don't look so worried,' he said. 'I'll be all right; I just need time.'

They found swimming things, bathing suits, goggles and snorkels in a cupboard, rather to Nelly's relief. She did not wish to offend local customs by appearing inadequately clothed on the beach, and chose for herself what looked like an English schoolgirl's regulation costume. She was surprised to see the label DKNY sewn into the back.

They ran across the short stretch of hot sand and waded into the water until it reached waist-level, then sank gently down and began to swim out to sea. After

217

a few minutes Nelly put down a foot and found that she could still touch the bottom, just. Hugo turned towards her, treading water. He smiled, squinting without his glasses, his short fair hair plastered against his skull.

'Tired?' said Nelly.

'Absolutely knackered.'

'Me too. Shall we have a sleep after lunch?'

'You don't think it would be a waste of our time here? Wouldn't you rather go and look at Lamu, or whatever?'

'Not particularly. Would you?'

'No.'

'That settles it, then. We'll have a good long sleep.'

The tinkle of a small bell floated over the water, and they saw Farah with his arm raised, while Mahommed laid out their lunch on the terrace. They began to swim back at once.

'Actually,' said Hugo, quite cheerfully, 'I really feel rather hungry.'

The rest of the day passed slowly and peacefully. They slept until six, then showered, put on clean clothes and came down to the sitting-room as the light was fading. Farah had lit all the lamps and the tiny flames from a dozen floating wicks leapt and sparkled in their white-washed niches; the whole room shimmered with colour from the red, blue and green glass reservoirs.

'How beautiful, how absolutely beautiful,' said Nelly, pausing on the stairway to look. She felt like a child seeing a Christmas tree for the very first time.

Hugo said nothing; in his mind's eye he saw Hester's room in Paris, glowing in scarlet and gold as her icons reflected the lamplight in the evening, with the sombre paintings of George like a ghostly human presence among them, silent but palpable. He saw Hester herself, bespectacled, alone on her sofa, a glass of Armagnac in her hand, and experienced a cold sensation, an acute feeling of loss, as if she too had died; was no longer there. 'It's lovely,' he said, and slipped his arm through Nelly's as they continued down the stairs together.

Farah had shown them a small fridge concealed behind an elaborate grille in the sitting-room and containing spirits of every kind, as well as juices, tonic and mineral water. There was ice, chilled glasses and a bowl of limes, freshly-sliced.

'What'll you have?' said Hugo.

'I think I'd like an extremely long gin-and-tonic, please.'

The terrace was lit by several insect-repelling lamps, so they were able to sit outside in the cool of the night. The heady scent of a flowering-tree that Hugo said was called Queen of the Night floated on the air. The tide was low and night was falling so quickly that they could only tell that the sea was there by the soft hiss and drag of the waves as they broke gently on the shore.

Presently Farah and Mahommed served their dinner, silently and with proper formality. They brought giant prawns in a fiery red sauce, with rice and flat, unleavened bread, then a salad of mango, pawpaw and pineapple in lime juice. In spite of his religious principles, Farah did not seem to mind offering them a perfectly-chilled bottle of *Pouilly Fuissé*. He poured the wine into delicate crystal glasses, and they flashed and sparkled like diamonds in the light of the tall candle which burned in its glass lantern, casting a wavering golden pool onto the table.

Hugo and Nelly ate slowly, saying little, enjoying the calm beauty of the night, soothed by the delicious food and wine and the unobtrusive service. She could not help reflecting rather ruefully on the difference in attitude between Farah and her various *au pairs* in London. Not one of them had been particularly willing or even pleasant, much less taken a pride in the job they were paid to do; a grim resentfulness seemed to be their dominant characteristic. She knew from what Hugo had told her that many of the old Kenya settlers had exploited their servants and farm-workers, paying them little and expecting much. She did not doubt that Farah, nowadays, was well paid by his Italian employer, but at the same time she had the feeling that such a man as he would have applied the same scrupulousness to his work, whatever the contract. After all, she thought, he does not *have* to be so kind and helpful to us; no-one will ever know whether he is or not, except us.

After dinner, they walked along the beach at the water's edge. The stars, huge and bright, came out one by one and made a faint silvery glimmer on the palm fronds, rustling stiffly above their heads in the slight cool breeze. Hidden among the palm-trees, occasional lights shone in the windows of other dwellings. There were one or two big old Arab houses and some small beach-bungalows, most of them dark and shut-up, forlorn-looking, slightly sinister. They turned and walked back to the house.

'I must ring up the hospital tomorrow, and tell them I'll be late getting back,' said Nelly, putting her feet in the prints she had left on the wet sand during their outward stroll.

'Will there be a problem?'

'I don't suppose so. I'm not indispensable; they'll manage. Anyway, I don't particularly care, one way or the other.'

'Oh?'

'This is more important.'

'You mean being here?'

'No. I mean your mum and dad, Hugo. Everything. I want to be with you; to help if I can.'

'You do help, Nelly. You always have.' He sounded polite, but curiously uninvolved, as if they were talking about other people.

Nelly sighed. She felt that she was not getting through to Hugo at all. It was as though there was a glass wall between them, a no-go area of his making.

'It's getting late,' she said. 'I don't know about you, but I'm quite ready for bed in spite of the afternoon sleep. I suppose we've got a lot of catching-up to do.'

As they came up from the beach and entered the house, Hugo stood uncertainly for a moment, wondering whether he should lock up before they went to bed.

Farah appeared silently from the kitchen archway. 'Will you go to sleep now, *bwana*?'

'Yes, I think so, Farah; it's been a long day for us. Thank you for the excellent dinner.'

'I am glad, *bwana*.' Farah inclined his head. '*Inshallah*.'

'Goodnight, Farah.'

'Goodnight, *bwana*.'

Later that night, wide awake, tense with misery and a deep feeling of outraged impotence in the face of his parents' tragedy, Hugo slipped quietly out of bed without disturbing Nelly and walked round the dark and silent house trying to find solutions to the problems that beset him. For the sake of his parents and his close boyhood friendship with Gabrieli, he wanted so much to be able to find a way of selling the farm to him.

'The problem, dear boy,' Colonel Tanner had said firmly, 'is our old enemy negative equity. There's no getting away from it.'

Hugo sat on the stairway and stared at the intricate starlit patterns of the grilles in the windows facing the sea. The trouble with me, he thought, is that I'm so pathetic; so completely useless at this sort of thing. I'm

221

sure Nelly would sort it all out for me, if I asked her, but I really must start thinking for myself. I am trying, but my bloody mind's a blank. All I can think of is poor Mum's face, that awful dark blood oozing through the bandages. He clenched his fists in agony as the horrifying pictures rose in his mind to torment him. I wonder which one they got first, Mum or Dad? Probably Mum, she would have woken first. Poor old Dad, did he try to save her? I expect they made short work of him, the bastards; he was just about as feeble as I am, poor old love. A hard lump constricted his throat, and tears fell unchecked down his face, splashing on his hands and running into the corners of his mouth, salt-tasting and bitter. After a while, he wiped his face with the palms of his hands and began to climb the stairs. His head ached, he still felt just as sad and confused, and was no nearer finding any answers to his problems.

On the landing he paused by a tall narrow slit, screened by a single shutter. He opened the shutter and looked through the slit. Down below, in a little compound half-hidden in the palms behind the house, he saw Farah and his family of three young children, as well as young Mahommed and the kitchen *toto* eating their main meal of the day beside a wood fire burning in a brazier. They sat at a low wooden table and a woman, presumably Farah's wife, sat with them. She wore the black *bui-bui*, though her face was uncovered and Hugo could see that she was rather beautiful, with dark eyes and long expressive fingers. Another liberated woman said Hugo to himself, smiling; quite right too. He closed the shutter silently, and went back to bed.

*   *   *

'Have they gone, darling?' asked Una-Mary, when Phyllida arrived with the breakfast tray.

'Yes. Alain just got back with Murphy, so they must have caught the launch all right.'

'Well, that's a relief. Goodness, a boiled egg, what a treat.' The old woman smiled tenderly at her favourite grandchild, who had behaved so sensibly if rather bossily to her sisters since the abrupt departure of their mother.

'You deserve a treat,' said the child kindly, putting down the tray and skilfully slicing the top off the egg.

'We all do,' said her grandmother. 'What shall we do? Have a picnic? Go to the beach?'

Phyllida sat on the foot of the bed. 'Granny?'

'Yes?'

'Are Mummy and Papa all right?'

'Of course they are, darling. I spoke to Mummy last night, they're fine. She sent her love, I told you.'

'I know, but where are they? In London?'

'No, not in London. In Nairobi.'

'Nairobi! Have they gone to see Gran and Grandpa Turnbull?'

Una-Mary hesitated a moment, and ate a spoonful of egg. She did not believe in lying to children, equally she did not want to cause them unnecessary pain, or to perform a task that was rightfully Nelly's or Hugo's.

'Yes, in a way,' she said quietly. 'You see, darling, there was a sort of accident.'

'Were they hurt?'

'Yes, they were.'

'Badly?'

'Yes, very.'

'Are they dead?'

'I'm afraid so.'

Phyllida stared down at her hands, folded in her lap. Then she looked at Una-Mary, her large hazel eyes serious beneath the fringe of red hair. 'I'm awfully glad it wasn't you, Granny,' she said.

'Oh, darling, that's only because you see so much more of me; you didn't know them very well. Think how sad it is for Papa.'

'Yes, poor Papa. He will be very sad.'

Una-Mary ate her breakfast and waited for Phyllida to speak, but she remained silent and preoccupied, picking her nails. 'Shall we go to the beach? Would you like that, darling?'

'Yes, let's.' Relieved, the child stood up.

'There's just one thing,' said her grandmother. 'Let's not tell the others about it, unless of course they ask me, like you did. I think we should let Mummy or Papa tell them when they get back, don't you agree?'

'Yes, they're too little to cope with it, aren't they?'

'It's a secret, then. Just you and me?'

'OK.' Phyllida picked up the tray and made her way to the door. 'I'll go and help Elsie make a picnic, shall I?'

'Thank you, darling. I'll be down soon.'

Chapter Twelve

Olivia picked up the small copper plate, its etched image already charged with ink, and dropped it into position on the bed of the press. Using the paper 'fingers' to prevent accidental marking of her expensive hand-made paper, she lifted a dampened sheet from the stack and took it over to the press. There, she lined up the paper on the registration marks and positioned it carefully over the plate, then covered it with a double layer of old blanket. She lowered the thin metal protective sheet into position, and began to wind the small wheel that drove the giant roller, the heart of the press. The great cylinder passed slowly and smoothly over the bed of the press and back again.

She raised the metal sheet and took off the blankets. Then she gently peeled the still-damp etching from the copper plate, and took it to the table to examine it. This was the moment of truth, and one which never failed to excite her, however many times a print had been struck. She looked at the sooty black image, each line, however fine, having the slight fuzziness peculiar to the process of burning metal with acid, and its special characteristic. 'Great,' she said softly, not with complacency but with a strong inner belief in herself.

She clipped the etching carefully to the wire line fixed overhead, then took the plate from the bed of the press and repeated the entire process. By six o'clock she had printed twenty-five perfectly, and had discarded three she considered flawed; she decided that she had completed an adequate number for an edition.

She poured herself a glass of wine, went into her little garden and sat down on an old basket chair in an advanced state of disrepair. She snapped off a sprig of lavender and rubbed it between her fingers, inhaling the sharp soothing fragrance. She could never understand why the English regarded lavender as an old lady's scent, fit only for soap and musty little bags for linen cupboards. To her, the smell represented all the warm beauty of the south and remained the favourite of all the other herbs that crowded her pots: thyme, basil and rosemary. For the first time that day, she thought about Basil. She considered him with affection, and with a certain joyful anticipation which sometimes became a deep longing. She had convinced herself that it would be a mistake to allow him to dominate her life, and in any case he had not telephoned her or written since his return to Paris, so it was quite possible that he had no desire to do so. She had not really expected that he would but felt slightly disappointed nevertheless. It would have been rather nice if he had, she thought; men are all the same, the brutes. She smiled a little wistfully, feeling rather mature and very street-wise.

She finished her drink and went back to the studio, examining her day's work critically. She went upstairs, took a shower and put on a clean T-shirt. Then she crossed the Place de l'Eglise to the Presbytery, to see whether she could cadge supper from her grandparents.

Hugo and Nelly spent their last evening on the beach beside a glowing fire of bleached driftwood, the narrow pure-blue flames sending a column of sparks straight upwards into the still night air. The tide was low and Hugo had built a ring of smooth grey stones on the damp sand as he remembered his father doing, to contain the fire. They had collected the pile of wood with the enthusiastic assistance of young Mahommed, who clearly thought them slightly mad not to be eating their dinner in a civilized fashion on the terrace, like proper *wazungu*. Nelly had consulted Farah about the menu and he had gone to the market that morning. He had returned with fresh fish which he had cleaned and dressed with oil, coriander and lime juice, and kept in a covered dish in the fridge until they were ready to cook. He had also prepared salad and fruit, and baked small flat loaves.

As the swift darkness began to fall, soon after sunset, they lit the fire and Farah came down the steps with the drinks tray, followed by Mahommed with a small folding table, which he erected close by. Farah put the tray down on the table.

'Thank you, Farah, you think of everything,' said Nelly.

Farah inclined his head. 'This fish, *sabu*? At which hour I shall bring him?'

'Oh, yes,' said Nelly. 'About eight o'clock, do you think?'

'At eight o'clock, *sabu*.' Farah cast an expert eye over Hugo's fire, decided that everything was under control and went back to the house with Mahommed.

'Aren't they amazing? You'd think they'd take the evening off and leave us to get on with it, wouldn't you?'

'It's not their way,' said Hugo. 'What'll you have, gin?'

'Yes, fine. Thanks.'

Hugo poured the drinks and sat down on a little mound, a cushion of dried seaweed, crisp and sea-wrack-smelling, redolent of his childhood. 'I wonder if we'll ever come back here,' he said, stirring the glowing red base of the fire with a bleached, pointed stick.

'Probably not,' said Nelly, 'unless you ever feel you really want to. It's too sad and painful. It always will be, won't it?'

He did not answer and they sat silently for a long time, spellbound beside the crackling fire, aware of the small sounds of the darkening night; watching the pale little land-crabs scuttling across the sand towards them, attracted by the light of the fire, standing on tip-toe, staring with their beady inquisitive eyes, poised for flight at the slightest movement. Then Hugo spoke softly, without looking up.

'Nelly?'

'Mm?'

'I think we need to talk; we ought to try to sort things out between us. There never seems to be a good moment at home, with the children, work and everything getting in the way. Perhaps here, in this quiet place, we could try.'

'What's on your mind, Hugo?' Nelly looked at him steadily. 'What is it you want to talk about?'

'Don't you know?'

'No.'

'What's on my mind, Nelly, is the question I've been asking myself for a long time.'

'Which is?'

'Why did you marry me?'

Nelly's heart stood still, but she spoke calmly. 'What do you mean, why did I marry you?'

'I mean, why did you choose me, and not Baz?'

'Why would I have "chosen" Baz, as you put it?'

'Well, you were in love with him, weren't you? And he with you?'

'Was I? What makes you think so?'

'You were sleeping with him; it wasn't a secret, was it?'

'I suppose I was a bit *in* love with Baz at one time, but it was you I really *loved*.'

'Is there a difference?'

'Of course there is. I loved you, and I thought you loved me. More than that, you needed me. Baz doesn't need anyone.'

'Does that mean,' said Hugo, speaking so quietly that she could hardly hear him, 'that you can only love dependent people who rely on you, like me, the children, your patients? Are you really only in your element when you're doing this kind of thing; supporting me through the nightmare of my parents' death? Taking charge?'

'Someone had to,' said Nelly, frowning. 'You're quite incapable of organizing anything on your own, you know that.'

'I do know that, and I'm grateful to you, of course, but perhaps that's exactly the problem.'

'Hugo, where the hell is all this leading? What problem?'

'Our problem. All right, the problem I have with you.'

'Which is?'

Hugo glanced at her briefly, then braced himself. 'Don't you realize, Nelly, that you've come to dominate us all completely? We get up, work, go to school, eat, take a walk, a holiday, whatever, when you say so. No-one dares step out of line, or disagree with you. You're always right.'

There was a long silence. Then Nelly began to speak, reasonably but firmly. 'From my perspective, Hugo, I see quite another picture. I realize that it's my choice, I don't need to, but I choose to work my tail off at the hospital; partly, it's true, for my own probably selfish

229

ambitions. But mostly I do it to make a real working contribution to our lives, for the children and for you. Obviously, a certain amount of organization is necessary, you must see that, otherwise our lives would be chaos.'

'I quite see that you feel you are acting in everyone's best interests,' said Hugo. 'But the fact is, I am sick and tired of being organized, and having to be grateful for everything, even our not very good sex, when you're always so tired.'

'That's a bit rich, coming from you, Hugo,' retorted Nelly. Then, suddenly angry, she added spitefully: 'And if you must know, Baz was a bloody sight better in bed than you've ever been.' She regretted the words the moment they were out of her mouth; it had been a moment of pure vindictiveness, intended to punish him for criticizing her.

'That doesn't surprise me,' said Hugo coldly. 'Your response to me since we were married has always been somewhat lukewarm, hasn't it? Perhaps you married the wrong man, if sex has such importance for you. You've certainly managed to keep him hanging round you long enough, haven't you?'

Nelly was silent, and stared into the fire, finding it difficult to believe that Hugo had come to dislike her so much. She had always felt very comfortable with herself on the whole, and perfectly confident that most people found her an attractive woman as well as a very able and dedicated doctor. This new image suggested by Hugo, of a sex-mad female bully, seemed totally alien to her idea of herself. Deep down, her common-sense told her it was rubbish and she knew she would reject it. Nevertheless, for the moment, she felt dismayed and deeply hurt by his remarks.

Farah came towards them, bearing a tray with the

prepared fish on a wire-mesh griddle with a long handle, ready for the fire.

'I'll do it,' said Hugo, getting up and taking the griddle from the tray. Mahommed, who was hovering behind Farah, removed the drinks tray, and Farah put the bread, the salad, the fruit, a dish of cut limes and the plates on the table.

'I will bring wine, *bwana*,' he said.

'Thanks,' said Hugo, and Farah and Mahommed went back to the house. Hugo knelt beside the fire and balanced the griddle on the hot stones. The heat from the glowing embers began to cook the fish almost at once, and a delicious smell rose irresistibly from them.

Nelly, sitting there rather sulkily feeling upset and angry, had made up her mind not to eat, to say she wasn't hungry. Now she changed her mind and got up and brought the plates to the fireside. 'Smells good,' she said.

'It does, doesn't it?' said Hugo. He smiled at her briefly, his face rosy in the firelight as he skilfully turned the fish.

Farah appeared with the wine, keeping cool in an ice-bucket. He examined Hugo's cooking of the fish. 'This fish smells good, *bwana*,' he said, and laughed.

'It may surprise you to know, Farah,' said Hugo, laughing too, 'that I am a pretty good cook.'

'God is good, *bwana*,' said Farah, departing. They could hear him, still laughing to himself as he went up the steps and into the house.

The fish was very good indeed, and they ate hungrily, their appetites sharpened by the night air. They ate everything that Farah had provided and drank the wine.

'I haven't enjoyed a meal so much for ages,' said Nelly. 'It was a nice idea, thank you.' She felt less angry now, and reminded herself that Hugo had been under a lot of stress lately, which could account for his uncharacteristic behaviour. She was anxious to put things right between them. 'I was very hurt, when you refused to come to Tuscany with us, Hugo. Did you realize that? Did you mind?'

'I realized you were angry, of course, but I thought you'd get over it. I needed to get away, Nelly. I told you that.'

'This Hester, Baz's mother, what does she mean to you?'

'A lot.'

'Are you lovers?'

Hugo looked at Nelly then, long and seriously, almost with contempt, certainly with pity. 'You simply have no concept, have you, of the idea that people can mean a lot to each other on any other terms than those of total possession?'

'That's a very complex question, Hugo, you might almost have written it. What do you mean, in simple language?' She sounded sarcastic, inside she felt miserable, and very unsure of herself.

'In simple terms, I like being with Hester because she expects nothing from me, and I expect nothing from her.'

'That's all very well, Hugo. But that's not marriage, is it?'

'No, it isn't, thank God,' said Hugo. 'That's why I have to go there sometimes.'

'To get away from me?'

'I suppose so, yes.'

'I see.'

Nelly stared into the heart of the dying fire, trying her best to understand this whole new development in their relationship. Thinking back over the past few months, she admitted to herself that she had failed to recognize Hugo's need to detach himself, to become less reliant on her. She realized that it was rather probable that she would have to try and understand his point of view, and appear to be relaxed about it, if she wished to keep him. Even a part-time husband and father is better than a totally absent one, she reasoned in her pragmatic way; I expect it'll work itself out.

She sighed and raised her eyes to Hugo's. 'What I'm going to say now will probably sound like blackmail,' she said. 'It's not meant to, and I wouldn't bring the subject up so soon, but it's my only chance, before you see the lawyers tomorrow afternoon.' Then she told him the plan that had been developing in her mind since the first night in Nairobi; that she should pay off his father's debts, to allow Hugo to sell the farm to Gabrieli, if that was what he really wanted to do. 'You'll probably tell me to get stuffed. I wouldn't blame you,' she went on. 'I realize it sounds like interference. I think you ought to know that I have had quite a struggle to make this offer, Hugo. If we do it, it will mean that I won't have the means to buy *Les Romarins* from Henry when my mother dies, which is what I've always planned to do. So you see, it's not quite as easy for me as you might suppose.'

Hugo stared at her for a long time, saying nothing. Then he stood up, took off his clothes, walked down to the water's edge and waded into the sea. Nelly watched as he swam away from her, leaving a long trail of sparkling pale-green phosphorescence in his wake. A yellow sickle moon was dropping down towards the west, just above the black silhouette of the palm-trees behind the house. Its weak light outlined the edges of the shallow waves and made a silvery patch on Hugo's head as he swam. She saw him turn onto his back and

233

float, and imagined him gazing up at the brilliant galaxies of stars that blazed extravagantly across the velvety black sky. Farah approached with the coffee, carrying a towel for Hugo.

'Thank you very much, Farah.' Nelly smiled at him and took the towel. 'You've been so kind, all of you. We've enjoyed ourselves so much.'

'*Inshallah, sabu*,' said Farah. 'I am glad.' He collected the dishes and returned to the house.

After what seemed like a very long time to Nelly, but was probably only twenty minutes, Hugo swam back and came close to the fire, glad of the warmth. He wrapped himself in the towel and sat down. Nelly poured his coffee and he drank it. Then he turned to her and took her hand in his. 'I don't know what to say to you, Nelly. It's your money, and the girls', and it's got absolutely nothing to do with me, thank God. Obviously, it's a tempting offer. It's difficult for me to think rationally at a time like this, and my gut feeling is that it wouldn't be a good idea. But there's one thing that I am absolutely clear about. I don't want you to deprive yourself or the girls of something that you desperately want to keep, like *Les Romarins*, out of a kind but quixotic desire to do good, either to me or to Gabrieli.'

'I've already decided.'

'Nelly, I'd much rather you didn't.' He released her hand. 'Whatever you do, it won't make me change my mind about how I choose to work and live. Going away when I need to; to Hester's or somewhere by myself, whatever. I'm not prepared to give up that freedom again, ever, for anyone.'

'Not even to help Gabrieli?'

Hugo hesitated, then shook his head. 'No, not even to do that.'

'Well, you've made it very clear, Hugo. At least we understand each other.'

'I hope you will understand, Nelly.'

'I think I do. It's not very flattering; I can't say I enjoy the feeling, but you need to get away from me sometimes?'

'Yes.'

'And what about the farm? The debts?'

'The lawyers will take weeks probably, sorting everything out; you know how these things are.'

'And Gabrieli?'

'He's perfectly capable of organizing things for himself, I imagine. Especially as he has a strong and capable wife.'

'Just like me?'

'Just like you.'

In the very early morning before it was quite light, Hugo woke and saw that Nelly was wide awake, lying on her side and looking at him. She smiled at him rather timidly when their eyes met. She looked young and vulnerable and Hugo felt moved, and strangely guilty at having destroyed so comprehensively her power over him, her self-confidence. He moved over to her side of the bed and put his arms round her, holding her close to him, feeling her warm body next to his. 'I do love you; I always will,' he said. 'You know that.'

'Do you, darling?' Suddenly, into her head came the startling memory of a similar moment with Basil, not so very long ago. Now, with a slight feeling of shame, she repeated to Hugo the question she had asked Basil. 'Would you like to prove it?'

Much later, while they were having breakfast on the

terrace for the last time, Nelly told Hugo that the cruel remark she had made the previous night, about Basil's being the better lover, had not been strictly true. She did not qualify this by adding that the improvement was extremely recent. He smiled at her kindly, but did not tell her that he did not particularly care, one way or the other.

Basil walked round Russell Square in his lunch hour, both for the exercise and to make some sort of attempt to clear his thoughts and get his priorities in the right order. He had been back in London for ten days, but had still not resigned from his job. He had begun to realize that it was important to get the new job sorted out first, he could not afford simply to walk away from his current one. The very small advance on his book was already spent. He had not saved any of his salary and had no other source of income. Equally, he was beginning to get cold feet about the idea of attempting to break into the unknown world of radio or television on the rather slender qualifications of having fluent Russian and French, as well as English. He supposed he could work as a translator, even a simultaneous translator with a bit of practice. But do I really want to do it? he asked himself. I imagine it's pretty demanding work, I couldn't just drift through the days doing the absolute minimum as I do here, with my mind on other things. And if I were to get down to it properly and make a serious career for myself, what happens to my ambitions, such as they are? How will I have the time or energy to carry on writing? It's all very well for Giò and Olivia to be so laid-back and confident about it, they've nothing to lose; they've got families to pick up the pieces if anything goes wrong. I've only got Hester, and it's *she* who should be able to lean on *me* if necessary, not the other way round. Still, I could always stay with her while I get settled into a job. *If* I get a job, that is. He sighed, feeling even more confused and unsure than before. I wish I could talk to Hugo he thought, I wonder when they'll be back?

A thin rain was falling and, turning up his collar, Basil began to walk towards the museum. He thought about his night out with Giò and shuddered at the memory, both of the mind-blowing nightclub and of his own subsequent humiliating behaviour. He was filled with shame, but also a huge relief at having been let off the hook. I wonder why, he asked himself. What the hell *is* it that I really want? He recognized his deep need for male love, in the way that he had always loved Hugo and had thought that Hugo loved him. He considered his relationship with Herbert and began to realize that although he had drawn a good deal of comfort from it at the time, a one-to-one permanent male partnership was not what he really needed, or sought. More than anything he wanted, had always wanted, what Hugo already had; a home, a wife and children, a family to live and work for. But who would want to take me on? he asked himself glumly. All the women of my age are already married, the good-looking ones, anyway. And I'm not much of a catch myself: no career and no money either. He climbed reluctantly up the steps of the museum, feeling thoroughly depressed.

After work that evening he went round to the Turnbulls' house to see if there was any sign of life. He had phoned every day but had only got the answerphone. Dusk was falling, and the outside security light was on. He peered over the area railings but the kitchen was dark and silent. He went up the steps and rang the front-door bell but no-one came. They can't be back yet, he thought. Poor things, they must be having a frightful time. He walked back to his flat, feeling sad for Hugo and Nelly, but lonely and sorry for himself, too.

He poured himself a vodka and sat down at his desk. He began to re-read the work he had done in Paris, but found it impossible to concentrate. He felt as if the silent brown walls of his room were leaning on him and was so lonely and depressed that for two pins he would have put his head down on the desk and howled with misery. Longing to talk to someone, he picked up the phone and dialled Hester's number. Her phone rang, the familiar long ringing tone of the French telephones.

'Hello?'

'Hi, it's me, Baz.'

'Hello, darling. How are you?'

'Pissed off and lonely.'

'Oh dear, poor you. Why?'

'Oh, I don't know. Just being back at work again after the holiday, I suppose, and all that wonderful weather. It's raining here, of course.'

'Actually,' said Hester, 'it's odd that you should ring now. I've just had a call from that nice girl you stayed with, Olivia something, she thought you might still be here. I gave her your number in London; she said she'd phone you there.'

'She is a nice girl, very. She's also potentially a very good painter. She's a great admirer of Dad's work.'

'Really?'

'Yes. I promised to bring her to meet you sometime, to see the paintings.'

'Why not? I'd like to meet her.'

'Well, good. You'll like her.'

'I'm sure I will. Her uncle Giò called again; he wants me to go and see his shop.'

'Will you go?'

'I suppose I should, though I feel a bit reluctant; I don't know why.'

'Don't you trust him?'

'Oh, it's not that. He makes me feel slightly ill-at-ease, that's all. I expect it's just me, I'm not used to dealing with people these days.'

'You seem to get on pretty well with Hugo?'

'Oh, Hugo; poor man.'

'Have you had a card or anything from him?'

'No, nothing,' said Hester. 'Have you?'

'No, not a word. They're not at the house, either.'

'Poor things, I can't stop thinking about them. I do hope they're all right. Africa, it's so far away.'

'I know. It's weird here without them, wondering.'

'I'm sure they're all right, really. It's just not knowing that's unsettling.'

'This is it,' said Basil. 'Well, I'd better not run up the phone bill, I suppose, though it's tempting. I haven't had a chat to anyone I really like since I got back.'

'My dear boy, you make it sound like Siberia. You'd better give yourself a drink.'

'It feels like Siberia, and I have got a drink.'

'Have another.'

'I will. Goodnight, then. Talk to you soon.'

'Goodnight, darling.'

Basil put down the phone, rather pleased at the thought of Olivia phoning him in Paris. He would have liked to call her back, but it was complicated having to leave a message for her at her grandparents' house. He went to the fridge to see whether there was anything at all edible for his supper, but the usual empty shelves confronted him, so he went down to the street to the Indian take-away. Coming back with the warm brown-paper carrier ten minutes later, he heard the telephone ringing as he climbed the stairs. He rushed up to his flat and snatched the phone off the hook.

'Hello?'

'Baz?'

'Olivia! How nice to hear you, are you still in Souliac?'

'Yes, but I'm coming back to Paris next week. How are you?'

'Fed up with being back here. I wish I was still with you.'

'I wish, too.'

'Do you?' said Basil softly.

'Yes, I do.'

'Well, what shall we do about it?'

'I was wondering, maybe you could come to Paris soon, for the weekend? Patrick will be back from Normandy then, and you could meet him.'

'That would be great, Olivia. But it wouldn't be the only reason for coming, would it?'

'Wouldn't it, Baz?'

'What do *you* think?'

Olivia laughed. 'The problem would be getting to be by ourselves,' she said. 'Too close to our respective parents, that's the difficulty.'

'I expect we can think of something, don't you?'

'I hope.'

'Shall we say not this weekend but the next? I can stay at Hester's, I want you to meet her anyway and show you my father's work.'

'Oh, Baz, I'd love that, I really would.'

'Right. Give me your Paris number, and I'll phone you as soon as I get there, OK?'

'Yes, terrific.' Olivia gave him the number, and then said goodnight.

'See you soon, my love,' said Basil.

'See you soon.'

Basil put down the phone and sat for a moment, filled with excitement and happiness at the prospect of being in Paris, and seeing Olivia again so soon. He stared at the telephone, amazed at how an unexpected call had the power to change his entire outlook. Then without warning he thought of his foolish escapade with Giò, and how easily he could have become seriously involved with him, and broke into a cold sweat. Dear God, he thought, I must have been out of my mind; what the hell did I think I was doing? He got up and poured himself another drink, and the neck of the bottle rattled against the rim of the glass as he did so. Then he took a fork from the drawer and ate his lukewarm curry straight out of the little foil boxes.

Olivia put down the phone very thoughtfully. 'See you soon, my love,' he had said. Did he really mean that, or was it just a typical bit of male casual friendliness? I mustn't over-react, she thought, or read too much into these things. Nevertheless, her spirits soared, she could not prevent herself smiling and hugged herself with joy at the prospect of being with him again. Her grandparents had gone out for the evening and she was alone in the Presbytery. She picked up a new copy of *Maison & Jardin* from the library table, switched off the lamps and went downstairs. She let herself out through the big double doors to the courtyard, locked them, hid the key in its special niche and walked across the Place de l'Eglise to her own house. There, she poured herself a glass of wine and made an omelette. She took her plate and glass to the little back garden, cool now and sweet-smelling in the night air. She ate her supper, looking at the pictures in *Maison*

& *Jardin* at the same time, but images of Baz, bearded, naked and beautiful floated across her consciousness in a very disturbing way. She finished her wine, and went up to bed. She lay on her stomach and slept, cooled by the breeze from her open window. In the middle of the night she cried out, and woke herself up; she had been dreaming about Baz, she knew, and she tried to recall the dream. But the harder she tried, the more elusive the memory became, though a curious, tender feeling remained with her. She turned onto her back and lay, wide awake, her hands linked behind her head, and stared at the big white moon that shed its cold white light on her as it rose above the trees in the square.

As she had reluctantly promised to do, Hester went to see *Le Patrimoine*. She walked along the arcade of the Place des Vosges, looking rather incongruous in that smart and luxurious *quartier*. As the September evenings were getting quite chilly she wore her old, rather shapeless Donegal tweed coat over her working clothes; baggy and faded denim trousers and a white cotton shirt. Her tanned face and grey-streaked dark hair gave her a somewhat gypsy appearance, emphasized by the shabby old leather satchel she carried with her everywhere. She had walked to the Place des Vosges, since the weather was fine. She was glad of the exercise, but the bag was heavy and she felt quite tired. She thought she might treat herself to a taxi home. The bank balance was pretty healthy, largely on account of Hugo's rent, so she reckoned the extravagance was probably justified and would be a reward for fulfilling a promise she regretted having made. She found the shop and walked slowly by, trying to take in as much as she could in passing.

'Oh, come on,' she said, 'don't be stupid.' She turned and went back to the big glass door and pushed it open. A slender young woman dressed in black got up from the desk where she had been working and advanced towards her, smiling politely but calculating Hester's social standing and finances with a rapid up-and-down movement of her eyes.

'*Puis-je vous aider?*' she asked, and Hester explained that she had come, by appointment, to see Mr Hamilton.

'*Ah, bon?*'

'*Oui. Je m'appelle Rodzianko.*'

'*Bien sûr, madame. Asseyez-vous, je vous prie.*' She went to the telephone, pressed some buttons and spoke. '*Giò, Mme Rodzianko est là. D'accord.*' She put the phone down. '*Il descend, tout-de-suite, madame.*'

Hester thanked her and sat down on an expensive-looking Louis XV settee, upholstered in an orchid-pink brocade trimmed with gold braid, which she privately thought rather hideous. She looked around her at the shop. She had to admit that it did have a lot of style and expensive good taste, but could not really visualize her icons in that particular ambience. Somehow, it all felt rather brittle and worldly.

A door opened, cunningly concealed in a book-lined wall in the second room of the shop and Giò came quickly through to greet her. 'How nice of you to come. I hope I haven't kept you waiting?'

'Not at all, I've just arrived.' She stood up, almost steeling herself to say at once that she did not think that her work would be appropriate for his shop, but he spoke first, taking the wind out of her sails.

'I expect you think all this is quite over the top, and far too glitzy?'

'Well, I did think perhaps . . .' Hester's voice trailed

243

off; she felt embarrassed and diffident, and did not wish to be offensive.

Giò laughed and took her arm gently. 'Come through here,' he said, and led the way to the small third section at the rear of the shop, currently decorated as a winter garden. It was full of mirrors and pretty wire garden furniture arranged round a small fountain, with many elegant potted palm-trees and a large flowering Tibouchina, its purple-blue flowers glowing against glossy green leaves.

'Goodness,' said Hester, 'how exotic!'

'Exactly, and quite unsuitable for you.' He invited her to sit and sat down himself. 'What I have in mind,' he said, 'is to turn this part of the shop into a small gallery. Very plain, no frills, almost monastic, but with state-of-the-art lighting, dimmers and that kind of thing. I would enjoy doing it and it would be nice to sell things that I really like myself, not just the stuff that appeals to the fashionable crowd.'

'But my icons are basically fakes,' said Hester, frowning.

'I don't see it like that,' said Giò. 'OK, you may be working in an old traditional style, but we're not going to be trying to pass them off as fourteenth-century or anything. I think people will buy them because they are beautiful, because they give comfort and reassurance in these rather godless times. It's like the sudden popularity of Gregorian chant. Strange, isn't it? The meaning and sound isn't any the less valid because it's on tape or CD, is it?'

Hester looked about her, wavering. 'But you'd need quite a lot, to mount an exhibition, wouldn't you?'

'There's no hurry. We could make a plan, decide on sizes and so on. Then you could begin the work. Obviously I would pay for each one as it's completed.

Then, when we have enough, say in two or three years' time, we set up the exhibition.' Hester still looked worried, doubtful.

'Come upstairs,' said Giò. 'I want to show you something.' He took her through the secret door and up the narrow winding stair to his apartment. They entered the big untidy room, filled with an eclectic array of old furniture in varying stages of disrepair, heaps of rugs and ancient fabrics, and tottering piles of books.

'Oh,' Hester exclaimed, 'this is much more my cup of tea, Giò.' She looked at the big, comfortable shabby red sofa and the beautiful French windows at the end of the room, overlooking the trees that grew round the *place*. 'I'm sorry,' she said, 'I misjudged you; it's lovely.'

'Don't worry about it,' he replied, smiling. 'Come in here, this is what I want to show you.' He led the way to his small white cell-like bedroom. On the wall, facing the foot of the bed hung a small icon of the Virgin and Child, blackened with age, with small patches of worn gilding on the haloes, and on the background. Her face was pale and serious, the baby looked as though he was already aware of his destiny.

'It's beautiful,' said Hester, rather moved.

'She means a lot to me. I don't know whether or not she's old, and I don't actually care. It's enough, that she exists. Do you understand?'

'Yes,' said Hester, 'I do.'

On her way home, the taxi stopped at her request in Rue St-Louis-en-l'Ile and Hester bought herself half a dozen oysters from a seaweed-filled basket, asking for them to be opened. Then she made her way rather wearily home and unlocked her door. As she closed it after her, she remembered that she had not looked in her post-box that morning. She unlocked it with the little black key and found a card from Hugo. It had a picture of elephants marching across a barren-looking plain with Mt Kilimanjaro in the background, seemingly floating in the blue sky. Hester turned it over and read the message, with some difficulty, on account of Hugo's microscopic black script.

'Hope to be back in London in a day or two. The inevitable frustrating delays for papers to be prepared for signature and so on. It has been a pretty rough time. N has been a tower of strength. Sorry I took off so precipitately; I didn't thank you for all your kindness, but I knew you'd understand. I hope to see you before very long. Much love, H.'

Hester read the card twice and slipped it into her pocket. She locked the post-box, went upstairs and poured herself a glass of wine. Then she opened the kitchen window to let in the evening air. She drank her wine and stared at the still-green lime-trees, thinking of Hugo, missing him, and missing George.

Chapter Thirteen

On their return from Kenya, Nelly went straight back to the hospital after interviewing three possible *au pairs* sent by the agency. In view of Hugo's antipathy to the tall blonde Inger she engaged a small jolly German girl called Eva, who had left her previous job in London and was prepared to move in straight away. Hugo offered to go to Florizel and bring the children home the following day.

His three daughters and Alain, with Murphy and the four-wheeler were at the harbour to meet the launch and they drove back to *Les Romarins* through the lanes, the trees already beginning to turn yellow and brown in the brisk September wind.

'We've missed two weeks of school, Papa,' said Sophie.

'I know. Awful, isn't it?'

'No, it's lovely,' said Gertrude. 'I hate school.'

'Do you really? Why?'

'I can't do the times tables, and I hate Miss Drabble.'

'Poor Miss Drabble, why do you hate her?'

'She's got hairy legs.' Hugo could find no answer to that, so he changed the subject.

'Have you had a lovely time here? What have you been doing?'

'Well,' said Phyllida, 'we've been to the beach a lot with Granny, and I can drive Murphy now, it's great.'

'Well done you.'

Murphy stopped at the entrance to *Les Romarins* and Phylly jumped down to open the gate. Alain drove the four-wheeler through, and waited while she closed the gate and climbed up again. He drove up to the front door and Hugo and the girls descended. Alain handed down Hugo's overnight bag and then clopped off round to the stable-yard. Una-Mary was not on the steps to greet them, so Hugo decided that now was probably as good a time as any to tell his children why he and Nelly had been away. He led the way to the flower garden and lawn on the west side of the house. Ten minutes later, Una-Mary, looking out for them through the drawing-room windows, saw the little group, red heads bent, sitting cross-legged on the grass close to their father. Hugo was talking, she could see, but very quietly and gently. She saw Phylly asking a question and Hugo replying gravely.

Poor boy, she thought, he looks so young to have to cope with all this. She waited a little longer to make sure that Hugo had finished talking to them, and then opened the French windows. Hugo and the girls stood up and came towards her and she went out to meet them. Wiggy and Pepys rushed past her and hurled themselves at the children, barking madly. It was a welcome diversion for them, struggling as they obviously were to understand the circumstances and sadness of their grandparents' death. Sophie and Gertrude chased the little dogs round a large clump of blue hydrangeas, but Phyllida held Hugo's hand as they approached.

'They know about it now, Granny,' she said seriously. 'Papa's told them.'

'Hello, Hugo. How are you?' said Una-Mary.

Hugo kissed her cheek. 'I'm all right, though I don't

think I could have coped without Nelly. And thank God the girls were here with you, that was a huge weight off both our minds.'

'Well, good,' said Una-Mary, smiling. 'And I don't think *I* could have coped without Phylly here, she's been keeping the others in order. She's so like Nelly, it's extraordinary.'

'Are you darling?' Hugo put an arm round his eldest daughter, nearly as tall as his shoulder now and hugged her.

'That's good, isn't it?' Phylly sounded anxious.

'It's very good,' said Hugo. 'Of course.'

Una-Mary smiled at him, her faded blue eyes full of sympathy and understanding, her white hair blown in wisps round her head by the wind. She wore an over-sized rather tattered Guernsey sweater, one of her late husband's, a shapeless tweed skirt and Wellington-boots. She looked, Hugo thought, exactly what she was, a real island woman.

'What about a drink before lunch?' she said. 'Elsie is cooking something, I hope.'

'She is,' said Phylly. 'Lancashire hotpot; I did the carrots.'

'Oh good.' She led the way into the drawing-room, where the drinks tray was already waiting. 'I'm afraid Elsie's repertoire is somewhat limited. It was lovely when Nelly was here. She cooked the most divine food every night, such a treat. What will you have, Hugo? Sherry, or gin?'

'I'd love a glass of sherry, thanks.'

Later that evening, when the girls had gone to bed, their packing done for the early departure in the morning, Hugo and Una-Mary had a bowl of soup, Baxter's Game out of a tin, and bread and cheese in front of the drawing-room fire. Hugo told her about their time in

Kenya, the inquest, the funeral, the meetings with lawyers. To his surprise he found it quite cathartic to talk about the whole horrible business, particularly as she did not interrupt, but listened, eating her supper quietly.

'We spent two days at Lamu on the coast, so it wasn't all total horror.'

'Oh, good. Were you able to relax there?'

'Yes and no.' Hugo looked at Una-Mary. He did not know whether she knew about his and Nelly's differences; how much, if anything, Nelly had told her. 'There's something rather worrying that perhaps you should know,' he said.

She looked up then, sharply and attentively. 'Oh?'

'Yes. In a way, it concerns you.' He told her about Nelly's offer to pay off the bank so that they could sell the farm to Gabrieli.

'Would you not wish to do that?'

'No. I've told her that I don't want her to use her money, or the girls', in that way, especially if it means her losing *Les Romarins* in the process, but you know how strong-willed she can be?'

'But if Nelly paid the debts and then you were able to sell the place to your friend, would the shortfall be so very great? Are we talking hundreds of thousands?'

'No,' said Hugo, and told her the estimated amount.

'Well, that's not a small sum, but neither is it vast, is it?'

'It is to me,' said Hugo, and laughed.

'Oh dear.' Una-Mary laughed too. 'Sorry, Hugo. I didn't intend to sound patronizing.'

'You didn't sound patronizing at all. Silly of me to mind, I expect.'

'Does it occur to you, my dear boy, that Nelly is

offering to do this as a means of holding on to you, making herself indispensable to you?'

'What do you mean?'

'She thinks you've stopped loving her. She is very unhappy, hurt and confused.'

'Has she told you so?'

'In a roundabout way, yes. You see, Nelly is exactly like her father, hard-working, ambitious and clever. If she had been a man, she'd probably have been a career diplomat, like him, with her eyes firmly fixed on getting her "K".'

'And what was *your* feeling about that? Weren't you delighted to be Lady T?'

Una-Mary laughed. 'No, I wasn't. I think the whole system is idiotic and élitist. I was perfectly happy being Mrs T. Even happier being Miss le Mesurier, to tell you the truth.'

'And what about Henry?'

'What about him? He's clever and boring, only interested in money. But Nelly is quite different. Clever and ambitious too, but also a bit of a do-gooder, and inclined to organize others, I'm afraid. In their best interests, of course.'

'You've noticed?' said Hugo, feeling disloyal.

'If you've lived with it yourself, you recognize the signs. Phylly will be the same, poor child.'

'Why poor child?'

'Well, worms turn and dominant people sometimes get rejected by those they love, as I rejected Arthur in the end. Bossiness doesn't necessarily preclude getting hurt or humiliated, Hugo.'

'You make me feel ungrateful; a shit, to put it crudely.'

'No, you're not a shit, my dear. As a matter of fact, much as I love Nelly and I do – she's my reason for living – privately, I think you are absolutely right to

251

stand up to her, and make it very clear that you too have rights in the marriage.'

'Do you really?' Hugo sounded astonished. 'And what about the farm business? What do you think I should do about that?'

'Well, it depends. If you really want to help your friend, it wouldn't be too difficult for Nelly. She could easily get a mortgage on your house, and pay it off quite quickly out of income. There could be tax benefits too, no doubt. And in any case, I'm not intending to pop off just yet.'

'But you see, the real problem is that I don't want to create a vicious circle of me having to be grateful to Nelly, and Gabrieli having to be grateful to me. I can't help noticing that people you've done a favour to, often end up hating you.'

Una-Mary looked at his tired, worried face and her heart bled for him, and for Nelly. She had been well over fifty years old before that dreary truth had dawned on her.

Basil took the last boat on Friday night and did not reach the Ile St-Louis until the early hours of Saturday morning. He felt slightly guilty as he rang Hester's bell, but she had been awake for some time as she frequently was in the middle of the night, and was reading. She came down to let him in.

'Sorry to get you up, old thing.'

'I wasn't asleep. It's good to see you, come in.'

They went upstairs to the kitchen and Hester put on the kettle. 'Cup of tea?'

'Yes, thanks, lovely.'

They sat at the table and drank the hot tea.

'I don't think I'll drive next time,' said Basil. 'It's tiring after a day's work and I could have had an extra evening here if I'd flown; I'm an idiot.'

'Why did you drive?'

'Why do you think? Money; it's marginally cheaper.'

'Money is a great bore, isn't it?'

'You're not kidding.'

Hester smiled and shook her head. 'Any news of Hugo? Are they back yet?'

'Yes,' said Basil, 'but I haven't seen them. I spoke to Nelly last week; she's back at work and Hugo had gone to Florizel to bring the children back to London.'

'How was she?'

'She sounded pretty low; tired, too.'

'Not surprising is it, poor things?'

'As a matter of fact, it *is* rather surprising for Nelly. She's a pretty strong woman, very positive, usually.'

'I suppose good doctors have to be?'

'I suppose.'

In the morning he telephoned Olivia and they arranged to meet for lunch at the *Café Procope*.

'I spoke to Patrick about you, Baz. Maybe he can come to lunch too, and meet you. I'll ask him.'

'It was good of you to speak to him, Olivia.'

'Not at all, delighted to help if I can.'

'I'd really much rather be lunching with you alone.'

'Me too, but business first, as they say. Plenty of time for the pleasure later.'

'Can't wait,' said Basil.

'*Moi non plus*. Twelve-thirty, *Café Procope*, OK?'

'Great, see you then.'

Basil had a bath, and washed his thick dark curly hair and beard, sinking under the deep hot bath-water to rinse out the shampoo. He sat up, squeezing out the excess water and wrapping a towel round his head. He got out of the bath and dried himself, then vigorously towelled his hair and beard. He looked in the mirror, before attacking himself with a spiky wire brush. His hair stood out round his head like a great brown bush. God, he thought, I look like an old-style hippie. I must get it cut.

He put on a clean white shirt, black cords and his black-leather jacket, then checked his pockets, took the spare key off the hook and let himself out of the apartment without disturbing Hester. He walked to the Rive Gauche, crossing the river by the Pont St-Michel, and making his way through narrow old streets and alleyways to the Cour de Rohan. A wrought-iron gate led to three linked courtyards, leafy, secluded and peaceful. In the second court was an exquisite Renaissance house, once the home of Diane de Poitiers, and Basil stood gazing at it with admiration and gratitude that such buildings still existed. The warm September sunshine penetrated the thinning crisp yellow leaves of the trees and he thought how fortunate were the inhabitants of Paris to have so many of these magical, secret little enclaves; the trick was, knowing where they were. He sat for ten minutes enjoying the tranquillity of the place, then an invisible clock struck the half-hour and he made his way to the Rue de l'Ancienne Comédie and the *Café Procope*. It was already packed and he peered over the crowded tables, shading his eyes, and glancing at the glass-fronted cabinets on the walls, displaying three-cornered hats, Phrygian bonnets, tricolor rosettes and other Revolutionary mementoes.

'Baz!'

He turned and saw Olivia waving to him. He threaded his way through the packed tables towards her. Her

254

sun-bleached hair fell over her shoulders and she wore a black chiffon head-scarf patterned with pink-and-yellow poppies, tied in the romany style. Gold hoops hung from her ears, and beneath the scarf her brilliant blue eyes, heavily lined with kohl, watched him, smiling as he approached. She was with a man, in his fifties Basil guessed, with cropped silvery hair, and steel-rimmed spectacles shading piercing pale-blue eyes. He was bronzed, and wore a mulberry-coloured polo shirt unbuttoned at the neck, and a grey-tweed jacket.

'Hello, Baz,' said Olivia as he arrived at the table, 'how lovely to see you. I want you to meet my step-father, Patrick Halard.'

'Sir.' Basil inclined his head politely.

'For God's sake,' said Patrick, 'don't call me that, please. Patrick will be fine.' He held out his hand.

'Basil Rodzianko,' said Basil, taking it, and quelling the impulse to say 'sir' again. 'How do you do?'

'Don't I get a kiss?' said Olivia.

'You do.' Basil bent and kissed her, holding her face in his hands.

'Hi,' said Olivia softly, her cheeks pink.

'Hi.' Basil sat down and Patrick looked from one to the other, touched to see Olivia so evidently in love.

'Glass of wine?' He picked up the bottle and looked inquiringly at Basil.

'Great, thanks.'

Patrick filled their glasses and signalled to the waiter, and they ordered the menu of the day – *Moules Marinière*, and a *Carbonnade Nîmoise*.

'Reminds me of Souliac,' said Olivia.

'Ah, Souliac,' said Patrick, smiling at her, and raising his glass before drinking some wine. Then he turned to Basil. 'You bear a famous name,' he said.

'I know, but I'm afraid I'm anything but famous myself, or ever likely to be.'

'Does that matter to you?'

'No, not in the least. I'm not particularly ambitious, all I ever really want is a reasonably well-paid job, an interesting one if possible, and some freedom to continue my writing, such as it is.'

'He's selling himself short,' said Olivia. 'It's so *English* of you, Baz!'

Patrick laughed. 'Modesty is not a thing you suffer from, is it, my love?'

'Not false modesty, no.'

'Well,' said Basil mildly, 'I've got plenty to be modest about and I *am* half-English, don't forget.'

'So am I,' said Olivia, 'but I do my best to conceal the fact.'

'What a nutter you are, Olly,' said Patrick. 'You'd argue the hind legs off a donkey, just to stir things, wouldn't you?'

'Yes, I would,' she said, and they all laughed.

The mussels arrived and for a few minutes they ate without speaking, each of them enjoying the delicious shellfish. Then Patrick put down his napkin and picked up his glass. 'Olivia has been telling me something of your present situation, Basil, and I have been making a few inquiries on your behalf. There may well be an opening for you in our group as a foreign correspondent, being posted to places where your languages, especially Russian, would be valuable. Do you think that might appeal to you?'

'Yes, it would, very much. But could I really do it, properly and professionally, I have to ask myself.'

'Obviously,' said Patrick, 'you wouldn't be thrown in at the deep end, just like that. You would have a suitable period of training, then be attached as assistant to a senior correspondent for a year, maybe more.'

'I see.' Basil felt very relieved to hear this, and began to feel much less unsure of himself. 'In that case, Patrick, thank you, I'd like to be considered for such an appointment.'

'Good. I'll set up an interview. You could fly over at pretty short notice, could you?'

'I think so,' said Basil. 'They're a very gentlemanly lot, my superiors.'

Patrick laughed. 'It's not like that here, I'm afraid.'

'At least you do know where you stand,' said Basil. 'With me, it's kind of in the corridor, if you know what I mean?'

'I do.' Patrick looked at him sympathetically. 'Not a comfortable place to be.'

After lunch they walked back to the river and when they reached the Quai des Grands-Augustins Patrick prepared to leave them and return to his family.

'It was very nice meeting you, Basil. I hope we'll be able to find something for you; I'll be in touch, quite soon.'

'It's very good of you to take so much trouble; I only hope that I won't let you down.'

'I'm sure you won't. They're not all media giants, you know.'

'Well, that's reassuring.' Basil held out his hand. 'And thank you for a terrific lunch, I nearly forgot.'

'Yes, I forgot, too. Thanks, darling Patrick.' Olivia threw her arms round Patrick's neck and kissed him.

'My pleasure,' said Patrick, and departed with a little wave of his hand. Basil and Olivia watched him as he walked along the *quai* towards his building.

'What a nice man.'

'The best,' said Olivia. 'My mother worships him, and they've got an ace little boy called Thomas.'

'And does Patrick worship her?'

'Oh, absolutely.'

'Lucky them,' said Basil.

They strolled across the Pont St-Michel and onto the Ile de la Cité, while Olivia told Basil the story of her mother's love affair with Patrick and her acrimonious divorce from her unpleasant English husband, Olivia's father.

'He sounds like a real pain.'

'He is, still.' Olivia laughed. They walked past Notre Dame and sat down in the Square de l'Ile de France, the little triangular garden at the very end of the island, overlooking the Ile St-Louis.

'What about *your* parents, Baz? Were they happily married?'

'Very. They were so close that it was impossible to imagine them as separate entities; they were always George-and-Hester. They were together for nearly forty years.'

'How amazing. And were you their only child?'

'Yes, and I think that was a bit of an accident.' He laughed, but it sounded rather bitter.

'Oh, dear. What do you mean?'

'Well, I think having children was not part of their plan. They didn't really need them, too wrapped up in each other, and their work. They got rid of me as quickly as they decently could; they sent me to school in London when I was eight and a half.'

'Is the half so important?' Olivia's voice was gentle, and Basil looked at her seriously.

'It is. I can't tell you how terribly rejected I felt, for years. Still do, in a way. I think Hester is fond of me, and so was my father, but in a very detached way. She doesn't seem to need me very much, even now that she's widowed.'

'Do you want to be needed?'

'I suppose I must. Luckily, I found a friend at school who was in much the same boat; his parents lived in Kenya. We went on to St Paul's together, and then Cambridge. He probably means more to me than anyone in the world.'

'Does he feel the same?'

'Hell, no, I don't think so. He's married to a rather rich woman, a doctor, and they have three adorable little girls.'

'What does he do?'

'He's a successful writer.'

'Like wot you want to be?'

Basil laughed, and kissed her. 'Like wot I want to be,' he agreed. The bells of the *quartier* struck four-thirty and Basil looked at his watch. 'It's getting late. What would you like to do?'

'Would your mother mind if I came to see your father's paintings? Will she be working, do you think?'

'Probably, but I don't think she'd mind. She said you sounded like a nice girl, on the phone.'

Olivia smiled. 'Really? Little does she know.'

'Don't worry, I won't tell her the awful truth. Come on, let's go and see her, shall we?'

'I wish we could go somewhere on our own, Baz. Somewhere private.' She leaned against him and he put his arm round her, holding her close.

'So do I. But I can't think of anywhere except the back of my car and that's a bit sordid, isn't it?'

'I suppose it is. God, I wish I had moved into my own apartment. It's time I left home, anyway.'

'Well, if I get a job here, I'll need to find a place. Perhaps you'd like to share it with me?'

Olivia looked at him, her blue eyes wary. 'Do you mean it? Are you serious?'

'Why not?'

'Well, we might not get on, we might fight.'

'In that case, we split up, no problem.'

'Oh.' She got up, brushing the dust off her long black coat, cut like a priest's. She tucked her hand into Basil's arm and they crossed the Pont St-Louis, and walked slowly along the Rue St-Louis-en-l'Île towards Hester's apartment. They opened the gateway into the *porte-cochère* and Olivia gave a little exclamation of pleasure.

'Oh, Baz, what a heavenly place!' She ran ahead, past Hester's modest door and into the courtyard and stood looking around her, admiring the beautiful buildings, their classical severity relieved by the fading green of the lime-trees. Basil followed her and they stood for a few moments, pointing out especially perfect details to each other. 'It *is* a lovely place,' said Basil, 'you're quite right. In spite of my whingeing about my lonely child-hood, it was marvellous to come here in the holidays.'

'And Ramatuelle?'

'Ramatuelle too, of course.' They turned, and looking up saw Hester observing them from her window.

She smiled and waved to them. 'Come up,' she called. 'Have you got the spare key, Baz?'

'Here it is.' He produced the key, then unlocked the door and they went upstairs and straight into the big room, where they found Hester washing her brushes, and screwing the lids onto her pots of pigment.

'I hope we're not interrupting,' said Olivia, as she came forward politely to be introduced.

'No, I was thinking of stopping anyway. It *is* Saturday, after all, isn't it?'

'I've always longed to do egg-tempera painting, and frescoes,' said Olivia, her eyes straying to the easel.

'Have you been to Florence, or Arrezzo?'

'No, not yet, but I must. I really want to go to Italy.'

'That's the place,' said Hester. 'Now, tea.' She was pleased that Olivia had not marched straight in as if she didn't exist, and started examining George's work as though the room were a gallery, as she seemed to recollect Giò doing. Perhaps he didn't, she thought, but it felt like it, somehow.

'I'll put the kettle on,' said Basil. 'You two relax, I won't be long.' He left the room, leaving them together.

'Come and sit down,' said Hester, going over to the sofa and switching on the big lamps. The room sprang into life, the warm colours of the textiles and the vermilion and gold of the icons vivid against the plain lime-washed walls.

'Oh!' cried Olivia, involuntarily, for she had been trying very hard to show restraint; not to gush, 'what a beautiful room.' She looked around her with shining eyes.

'And you are a beautiful girl; the room suits you.'

'What a nice thing to say. Thank you.' Olivia spoke very quietly, almost shyly, and came and sat beside Hester on the rug-covered sofa, with the mellow kilim cushions.

Basil came in with the tray of strong Russian tea in glasses, with lemon. 'Is this all right, Olivia? Do you prefer milk?'

'No, lemon is perfect, thank you.'

They drank the tea, and Basil told Hester about their lunch with Patrick, and the possibility of his moving to Paris.

'Good,' said Hester. 'That would be very nice. But wouldn't you miss the Turnbulls?'

'I don't think so, really. They have their own life to lead, and I daresay Hugo will come over to stay with you from time to time, he seems to love being here.'

'I love having him,' said Hester, and smiled at her

son. 'I hope you won't be thinking of claiming your room back?'

Basil laughed. 'So much for mother-love,' he said. 'No, I'll find a place of my own, don't worry.' He covered Olivia's hand with his, briefly.

'Olivia,' said Hester, 'would you like to look at my husband's paintings?'

'I would, very much, thank you.'

'Carry on,' said Hester.

Olivia put down her glass and went slowly and silently round the room, while the other two remained where they were, talking comfortably together. At last she came back to the sofa and sat down. She looked subdued and quite sad. 'They're such satisfying paintings; they're so logical, so complete, with so much condensed experience, like a Bach prelude. Thank you, it was a privilege to be allowed to see them.'

Hester looked at her intently, her grey eyes thoughtful. 'Would you like to see more of them? And some etchings?'

Olivia sat up, electrified. 'I would,' she said. 'I really would. I knew his output was quite small; I thought this was all you had.'

'I have about forty in store in a friend's studio in Pigalle, and a plan-chest full of etchings. I could phone Maurice and see whether you and Baz could go over tomorrow and see them. How would that be?'

'Unbelievable,' said Olivia, 'I feel as though I'm dreaming.'

Hester went to the phone. 'I'll see if I can get him now.' She dialled the number. 'Maurice? Hello, it's Hester Rodzianko – I'm fine; busy. How are you? – Really? Well, lucky you. When do you leave? – tonight? As soon as that?' Basil looked at Olivia, whose face clearly expressed her disappointment. 'Well, Maurice, have a marvellous trip, but I wonder whether you'd mind me coming over to check out George's paintings and the plan-chest, every now and then? Especially as the studio won't be heated while you're away, will it? – Oh, good. Thanks. Yes, I've got a key – I can't think of anyone off-hand, but I'll try and find someone for you. Send me your address and phone number when you're settled, won't you? – You, too. Bye.' She put down the phone and came back to the sofa, smiling. 'Lucky old thing is off to Algeria for the winter, he's flying out tonight. But it's all right, you can go tomorrow, I've got the key. Just as well I rang, it's typical of him to leave everything in the cold and damp for months, though he says the night-storage heating is on low. Now I can go over and air the place, and make sure the etchings aren't getting foxed.'

'Ghastly thought,' said Olivia, wincing.

'Isn't it? He's been looking for a suitable tenant, he says. You know, low rent to responsible person, that sort of thing.'

'What about me?' said Basil. 'That is, if I get a job.'

'Better have a look at it first, it's rather big and draughty, though he loves it.'

A feeling of excitement was beginning to flow through Basil's veins, almost of confidence and belief in himself. For the first time in his life he began to experience the joy of feeling that he was in the right place at the right time, that anything was possible. He stood up and addressed the two women formally. 'Since your father so kindly paid for our lunch, Olivia, I am still feeling fairly solvent, so I would be very honoured if you two ladies would allow me to take you out to dinner.'

'All right,' said Hester, 'but I'll have to smarten up a bit.'

'You look fine to me,' said Olivia, truthfully.

'Yes, but even I draw the line at paint on the shirt, it's a bit affected, don't you think? Naff, as you young people say?' She rose from the sofa. 'You two open some wine, and there are olives and some *anchoïade* in the fridge, if you'd like to make some toast. We'll have a drink before we go out.'

On Sunday morning Basil walked to the St-Michel *métro*, where he found Olivia waiting for him. They took the train to Pigalle station, crossed the *place* and walked down the Rue Pigalle.

'We have to find number sixty-four.' Basil took Olivia's arm protectively as they made their way down the sleazy street, with its sex-shops and porno-cinemas. Tired-looking prostitutes lurked in doorways, or walked the street, exercising little dogs. They found the number and looked uncertainly at the building.

'Is that it, do you think?' said Olivia, looking very unimpressed.

They approached the entrance, looked in, then slipped through as unobtrusively as they could. They found themselves in another world, a curious time-warp, a jumble of linked courtyards. Tall Victorian tenement-blocks rose beside small older-looking cottages with wooden shutters. Some dwellings had obviously been gentrified and were smart with new paint and pots of clipped-box at the doors, while others were still seedy and run-down, with strings of washing hung from high windows. Following Hester's instructions, they passed through several courts and then arrived at the building they sought.

'It's a leg-job, I'm afraid; no lift,' said Basil. 'Poor Hester, no wonder she doesn't come here very often.' They climbed the four long flights of steps to the top of the building, and arrived at Maurice's door. His name was written in pencil on the wall beside the bell. Basil rang the bell just in case anyone was still there, then he unlocked the door and they went in, feeling rather like criminals.

They stepped straight into an enormous square light room, with brick arches leading into a glass conservatory stretching along the whole of one wall. Basil closed the door behind them and they looked around, slightly overawed by the big silent place. On the left-hand wall hung an extremely large painting, though construction might have been a more appropriate description. The work appeared to be composed of books, their spines stuck to the canvas, the loose pages burnt and brown at the edges, the whole sprayed densely with a coating of thin plaster, through which the charred pages of the desecrated books were still visible and seemed to quiver slightly in the air. The effect was disturbing, and rather depressing. Straight in front of them, across the seeming acres of wood-block flooring, the fireplace had been filled in and shelves fitted. These contained art books, maps, an English dictionary and some paperbacks, including the entire works of Camus. On the top of the fireplace was propped a row of David Hockney polaroids. In the niche on one side of the chimney-breast was a tall walnut bureau, inlaid with ebony. On it stood a large bronze head, beside a Victorian painting on a pretty miniature easel. In the niche on the other side of the chimney stood a plan-chest.

'The etchings, Baz!' Olivia ran across the room and with Basil's help pulled out the heavy top drawer of the chest. Inside, sure enough, were George's etchings, each one carefully interleaved with blotting paper and each separate edition wrapped in fine tissue paper.

Carefully, she took out each packet and laid it on top of the plan-chest. Then, first checking her hands to make sure that they were clean, she lifted the blotting paper to examine each print.

'God, they're wonderful,' she said softly, gazing at a postcard-sized image, a still-life of some semi-abstracted, one-dimensional bottle shapes. They worked their way through all five drawers of the chest. Olivia made sure that the last drawer was tightly shut and then stood up. She leaned against Basil wearily and he put his arms round her.

'Tired?'

'Knackered. Haven't you noticed how exhausting it is, when you go to exhibitions?'

'Yes,' said Basil, 'except that I don't, very often.'

'Now, where are the paintings, I wonder?' Olivia looked around the room. There was a door beside the massive 'books' construction, which proved on examination to lead to a small functional kitchen. She closed the door, crossed the room and went through one of the brick arches into the conservatory. The glass windows on the long wall looked out over a roofscape of grey roofs and chimneys. A large bushy jasmine grew in a deep pot and was clawing its way up a brick pillar and across the glass roof. At the narrow end, to the right and facing north, a deep round-topped window, with a plaster-cast of a pair of hands on the sill, looked out over the rooftops and up through chimneys to a glimpse of the white pepperpot-spires of the Sacré-Cœur above. To the right of this window was a narrow door, which they discovered led to the bedroom.

Here was a total change of ambience, and the room was full of warmth and colour. The walls were painted a soft glowing apricot and were hung with many paintings. A deep carved wooden cornice ran right round the room, separating the walls and ceiling, which was painted a paler shade of apricot. The big bed was covered with a stitched quilt, patterned with bunches of faded-red roses with khaki-green leaves on a cream ground. A pile of square white pillows, together with several smaller square cushions covered in red-and-beige-striped silk, were heaped at the bedhead. Small round tables, covered in tapestry cloths and carrying large ornate brass lamps with cream parchment shades, and stacked with books, stood on either side of the bed. At its foot a long, needlework-covered footstool carried more books and magazines, and in front of the stool a beautiful though damaged Persian rug glowed on the bare polished floorboards. They stood together for a moment, completely taken by surprise.

Olivia was the first to speak. 'Baz?'

'Mm?'

'Do you realize that all these paintings are your father's?'

Basil looked again, more carefully. 'Good Lord, so they are.'

'Aren't they unbelievable?'

'Are they? I don't think I'm capable of judging.'

The many canvases, all in George's familiar subdued palette, some large and set off by slender gilded frames, some smaller in beautiful antique carved wooden frames, and all hung very close together seemed to burn with life against the warm colour of the walls. Olivia went slowly round the walls, looking at the paintings as though they were old friends. At last, she turned to Basil and looked at him as if he, too, existed for her. She took off her coat, folding it carefully on the foot-stool, then she stepped out of her boots, putting them neatly side by side in front of the stool. She came to Basil and wrapped her arms around his waist beneath

267

his coat, burying her face in his shirt front, inhaling the smell of him.

'What do you think?' she said, her voice muffled.

'I thought you'd never ask.' He hugged her tightly against him and kissed the top of her head.

'Well, now I have.' She raised her face to his.

'Yes, now you have.' Basil's hands shook as he undid the buttons of her shirt, one by one, so fierce and sudden was his desire for her.

Chapter Fourteen

Nelly drove slowly down Hammersmith Road in the rush hour, glancing at the clock every few minutes, hoping to get home in time to sit with the children while they had their supper. She and Hugo had been back from Kenya for nearly three weeks now and things seemed to be settling down pretty well, to her intense relief. Eva had turned out to be an excellent choice and the children liked her. She was quite firm with them, but kind and funny too. She understood that peace and quiet for Hugo meant exactly that, and never let the children roar about during his working hours, or play pop music on the kitchen radio. Sometimes, late at night, Eva played her own CDs very quietly in her room; Schubert and Bach seemed to be her favourite composers. It all sounded rather sad for such a jolly girl, Nelly thought. Since their return home, neither she nor Hugo had raised the subject of their matrimonial problems. Sometimes she wondered whether their conversation on that far-away beach had actually taken place at all, and wasn't just a figment of her imagination. She was anxious to forget it, and rather hoped that both would manage to carry on as though nothing serious had happened. Nevertheless, without consulting Hugo, she had been to see her bank and arranged to take out a mortgage, putting the money on deposit until it was required.

The last set of traffic lights turned green and soon afterwards she arrived at her turning. Thankfully, she began the last part of her journey, driving through a maze of back streets to her own quiet little square. She parked in her parking space and got out, taking out her bag and her medical case, locking the car carefully and turning on the alarm. She walked across the pavement and looked over the area railings through the kitchen window. She saw her three daughters sitting with Hugo, eating their supper, all of them laughing, their eyes on Eva as she sat at the head of the table, in Nelly's place, recounting some interesting tale with great intensity and a lot of elaborate pantomime. For a second, Nelly felt a sharp little pang of irritation, even jealousy. Don't be ridiculous, she thought, and marched up the front steps and let herself into the house. She dumped her bags and jacket, then went to the top of the basement stairs and paused for a moment, listening. A soft, thrilling voice, speaking half-English, half-German reached her ears, punctuated by delighted laughter from the audience. Nelly went down to the kitchen. Eva stopped talking when she saw Nelly, and three pairs of bright hazel eyes looked up as she entered the room.

'Hello, Mum,' said Sophie, waving a fish-finger at her.

'Hello, my family.' She sat down and looked across the table at Eva, who smiled at her and stood up, shyly.

'I thought you were here to speak English, Eva,' said Nelly, in what she hoped was a light tone.

'Oh, I'm so sorry. I was just telling a little story.'

'Go on with the story, Eva,' said Hugo. 'You can't just stop in the middle like that.'

'No, no. Another time perhaps.' Looking mortified, Eva went to the fridge, got a carton of milk and filled the girls' mugs. Then she picked up the empty plates, took them to the sink and began to wash up.

Nelly looked at Hugo, who stared back at her with pained blue eyes, saying nothing. She knew that she should apologize to Eva at once; explain that she was irritable and exhausted after her long day's work, and ask her to carry on with the story. The children drank their milk in silence. Then Sophie slid off her chair and went to Eva, tugging her skirt insistently.

'Please, Eva, will you tell us the rest in bed?'

Eva shot a worried glance at Nelly, who sighed.

'Yes, of course. Please do.' She did her best to smile reassuringly at Eva.

'If you're sure?' said Eva quietly.

'Please.' Nelly spoke through gritted teeth.

The girls all got up from the table, and kissed their parents. 'Goodnight, Papa,' said Gertrude. 'I'll tell you the rest tomorrow,' she added in a hoarse whisper.

'Great, I'll look forward to it.' Hugo gave them all a hug and they departed, followed by a subdued-looking Eva.

'Do you want a drink?' said Hugo, getting up.

'Yes, please.'

He poured her a gin and tonic, and sat down again. 'What the hell was all that about?'

'I don't know.' Nelly put her head on the table and began to sob as if her heart would break.

Basil drove through the night to Calais to catch the last ferry to Dover. It was raining, and although the *auto-route* was clear the drive was tiring, and the fast swish-swish of his rather primitive windscreen wipers got on his nerves. Once on the ferry, he bought a coffee and took a walk round the boat to wake himself up and stretch his legs. He began to re-live the week-end in his mind. He still felt astonished that Patrick

Halard had considered him a suitable candidate for training in TV reportage, and felt both very excited and quite alarmed at the prospect. He thought about the extraordinary apartment in Pigalle, and allowed himself to dream about the possibility of sharing it with Olivia, when and if he managed to get the job that seemed to be almost within his grasp. He remembered their last few hours together and then saw in his mind's eye Olivia's slender silhouette as she disappeared through the entrance to her building on Grands-Augustins after he had dropped her off at her door.

He lay down on an empty bench in the motorists' lounge and closed his eyes. He was woken by the crackle of the public address system announcing the approach to Dover. He sat up, yawned and made his way slowly back to the car-deck, waited until the door was unlocked and got back into his car. For once, it was not raining in England and he drove through the Kent countryside in silvery moonlight. He felt very sad to have left Paris and Olivia for the moment, but at the same time enormously exhilarated by the promise of the amazing opportunities that seemed to lie ahead.

On Monday evening Giò telephoned Hester to see how she was getting on with the icons.

'The short answer is, Giò, that I'm not.'

'Oh. Any problems?'

'No, no problems; and I *am* getting on, but it's going rather slowly, I've had quite a few distractions, one way and another.' Hester paused, then thought that perhaps she should elaborate further. 'I've had Basil coming and going from London, then he and Olivia took me out to dinner, and then they both had supper here last night, so you see I've been quite busy, for me.'

'Sounds like it.' Giò did his best to sound only mildly interested in this account of Hester's social life. 'Any special reason for his visiting you again so soon?'

'Yes, he came to meet Olivia's stepfather. It's possible he might be moving to Paris, if a suitable job is forthcoming.'

'Oh, I see. And is Patrick giving him a bunk up the ladder?'

'I think that's the general idea.'

'Well, best of luck to him. Now, when will you have something to show me?'

Hester closed her eyes and tried not to feel that she was being pressured, as indeed she was. 'Giò,' she said, 'please don't hassle me. I can't work like this, and if you feel that I should then I shall have to cancel our arrangement.'

'I'm sorry. I wasn't intending to hassle you in any way.'

'The best thing will be for *me* to contact *you* when I've done the first batch; then we can decide whether we both want to continue, or not.'

'Yes, all right. If that's what you'd prefer.' Giò sounded contrite, but not very.

'I was perfectly happy with my crooked old dealers, you know.' Hester spoke quietly but firmly. 'This whole thing was your idea, Giò, and I'm still not really convinced that it will work. In fact, I shall continue to sell the odd one to them; I don't want to be left with no dealers at all, if you decide to drop me at the end of the day.'

Giò was taken aback by Hester's assertiveness and for two pins would have told her to go to hell. But his natural good sense prevailed, and he laughed. 'Don't worry, it'll be fine,' he said. 'I'll look forward to hearing from you, Hester.'

'Fine. Goodbye.'

'Goodbye.' Giò put down the phone, feeling dismissed, and drank the remains of his coffee, now grown cold. Silly old bat, he thought, who the hell does she think she is? He went to the French windows, opened them and stepped out onto the balcony. The air smelt faintly autumnal, acrid and sad. Why didn't Baz get in touch? I can't believe he's forgotten me, he thought miserably. How could he? A breeze stirred the trees across the road and a shower of yellow leaves drifted to the ground, but Giò stared through them with blank unseeing eyes. It's that bloody Olly, he thought with a flash of anger, she's got her hooks into him, the scheming little cow. I suppose she reckons that if she gets him a job with Daddy, she can do what she likes with him. Well, I'll soon put paid to that. He went to the phone, picked it up and dialled Olivia's number.

'Olly?'

'Giò. Hi.'

'How are you?'

'Great, how are you?'

'Oh, fine. Olly, I was thinking of going out to Père-Lachaise tomorrow afternoon to give old Oscar a tidy. Do you want to come? We could have a drink together afterwards, perhaps?'

'Yes, OK. Why not?'

'Good. See you at the main gate about five?'

'Right. What time do they shut?'

'Six, so don't be late.'

'I won't. See you then. 'Bye.'

' 'Bye.'

Olivia left her life-class early, pleading an appointment with the dentist. She stowed her equipment in her locker, put on her long grey sweater, left the building, and began to walk swiftly towards the *métro* at St-Germain-des-Prés. She was rather irritated with herself for having forgotten that today was the life-class, when agreeing to go with Giò to Père-Lachaise. Although she anticipated that her own work would eventually tend towards the abstract and intellectual, rather than purely figurative, she nevertheless greatly enjoyed the discipline of translating the arms and legs, bottoms and backs she saw before her in the cold, cruel light of the studio to as close a realization as she could manage on paper or canvas, in pencil, or charcoal, or paint. She would really very much rather have finished her class, gone out for a drink with her friends and then gone home to Grands-Augustins to cook supper, and do some more work.

As she left the station at Père-Lachaise she looked at her watch: five past five. Damn, she thought, it always takes longer than you think. She ran down the road towards the entrance to the cemetery, knowing that Giò would be annoyed with her for being late. I don't know why I do this anyway, she thought. Just habit, I suppose.

Giò stood waiting at the gate, with the plastic cleaning-bag in one hand, and a spray of bay-leaves in the other.

He smiled as she came running up, red-faced with exertion. 'Where's the fire?' he said.

'I thought I was late?'

'You are: what's new? It's OK, there's time, just.'

'Oh. Good.'

They set off, walking briskly up the Avenue Princi-pale towards Oscar Wilde's tomb. Olivia glanced at the bay-leaves. 'Couldn't you get any flowers?'

'No; it's all horrid chrysanthemums. Or lilies, too

275

gloomy. Actually, I thought bay very appropriate. You know, laurels and all that?'

'Yes, that figures.'

They arrived at the tomb and removed the dead flowers, not the roses from their last visit, but a rather large wreath of arum lilies, looking sad and smelling worse.

'See what I mean?' said Giò. 'Disgusting.'

Olivia laughed and swept all the dead leaves and rubbish off the tomb, using Giò's little dustpan and brush. He placed the bay-leaves on the stone shelf below the torso of the winged figure, and they put the dead wreath into the plastic bag with the rest of the garbage to dump in a bin on their way out. Then they hurried back to the entrance with five minutes to spare before the gates were shut for the night.

As they walked in a more leisurely way back to the *métro*, Giò decided to reveal his real reason for their meeting. 'God, I'm thirsty; let's have a drink here.' He led the way to a café with a couple of tables on the pavement. 'Do you want to sit here, or inside?'

'Here's fine.' Olivia sat down, quite glad of a rest.

'What'll you have?'

'I'll have a beer, thanks.'

'Good idea, so will I.' A waiter appeared and Giò ordered the drinks, and a packet of crisps, then he leaned back in his seat and looked at Olivia. 'Basil was here at the weekend.' It was a statement, rather than a question.

She looked at him warily, but his face revealed nothing. 'That's right,' she said. 'He came to see Patrick. He might be able to help him get a job.'

'Yes, so his mother told me.'

Jesus, thought Olivia, what else did she tell him? 'It will be fun if he comes to live in Paris, won't it?' She spoke casually and lit a cigarette. 'He seems a nice chap.'

'Only "nice"?' Giò looked at her with hard narrowed eyes. 'What exactly do you mean by "nice", Olly?'

'Very amusing; OK. What do you think I mean?'

'I think you fancy him.' The waiter arrived with the beer, but this small diversion failed to conceal the alarm in Olivia's eyes. She took a swig of her beer and a deep drag of her cigarette, and told herself to stay cool. 'Don't you?' said Giò.

'Don't I what?'

'Fancy him.'

'What *is* all this, Giò? Why do you want to know?'

'Don't be naïve, Olly.'

'I don't think that I am being naïve, at all.'

'No? Well, perhaps I should warn you, my dear. Basil is gay.'

What a shit he can be, thought Olivia, stubbing out her cigarette angrily. He'd invent anything to warn me off, and leave the field clear for him. She finished her beer, put the glass down on the table and looked at him steadily with a faint smile. 'That's a load of crap; you can forget it,' she said calmly. 'But thanks for the kind thought, anyway.' She stood up, ready to depart.

'But it's true; it's perfectly true!'

Olivia turned to Giò furiously. 'It is *not* true! Baz is *not* gay! I *know*!'

'*How* do you know?' Giò shouted, equally angrily.

'How do you *think* I know, you stupid old cretin?' Tears of rage filled Olivia's eyes, and she turned away abruptly and marched off in the direction of the *métro*, her bag clutched to her breast, her long skirt flapping behind her as she went.

Giò remained where he was, shocked and trembling. He tried to tell himself that Olivia had been bluffing, but deep inside himself he knew that she had not.

By the time she reached St-Michel station Olivia's anger had largely evaporated, but she knew exactly how ruthless Giò could be when he really wanted something. She began to plan a strategy to steal a march on him and consolidate her own position, both with Basil, and even more importantly her instinct told her, with Hester. She remembered very well what Baz had said about feeling rejected by his parents and guessed, rightly, that Hester's opinions and beliefs, even her prejudices, still meant a good deal to him; perhaps all the more so because they were not at all dogmatically expressed. It had not escaped Olivia's notice when they had all been out together, that Basil treated his mother with an affectionate consideration; respect, she supposed. Not at all like most of the young men of her own generation, who all seemed gerontophobic as far as their parents were concerned. She walked rapidly along the Quai des Grands-Augustins towards her door, and found Patrick in the lobby, carrying a bouquet of yellow lilies and waiting for the lift to arrive.

'Not walking up?' she asked, kissing him.

'No, I've been on my feet all day. I've had quite enough exercise, thanks.'

'Me, too. I'll ride up with you.'

When they reached the top floor Olivia hesitated, then touched Patrick's arm. 'Could you spare a moment?' She knew he would be longing to be with Anna and their small son, who would probably be having his bath.

'Yes, of course. What's the problem?'

'Come in for a second.' She unlocked her door, just across the landing from her parents' apartment, and he followed her into her room. She dumped her bag and pulled off her sweater, and they sat down on the squashy old flea-market sofa.

'Fire away,' said Patrick, putting his lilies on the floor beside him.

'It's difficult.' Olivia looked at him shyly.

'Does it by any chance concern Basil Rodzianko?' Patrick smiled sympathetically.

'Yes, it does in a way. The thing is, we went to look at an apartment in Pigalle. It's for rent, quite cheap.'

'And you want to move in with Basil if he gets a job here? That's very understandable.'

'Yes. But there's something else I want your advice about.'

'Go on.'

'The apartment is absolutely crammed with Baz's father's painting and etchings. There must be at least forty or fifty paintings and dozens of etchings, in editions. I find them absolutely amazing, incredible.'

'How extraordinary. I understood that he often refused to complete paintings, and destroyed most of his stuff.'

'Do you think you could spare some time to come and see them? The apartment belongs to an elderly painter, you may have heard of him, he's called Maurice Coburg. He's an old friend of the Rodziankos; he's gone to Algiers for the winter.'

'Why are the paintings at his place?'

'Because there isn't any more room at Hester's. There are loads there, too.'

'Why do you specially want *me* to see them?'

'Because I trust you. You'll tell me if we should do something about them, or just leave things as they are.'

'Do *what* about them, Olly?'

'Maybe a little piece in one of your programmes?'

'Isn't it too late now? The poor chap's dead.'

'But Hester isn't, and Baz isn't. It would be a

justification of her belief in him, wouldn't it? And great for Baz, too.'

'That's true.' Patrick leaned across and kissed her on the forehead. 'I can't promise anything, but we'll go and look at them, anyway.' He took out his diary. 'What about Thursday evening?'

'Brilliant,' said Olivia. 'Thank you. I'll get the key from Hester.'

At the door, he turned towards her. 'See you Thursday, then. Maybe I'll have some news on the job front by then, so fingers crossed.'

Olivia watched him as he opened his own door and disappeared through it to screams of welcome and laughter from his family. She closed her door, smiling, and put a tape in the machine; a Beethoven cello sonata. Then she lay on her sofa, listening to the music and congratulating herself on not blurting out to Patrick her fears concerning Giò. He was after all her mother's greatly-loved twin brother, and until this moment, greatly loved by Olivia herself. She had no wish to make trouble, but this was not going to prevent her from defending her own territory in any way she thought proper.

Hugo sat in front of his word processor, transcribing his book from manuscript to typescript. As he had never learnt to type properly he did not work particularly fast, or even accurately. This did not worry him unduly as it was so easy to correct the errors, and only he knew how extremely often these occurred. Equally, his lack of speed made it possible to edit the text, fine-tuning it even more as he went along. It was very tiring work for him, and hard on his weak eyes too, and from time to time he stopped and walked round the room to stretch his legs and give his eyes a rest.

He opened the French windows and stepped out into the garden for a moment to get some air. The leaves of the almond tree were now wizened and yellow and occasionally one of them fell, spinning slowly to the paving-slabs below. A few had come to rest on the iron table and were leaving rusty stains on the white-painted top. Hugo brushed them off, and then absent-mindedly wiped his hand on his trousers. He sat down on a chair, checking that the seat was not wet, and looked up at the grey-brick walls of the house, with their regular white-painted windows. Neat and orderly, like a doll's-house, he thought. He did not often allow himself to sit alone, doing nothing like this. If he did, he began to think about his parents and could not stop himself from going over the entire nightmare yet again, and sinking into a mood of grieving depression that sometimes felt rather like guilt to him. Common sense told him that this feeling was both masochistic and ridiculous, but he knew that he badly needed to talk about it.

Talking to Una-Mary had been quite comforting, largely because she was so old that although she listened and sometimes offered a quiet opinion, she remained totally uninvolved. He did not think that anything could really get to her any more, and in a sense envied her that emotional freedom. He was resisting taking the obvious course of telling Nelly about his feelings, though he was sometimes extremely tempted to do so, particularly late at night, in bed. He guessed that if he cracked and unburdened himself of all his rage, guilt and sorrow to her, he would reveal himself as the still-vulnerable man he knew himself to be, and she would subtly re-establish herself as the dominant, strong, supportive partner.

Hugo was perfectly well aware how childish and unimportant his small rebellion probably seemed to Nelly; stupid, unnecessary and ungrateful. But a deep streak of stubbornness, probably the same illogical refusal to submit to a superior force that had informed his father's later years, forced him to go on with the silent battle. Whether Nelly had given the matter much thought since their return home, he did not know and was certainly not going to ask. She was so busy at the hospital, in any case, that it was doubtful she had thought about it at all. I wish I could think of a good enough reason to hop over to Paris, he said to himself, that's what I'd really like to do. Well then, why don't you just do it, you fool? You don't need an *excuse*.

He returned to his room, leaving the garden door open and continued with his work. At six o'clock he decided to try Hester's number. Allowing for the time difference, she should be back from her evening's shopping by now. He dialled the number. The phone rang five or six times and he was beginning to think that she must be out, when she answered.

'Yes?' Her voice was quiet; wary.

'Hester? It's me, Hugo.'

'Oh, Hugo, thank heaven! I thought it was a boring man who's nagging me about work. How are you, my dear boy?'

'So-so. You know.'

'Yes, I know.'

'I was wondering, could I come and see you? Stay a night, maybe?'

'Yes, I think so. When do you want to come?'

'Any time that suits you. I don't want to be a nuisance. Say no if you're awfully busy.'

'It's not that, it's Baz. He keeps coming over at short notice, he may need to come for an interview. Could you come this week, say Friday? I don't think he'll be coming again for a week or two.'

'Friday would be great, if you're sure? Really?'

'Yes, I'm sure. In any case, if he did turn up one of you could always sleep on the sofa, so it's absolutely not a problem.'

'Thanks so much, I'll be there about seven, is that OK?'

'It's fine, Hugo. I look forward to seeing you again.'

'So do I, very much. See you on Friday.'

'See you then. Goodbye.'

Hugo put down the phone, feeling better, carefully saved his day's work, and switched off the word processor. He put the cover on the machine, and tidied his manuscript and notes. Then he went down to the kitchen to sit with his daughters while they had their supper, mentally rehearsing what, if anything, he would tell Nelly when she got home.

After supper, Eva went out to see a friend, leaving Hugo and Nelly with their coffee, watching the *Nine O'Clock News* without much interest.

'How was your day?' asked Hugo, after a few minutes.

'All right.' Nelly glanced at him briefly. 'Tiring as usual. What about you?'

'OK. I got quite a lot done. Eva's very good with the girls. I hardly know they're there sometimes. It makes me feel quite guilty, poor little things. It seems unfair that their lives are so restricted, doesn't it?'

'Well, what else can we do?'

'Nothing, of course. I just keep thinking of my own early childhood, and yours on the island. So much space and freedom, one feels they're missing out.'

'Well, they get plenty of that in the holidays. They're lucky, compared with some city children.'

'But ours aren't "some city children", are they?'

283

Nelly could see which way the wind was blowing; Hugo was about to start riding his most recent hobby-horse, that for the sake of the children they should sell the London house and move to the country. He's so incredibly selfish, she thought. He really does seem to think that I should be quite prepared to give up my job, my career, go to the country, just like that. If I were a man, such an idea would never enter his head for a moment; so much for equality between the sexes. She stood up with an elaborate yawn, and put the coffee-cups in the dishwasher. 'I must have a bath and wash my hair. I'd better do it now, or I'll be too sleepy later,' she said.

Hugo smiled at her. 'By the way, I'm going to Paris on Friday, for a couple of days.'

'Oh?' She paused for a moment, and considered telling him that she was not on duty this weekend, that it would have been nice to spend it together and take the girls somewhere, then changed her mind and continued up the stairs without another word. Hugo watched the rest of the news, and the weather forecast. Then he switched off the television and the kitchen lights, and went up to his room to work for an hour or two.

'God, I'm glad I don't have to do this every day,' said Patrick, as he and Olivia toiled up the four sordid flights of stairs to Maurice Coburg's studio.

'Here we are.' Olivia took the key from her pocket as they reached the top floor and led the way to the door. 'In here.' She unlocked the door and they went in.

'Good Lord, how amazing.' Patrick looked around him at the enormous white room, so impressively ascetic. 'What a surprise, I was rather expecting the old *vie de bohème* bit.'

Olivia laughed and crossed the room to the plan-chest. 'The etchings are all in here, loads of them.'

'And the paintings?'

'Which do you want to see first?'

'The paintings.'

'Right. Come with me.' She led the way to the conservatory, and opened the door to the bedroom. 'Here they are.' She switched on the lights and sat down on the bed, while Patrick went slowly round the room studying each painting minutely, without comment.

At last he turned to her, and smiled. 'Well done, Olly. What a find.' He sat down on a chair beside the fireplace and gazed at the very large painting that hung above the bedhead, an allegorical group of figures in a series of apparently empty rooms, one leading into another. Some of the figures were clothed, some not, and this, combined with the drab palette, the broken-whites, greys and taupes so recognizably the signature colours of the artist, gave the work a curiously disturbing impact.

Patrick shook his head. 'Why, one asks oneself, are the paintings all here, in this one room? And all so beautifully framed and sensitively hung?'

'Don't ask me. Perhaps Coburg just admires them?'

'Maybe. Anyway, it doesn't matter. They're here. They exist. That's the important thing.'

'So?'

'So, I'll have to think about it. Look again at next year's schedules, see whether I can fit him into a suitable slot; I'd certainly like to. Do you think his widow would co-operate, allow us to film, bring cameras here, and so on?'

'Hester? I don't know. I should think she would, if

she thought that you considered the work was really worth taking seriously, even posthumously. In his lifetime he got a lot of abuse from the critics, she's very sensitive about that. She'd need to be very sure.'

'How do you get on with her?'

'Fine. I like her very much. Her apartment is beautiful, you'd love it. There are quite a lot of paintings there too, as well as her own work.'

'She paints too?'

'She does the most exquisite bogus icons in tempera. They're quite marvellous, jumping with life, I love them.'

'*Bogus?*'

'Yes, bogus.' Olivia laughed. 'She sells them to the rat-bag dealers; she has to. No other means of support, isn't that the expression? So next time you see a Novgorod Virgin and Child in some auctioneer's catalogue, it's quite probably one of Hester's.'

'So a revival of interest in Rodzianko's work could be a good thing for her, in more ways than one?'

'I suppose so.' They turned to the big white studio, and Patrick looked at the 'books' construction, its charred pages quivering in a faintly menacing manner.

'I take it this is Coburg's work?'

'It must be. Do you want to see Rodzianko's etchings?'

Patrick looked at his watch. 'I don't think so, not at this stage. I'll take your word for it that they're in the same league.'

As they walked back up the Rue Pigalle towards the *métro*, Patrick looked about him with some distaste. 'I don't really feel awfully happy about you living in this district, Olly. Not the most salubrious of areas, is it?'

'Well, I won't be, unless I share it with Baz. And he'll look after me, won't he?'

'I hope so.' Patrick sighed. 'Why are children such a

worry? Your brother in Prague, and now you flying away.'

Olivia gave his arm a little squeeze. 'Good job you and Mum have Tom, isn't it?'

As he was only carrying a briefcase and in any case felt a great deal more confident about getting about Paris now, Hugo took the *métro* to the Pont Marie and crossed the bridge to the Ile St-Louis. Walking down the Rue des Deux-Ponts towards the Rue St-Louis-en-l'Ile, he saw Hester crossing the street at the corner carrying her shopping, and ran to catch up with her.

'There you are,' she said, without surprise.

Hugo kissed her and relieved her of her heavy basket. 'Is this it? Or have we more shopping to do?'

'No, this is all, except the bread, and that's on our way. I've got a little *rôti de porc*. I hope you haven't got a thing about fish on Friday?'

'Certainly not.' Hugo laughed. 'Sounds great. In any case, I'm a bona fide traveller, so that makes it OK, doesn't it?'

After supper, Hugo washed the dishes, while Hester made coffee, and poured the remains of the wine into their glasses. Then she picked up the tray and led the way into the sitting-room. It was almost the middle of October and she allowed the heating to be on for a couple of hours in the morning and evening; with such low ceilings the *entresol* was not difficult or very expensive to keep warm. She switched on the lamps and Hugo looked around the familiar room with affection.

Hester sat down and poured the coffee. 'It's a bit too warm in here, isn't it? Shall we open the window for a few minutes? The air's lovely this evening, and it's not cold.'

Hugo opened the window behind Hester's work-table and stood for a moment looking down through the thinning foliage of the trees to the courtyard below, remembering the evening Giò Hamilton had come looking for Hester, or had it been Basil?

'Did that chap Hamilton find you in the end?' He crossed the room and sat down in his usual low chair.

'Yes, and I often wish he hadn't.' She handed Hugo his coffee, frowning.

'Oh dear, why?'

'It's quite boring, are you sure you want to hear it?'

'Certainly, I do.'

Hester told Hugo about her visit to *Le Patrimoine* and how she had been persuaded against her better judgement to work for Giò.

'And why is it against your better judgement? What's the problem?'

'The problem is me, Hugo. When I do the icons and sell them to my weird little men, that's it, the deal is done. What happens to them afterwards is not my concern, and I really don't want to know where they finish up, they're no longer part of me. But this new man is something else. He wants me to do enough to mount a kind of exhibition in a special little gallery at the back of his shop, got up to look like a chapel in Old Russia. The more I reflect on it, the more *kitsch* the whole idea seems to me; it feels like even more of a con than my present line of business.' She looked at Hugo, her grey eyes perturbed. 'Do you understand?'

'I understand perfectly.'

'The worst thing is, he keeps phoning to see how I'm getting on. It's making me feel quite threatened, as if my life's no longer my own.'

'Well, you know what to do, don't you?'

'What?'

'Tell him to get lost.'

'Could I?'

'Why not? You haven't signed a contract, have you?'

'No.'

'Well then, you're in the clear. Say you've changed your mind.'

'It's quite embarrassing, he's rather a friend of Baz's.'

'Tough,' said Hugo, and Hester laughed.

'Thank you; you're quite right. What a relief. I shall do exactly as you say, Hugo, how sensible you are. Now, let's have an Armagnac and stop talking about me, shall we?'

Hugo fetched the bottle and the glasses, poured the drinks and sat down again, warming the glass in his hand. Then, very quietly, so that sometimes Hester found it difficult to hear him, he began to tell her about Kenya, about the visits to the mortuary and to the ransacked farm; about the inquest and the funeral. He described the interview with his father's lawyers and the bank, and their cold and inflexible attitude to his father's financial situation at the time of his death.

'You must both have had an awful time,' said Hester. 'I expect you still are?'

'Yes, I feel absolutely haunted by it all; I can't get it out of my mind. Every time I turn on the news, I see pictures of mutilated bodies; or if I watch a film, there always seems to be a funeral in it. The other day I watched a clip from an old *Monty Python* show, and it was a *joke* funeral, bodies falling out of the coffin, that sort of thing, horribly *unfunny*. I felt sick.'

'Of course, one would.'

'Then there are the photographs. Gabrieli searched

the house after we'd gone and found quite a lot. They arrived in the post the other day. I don't know whether I feel comforted by them, or whether they just add to the sense of loss, the awful waste.' He looked at Hester, taking off his spectacles and cleaning them on his sweater. 'I brought them with me. Would you like to see them?'

'Would you like me to see them?'

'Yes, I would.' He went to Basil's room to fetch them. Hester sighed sadly, and poured some more Armagnac. On his return Hugo sat down beside her on the sofa and took the sheaf of photographs out of a large brown envelope. He passed them to her, one by one. She said very little, seeming to know who the various people and places were, without being told. The last photograph, a large faded sepia-print showed a white, palm-fringed beach, empty except for a man and a woman, and a little fair-haired boy. The man was wearing a kikoi and a bush-hat and was cooking a large fish, impaled on a stick, over a driftwood fire on the sand, with the woman and the little boy close by.

Hester examined it closely, then looked at Hugo and smiled. 'You must be very glad to have this?'

'Yes, but at the same time it breaks my heart.' She gave the photograph back to Hugo, and he put it carefully back in the envelope with the rest.

'You know, Hugo, when George died, it was a stroke that killed him. We were having a few people in for drinks to celebrate the birthday of our old friend Maurice. I was in the kitchen, carving a piece of smoked salmon into thin slices, and he was in here arranging the drinks and things. Suddenly, I heard a fearful crash, and I knew at once what had happened. I rushed through and found him lying on the floor, just there, by the big table.'

'How awful; you poor thing, what a shock. He was dead, of course?'

'Luckily, yes, poor darling. At least he didn't have to suffer the humiliation of the paralysis thing, or not being able to speak. I have to be thankful for that.' She looked at Hugo thoughtfully. 'It was what you said about being haunted that reminded me. For months and months afterwards I couldn't pass a delicatessen without beginning to shake. Even now, I can't eat smoked salmon; I doubt I will, ever again.'

'So the haunting is something you just have to live with?'

'Yes, I think so. When you can accept it, even welcome it, it gets a bit less painful, but not much. It's always there, whatever they tell you.'

Down below in the courtyard, Giò stood miserably gazing at Hester's windows, listening to the muffled voices, watching the shadows moving from time to time over the lamplit beams of the low ceiling. He was slightly drunk, and full of jealous anger. He would have given much to know if it was Basil up there with Hester, but did not quite have the brass neck or the courage to ring the bell and find out. He stood there, undecided, until the lights were switched off, and silence crept over the entire courtyard. Then he put up the collar of his coat and walked slowly back to the Place des Vosges.

Chapter Fifteen

It was Eva's free weekend, so Nelly spent Saturday alone with the children. She took them to the zoo, which they seemed to enjoy, particularly the elephant house.

'It's such a lovely tall house, isn't it?' said Phyllida. 'A tall house for tall elephants.'

'And the walls look like elephant's skin, don't they?' said Sophie. 'Sort of crinkly, like prunes.'

'Yes, like in the bath when you've been in too long,' said Gertrude, 'only grey, of course.'

'Grey what?' said Nelly.

'Elephant's skin.'

'Oh, yes. I see.'

After they had seen enough animals behind bars they took a long walk round Regent's Park, then caught the underground back to Notting Hill Gate and had lunch in a pizza place. After lunch they walked up Portobello Road and spent a happy couple of hours trawling through the stalls of the flea-market. On the other side of the road Gertrude noticed a white bull-dog puppy in a pet-shop window and turned her big pleading eyes on her mother.

Nelly smiled and shook her head. 'I wish we could, darling, but it wouldn't be fair, would it? Who would take him for walks? And what about when we go on holiday? It's too difficult, honestly.'

'Mum's right,' said Phyllida censoriously. 'It's cruel to keep pets in town, my teacher says so.'

'I s'pose so.' Gertrude sighed noisily. 'But I would've so *loved* him.' Nelly gave her a pound to put in a blind man's hat, and they wandered back down the road again, crossed over to Kensington Church Street and walked slowly home. They sat in the kitchen and watched television. It was *Tom and Jerry* and Nelly endured without complaint the raucous sound-track that accompanied the cartoon. She looked in the fridge to see what she could make for their supper. There was half a cold chicken, a sadly-wilted bunch of celery and a bowl of solid-looking rice pudding. Vile, she thought and looked in the freezer. There she found a good selection of dishes from Marks and Spencer. Good old M and S, what would I do without you, she said to herself. She chose moussaka for the girls and frozen French bread. What about me? she thought. All these dishes are for two or four; I don't want to eat dreary cold chicken all on my own. She stared into the freezer, feeling lonely and resentful without Hugo. Then she picked up the telephone and called Basil.

He answered at once. 'Hello?' He sounded eager, almost as if he were expecting a call.

'Baz, hello. It's me, Nelly.'

'Oh. Nelly. Hi.'

'Sorry, you sound disappointed!'

'No, no, not at all. It's nice to hear you, how are you both?'

'All right. Well, not very, really.'

'Hardly surprising, you poor things.'

'Baz, I was wondering. Hugo's in Paris for a couple of days, with your mother. Would you like to come to supper?'

'What, tonight?'

293

'Yes.'

There was a slight pause.

'Is there a problem, are you busy?' said Nelly.

'No, not really. I'm expecting a call from Paris. I could come after that, if you want me to?'

'No hurry. I've got the girls to deal with first. You know, baths, supper, all that. Come when you're ready.'

'OK, Nelly, see you later.'

She put down the phone. The cartoon was finished, and the girls sat transfixed in front of a programme that reminded Nelly of *Top of the Pops*. She looked hopefully at the kitchen clock. 'Time for baths,' she said and switched off the TV.

'Oh, Mum!' wailed Sophie, 'you are mean. Can't we see it to the end?'

'Absolutely not,' said Nelly firmly. 'Go up and get started while I put your supper in the oven, OK? I'll be up in a few minutes.'

With exaggerated sighs of frustration, knowing that it was pointless to argue with their mother, the girls gave in and departed noisily, crashing into the furniture as they went.

Then Sophie reappeared at the foot of the stairs. 'Can we have some of your *Bluebell* stuff?'

'Yes, but just the tiniest bit, it's awfully expensive.' Sophie thundered up the stairs after her sisters.

Nelly ripped the packaging off the moussaka with some difficulty and put it in the oven. She set the timer, and then looked in the freezer again and took out salmon steaks with a green sauce, prepared new potatoes and *mange-tout* peas. She decided not to give the children the cold rice pudding, but got out a tub of chocolate-chip ice-cream instead. Then she went upstairs rather wearily to supervise the baths, and long before she reached the children's bathroom an overpowering smell of bluebells floated down the stairs towards her.

At about eight-thirty the front-door bell rang. Nelly opened the kitchen door and shouted up the steps: 'Baz?' His shaggy head appeared above the black iron railing. 'Come down this way: I'm too pooped to come up and let you in.' He came down the steps and into the kitchen, pulling off his leather jacket. Smelling of cold evening air and maleness he embraced Nelly, and she clung to him for a second, remembering, then released him.

He took a bottle wrapped in tissue-paper from his pocket, and put it on the table. 'It's probably horrible, but it's the best the off-licence had.'

'I'm sure it's fine.' She took off the wrapper, revealing a bottle of *Mouton-Cadet*. Not too brilliant with salmon, she thought, and then smiled at Basil. 'Wicked man, how extravagant of you, it's lovely. Will you open it?' The timer rang and she went to open the oven door. The salmon steaks looked excellent, just faintly touched with golden-brown, the green sauce in the hollow of the steak bubbling, and a delicious smell filled the kitchen. Pleased, Nelly took out the dish and put it in the lower oven to keep warm, while she drained the potatoes and peas. The table was already laid, and Basil filled the glasses while she lit the candles, a thing she hardly ever bothered to do. She brought the plates to the table and they sat down.

'God, I'm ravenous,' said Basil, picking up his knife and fork.

'So am I, for once. Usually, I'm too tired to feel very hungry. Especially for German food which is what we mostly have at the moment.'

'Oh; why's that?'

'It's Eva, our new *au pair*. She's a real treasure, the

girls love her, but cooking's not really her thing.'

'Well, I suppose the important thing is how she gets on with the children and Hugo. I take it this girl doesn't traumatize him, like the dreaded Inger?'

Nelly laughed. 'No chance. She's a dumpy little thing, like a bun, but a real pussy-cat.'

Basil shot her a wary glance, wondering whether she was being sarcastic, and drank some wine. 'Tell me about Kenya. That is, if you want to.'

'I want to. Hugo refuses to talk about it. I can't say I blame him, it was ghastly.' Quietly she recounted the whole sad story, leaving out the trip to Lamu, but including the painful sessions with the lawyers and the business of the negative equity.

'So what? That's no fault of Hugo's; it's not his responsibility. Let the bloody bank suffer the loss, God knows they can afford to.'

Nelly looked at him, frowning. 'That's just what Hugo says, but I don't agree. I don't like the idea of my father-in-law being in debt like that, even when he's dead. In fact, I intend to pay it off.'

'Oh? What does Hugo think about that?'

'He doesn't want me to do it, of course; you know how touchy he is. But what's the point of my having money if I'm not allowed to make good use of it? It's not a vast amount, anyway.'

Basil felt inclined to warn her that she was playing with fire, but decided against it, having no wish to provoke her. Instead he turned towards her, smiling, his eyes bright. 'You haven't asked me how *I* am. Don't you want to know?'

'Oh, Baz, I'm sorry. Yes, of course I do. What have you been up to?'

'Well, two things. One, I'm waiting for a call from Paris about an interview for a job. And two, I'm in love.'

For a second Nelly felt quite sick, as if the ground were crumbling under her. Then she smiled bravely and even managed a little laugh, albeit a slightly wobbly one. 'Baz, how terrific, on both counts. Tell me about the job, and the lucky woman.'

'I'm rather embarrassed to tell you. She's still a girl, she's only nineteen.'

'Good heavens, Baz! I never thought of you as a cradle-snatcher. What's her name? Is she rich, or something?'

Basil decided not to react to this insulting suggestion. Instead he smiled at Nelly, his grey eyes soft. 'You make me sound like Vlad the Impaler,' he said mildly. 'You don't have to worry on her account, she runs rings round me. Her name's Olivia, she's very wise for her age and seriously talented, and I love her. It rather frightens me, but I do.'

'Well, what a surprise. That's wonderful; congratulations. And the job?'

He told her about meeting Patrick and the possibility of a job. He did not mention the fact that Patrick was Olivia's stepfather, as he well knew what inference she would draw from that.

'Well, good. I hope you get it, Baz. What about your poetry?'

'Oh, I'll go on with that, when I can. Olivia will keep my nose to the grindstone, I'm sure.' He smiled tenderly, rather to Nelly's exasperation. 'She seems to have a much higher opinion of my capabilities than I have myself, though that wouldn't be very difficult. Still, it's a nice feeling, someone believing in you, isn't it? Like your belief in Hugo.'

It was Nelly's turn to smile, but it was not with tenderness.

They sat at the table, drinking coffee and finishing the

wine, with a slight feeling of constraint between them, of things left unsaid, and she wished she had not invited him to supper. At ten o'clock Basil said that he must go and Nelly did not try to detain him. She followed him up the area steps to the street for a breath of air.

'Nelly?'

'Yes?' She looked up at him, tall, bearded and somehow formidable in his black-leather jacket.

He put his hand on her shoulder and touched her lips briefly with his. 'Don't do anything that will hurt Hugo, will you?'

Nelly stared at him, and Basil could see by the light of the street-lamp that her eyes were hard and angry. 'Goodnight, Baz. It was nice seeing you again.'

Before he could say anything else she had run down the area steps and slammed the kitchen door. Basil turned and walked thoughtfully down the street, glad to be alone, full of apprehension for Hugo.

On Saturday night Hugo insisted on taking Hester out to dinner, as she had refused to let him pay for a stay of only two nights. 'But you will let me pay as usual if I come to work for two weeks in December?'

'Yes, of course. I'll be glad of the money, just before Christmas.'

'Good, that's settled then. Now, where would you like to eat?'

'Would you think it very dull if we went again to *Au Gourmet de l'Isle*? I really love that place.'

'Suits me, Hester. I love it, too.'

They arrived at the restaurant a little before eight-thirty and ordered oysters and *Lotte à l'Armoricaine* and a bottle of *Pouilly Fumé*. The oysters arrived on plates piled with seaweed and cracked ice, with fat wedges of lemon. The waiter brought the wine, showed it to Hugo and opened the bottle, pouring a little into his glass for him to taste.

He passed the glass to Hester. 'You taste it; you know a lot more about wine than I do.'

'You have a touching faith in my capabilities, considering that I am a dedicated consumer of *vin ordinaire*.' She tasted the wine and pronounced it perfect. The waiter poured the wine, wished them *bon appétit* and departed.

Hugo looked at his oysters. 'They look so beautiful, I can hardly bear to eat them.'

'But you'll twist your own arm, I'm sure?'

He laughed, squeezed lemon over the fish and tipped the first one into his mouth, slowly savouring the exquisite taste of the sea. 'The pleasure principle,' he said, smiling. 'I'm totally in favour of it, aren't you?'

'I am. But it's all the more enjoyable if the high points, like this, are rather infrequent.'

'I couldn't agree more. If one has the financial clout to buy whatever one wants, it can become counter-productive. Nothing is a treat any more.'

Hester smiled. 'Are you speaking from personal experience, Hugo?'

'In a vicarious way, yes.'

'Oh. You mean Nelly?'

'Yes, I mean Nelly.' He began to tell her about his father's debts, Gabrieli's wish to buy the farm and Nelly's determination to pay off the bank, to make it possible for Hugo to sell it to Gabrieli at the current market price.

'And how do you feel about that?'

'I would much rather she didn't. It's very generous of her, she means well, but I feel quite strongly that it's not the right thing to do at all.'

The waiter took away the empty plates and brought the *Lotte* in its fragrant red sauce. He put a dish of plain boiled potatoes on the table and a fresh basket of bread. He filled their glasses, put the bottle back in its cooler and left them. They ate in a pleasurable silence for a while, concentrating on the delicious food. Then Hugo put down his fork and looked at Hester seriously, his blue eyes misty behind his spectacles.

'Does it worry you, me talking about all this? Am I spoiling our dinner?'

Hester looked up, surprised. 'No, not at all. I've never been much of a one for polite social chit-chat myself. And talking seriously has never interfered with my intense enjoyment of food.' She smiled and took a sip of wine. 'Do go on, Hugo, please, if it helps to talk.'

'The thing is, I just feel that brandishing the cheque-book like that will result in two things. One, I shall be under an even greater obligation to Nelly than I already am. Don't forget, she has already shelled out a bomb for air fares, hotel bills and so on, in addition to paying the bulk of the bills at home, all the time. I'm not proud of that, but left to myself I wouldn't have such a grand lifestyle, obviously.' He looked at Hester with a wry smile. 'My earnings are modest, and that's a gross exaggeration.'

'And the second reason?'

'The second reason is Gabrieli. He is so dear to me, I can't bear the thought of not treating him as an equal, which he is. If I let Nelly do this for him, and me, it will be a typical piece of colonial paternalism; I know he would resent it bitterly.'

'So what do you think is the best way of dealing with the problem?'

'I think Gabrieli should offer the market price for the farm, and then tough it out. Apart from everything else, he has a highly-qualified accountant for a wife, a most impressive woman. They don't need any favours from me.'

The waiter came back, removed their plates and brought a flat basket of cheeses. Hester took a piece of *chèvre* and a piece of *Livarot*, and thought for a moment before replying. 'I can understand why Nelly wants to do this. I don't know her, of course, but from what you have told me she seems to have what I can only describe as a highly developed social conscience, and a feeling of shame about her wealth. She needs to share it, to make herself feel less guilty.'

'So you think I should let her do it?' Hugo spoke very quietly, without looking at her.

'No, I don't. I think you're quite right to resist. I'm just saying that I *understand* her point of view; that doesn't mean I think she's right.'

After dinner they walked slowly home through the narrow, ancient streets and Hugo told her about his tentative idea of writing a life of Marguerite de Valois.

'What a subject to choose. They were a really wild lot, the Valois. If they weren't murdering people, they were jumping into bed with each other.'

Hugo laughed. 'I know, that's what tempts me. It'll be fun, after the serious business of politicking clerics, won't it?' He did not add that it would also be the perfect reason for his continuing visits to France.

Later, lying in Basil's narrow bed, Hugo realized that this was the first time since his parents' death that he had felt comparatively happy, and the thought saddened him.

At the end of October Basil got a call from Patrick, inviting him to an interview with the newsroom chiefs.

301

He flew to Paris the next day and attended the interview. There had not been time to get a haircut or worry about what to wear, so he turned up looking his usual shambolic self and did his best to feel as relaxed as he looked. He was spoken to at length by various people in his three languages, switching rapidly from one to another, then did some voice tests. Then they told him to go and sit in the corridor. After twenty minutes a girl dressed in jeans and carrying a clip-board appeared and told him to come back. She smiled at him quite reassuringly, and he followed her back to the interview-room. They offered him a six-month trial as a trainee, and mentioned a starting salary far greater than his present one. He accepted without hesitation, shook hands with everyone, agreed to start work at the beginning of December, and left, feeling as if he were walking two feet above the ground. He asked the kind secretary the way to Patrick's office, and she took him there.

'He may not be there, he may be editing or something.' She knocked and poked her head round the door. 'Oh, good, you're here. You've got a visitor.' She held the door open for Basil, who thanked her and entered the room.

'I can tell by your face that it went well.' Patrick smiled kindly and shook Basil's hand.

'Well, it's only a six-month trial, but I'm delighted, of course.'

'Congratulations. That's all you need, the foot in the door. You'll be fine, you'll see.'

'Well, I hope so. God, talk about metamorphosis! One moment I'm rather feebly beavering away among a lot of dusty documents, and the next I'm in this extraordinarily exciting place, in an unbelievable job.'

'It'll be pretty believable when you're dead tired,

hungry, needing a bath and probably scared stiff in some of the hot spots in which you may find yourself before very long.'

'But think of the money,' said Basil and they both laughed.

Patrick looked at his watch. 'Let's get a cab, and go and winkle Olivia out of the Beaux-Arts, and have a drink to celebrate, shall we?' Before leaving, he picked up the phone, got an outside line and dialled a number. 'Anna? I'll be about half an hour late. I'm just taking Basil Rodzianko and Olly for a drink at the *Flore*. Yes, he got the job; great, isn't it? Yes, I'll tell him. I will. I do, too. OK, darling, 'bye.' He replaced the phone. 'Anna sends *félicitations* and says you must come and dine, once you're settled here.'

'How kind of her. I'd love to.'

They got a cab and drove to the Rue Bonaparte, arriving at the art school just as a gaggle of students emerged from the building and congregated in the courtyard in chattering groups. Basil leapt out of the cab and ran towards Olivia, who was standing with her back to him talking to two young men. Her long fair plait, tied at the end with a twist of fabric, hung down her back over her grey pullover, which reached almost to the ankles of her Doc Marten boots. Basil's heart turned over when he saw her. He came up behind her and touched her lightly on the shoulder.

'Olivia?'

She whirled round, dropping her files and books and then flung herself into his arms. He held her close, ignoring the smirks of the two young students. 'You got it?'

'I did.'

'Oh Baz, that's great; that's terrific. I knew you would.'

'Come on, Patrick's here, in that taxi. We're going to have a drink, to celebrate.' Basil gathered up her papers and books, and they ran to the cab together.

At the *Flore* Patrick bought champagne and he and Olivia raised their glasses to Basil and wished him a great future.

'I couldn't have got even this far without your help, both of you. Thank you, from my heart. I just hope that I won't let you down.'

'You won't, I know.' Olivia leaned sideways to kiss Basil.

'No, you won't, I'm quite sure.' Patrick rose to his feet. 'I'm going to leave you two to get on with your celebration; it's quite obvious you don't need me. We're off to Normandy first thing in the morning for the weekend, so I probably won't see you again, Basil, until you start work. I'll look forward to that, and say goodbye for the moment.'

Basil stood up, shook hands with Patrick and thanked him again.

'It's nothing.' Patrick kissed Olivia, flagged down a passing cab and drove away.

'What an amazing man,' said Basil. 'You're lucky to have him for a stepfather, Olivia.'

'You don't have to tell *me* that Baz; I know.' She looked at him over the rim of her glass, her blue eyes shining. 'When I was a child, I was rather in love with him. Still am, a bit.'

'More than with me?'

'No, Baz, not more than with you. I'm not longing to go to *bed* with Patrick. I just love him, that's all.'

'I hope you're still longing to go to bed with me?'

'What do you think?' She leaned against him, and he turned his head and kissed her. 'Talking of which,' said Olivia, 'it's a bit of luck they're going to Normandy, isn't it?'

'I'll drink to that,' said Basil, and raised his glass. They sat holding hands, talking, happy to be together, until the bottle was empty. 'I feel slightly pissed,' he said. 'I don't know whether it's the champagne, or being here with you, or what.'

'We should eat; it's half past eight, anyway.'

'Where would you like to go? Is there somewhere nice that's pretty close?'

'Why don't we have bacon and eggs here? It's one of their specials.'

'Are you sure? Wouldn't you rather go to a proper restaurant?'

'Not specially. As a matter of fact, I absolutely adore bacon and eggs. In my view, a real English breakfast is one of the great classic meals; though not necessarily at breakfast time.'

They ate double helpings of bacon and eggs, most of a baguette and some cheese, and drank coffee. Then they walked slowly to the Quai des Grands-Augustins, their arms round each other.

'Now that I'm gainfully employed, I'll get Hester to write to Maurice Coburg about renting the apartment, shall I? Is that what you'd like?'

'Yes, Baz, it is.'

'Really? You wouldn't rather be somewhere round here, nearer the Beaux-Arts?'

'No, I think it would be much nicer to be on our own, not always bumping into people, don't you?' She slid her arm round Basil, underneath his jacket, and lifted her face to his. 'Shall we go out there tomorrow,' she said, 'and look at it again?'

Basil kissed her and held her close to him. 'Yes, let's do that.' At the door to her building he handed over her files and books. 'Goodnight, my love. I'll call for you about ten, OK?'

'Yes, great. I'll see you then.' Someone emerged from the creaky old lift in the hall, and Olivia ran to grab the gate before it could close and begin its ascent without her. 'Goodnight,' she called, as the gate gave its soft metallic clang and the lift took her up and away from him.

Basil walked quickly away, across the Pont St-Michel and along the riverside to Notre Dame, floodlit and beautiful. He walked round the cathedral to the Pont St-Louis and down the Rue St-Louis-en-l'Ile to Hester's little street. He rang the bell, and in a few minutes she appeared.

'Oh, hello, it's you, Baz. What a surprise. Come on up.'

'I tried to phone you last night, but you were out. I thought of trying again later, but I thought you might have gone to bed. I flew over this morning, for an interview.'

'And?'

'I've got the job. Well, actually, it's a six-month trial to start with.'

'Well done; clever old you.' Hester kissed him.

'I hope.'

'When do you start?'

'Beginning of December. This flat of Maurice's at Pigalle, could you propose me as a tenant? I'm going to be quite well paid, thank God, so I'll be able to afford it.'

'Of course,' said Hester, rather relieved that he didn't want to move back to his old room permanently. 'I'm sure he'll be delighted. He said low rent to right person; you'll be excellent.'

* * *

In the morning, Basil took the key to the Pigalle apartment and walked back across the islands in the crisp autumn sunshine to Grands-Augustins. The little lift seemed unwilling to appear, so he climbed the stairs to the top floor, found Olivia's door and knocked. There was no response. He waited for a few moments, then knocked again, louder. He heard noises within, then the door opened a crack, still on the chain, and Olivia's blue eyes peered out. She undid the chain and opened the door. She appeared to be wearing nothing but a towel.

'Hi,' she said, 'come in. You're early, I was just having a bath.'

Basil entered the room and she closed the door. She turned towards him and he took her in his arms and kissed her. 'Olivia, my darling, how do you expect me to keep my hands off you, dressed like that? Or rather, not dressed?'

Olivia laughed and let the towel drop to the floor. 'Do you want to keep your hands off me?'

'No, of course I don't.'

'Well, what are we waiting for?'

At noon, they ate a curious lunch of dried sausage, oatcakes and olives in bed, and drank a glass of white wine. Happy and relaxed, Basil leaned against the pillows and gazed around him at Olivia's room, taking in the extraordinary collection of junk, an eclectic mix of retro-camp and real treasures that formed the background to her private, secret life. Several years of enthusiastic hunting in flea-markets had resulted in the bizarre accumulation of her possessions. From the exposed roof-timbers of the attic room hung many rusty iron bird-cages, their doors standing open, a few housing pots of ivy, their long trailing stems carefully threaded through the narrow bars to descend in luxurious green showers. On a small round walnut table near the shuttered window stood an alabaster bust of a *belle époque* beauty, swan-necked and with a delicately straight, though damaged nose. Her heavy mass of sculpted hair was piled on top of her head. Olivia had wound an orange-and-yellow chiffon scarf *à l'indienne* around her forehead, and when the shutters were open she gazed longingly across the *quai* to the Ile de la Cité. The walls were covered in exhibition posters, unframed prints and a few small valuable paintings in gilded frames. The big shabby sofa was piled with soft cushions, some covered in threadbare antique fabrics, some in *gros-point*, and a frayed cashmere shawl was draped over the back. Books and magazines were piled everywhere, on the floor and on the long, low glass coffee-table in front of the sofa, with large chrome 1930s lamps on either side. Facing the window, and beside the small *coin cuisine* was a life-size wooden statue of a bishop in full ecclesiastical robes and mitre, his left hand carrying a crozier, his right hand raised in blessing. His rather stern Byzantine face was blackened with age and dirt, as were his hands, but the mitre and vestments still revealed traces of their original bright paints and gilding. Next to the bishop, a human skeleton was suspended from the ceiling, his thin arm draped in a friendly way round the bishop's neck.

'Love the bishop,' said Basil, smiling, 'not too sure about his chum.'

Olivia laughed. 'Daft, isn't it? A terrific cliché too. It was Josh's idea. I got the skeleton from a sale of medical-school stuff, I needed it anyway for anatomy, and Josh helped me rig him up. He wanted to put a rope round his neck, but I drew the line at that.'

'That's your brother, yes? Does he still have a room here?'

'Yes, it's the door next to mine on the landing.'

'Is it as fantastic as this place?'

'No way. It's a stark white cube, just a single bed with a black blanket, stainless steel shelving, black music-system, black-leather Mies Van der Rohe chair. Tiny white shower and loo; gas-ring and black kettle. That's it.'

'Mr Minimalism?'

'Absolutely.'

'The studio at Pigalle is a bit like that. Not terribly cosy, is it?'

'No, but it's a great space to work in. I expect we'll spend quite a lot of our time somewhere else, don't you?' She looked at him, smiling provocatively, her slender arms folded behind her head as she leaned against the pillows.

'Come here, you naughty thing.' He pulled her to him, laughing. 'You're insatiable, aren't you?'

'Isn't it lovely?'

'Yes, that's exactly what it is.'

They spent a happy afternoon at Pigalle, planning small changes to make the apartment seem more like their own place, less redolent of its owner.

'It will be fine with some rugs and books, and the heating on. More plants would be good too, and my music-system. It could be lovely.'

'You're right,' said Basil. 'I've got hundreds of books in London. There's loads of room for them here; we could easily fix some shelves without touching his pristine walls.' He looked coldly at Maurice's construction. 'I wonder how many books were destroyed to make that thing?'

'I wonder.' Olivia looked at it seriously. 'It does have something to say though, doesn't it?'

'Yes,' said Basil sternly, 'lots of burnt books. It's an exercise in vandalism.'

'Perhaps they were just cookery books or railway timetables?'

'Or the Bible?'

'Baz!'

'Well, you know what I mean. It's the principle I care about.'

'I know.'

They watered the plants carefully, checked the windows and left the apartment, double locking the door. They ran down the ugly concrete stairs, and walked in the twilight back up the Rue Pigalle towards the *métro* station, catching a glimpse of the *Sacré Cœur* perched high above them as they went.

They got off at Cité, where they parted temporarily, Olivia to go ahead to Grands-Augustins where she said she had something to do, and Basil to buy the food and wine for their supper. He hurried along the Quai aux Fleurs and across the Pont St-Louis to the smaller island to shop at the little establishments he knew best. He bought bread, butter, cheese, salad and two little tournedos. Then he bought ceps and two beautiful golden pears, freckled and honey-smelling. He chose some wine, and then saw a large wicker basket outside the mini-market, filled with seaweed and ice and still displaying a few dozen oysters. Unable to resist, he bought a dozen, and some lemons. Laden with his shopping, he made his way back across the Pont St-Louis. He hurried along the Rue du Cloître

Notre-Dame, scarcely noticing the cathedral in his desire to get back to Olivia as quickly as he could. As he turned the corner into the Place du Parvis, a figure stepped out of the shadows just in front of him.

'Baz?' It was Giò.

'Giò! What are you doing here?'

'I might ask you the same question, Baz.'

'I live here, remember?'

'Really? Aren't you going in the wrong direction?'

'What is all this, Giò? Are you keeping tabs on me, or what?'

Giò looked miserably at Basil. 'I'm afraid I have been, yes. I know I shouldn't do it, but I can't stop myself.' His voice shook, he sounded close to tears.

'Giò, please. Don't be upset.'

'I can't help being upset. You keep coming to Paris, and you don't get in touch. Why?'

'Let's go and sit inside for a minute,' said Basil gently, touched by the misery of the other. They went into the cathedral, where Vespers was being sung in the choir at the far end of the great echoing building. The sound of the beautiful polyphonic music seemed to float high into the upper air and reverberate around the encircling stone cloister. They sat down in a row of empty seats at the back and Basil stowed his shopping bags out of sight. They sat together without speaking for a few minutes, listening to the music, then Giò spoke, his voice scarcely more than a whisper.

'Baz?'

'Yes.'

'Why are you avoiding me?'

Basil shifted uncomfortably in his seat and sighed. 'I haven't been avoiding you particularly, Giò. I've been busy.'

'Too busy to make a phone call? To come out for a drink?'

Basil stared at his feet, but did not reply.

Giò touched his arm, forcing Basil to look at him. 'I thought we were friends? Perhaps more than friends? If that's not the case, why did you come out with me in the first place? Why did you lead me on?'

'I don't know,' said Basil uneasily. 'It was stupid of me and I'm sorry if I hurt you.'

'So that's it, is it? End of story? We can't be friends? You've changed your mind, just like that?'

'I didn't say that,' said Basil, feeling appallingly guilty and embarrassed. 'There's no reason why we can't see each other from time to time, is there?'

Giò turned to him, his face alight with hope. 'Come home with me now, Baz, please?'

'I can't, Giò. I'm busy.'

Giò's face fell. He looked at the shopping bags and flushed angrily.

'With Olivia?'

'Yes.'

'And after supper?'

'None of your business, Giò.'

'It *is* my bloody business, you bastard! And in any case, you won't get away with it,' he added spitefully, 'I told her you were gay.'

'Really? In that case, Giò, you might force me to drop you.'

At this threat Giò's anger crumbled. 'I'm sorry, I don't want to make you angry or to alienate you in any way. It's OK if we're just friends, nothing more, really. Just don't drop me altogether, Baz, it's all I ask.' He pulled a handkerchief from his pocket and blew his nose, and the sound echoed round the building. He gave a little snort of nervous laughter, and looked at Basil, red-eyed and humiliated.

Basil's heart melted with pity, he put his arm round Giò's shoulder and hugged him. 'I won't drop you, I promise.'

They left the cathedral and parted at the door, Giò towards the *Rive Droite* and Basil to Grands-Augustins. The lift took him slowly up to the top floor, and Olivia. He tapped on the door and she let him in, taking the shopping bags from him.

'What kept you? You've been ages.'

'Have I? I suppose I'm not a very efficient shopper yet. I live on Indian take-aways in London.' Basil looked around him, thankful to be back in this warm, safe haven. Olivia had lit night-lights in all her bird-cages and the little flames sent moth-like flickering shadows across the low ceiling. She had set the coffee-table for two, with candles burning inside tall glass lanterns. The room looked comfortingly domestic and intimate, and Basil took off his jacket, beginning to calm down, to unwind and forget the disturbing image of Giò's ravaged face.

'Could you open the wine, Baz?'

He crossed the room to the *coin cuisine*, where Olivia was unpacking the shopping and setting out the elements of their supper on the white tiles of the work-top. It looked beautiful, like a still-life. Basil put his arms round her and covered her breasts with his hands, holding her body against his, inhaling the smell of her hair. 'God,' he said quietly, 'I am so *glad* to be here; you have no idea.'

She twisted round in his embrace and folded her arms tightly around his neck. 'Are you really? Truly really? Absolutely truthfully really?'

'I love you, Olivia. Will that do?'

'Yes, that'll do.' She lifted her face to his and as they kissed, Olivia noticed a faint, familiar scent; it was Giò's after-shave, the unmistakable *Rose Geranium*. For a second, she was gripped by a sickening fear and revulsion, and very nearly recoiled from his embrace. Then her natural common sense reasserted itself. That's impossible she told herself; if they did meet, it couldn't have been for more than a few minutes, certainly not long enough for anything to happen. Fleetingly, she was tempted to ask him outright: have you just seen Giò? but dismissed the thought at once. Stay cool Olivia she said to herself, no need to make a drama out of nothing. She put her hands on either side of his face and kissed him again. 'Let's eat shall we? I'm starving.'

'Me too,' said Basil, releasing her reluctantly, 'I'm absolutely ravenous.'

Chapter Sixteen

On Sunday evening Basil flew back to London to work out his notice at the British Museum. His mood of excitement and euphoria at having got the job in Paris extended into his daily life and he quite enjoyed the work he had previously found so boring and pointless. The days passed comparatively quickly and in the evenings he sorted his books, cleaning them all carefully, and packing them tidily into small tea-chests. He did not want to worry Olivia with the business of receiving them and getting them to Pigalle, so he arranged with Hugo to leave the chests with him, to be collected by a carrier and delivered to the new flat after he and Olivia had moved in. Nelly looked with some disfavour at the stack of tea-chests in her hall that grew larger as the days passed, but said nothing. Basil left his father's painting until his own departure, intending to carry it with him in the car and give it to Olivia as a demonstration, if she needed such a thing, of his serious feelings towards her. He telephoned her nearly every night, with a total disregard for the day of reckoning when he would have to pay the bill.

He was so busy that he did not have much time for introspection, but sometimes as he lay in bed late at night he thought about Giò and felt a bit sad and guilty, but he did not write or phone him. Much more, he thought about Olivia, longing to be with her, to be part of the stimulating and creative world which she seemed to believe belonged to them quite naturally, like breathing, or eating, or making love. He worried that he had not been totally straight with her and would have given much to know what her reaction had been when Giò had told her that he thought Basil was gay. Every time he thought of that he felt a stab of fear and pain. He was haunted by the possibility of losing Olivia, and Patrick, the new job, the apartment and everything that offered him such a huge and wonderful chance of happiness.

In the middle of November Patrick tapped on Olivia's door and told her that he had found a suitable slot in the following year for a piece about George Rodzianko. He had developed the idea into a programme about three neglected but important painters, and he thought there was a possibility of a simultaneous exhibition, first in Paris, followed by a tour of several cities.

Olivia's eyes widened in surprise and admiration. 'You don't do things by halves, do you?'

Patrick laughed. 'No, I don't, but I do things one step at a time. Could you arrange for me to meet Hester Rodzianko, and maybe prepare the ground a little? I don't want her scared off. From what you tell me, she's a proud and very reserved woman.'

Olivia agreed to arrange an appointment with Hester and at the end of the week she took Patrick to meet her. As they walked together on a misty, grey and rather chilly evening towards the Ile St-Louis, Patrick asked Olivia to be very discreet, not to express her own enthusiasm for the painter's work. His plan was to approach the subject through Hester herself, to allow her to talk about her husband's work and life, his childhood and so on, in her own words and in her own time.

From the beginning it was obvious to Olivia that Hester felt an immediate rapport with Patrick, so she sat quietly on the window-seat looking down through the bare branches of the lime-trees to the courtyard below, while Hester went slowly round the room with Patrick, pausing in front of each painting and talking easily to him, as if she had known him for years. Olivia was not at all surprised; she had observed how Patrick had this curious ability to attract the confidence and trust of people, at the same time himself remaining the most intensely private of men. Only two people, she knew, had an absolute emotional reality for Patrick: her mother, Anna and their little boy, Thomas. Sometimes Olivia had felt slightly excluded, and a little jealous of their happiness and commitment to each other, but in her heart she knew that Patrick was the best and kindest of fathers. She loved him dearly and his strong supportive presence in the background of her life was of immense importance to her.

Hester and Patrick finished their tour of the room, then she led the way to the sofa. 'Would you care to join me in a glass of wine?' She spoke politely, rather formally.

'Thank you, that would be very nice.'

Olivia got up from her seat and came towards them. 'May I help? I can get the wine.'

'Thank you, dear. You know where everything is, of course.'

'Won't be a minute,' said Olivia and went to the kitchen.

Hester sat down on the sofa beside Patrick and smiled at him, her large grey eyes bright behind the horn-rimmed spectacles. 'What a beautiful creature she is, isn't she?'

'Yes, she is. And yet as a child she was quite plain; there was no indication of what was to come. In a sense she invented herself, and re-invents herself all the time. It's the same with her work; it's a process of continual exploration for her. I think she has a lot of talent, and ambition.'

'She has only shown me a few things, some etchings, and life drawings, but I think you're right.' She looked at him, hesitating slightly. 'It was a lucky day for Basil when they met, and kind of you to help him.'

Patrick smiled. 'And a lucky day for Olivia too, perhaps?'

'One hopes so much for the young, and is anxious for them too, at the same moment.'

'But we can only do so much for them, they have to discover everything for themselves in the end, don't they?'

'Absolutely.'

Olivia came back with the wine and three glasses on an old black lacquer tray, with a gilded picture of St Petersburg on it. She set the tray down on the table at Hester's side, poured the wine and handed the glasses. Then she sat down on the little low chair that Hester now thought of as Hugo's.

Patrick took a small loose-leaf file from his pocket, and began to demonstrate to Hester how he proposed to make the film about George, and their life together. He explained that it would be necessary for her to go with his team to Pigalle, to film all the big important pictures with which he intended to illustrate his interview with Hester herself. The filming of the actual interview was to be here in the apartment, and would follow an informal question-and-answer format between Patrick and Hester, intercut with examples of the paintings. He promised to send her a list of the questions, so that she could decide for herself how she wished to reply, either briefly or in greater depth, or not at all, it was to be entirely up to her.

'Well,' said Hester, 'that all seems pretty straight-forward; not half as frightening as I feared.'

Patrick laughed. 'I'll try to make the whole thing totally unfrightening, and with any luck you might even enjoy yourself. And don't forget, any bits you're not happy with can be cut.'

'Thank you, that certainly makes me feel more confident.'

Patrick closed his file. 'There's just one more thing,' he said.

'Yes?'

'If you agree, I want this room to stay exactly as it is. I love the juxtaposition of your own work with that of your husband. It seems to me that they complement each other perfectly, and express exactly your relation-ship with each other.' He looked at Hester rather anxiously, fearing that she might consider this too invasive of her private life and feelings, and prepared to back-track at once if she objected.

Instead, she gazed thoughtfully into her glass for a moment, then looked at Patrick, and smiled. 'Thank you; I should like that very much.'

When they had gone, Hester looked at her watch: seven-twenty. I'd better shop for supper now, she thought, it's getting late. She got her coat and bag, and set off towards the shops. The chill November mists rose from the river and drifted wraith-like through the narrow streets, smelling of fog. Hating the thought of the approaching winter, Hester shivered and fastened the top button of her coat.

On his last night in London, having handed over the keys to his flat to the new tenant, Basil put his suitcases and his father's painting, carefully wrapped in corrugated cardboard, into the boot of his car and drove round to the Turnbulls. He was to have supper and spend the night with them, and drive to Paris in the morning. The children were on their way upstairs with Eva when he rang the front-door bell.

Phyllida opened the door and let him in. 'Hello, Baz. You're just in time to say goodnight, we've got to go to bed. Boring old school tomorrow, and all that.'

'Shame.' Baz kissed her, and Sophie and Gertrude ran down the stairs again to be kissed, too.

'Come on, children,' said Eva, smiling shyly at Basil. 'Say goodnight to your uncle and come along, please.'

'He's not our uncle, he's Baz,' said Sophie.

'Baz,' echoed Gertrude softly, holding his trouser leg.

'He's called Basil Rodzianko,' said Phyllida. 'And this is Fraülein Eva Schwartz.'

'How do you do?'

'How do you do? Come along now, girls, please. It's my evening off, don't forget.' She turned to Basil. 'Dr Turnbull is not home yet, but Hugo is in his room. You can go in, please?'

'Thank you.' Basil said goodnight to the children, then tapped on Hugo's door and went in.

Hugo looked up from his work, saw Basil and smiled. 'Come in.' He looked at his watch. 'Good heavens, is it as late as that? I must stop.' He put down his pen, and waved a hand at the chair on the other side of the desk. 'All done? Ready for the off?'

'For a wonder, yes. I bet you'll be glad to get rid of all those tea-chests. I've arranged for the carrier to collect them next Wednesday, is that OK?'

'I'm sure. I'll be here anyway, and Eva too, probably.'

'Thanks, that's great. You don't realize what a lot of stuff you've got, especially books, until you move.'

'I suppose that's right.' Hugo looked rather vaguely round his book-lined room. 'God knows how many I've got here, and there are more upstairs.'

Basil looked at Hugo and suddenly realized that he and his oldest friend were about to be parted, for the first time. 'I'm going to miss you, Hugo.'

'You won't get rid of me as easily as that, old dear. I'm coming over to Hester's next week, to go through my copy-editor's notes, so I expect I'll see you then?'

'Great. You must come and see the apartment at Pigalle, and meet Olivia.'

'Ah, Olivia. The sister of that chap Joe Whatsit.'

'Niece, as a matter of fact.'

Hugo looked startled, but he said nothing, simply smiled.

'Don't *you* start, Hugo. It's quite OK, you'll see.'

'I didn't say anything,' said Hugo.

'You didn't have to; the face spoke volumes.' They laughed, and Hugo took a bottle and glasses from a drawer in his desk, and poured whisky for them both.

'Best of luck in the new job, Baz. I envy you going to live in Paris.'

'It's marvellous. I can still hardly believe it, myself.'

The front door slammed. In a moment they heard footsteps and Nelly put her head round the door.

'Hello, Baz. You've got everything organized, then?'

'Hello, love. Yes, it all seems to be under control.' He got up and embraced her.

'Drink?' said Hugo, picking up the bottle.

'No, I can't. Eva's going out, so I'm duty cook tonight.'

'Can't we help?' said Basil.

'No, no, it's OK. There's not much to do, really. You two come down in about half an hour, when the dust has settled.'

'Are you sure?' said Hugo.

'Quite sure.' She left the room, closing the door quietly behind her.

'It doesn't seem very fair to let her do it all,' said Basil, 'especially after a hard day's work in that vile hospital.'

'She prefers it this way. She'd say if she wanted help.'

Basil decided to change the subject, sensing uneasily the coolness between his old friends. 'What are you planning for Christmas, anything exciting?'

'We're going to Florizel, as usual. My mother-in-law will be on her own otherwise. Not that she seems to mind that, but Nelly doesn't like it. And the children love it there, even in winter.'

'So Nelly won't be on duty this year?'

'No. She'll be working right up to the holiday, then fly over on Christmas Eve. I'll be going on ahead with the girls as soon as they break up. That means Eva can have a couple of weeks off, with her family.'

'Well, sounds a good plan.'

'Should work well. Eva's been a terrific help, she deserves a proper break.' Hugo poured more whisky. 'You go down and chat to Nelly, Baz. I'll just run up and settle the girls, and tell them a story.' He turned off his working-light and they went into the hall, carrying their glasses.

Basil looked at his suitcases, and then at Hugo. 'I wish you were coming to Paris with me.'

'Christ, don't tempt me! So do I.' Holding his glass carefully in front of him, Hugo mounted the stairs, and Basil went slowly down to the kitchen. He found Nelly making a dressing for the salad, already washed and arranged in a deep china bowl, resembling green overlapping cabbage leaves.

'Pretty bowl,' said Basil, sitting down. 'I don't remember it.'

'It was Papa's. I don't use it often, it's rather precious. But on special occasions it gets an airing.'

'Is this a special occasion, seeing the back of me?'

Nelly smiled at him gently, pushing the copper-coloured hair from her eyes. 'You know, Baz. End of an era and all that. We shall miss you.'

'And I shall miss you; all of you.'

Nelly laughed. 'I don't suppose you will, at all. You'll be far too wrapped up in your new job, and with Olivia, for that.'

'How's it going, Nelly? You and Hugo seem to have got over the Kenya thing pretty well?'

'Yes and no. We don't talk about it, but the money side still isn't sorted. Lawyers never hurry themselves, do they?'

'So you're just letting things take their course, then?'

'Sort of.' She flashed a quick look at him, poured the dressing over the salad, and began turning the leaves, coating them carefully with the garlic-smelling oily mixture. 'All I *have* done is write to the lawyers and asked for a written breakdown of the figures. I felt that it was important that Hugo should be in full possession of the facts of the situation, whatever the outcome.'

'I see. Well, good.' He did not dare to ask whether or not Hugo knew about her letter; he thought that very probably he did not.

Nelly lifted the lid of the pan of potatoes and prodded them with a fork. 'Nearly done.' She put a bottle of wine on the table and handed the corkscrew to Basil. 'Could you? I'll just get out the casserole.' She took the big black cast-iron pot from the oven and set it on the work-top. She lifted the lid and a delicious smell of garlic, herbs and wine filled the kitchen.

Basil sniffed appreciatively. 'Mm. That doesn't smell like good old Marks and Sparks.'

'It isn't. I had this brilliant idea and got an Elizabeth David paperback for Eva, on the pretext of its being very good for her English.'

'It seems to have worked.'

'Absolutely. And she always makes such vast quantities that there's always plenty for the girls next day. I don't really approve of fish-fingers and tinned spaghetti all the time.'

'And the girls?'

'They love it, thank God.'

They heard Hugo's steps on the stairs. Nelly straightened the knives and forks on the table and drained the potatoes.

'Smells good,' said Hugo, putting his whisky glass on the draining board.

'Venison stew, courtesy of Eva.'

'My, she's a fast learner.'

'Well, she can read a cookery book, can't she?' Nelly handed Hugo the serving spoons. 'There you are. You dish, while I run up and say goodnight to the girls, OK?'

The first week of December was a busy one for Basil. His days passed chaotically but satisfyingly as he tried to commit to memory, later writing up, all the technicalities of his new profession. He would have liked to discuss things with Patrick, but thought it important to stand on his own two feet, like any other newcomer. He was reluctant, in any case, to reveal to his colleagues the part played by Patrick in getting him the interview in the first place, so if he caught sight of him in the canteen or in the muddling and endless corridors, he either pretended not to see him or merely gave a small wave of his hand. For his part, Patrick understood perfectly what was in Basil's mind and took equal care not to embarrass him.

The evenings at Pigalle were just as busy. Basil was erecting angle-iron shelving to house his books. It was not a difficult task, but needed a lot of time tightening the many nuts and bolts, to make sure that the shelves were perfectly rigid. They had brought over Olivia's music-system and some rugs and cushions from Grands-Augustins. She had also been to the street market in the Rue de Buci and bought several large green plants to embellish the apartment, and they transported them to Pigalle in the back seat of the Riley, with the hood down. Humping them up the four flights of stairs was not so easy, but worth it for the softening effect they had on the severity of the studio. At last the work was finished, and the books unpacked and stacked on the shelves.

'That's better,' said Basil, 'it feels more like home now, doesn't it?'

'It's great. All we need now is a couple of friendly lamps and a chair or two.'

'There's just one more thing, Olivia. Open that package, it's for you.'

She had been wondering about the corrugated-cardboard parcel, tied with string. Now she undid the knots and unwrapped the package. Inside was one of George Rodzianko's early paintings, of a small boy standing on the edge of a grey sea, which became a paler grey sky. She looked at it for a long time, then raised her eyes to Basil, sitting cross-legged on the floor a little way away.

'It's you, isn't it?'

'Probably, I don't know.' He smiled. 'You'll have to ask Hester, she'll know.'

Olivia put the painting carefully against the wall, and then knelt in front of Basil. She took his face in her hands and kissed him gently, almost chastely, as a mother might a child. 'Thank you, Baz, very, very much. You couldn't have given me anything in the world I'd treasure more.'

'I treasure it too. That's why I've given it to you; I want it to be the most treasured possession of both of us, always.'

Olivia stared at him. 'Do you mean that, Baz? Really?'

'I do. Really.'

'Really always?'

'Yes, if you'll have me.'

She leaned against him, her eyes closed, not wanting to break the spell. After a few minutes, Basil lifted her face towards his and kissed her softly. 'I could sit here all night, just holding you like this, but we have Hugo and Hester coming to supper, remember?'

'My God, I'd quite forgotten.' Olivia sat up. 'What's the time?'

'Nearly half past.'

'Half past what?'

'Six.'

'Is it really? We haven't even shopped yet. They might come when we're out.'

'Don't panic,' said Basil, 'it's all in the fridge.'

'Baz! I don't believe you.'

'Go and look.'

Olivia scrambled to her feet and went to the tiny kitchen. In the fridge she found what looked like the entire contents of a delicatessen. Russian salad, *blinis* with sour cream and caviare, prawns in a herby vinaigrette, oatcakes, several cheeses, butter, *saucissons secs*, vodka and champagne chilling in the door.

'You forgot the bread!'

Basil exploded with laughter and grabbed her from behind, closing the fridge door at the same time. 'I did not forget the bread, miss. I'm going out now to get it, while you have a bath and put on something ravishing.'

'Good thinking; I'm filthy from all these beastly books. If you like, you can come in with me.' She put her arms round him and hugged him. 'Thank you, darling Baz, it was a wonderful surprise; two wonderful surprises.'

'I'd love to share the bath with you, but duty calls. I must go *now*, at once, and do my shopping.'

When he came back with the bread Olivia had set the table in the conservatory and lit candles. Some she had put on the table, others were stuck in glass tumblers and placed around the studio. With most of Maurice's spotlights turned off the effect was magical, with the added bonus of the starlit view over the rooftops from the conservatory, and the floodlit wedding-cake spires of the *Sacré-Cœur*, glimpsed through the narrow window by the bedroom door.

'You've got ten minutes,' said Olivia, 'just time for a quick bath?'

Basil looked at her, stunning in the long Indian coat in which he had first seen her. She still wore the little red slippers, but the old jeans had been replaced with soft baggy white silk trousers. Her hair was loose and tied round her head with the piece of scarlet silk he remembered so well. He went to the kitchen and found that she had arranged all the food on plain white dishes, ready for the table. He put down the bread, then took champagne from the fridge. He carried the bottle to the conservatory, opened it and filled two glasses, handing one to Olivia.

'To you, Olivia.'

'And to you, Baz.'

He managed to have a quick wash, brush his hair and put on a clean shirt before the doorbell rang to announce the arrival of Hester and Hugo, she slightly out of breath from the climb up the stairs. They sat round the table in the conservatory, since the only other place to sit was the floor, and drank champagne.

Hugo was enchanted by the apartment and the view, and said so at once. 'How clever of you to find it.'

'We didn't,' said Baz, and explained about Maurice. 'A hell of a lot of my father's paintings are here. We'll show them to you later; is that OK, Olivia?'

'Of course; delighted.' She smiled at Hester, who smiled back. Neither of them had told Basil about the projected film, Hester preferring to wait until all the details had been finalized, the script approved, and Maurice's permission obtained to bring cameras to his studio.

Basil and Olivia brought the food and the vodka from the kitchen, and placed the dishes on the table.

'It's only a picnic, I'm afraid,' said Basil.

'But a very *grand* picnic,' said Hester, 'it's lovely.'

It was after midnight when the guests departed. 'Thank God it's Sunday tomorrow, we don't have to get up early,' said Basil, carrying the dishes through to the little kitchen, where Olivia was loading the dishwasher, one of the pleasant surprises of the apartment. 'Typical of a man,' Olivia had remarked, 'dishwasher, yes; washing-machine, no.' However, they had found an old-fashioned *blanchisserie* quite close by and they took the sheets and shirts there to be washed.

'You go and have your bath, Baz. I can finish all this, it won't take a minute.'

'Sure?'

'Absolutely.'

When she had finished the clearing-up Olivia wiped down the table carefully, then sat for a few minutes gazing out over the rooftops and chimneypots. She thought about Basil. He was obviously stimulated and increasingly engrossed in his new work, and seemed very happy to be sharing the apartment with her. As the days passed she was becoming less doubtful about his feelings for her, more sure that he did in fact love her; though whether he would ever love her as much as she knew herself to be capable of loving him, she neither knew nor particularly cared. What's the point? she asked herself. One either does or doesn't, it's not a competition. You can't measure it, like milk, can you? The trick is to grasp the moment, be happy.

She got up and went to the bedroom. She could hear Basil sloshing around in the bath, and smiled. She undressed, hanging her clothes up carefully, and got into bed, enjoying the cool embrace of the cold sheets on her naked body. Bliss, she said to herself.

Basil lay in his bath with his eyes closed, and thought about Olivia. He had never before shared his home with a woman, except of course Hester but that didn't count. He was surprised and delighted at the discovery that the actual domestic bit, quite apart from the sex bit, was so much fun in itself, and he knew that he was definitely planning a future for himself and Olivia. A future, if he managed to become as successful as he hoped and intended to be, that would include a proper house, perhaps a small vineyard in the Touraine for quick access to Paris, maybe children? Throughout his last month in London Basil had become increasingly obsessed with this vision of an enchanted family life with Olivia. Although he had never had unprotected sex with Herbert, he had decided to have himself screened for HIV, to be absolutely sure that it would be safe to think about having children. He had felt unbelievably happy and thankful when the tests had proved negative. Dear old Herbert he thought, maybe it was a one-off for him too?

In spite of his new-found confidence and optimism there still remained a nagging uneasiness at the back of his mind, a consciousness of a grey area in his relationship with Olivia, of important things left unsaid. Sooner or later, he knew that he would have to be honest about his past, even at the considerable risk of her ending their association. The thought of such an eventuality pained him deeply, and the dream of the creeper-covered farmhouse, with vines marching right up to the buildings of the domaine filled his mind. He saw Olivia, followed by a gaggle of little blond children, her own beautiful hair floating behind her, walking along the edge of a hayfield, full of poppies and dog-daisies. What a sentimental fool you're becoming Baz, he said to himself, you sound just like an ad for shampoo. Nevertheless, the general idea was immensely appealing and he knew he wished it more than anything, in the fullness of time.

The water was getting cold and he got out of the bath, dried himself carefully, brushed his teeth and went through to the bedroom, his bare feet silent on the soft Persian rugs. Olivia's eyes were closed, but as he got quietly into bed beside her she opened them and turned towards him, smiling.

'Hello,' she said.

'Hello.' He gazed at the face which had become so

dear to him and decided to speak about Giò, now, before
his courage failed.

'Olivia?'

'Yes?'

'You remember that time when I went shopping
for supper, and when I got back you said "what kept
you"?'

'Yes, I remember.'

'Well, what kept me was Giò.'

'I know.'

'What do you mean, you know? How could you?'

'You smelt of him; of his scent.'

'Christ, how awful. Did I really?'

'Yes, you did, my love.' She reached across the gap
between them and laid her hand on his neck. 'I guessed
you must have bumped into him on the island. What
happened, exactly?'

'He waylaid me on the way home, coming back with
the shopping. He was drunk and upset. I couldn't just
leave him there. We sat in Notre Dame and talked for
a bit, till he felt better. It was awful, as a matter of fact.'

'Yes,' said Olivia slowly. 'I could see you were upset
about something; now I understand.'

'Do you really?' said Basil quietly. Then, determined
to be as truthful as he possibly could be, he told her
first of all about his long-ago relationship with Herbert,
and then about his horrendous night out with Giò.
Finally, he told her of Giò's pleading with him to go on
seeing him, and of his own reluctant promise not to
drop him entirely.

'Poor Giò, how sad he is,' said Olivia. 'I wish he could
be happy.'

'Yes, he is sad, that's the right word for him. It must
be dreadful to be so dependent on others, to have so
little self-reliance.'

331

They were silent for a few minutes, each thinking rather soberly about Giò. Basil, because he felt guilty at having encouraged him; Olivia, because she loved Giò in spite of his occasional malign behaviour. She put her arms round Basil and folded herself against him, feeling small and cherished against his big, comforting body.

'So, how come you smelt of his scent?'

'I imagine because I hugged him.'

'What, in the cathedral?'

'Yes. He looked so desperate, I couldn't bear to leave him like that.'

'You know what they say, don't you?'

'What?'

'Beware of pity.'

Basil tightened his arms round Olivia, and kissed her. 'There's no pity in my relationship with you; that's the last thing that's in my mind. What *is* in my mind though, is how will all this affect us, how do you feel about it, truthfully?'

Olivia thought for a moment, her eyes closed, her cheek against his chest. She could hear his heart beating, loudly and rather fast. He is afraid, she thought, he doesn't want to lose me any more than I want to lose him. 'I don't feel anything, especially,' she said, 'except incredibly happy to be here with you. What happened in the past is one's own business, mine as well as yours; we all have private bits of ourselves. What happens in the future is anyone's guess. It's a risk we all take, don't we, when we love someone?'

There was a long silence, and then Olivia lifted her head and looked at him. He looked back at her seriously, unsmiling. She saw that his eyes were full of tears. 'Olivia, my darling,' he said, 'will you marry me?'

Olivia laughed and kissed him. 'Is it only to ward off the Giòs who fancy you?'

'No, it's because I love you. I would love us to have children; I fantasize about it all the time. I would never betray you, I promise.'

'No,' said Olivia softly, 'I don't believe you would.'

Chapter Seventeen

Hugo looked down through the window beside him and watched the rippled grey sea below become white cliffs and green fields as the plane crossed the English coastline. He was happy that he had had his two weeks with Hester and had seen Basil's new apartment, not to speak of his beautiful young girlfriend. As the aircraft began to lose height and approach the airport, he felt relaxed and quite pleased to be spending Christmas on Florizel, and made up his mind to devote all his energies to his children during the holiday, and to Nelly too, if she would let him.

From Heathrow, he took the underground to Hammersmith and then got a cab home. The house was quiet as he let himself in; Eva and the girls were obviously not back from school yet. He took off his coat and hung it up, picked up the stack of mail on the hall table and went to his room. He sat down at the desk, riffled through the envelopes and extracted a large, official-looking one with a Kenyan stamp and a Nairobi postmark. It was typewritten and addressed, irritatingly, to Dr and Mrs Turnbull. They are so unbelievably inefficient; you'd think they'd manage to get as fundamental a fact as that correct, he said to himself, as he opened the letter. The letter was brief and had a thick wad of enclosures which appeared to be photo-copies of correspondence relating to the farm, together

334

with bank statements. Hugo frowned, switched on his working-lamp and read the letter.

'Dear Dr Turnbull,

Further to your letter of 27th November, in respect of the estate of your late parents, we enclose herewith copies of the documents requested by your good self and look forward to hearing from you further.'

Hugo read the letter twice, and flicked through the photocopies. Then he laid the letter on the desk in front of him, flattening it carefully with his hand. He felt cold and empty, numb with anger and shock. Bloody interfering cow, he thought, I hate her; I really do hate her. The front door banged and he heard the cheerful voices of his daughters and Eva as they took off their coats in the hall. He braced himself to behave normally, if they should notice his coat and come in to see him. But they did not, and thumped down the bare wooden stairs to the kitchen, perhaps to watch the telly before their supper. He poured himself a whisky, and waited.

Three-quarters of an hour later, the front door banged again and Nelly came in. 'Hello, darling,' she said, 'you're back.'

'Yes, I'm back.' Hugo stared at her with cold, stony eyes. Then he pushed the letter across the desk towards her. 'What is the meaning of this?'

Nelly picked the letter up and looked at it. 'They've sent it to the wrong person, stupid things.'

'I see. So you intended that I should be unaware of your correspondence with the lawyers about a matter that concerns no-one at all but my father and me?'

'No, I would have told you at an appropriate time.'

'But what the hell has it got to do with you at all? How many times have I got to tell you to get off my back, for Christ's sake?'

'I was just trying to help, darling.'

'Don't call me darling, especially now when I hate, loathe and detest you and wish we had never met.'

'Hugo, you know that's not true!'

'It *is* true. You are a bossy, domineering and obstinate woman. What seemed attractive when you were a girl is very much less appealing, now that you are older. And it's not just me that thinks so.'

'Oh, really? And who else sees fit to criticize me?'

'Baz, for one. Your mother, for another.'

Nelly folded the letter, and sat down in the chair on the other side of the desk. 'Let's not quarrel,' she said calmly. 'I'm sorry if I hurt your feelings, my dear. Of course, you must do what you think is right.' She looked at the letter, and put it back on the desk. She looked at Hugo and smiled kindly, as if humouring a fractious child. 'But it *is* quite useful to have all the facts and figures, isn't it?'

Hugo crashed his fist down on the desk, upsetting his glass as he did so. 'You never learn, do you, you stupid, obstinate, bloody cow?'

Nelly looked at Hugo, his face white with rage, his body trembling, and stood up. She began to speak, but he cut her short. 'Get out of here and leave me alone, for Christ's sake!'

She went to the door, paused for a second and then left the room, closing the door silently behind her. She went quietly downstairs to the kitchen. Four pairs of eyes looked at her anxiously and she realized that they must have overheard quite a lot.

'Is everything all right, Eva? Have you had a good day?'

'Yes, fine,' said Eva, 'thank you.'

'Had a good day, darlings?'

'Yes, Mum, we're OK,' said Phyllida.

'I think I'll pop up and have a bath, then.' Nelly

poured herself a gin and took it upstairs with her.

'Tell us a story, Eva, please,' said Sophie.

'Which one?'

'Billy Goats Gruff,' said Gertrude.

The next day school broke up, and Eva packed for the children. The day after, she flew to Germany and Hugo took his daughters to Florizel. He had not spoken one word to Nelly, and had coldly ignored her attempts to communicate with him. He had slept in the spare room and worked at his desk in the evenings to avoid any contact. Still full of anger he had sent a fax to the lawyers in Nairobi informing them that Dr Turnbull was his wife, and that he did not wish them to communicate with her in any shape or form, in view of the fact that his father's estate had nothing whatso-ever to do with her. After sending the fax, he left the original on his desk, for Nelly to see if she came snooping in his absence. Rather spitefully, he very much hoped that she would.

During the next few days Nelly was extremely busy at the hospital, and had little time to dwell on her private problems. But at night, coming back to the dark, empty house, anxiety and confusion engulfed her the moment she stepped through the door. She tried to convince herself that Hugo would eventually calm down, and come to understand that her efforts on his behalf were genuine, and made with the best intentions. She sat at the kitchen table, forcing herself to eat but tasting nothing; half-listening to the news or some current-affairs programme of an investigative nature, which would normally have been of riveting interest to her, but now seemed only peripherally absorbing. She drank more than usual and went to bed as late as possible in the hope of getting to sleep quickly, but as soon as she put down her book and turned off the light, she began to ask herself miserably what it was that drew Hugo so frequently to Paris, what was the exact nature of his relationship with a woman old enough to be his mother? Equally, she was tormented by visions of Basil with his new young lover. She felt rejected not only by Hugo, but by the faithful Baz as well, and recognized, painfully, the symptoms of jealousy. She did her best to rationalize the situation, to accept the fact that she was no longer the brilliant, rich and above all young Nelly Tanqueray to whom it came easily to be the most important and desirable person in her peer group. She wished fleetingly that she had a girlfriend to talk to, but such relationships had never had any appeal for her. For one thing, she had always been too busy, preoccupied with her career and her family; for another, she had always regarded Baz as her great friend, almost her private property, and it had been his willing role to listen to her problems and support her in every way. She had not needed a girlfriend.

Now, with a slight feeling of guilt, she acknowledged that it would not have been much fun for Baz to spend the rest of his life in a dull job, and in an on-off relationship with her. She missed his presence in her life, and the reassurance he had always given her of her undiminished powers of attraction. At the end of the day she knew that she should be glad for him, but had to admit that she was not, and unreasonably, felt that Baz had betrayed her.

And Hugo, what of him? He was, after all, her husband and the father of her daughters. She had given him everything, a home, children, freedom from financial worry. What else did he want, for God's sake? Why did he keep going to Paris, to the woman Rodzianko? Why? She lay in the big, lonely bed, trying to find answers to these questions, and could not. Eventually, she turned on the light and went downstairs to make some tea. She carried the mug upstairs and got back into bed. She drank the tea, her eyes wandering round her beautiful bedroom, at the silver-framed wedding photographs, pictures of the children and Hugo, of her mother with Wiggy and Pepys in Florizel, of her father at the Palace. This is stupid, she thought. I don't want my marriage to disintegrate. It's a good one, and worth fighting for. Tomorrow, or rather today, was Thursday, her free day.

'I'll bloody well fly to Paris and see this woman,' she said loudly to the empty room. 'I'll sort her out, once and for all. I'm sick and tired of being messed around, not really knowing what's going on, or where I stand.'

Hester was in the delicate process of floating gold-leaf onto a halo when the doorbell rang. 'Damn,' she said, 'who the hell is that?' She held her gilder's tip bearing its trembling feather-light leaf of gold above the icon, and waited for a few moments, willing the caller to go away. The bell rang again, insistently. She sighed and put the tip carefully down on the calfskin pad. Then she went downstairs and opened the door. A young woman stood under the *porte-cochère*. She had red hair cut in a fringe, and wore an expensive-looking brown suede coat. Hester guessed at once that it was Nelly Turnbull, and immediately sensed trouble. She frowned.

'Yes?'

'Mme Rodzianko?'

'Yes.'

'I'm Nelly Turnbull, Hugo's wife. May I come in?'

Reluctantly, Hester inclined her head and stood aside for Nelly to enter, and climb the narrow staircase. Hester closed the door and followed her up to the landing. 'In here,' she said, going into the kitchen. She indicated a chair and Nelly sat down. Hester seated herself on the other side of the table, folded her hands and waited.

Nelly looked at her levelly. 'I expect you know why I've come here?'

'No, I do not.'

'It's about my husband.'

'Hugo?'

'Yes, Hugo.' Nelly had been going to ask Hester point-blank whether she and Hugo were lovers, but somewhat to her surprise she found herself intimidated by the calm self-assurance of the older woman in her dirty, paint-spattered shirt and baggy old skirt. Her courage failed her; she looked down at her hands, twisting nervously in her lap and tried to think of a less offensive way of approaching the subject.

In the event, Hester spoke first. 'You want to know whether Hugo and I are lovers, don't you?'

'Yes.' Nelly's voice was little more than a whisper, and a dark flush crept up her neck and into her cheeks.

'The answer is we are not, we never have been and never will be,' said Hester sternly.

'I'm so sorry,' said Nelly, and a tear rolled down her blazing cheek. 'I do beg your pardon.'

'It's of no importance.' Hester looked at Nelly and felt a twinge of pity for the younger woman's distress. 'My poor child,' she said gently, 'whatever is the matter?'

At this, Nelly's control deserted her completely and she buried her face in her hands and began to cry, messily and noisily, like a child. Hester let her weep, and after a while she became less hysterical, and in a rather incoherent way, with tears still pouring down her face, she tried to tell Hester about the letter from Nairobi; about Hugo's rage and hatred of her; of her own anger and hurt; and above all, of her own overwhelming desire to do the correct, responsible thing. Rather abruptly, she ran out of words, and blew her nose. She looked at Hester forlornly.

'Sorry about that; it's not like me, at all.'

'Maybe that's the problem?'

'What do you mean, what problem?'

'Maybe it would be better if you didn't always try so hard to be indispensable, to provide all the answers.'

'I don't understand.'

Hester hesitated, then looked at the troubled young woman, red-eyed beneath the shining fringe of coppery hair. 'You know, Nelly, I was a child of the manse, if you know what that means? My father was a vicar, and his church was the central and only real thing in his life. To him, there was never any question of a conflict of beliefs or ideas. If the Bible said something, it was true.'

'But what's that got to do with me?'

'Well, it's just a thought, but I used very often to have the feeling, as a child, that Jesus must have been quite a tiresome man in many respects, always doing what he believed to be right; always absolutely confident that he *was* right; that sort of implacable authority, the high moral ground; the faith thing.' She looked mildly at Nelly, who stared back at her uncomprehendingly. 'You know,' Hester continued, 'I've always found St Peter a much more sympathetic character, personally.

341

Full of human weakness and frailty; but he got himself crucified too, in the end, didn't he?'

Nelly looked mutinous, and stared at her hands. 'You're confusing me,' she said sulkily, 'I don't see where all this is leading.'

'Don't you?'

'No, I don't. In any case, I rather think I'm an agnostic, so it's a pointless line of argument.'

'Don't be disingenuous, Nelly.'

Nelly coloured angrily, and raised her eyes to Hester. 'OK. What do you think I should do, then? Be an uncaring shit, and walk by on the other side?'

'Try doing absolutely nothing. Try letting people go to hell in their own way.'

'You mean Hugo?'

'Of course I mean Hugo; who else? Try not to emasculate him, so to speak. Don't reduce him to being inadequate, either in your eyes, or his own.'

'But I've *never* thought him inadequate. Never, ever.'

'Haven't you?' said Hester quietly.

'Is that what this whole thing has been about?'

'What do *you* think, Nelly?'

Hester looked at the kitchen clock: twenty past one. 'Have you eaten?' she asked.

'I had a coffee on the plane.'

'Are you flying back today?'

'Yes, I'm on duty tomorrow. I've got a flight this evening.'

'Well, I don't know about you, but I'm rather hungry. Shall I make an omelette?'

'How kind of you; thank you.'

While Hester prepared the omelette, Nelly poured two glasses of wine, following Hester's instructions, and put bread and cheese on the table. After they had eaten, Hester made coffee and took Nelly into the sitting-room.

342

Both women felt tired and rather bruised by their encounter, and Hester quite wished that her visitor would now go, and allow her to regain her usual internal composure. But Nelly, apparently oblivious of the fact that she was seriously interrupting Hester's working day, showed herself to be in no hurry to depart. She sat silently in Hugo's chair, allowing herself to be soothed and refreshed by the peaceful atmosphere of Hester's room, and beginning to understand what it was that brought Hugo back here so frequently.

Hugo and his daughters sat on the floor in front of the drawing-room fire at *Les Romarins*, playing Racing Demon. In spite of the fire and the comparative mildness of the weather, the house felt damp and cold and the children wore thick sweaters with their cord trousers, even indoors, and sometimes Hugo had the feeling that it was actually colder inside the house than out. Una-Mary seemed unaware of the chill and wore more or less her usual attire, give or take the odd extra cardigan or muffler. It was warmer in the kitchen, where Elsie was preparing lunch, and would be warmer still when Nelly arrived and got the old black range going. Hugo did not feel capable, or even much inclined to have a go at it himself, dreading the probable outcome, a kitchen full of evil-smelling black smoke, and frightful floating black smuts all over the ceiling and walls, and clinging to the several dozen ironstone plates arranged on the long shelves of the dresser.

At one o'clock sharp, they sat down to lunch in the freezing dining-room. Una-Mary sat at the head of the table, while Hugo served the stew and potatoes from a sideboard, with Phyllida carrying the plates to the table.

Hugo sat down in his place opposite his mother-in-law and shook his napkin over his knees. Una-Mary said grace and they began to eat. At once, Hugo noticed that Gertrude had not picked up her knife and fork. She leaned against the back of her chair, looking drowsy.

'What's up, Gertie?' he said. 'Not feeling hungry?' Gertrude looked at him vacantly, as if wondering who he was. 'Don't you feel well, darling?' Hugo got up, felt the girl's forehead, and looked anxiously at Una-Mary.

'Temperature?'

Hugo nodded. 'Yes, she's awfully hot.'

'Phylly,' said Una-Mary, 'run up to my bathroom, please darling. There's a thermometer in the cabinet. Don't drop it, will you, and don't run.'

In a couple of minutes Phyllida returned, and Hugo took Gertrude's temperature: 40. He showed the thermometer to Una-Mary, without shaking it down.

'Better not take any chances, Hugo, especially in the winter; a fog might come down at any time. Look on the hall table, you'll find the emergency services number. Ring them and they'll send the helicopter and get her to St Peter Port and the hospital. I'm sure that's best.'

While Hugo was phoning, Una-Mary sent Sophie to fetch Gertrude's woollen dressing-gown, and the plaid rug from her own dressing-room. She took the sick child onto her knee and cradled her in her arms, while Phyllida fetched a bowl of cool water and a flannel, and bathed Gertrude's burning forehead and hands, in the hope of reducing the fever. She seemed to be slipping into unconsciousness, and her breathing was rapid and laboured. Hugo came back into the dining-room, nodded to Una-Mary and held up five fingers, twice.

'Pack a bag quickly, Hugo. You must go with her, of course. Phylly and I will cope here, don't worry.'

Hugo went to the kitchen, took the torch from its hook by the back door, explained the situation to Elsie, and asked her to go and stand outside the garden gate, and start flashing the light on and off as soon as she heard the helicopter approaching the island. She took the torch and ran outside without a word, and disappeared round the side of the house towards the garden gate. Hugo raced upstairs, flung his pyjamas, dressing-gown and shaving things into a grip, and hurried down again just as the clack-clack of the helicopter's rotor-blades announced its arrival in the field on the other side of the garden wall. Hugo picked up Gertrude, followed by Phylly with the grip, and ran towards the garden gate, just as it opened and two paramedics carrying a stretcher came through it.

'It's all right,' said Hugo, 'I've got her.'

'Right, sir, carry on,' said the senior man, taking the grip from Phyllida and running after Hugo.

In two minutes they were airborne and clacking away over the dull grey sea to Guernsey. Phyllida watched until the helicopter became a tiny speck in the sky, then she took Elsie's hand and went back into the house.

'We must finish our lunch,' said Una-Mary, robustly.

'Must we?' said Phyllida. She felt as though she had a stone in her stomach.

'It's better,' said her grandmother, 'really.'

Sophie opened her mouth to complain that the food had gone cold, met her sister's stern, forbidding gaze, changed her mind and began to eat.

'It could be meningitis, or it could be a particularly nasty virus. It's difficult to tell when the child is semi-conscious and unable to co-operate in assessing

345

the symptoms. She's obviously very dehydrated, so we'll put her on a drip. I've taken some blood and sent it to the lab for analysis, but we'll treat her with antibiotics in any case, to be on the safe side, and keep her under observation.' The doctor looked at Hugo kindly. 'I have young children myself, I know how you must be feeling; you must try not to worry. Is your wife not with you?'

'No,' said Hugo tiredly. 'She's a doctor herself. She's on duty at her hospital in London until Christmas Eve, then she'll be here.'

'I see. Well, if you want to telephone her, please use the phone in my office, it'll be less public.'

'Thank you, that's very kind. I'll do that.'

He sat with Gertrude, who now seemed to be deeply asleep although still breathing heavily, and watched the saline pack, suspended on its chrome hook, dripping hypnotically into the tube attached to the hypodermic needle inserted into the back of her hand, held in place by a thick adhesive bandage. A nurse came in carrying a stainless steel kidney-shaped dish containing a syringe. She switched off the drip, detached the tube and slowly administered the antibiotic through the hypodermic needle, a massive dose to Hugo's untutored eye.

'That should do the trick,' she said cheerfully, reconnecting the drip and smiling reassuringly at Hugo.

'I wonder if you'd mind staying with her for a few minutes? I must phone my wife, she's in London.'

'Of course. Don't worry, we'll keep an eye on her.'

Hugo took his pocket-book from his jacket, and went to the doctor's office to telephone Nelly at the hospital. After a long wait, while they tried to locate her, he was put through to the ward sister.

'I'm sorry, Dr Turnbull isn't in today, it's her day off.

346

She'll be in tomorrow, though, or would you like to leave a message?'

'Oh, how stupid of me, I should have thought of that, I'll get her at home. I'm so sorry to have been a nuisance.'

'No problem,' said the sister. ' 'Bye.'

Hugo rang off, then dialled his home number, but there was no reply. He looked at his watch: twenty-five past two. She must be out, he thought, probably Christmas shopping, I'll try again in an hour. He tried the number at half past three, and again at four, with no success. He thought of Una-Mary and the two girls anxiously waiting for news at *Les Romarins*, and dialled the number. Una-Mary must have been hovering quite near to the telephone, for she answered almost at once.

Hugo explained to her what was happening. 'She's asleep, but still very hot, poor little thing. I expect it takes a bit of time for the antibiotics to work.'

'Yes, it would do. Thank heaven you got her into hospital.'

'There is just one thing,' said Hugo. 'I don't like to take over the doctor's telephone. I've been trying to contact Nelly all afternoon. Apparently it's her day off, but she's not at home, either. I wonder if you could keep on trying the number for me, and tell her what's happened?'

'Yes, of course I will, gladly. And when I get her, I'll give her the hospital number and she can phone you direct.'

'Thanks very much. I really don't like leaving Gertie, even for five minutes, though the staff are very good; she's in safe hands.'

'I'm sure she is.'

'I'd better go; love to the others.'

'And love to you, my dear.' Una-Mary put down the

phone. Phyllida and Sophie stood close to her, looking anxious. 'Try not to worry, darlings, she'll be better soon,' she said, sounding a great deal more confident than she felt.

'I wish Mummy was here,' said Sophie, looking as though she might cry.

'She soon will be,' said her grandmother briskly. 'Phylly, pull up that chair for me will you, darling? Sophie, you go and ask Elsie to make us a cup of tea, there's a good girl.'

Sophie departed, glad to have something to do, and Phyllida brought the chair so that Una-Mary could sit while she telephoned. For the next hour she dialled the London number every ten minutes, with increasing exasperation and anxiety. She even got the engineer to check that the line was working properly. She sat staring at the big black silent telephone, feeling helpless. Then quite suddenly, she guessed where Nelly was. She remembered the name: Hester Rodzianko; the friend with whom Hugo had been staying in the south of France when Nelly had to phone him with the news of his parents' murder. That's it, she thought, that's where she'll be. The silly child has taken advantage of Hugo's absence to have a day-trip to Paris and warn this woman off. Quite calmly, she got through to continental directory enquiries, gave the name, said she thought the person lived on the Ile St-Louis in Paris, and in a couple of minutes the helpful girl gave her the number and the codes. Una-Mary sat for a moment, looking at the number she had written on the message pad, then she picked up the phone once more, and dialled.

'*Oui?*'

'Mme Rodzianko?'

'Speaking.'

'My name is Tanqueray, I am the mother of Nelly

Turnbull. Please forgive me if I am disturbing you unnecessarily, but I am trying to contact Nelly; her little girl is in hospital. I thought that she might possibly be with you?'

'I am so sorry to hear it. Hold the line a moment please, I'll get her for you.'

The next two days crawled by at *Les Romarins*. Nelly had flown straight from Paris to Guernsey which was a great relief to Una-Mary; nevertheless she did not wish to be far from the telephone, and Phyllida and Sophie seemed anxious to remain close to her. She managed to persuade them to go out into the garden and help Alain dig up the Christmas tree from the vegetable-garden, plant it firmly in its big plastic pot and carry it into the drawing-room, ready for decorating. Alain had grown on this tree for a good many years now, and every Twelfth Night he replanted it outside, with a good dollop of well-rotted manure to encourage its survival. It was not a particularly beautiful specimen, but the children were attached to it and would have been sorry if it had died. Alain and Elsie untangled the fairy-lights and tested them, before festooning them through the branches of the tree. Then the two girls began the task of decorating it, which occupied the major part of a day, since they both had strong ideas about the correct disposition of each shining coloured-glass ball, golden angel or silver star. At last it was finished, but they did not fix the big tinsel star to the top of the tree, or switch on the lights. Christmas Eve was the proper time for that, and in any case, no-one felt like doing it until they had better news of Gertrude.

The next day was Christmas Eve, and the two girls

sat on the floor in the drawing-room making pink, mauve and green chains from packets of gummed paper bought specially for the purpose at the village store. With a good deal of mild bickering, and bossiness on Phyllida's part they managed to produce a dozen long chains. These had rather a tendency to come unstuck and had to be reconnected with the help of a Pritt stick, some of which mysteriously transferred itself to the carpet. At last the job was finished and they asked Elsie to come and help them pin up the decorations, which she did with her usual good humour. She too was glad of any diversion, for Gertrude had always been her own particular favourite of the girls, and she was gripped with a horrible, stomach-churning fear. Una-Mary looked around her drawing-room, made hideous by the ugly paper-chains, so laboriously manufactured. She smiled tolerantly, but could not help regretting that Nelly's guiding hand had not been there to help them avoid the worst excesses.

That night, while the girls were having their bath, Hugo telephoned to say that Gertrude was conscious, and her temperature had come down.

'Thank God,' said Una-Mary, and tears pricked her eyes.

'Amen to that,' said Hugo.

'Happy Christmas, my dear boy.'

'And to you; and thank you for everything, you've been wonderful. I'll get Nelly to ring later, if I can. Trouble is, she won't leave Gertie, even for a minute.'

'Don't worry about it; don't bother her. We'll all talk tomorrow. Goodnight, Hugo. Thanks so much for ringing.'

'Goodnight, and love to Phylly and Sophie.'

Una-Mary put down the telephone and stood up. She

picked up her stick and walked quite briskly to the kitchen, where Elsie was preparing supper: fried fish and chips. She was cooking the chips in the hope of tempting the appetites of the anxious children, and even Una-Mary now found that the smell made her feel hungry.

'Good news, Elsie. She's conscious, thank God, and the fever is less.'

'Oh, ma'am, thank heaven!' Elsie turned towards Una-Mary, her eyes bright. 'I've been that worried.'

'So have I, very worried indeed.' She went to the fridge and took out a cold bottle of tonic. 'I think we both deserve a drink, Elsie. Gin all right for you?'

'Thank you, ma'am. A gin would just settle me nicely.'

At the hospital Christmas Day passed slowly. Gertrude lay quietly, dozing most of the time, not speaking very much as her throat was still painful and it hurt her to talk. Her temperature was now sub-normal, which Nelly said was par for the course after a very high fever. She and Hugo sat on either side of her bed, saying little, Hugo holding Gertrude's free hand and both smiling at her reassuringly whenever she opened her eyes. In the afternoon, they heard carols being sung in one of the wards, and a little later a priest put his head round the door, then came into Gertie's room, stood at the foot of the bed, said a short prayer, blessed them and left them alone. It was all too much for Nelly, and tears began to slide down her face. She got up from the bedside, desperate not to let Gertrude see her upset, and went and stood in the corridor. After a few moments, Hugo came out of the room and put his arms round her, holding her close.

'It's all right, darling,' he said quietly, 'she's going to be all right, don't cry.'

At this, Nelly began to weep again and she buried her face in Hugo's chest, soaking his shirt with her tears. 'I feel so guilty,' she sobbed incoherently, 'I should have been here.'

'It doesn't matter, you're here now. We're all together, that's the important thing, isn't it?'

Nelly looked at Hugo sadly. 'Is it really the important thing?'

'Of course it is.' He tightened his arms round her.

'I was so terribly frightened,' she said.

'So was I,' said Hugo, and kissed her.

'But it was you who coped, Hugo.'

'So it was,' he agreed, sounding surprised, 'so it was.'

Nelly put her hands on either side of his face and kissed him. 'I'd better phone Ma and the girls, hadn't I?'

'Good idea,' said Hugo. 'Give them my love.'

In Paris, the Christmas season was being celebrated with the usual brilliance and excitement, the shops and restaurants blazed with light, and beautifully arranged special promotions brightened every street. The Ile de la Cité and the Ile St-Louis looked even more ravishing than usual, seeming to float on the river in a sea of light. Basil and Olivia spent a happy couple of hours shopping together in the Rue St-Louis-en-l'Ile, buying their contributions to the Reveillon dinner they were planning to share with Hester. They had discussed the question of whether to have an English, French or Russian Christmas and had settled on an English one, but on Christmas Eve rather than on the actual day. The Russian festival was in any case two weeks later, and none of them had particularly strong feelings about it, one way or the other. Basil was feeling delightfully affluent, still a novelty for him, and he bought a glass jar of *foie-gras semi-conserve*, containing two lobes of the goose-liver, pink and luscious, lying in its pale blanket of fat. They bought two dozen oysters, a bottle of vintage champagne, and two bottles of St-Emilion to go with Hester's pheasants.

'What about a present for Hester?' Basil stopped outside a florist.

'I've got something for her; it's in my bag.'

'Oh, good. Shall I get her flowers?'

'What about that nice big white azalea? It's lovely, like snow. She'll love it, I know.'

'Are you sure?'

'Sure.'

Basil went into the little shop and bought the white azalea, and a small, fat bunch of violets for Olivia. 'This is getting out of hand,' he said. 'We can't carry any more.'

Laden with their shopping, they walked round to Hester's apartment, the December air clear and cold, the pavements wet from recent rain, but brilliant with reflected lights and cheerful with the bustle of last-minute shoppers and the magpie chatter of excited children. They found Hester preparing her brace of pheasants ready for the oven, and the kitchen smelt warm and aromatic with garlic and herbs. They put the *foie-gras* and the wine on the table, and Basil put the oysters and the champagne into the fridge.

'Good heavens, how extravagant!' said Hester, examining the *foie-gras*. 'But lovely, what a treat.'

'Not worried about the awful force-feeding thing?' said Olivia teasingly.

'No,' said Hester. 'I can easily turn a blind eye where food is concerned.'

353

'Quite right,' said Basil, laughing. 'So can I. Where do you want this? It's my rather modest seasonal offering to you.'

Hester took the shiny, star-spangled gift-wrapping off the package, revealing the white azalea, its frilly white petals faintly tinged with palest pink at the centre. 'It's really beautiful, Baz. Thank you, darling.'

Basil gave his mother a hug, and he and Olivia exchanged pleased smiles. 'I should think it probably needs a long drink, poor thing,' said Olivia.

'Good idea.' Hester took a large Chinese bowl from the cupboard, and gave it to Olivia. 'Put it in this bowl, on my work-table, near the window. It shouldn't get too warm, should it?'

Olivia put the plant in its terracotta pot into the Chinese bowl, gave it half a litre of water and carried it through to the sitting-room.

'Shall I open the oysters?' said Basil.

'Yes, please do.' Hester had put her best Moustiers service on the table, and he prised open the oysters and arranged eight in their half-shells on each plate. Hester cut two lemons into wedges, arranged them with the oysters and put the plates in the fridge.

'Your fridge is far too small,' said Basil.

'It suits me when I'm on my own.'

'Well, you're not always on your own now, are you? I must get you a new one.' He looked at the clock. 'It's nearly eight o'clock; what time are we eating?'

'About nine-thirty, I thought. With all this lovely food and drink, it will be Christmas Day before we finish, won't it? What do you think?'

'Great. I'd rather like to take Olivia to Dad's church. Not especially to a mass or anything; just so that she has a feeling of the atmosphere. I've never forgotten going there with you and Dad.'

354

'Why not? Good idea.'

'Do you want to come?'

'No, no. I'll stay here, and get on with the dinner.'

'Sure?'

'Quite sure. I'll be fine here, Baz. Thanks all the same.'

Olivia and Basil took the *métro* to Courcelles and walked down the Rue Daru to the Russian Orthodox Cathedral. Behind its protective black railings, the tall white building rose cliff-like into the night sky, its gilded onion-domes shimmering in the light of the street-lamps. Inside, the dark interior was partially illuminated by the glimmer of hundreds of orange-coloured tapers, burning in large brass circular stands. They stood for a moment, their eyes adjusting to the gloom. Presently they became aware of the life-size icons of the saints painted on the walls behind the banks of guttering orange candles. The icons seemed to take on a palpable reality, and almost appeared to move behind the warm leaping flames of the burning tapers. A few old ladies were lighting candles and saying their prayers in fast, sibilant whispers, crossing and recrossing themselves as they did so, occasionally bending down to touch the ground. The wavering smoke from their candles carried their prayers up into the dome, high above their heads to the smoke-blackened, barely visible icon of the Creator. Basil and Olivia walked slowly and quietly from one candlelit shrine to the next, taking care not to disturb anyone.

'Is it OK if I light a candle?' she whispered.

'Yes, of course.' Basil put money in the box, chose two long candles and gave one to Olivia. They lit them from the little flame that burned in a small brass reservoir, and stuck them into two empty sockets. They stood side by side, watching their candles burning, thinking of their own dreams and desires, then Basil put his hand into his coat pocket, his fingers closing over a piece of stiff white paper folded many times to form a small, square package. He held it concealed in the palm of his hand for a moment, then turned to Olivia and offered it to her. She took the little package, giving him a quick, questioning glance.

'Open it,' he whispered.

Slowly, she unfolded the paper, finally revealing two plain gold rings, one smaller than the other. She picked up the larger ring. 'Is this one for you?'

'Yes, if you will give it to me.' They looked at each other seriously for a long moment, then he held out his hand and she slid the ring onto his finger. He took the small ring and put it onto Olivia's finger. It fitted perfectly. He bent and kissed her. 'Happy Christmas, darling,' he said softly.

She looked up at him, her face rosy in the hypnotic glow of the candles, her blue eyes full of love and trust. 'Happy Christmas, Baz.'

A few minutes later, as they walked back towards the *métro*, Olivia admired her ring, shiny and new in the lamplight. 'How did you guess the right size, Baz?'

'It wasn't a question of guessing, I just knew.'

'How could you?'

'I reckon I know my way around you without a map, now.'

'Baz! That's very sexist of you!'

'Is it really? Sorry, do you mind?'

'No, I don't.' She laughed, and began to run. 'Come on, race you to the *métro*.'

Hester opened the jar of *foie-gras*, and carefully extracted one of the two lobes of the whole goose-liver. She cut it into fat diagonal slices and arranged them on a dish. With so much other rich food, she thought, it'll be best to eat it quite simply, with warm toast, and of course, the champagne. Then would come the oysters, and after that the pheasants, now roasting slowly in the oven. She had made creamed potatoes to go with the birds, and these were keeping hot in a covered dish, along with the dinner-plates. She opened the oven door and basted her birds carefully. They smelt delicious and were turning a delicate golden colour under their jackets of fat bacon, and a thin fragrant gravy was already collecting in the roasting tin beneath the trivet. She washed up all the dirty cooking-pans, and put everything away. Then she opened the window for a few minutes to let out the steam, and began to set the table for dinner. She spread the beautiful linen cloth, and put the old Russian silver candlesticks in the middle of the table, with new tallow candles. She set out her mother-in-law's ornate silver knives and forks, the best glass and china, and the silver salts.

When the table was finished, she poured herself a glass of wine and went to the sitting-room, taking with her two heavy glass tumblers and two candles. Carefully, she stuck the candles into the tumblers, lit them and set one on each of the deep window-sills. They shone out into the night, just as her mother's Christmas Eve candles had done in England, so long ago. She opened the window next to her easel, making the candle leap in the draught, and sat for a few minutes drinking her wine and enjoying the cool, reviving air.

She looked up at the cold starry sky, through the bare branches of the lime-tree, and thought of Hugo's little girl, lying ill in hospital. Dear God, she thought, haven't they suffered enough? Don't take the child from them, too. Turning from the window, her gaze fell on the beautiful white azalea, which Olivia had placed next to the photograph of George as a little boy, holding the hand of his mother. She closed her eyes and willed him to fill the room and give back to her his warm, bearded, comforting presence: to let her smell his smell, and feel his strong arms around her once more.

Slowly, painfully, she realized that he had gone from her; was no longer there. A dull fear engulfed her, and anger. Why have you left me here all alone? she asked her dear, dead husband. I suppose you think I don't need you any more, that you're free to go? Perhaps you *want* to go anyway, how the hell do I know? Tears of grief and regret for the lost past filled her eyes. It's my own stupid fault, I've let other people crowd him out. I've allowed myself to become involved again, with Baz and Olivia, with Hugo. What a fool I am. I was perfectly happy all alone here with George, I was managing very well. Hester blew her nose and finished her drink in one swallow. Bugger it, she thought with a flash of irritation, now I have to start all over again, worrying about people, caring, getting hurt. It's only when you've lost everyone you care about that you become bomb-proof and cease to be vulnerable, she thought sadly, knowing that fundamentally she deeply regretted the loss of that quiet, desirable state.

And yet, when she heard the footsteps of Baz and Olivia in the courtyard below, and their laughter, she smiled. She went to the window and looked down at them, Baz so like George at that age, Olivia a little bit like herself. They looked up at her, their arms round each other, smiling.

'Merry Christmas, Hester.'

'You too, my dear ones.'

Chapter Eighteen

Giò remained in Paris for Christmas. Anna and Patrick had invited him to go to Normandy with them, and spend the holiday with Patrick's father, but he had refused, preferring to hang around, watching the comings and goings of Baz and Olivia from a discreet distance. When he wasn't doing that, he lay on the big red sofa in his apartment in the Place des Vosges, willing the telephone to ring, desperately hoping that Baz would keep his promise to come round and see him. But Baz did not telephone and he did not come. Giò did not dare to phone him at Hester's number, and there was no reply from Olivia's phone at Grands-Augustins. He felt himself slipping into a deepening black hole and did nothing to prevent it. He did not eat, but drank quite a lot and slept very little. He had a disgusting taste in his mouth but did not clean his teeth. He thought he had never been so unhappy in his life, and had never felt so totally apathetic and powerless to drag himself out of his depression. He wished fervently to die; to go to sleep and not wake again to this anguished state of mind. Even his little cat had deserted him, and had been absent since Christmas Eve. Probably dead, lucky thing, he thought.

Giò always closed *Le Patrimoine* for Christmas, partly to give his assistant a decent break, partly because very few people were looking for antiques during that period.

By the fifth day after Christmas he felt so ill, so light-headed with starvation, that when the telephone did ring he could only just manage to get up from the sofa and answer it.

'Hello?'

'Giò?' It was his mother, in Souliac. Disappointment flooded through him. He tried to speak, but could not.

'Giò, darling? Are you all right? Are you ill?'

'Just flu,' he croaked.

'Oh darling, poor you. Is there no-one to look after you?'

'No, everyone's away.'

'Giò, get a taxi and get the next TGV. We'll be at Avignon to meet you. Can you manage that?'

'OK, Ma. Thanks; perhaps I should.'

'Good. Don't hang about, now. Come at once. Do you hear me, Giò?'

'I hear you.' He heard a scratching at the French windows and saw his cat peering through the glass. It saw him and stepped delicately through the cat-flap. 'Is it OK if I bring Cat?'

'Yes, of course, darling. Just come.'

'OK, I will.'

Even before the train reached Avignon, he felt a little better. He had eaten a sandwich and had a coffee, resisting the temptation to have another drink. Cat was imprisoned in his travelling basket, growling furiously under the lid, making both Giò and his fellow-travellers slightly nervous. But soon after Lyon the sky became blue, warm sunshine poured into the carriage and in spite of himself, he began to feel his spirits lifting a little.

Robert, his father, had laid the fire in the *salon* before going to meet the train, and after supper the three of them took their coffee up there and settled themselves comfortably beside the blazing oak logs. Stroking his sleek little cat, which had recovered its self-possession, Giò sat on a cushion on the floor, practically inside the great carved limestone chimneypiece. Domenica sat close to Robert on the sofa, and studied her son covertly, recognizing the signs of anguish, the hollows under his cheekbones, the blue shadows beneath his eyes. In the rosy light of the fire his pallor was not so evident, but she observed with a touch of sadness how much greyer his hair had become since the summer, when he had last stayed with them. His nose looked narrow and rather pinched and had permanent little red marks on either side of the bridge, caused by the spectacles he now wore for reading. This too was a new departure and Domenica leaned against Robert, closed her eyes and sighed. Giò, her best-loved child and adored son was getting old at last, was no longer beautiful. He looked worn and tired, frayed at the edges, forlorn.

'Sleepy?' Robert put his arm round her and kissed the top of her head.

'Mm. It's the fire, and the lovely food and wine.'

'Yes, Dad, thanks.' Giò raised his eyes and smiled at his father. 'You've become a really terrific cook, it was great.'

Robert laughed, but he looked pleased. They sat quietly for a little longer, lulled by the peace and the warmth. Then Domenica gave a slight snore.

'Come on, old thing, it's past your bedtime,' said Robert, and they got slowly to their feet, putting their glasses and cups on the tray. They looked at Giò, still sitting by the fire, nursing his cat.

'Goodnight, old chap. Sleep well,' said Robert.

'Is it OK if I sleep here, in front of the fire? I used to love doing that when I was a kid, and ill.'

'Of course, whatever you like, darling. But do get yourself a couple of blankets, won't you?' Domenica looked at her son, slightly concerned. 'Do you need aspirin or anything? Sorry, I'm treating you like a child.'

'Sometimes,' said Giò, 'it's quite nice to be treated like a child.'

The next day was New Year's Eve. After a cold and misty start, the sky became a deep flawless blue and the courtyard of the Presbytery was filled with warm golden sunshine.

'Bliss,' said Robert, opening the kitchen door to the courtyard, 'thank God we live here all the year round now.' He made tea as usual and took it upstairs to Domenica, casting a quick eye in passing at his son, still curled up on the sofa, fast asleep. He put the tray down on the bed-side table, rattling the cups to encourage Domenica, who untangled herself from the duvet uttering her familiar groans as she came to the surface. Robert flung open the shutters and the sunlight flooded in. 'Giò's still asleep,' he said, 'I'll leave him, shall I?'

Domenica sat up, looking thoughtful. 'Poor old love, he does look ghastly, doesn't he? I don't really believe the flu story, do you?'

Robert poured the tea, frowning. 'What do you think it is, then?'

'Same old thing, I imagine. Another duff affair.'

'Oh dear, poor old Giò. Are you sure?'

'The signs are pretty obvious, aren't they?'

'Well, we must do something to cheer him up, mustn't we?' said Robert. 'Maybe we should go out tonight, celebrate the New Year. Trouble is, everywhere will be booked solid, won't it?'

'Don't worry. He just needs time to get over it; a bit of peace and quiet. He should have sun, fresh air and exercise.'

'You make him sound like a dog, darling. Are *you* going to take him for walks, by any chance?'

Domenica laughed. 'No, my love, *you* are. You know you'll love it, anyway.'

'Well,' said Robert, 'that's true. It'll be a pleasant change to have someone to help me get the logs up, and dig the potatoes. Which is more than you ever do, you lazy old bag.'

'Not so much of the old,' said Domenica. 'I'm ten years younger than you, remember?'

After breakfast, Robert and Giò went to Honorine's vineyard, now Olivia's, to get salad and vegetables for the day, with the little cat running along beside them. The neighbour who had cultivated the vines for Honorine was now dead and the five hectares of land, situated about half a kilometre down the lane behind the village, had become sadly neglected. In any case, the vines were very old and almost totally unproductive. The adjoining properties had been newly planted with fresh young vines and looked in good heart.

'They've all taken the EU subsidy to grub up the old stock and replant,' said Robert. 'I believe there's talk of the wine getting its own *Appellation Contrôlée* in a few years, it'll be good for the growers and good for the consumers; much better wine.'

Robert was cultivating a patch of about ten square metres and was growing potatoes, carrots, onions and salad under plastic tunnels. He had a row of asparagus-crowns, also protected by the unsightly but useful polythene, and a row of melons, the small round orange-fleshed Cavaillon variety, sweet and honey-smelling. The dried wreckage of their summer stems and leaves lay on the ground, like driftwood on a shore, waiting to be raked up and burned. He dug up some potatoes and Giò brushed off the flakes of earth with his fingers and put them in the vine-basket they had brought with them. Robert extracted some carrots from the clamp he had constructed in September, then cut a *frisée* and pulled a handful of lamb's-lettuce from the tunnel. He picked three rather small specimens from the tomato-vine, now almost ceasing production.

'In a couple of weeks, I'll start sowing seeds if it's not too wet,' he said cheerfully, putting the tomatoes carefully into the basket with the rest of the produce.

Giò looked at his father's face, so brown and wrinkled under the tattered old khaki bush-hat that protected his balding head, and thought that he had rarely seen a man look so happy, so content with his lot. 'You really do love it here, don't you, Dad?'

Robert drove the fork into the soft beige-coloured earth and looked around him at the vineyards, the *garrigue* and the blue mountains of the Cévennes beyond. 'I do, Giò. My only regret is that I didn't get my roots down here a lot earlier, before I was too knackered and old to cultivate a real vineyard. That's what I would really love to have done.' He looked around at the ruins of Honorine's vines and shook his head sadly. 'Too late now, I'm afraid.'

The cracked bell of the church clock struck twelve and they walked back to the Presbytery together, up the lane to the gate in the rear wall. They went in through the garage to the back courtyard, where Domenica had already set the table for lunch under the fig-tree.

She emerged from the kitchen carrying a steaming

364

black pot of pasta and beans. 'Good timing,' she said, putting the heavy pot in the centre of the table.

'*Pastis?*' Robert looked at Giò, the bottle poised.

'Thanks.' Giò picked up the *carafe* of water and slowly poured some into his glass, watching the clear fluid turn a milky greenish-white. He took a sip of the anise-smelling drink and felt its warmth as it ran down his throat and into his stomach. The sun felt hot on his shoulders, almost burning the skin through his cotton shirt, and he was surprised by the realization that he was no longer in quite so much pain. He sat down hungrily, and began to eat.

After lunch he took the dishes to the kitchen, refusing offers of help. Then he fed his cat and went back to the courtyard. His father and mother lay in their old cane chaises-longues, she dozing in the sunshine and he reading the previous week's *Sunday Times*. Robert looked up as Giò approached. 'Don't know what the UK is coming to,' he said. 'I'm glad I don't live there any more.'

'Why bother to buy the paper if it gets up your nose?'

'Don't ask me; just habit, I suppose. The book pages aren't bad.'

'Do you buy the books?' asked his son slyly.

'No,' said Robert, and laughed. 'No time for reading, too much to do.'

'I think I'll just go for a walk,' said Giò. 'It's ages since I went right round the *périphérique* and I could use the exercise. Come on, Cat.'

He went out through the garage to the back lane, followed by the little black cat, which bounced along, enjoying the space, the lack of traffic and absence of people. When he reached Honorine's vineyard, Giò sat down on a rocky outcrop projecting from the grass verge and looked around at the run-down, weed-choked field, with Robert's little patch so neat and trim in one corner. All through lunch, an idea had been slowly developing in his mind and he began to weigh up the pros and cons. What if he were to buy or rent the vineyard from Olivia, grub up the old vines and replant with better stock, like the other growers in their district, and profit by the *Appellation Contrôlée* status in due course? Maybe negotiate to buy more land, increase the holding? *Le Patrimoine* marched along pretty steadily these days and his assistant was more than capable of running the place on her own. In the old days Domenica had spent the greater part of her time combing the countryside for antiques, and Giò had brought the van from Paris every couple of weeks and taken the stuff back to the shop. This system had worked well until his parents had decided to live together again, first in London, then permanently at the Presbytery. He had been happy for them, but it had made life much more difficult for him. He had tried employing local runners, but inevitably they ripped him off and his profit margins had grown correspondingly smaller. He looked at Cat, sitting on the ground beside him, his ears twitching, contemplating the view.

'What if I did the searching myself, Cat? Drove the van up every couple of weeks, stayed at Place des Vosges for a week or two? I could deal with the correspondence, the restorers, the accounts, all that; check out the display, plan the new one. We wouldn't want Charlotte taking over in that respect, would we?' The cat looked up at him, his green eyes like jade, and as inscrutable. 'What do you think? I reckon you'd like it here, part-time, Cat.' And so would I, he said to himself. He folded his arms round his legs as he crouched on his rock, resting his chin on his knees and gazing thoughtfully across the weed-infested vineyard.

The sun was beginning to sink in the west and the sky was slowly turning pink above the blue mountains. The black, gnarled, hairy stumps of the leafless winter vines cast long sharp shadows across the neglected field. Yes, he thought, I would love to be a *vigneron*, especially with Dad; I really would. In his mind's eye he saw the rehabilitated vineyard in summer, the brilliant emerald-green leaves of the vines speckled with blue copper-sulphate, the heavy bunches of purple grapes half-hidden beneath the sheltering foliage. It would mean back-breaking work he knew, and was not a job for a faint-hearted dilettante. But it's no harder than lugging sodding furniture around he said to himself, and a hell of a lot more satisfying than selling the stuff to silly rich cows who don't even appreciate what they're buying.

More importantly, Giò realized that it would be a means of distancing himself, at any rate for some of the time from the beautiful, cynical and seductive arcades of the Place des Vosges, with its beautiful, cynical and seductive inhabitants. After all, he would still be living there part-time; he would still be able to see his friends, maybe even Baz, but in a much less obsessive and humiliating way. I really must learn not to fall into the trap every time, he thought sadly. At my age, it can't be an edifying spectacle. Why can't I be just a little bit in love, not be utterly consumed by it like a silly teenage girl? Why not indeed? He looked down at his little cat, sitting so companionably beside him and smiled ruefully. 'You're such a clever old thing,' he said, '*you* tell *me*.'

He got up from his rock and stretched his legs before continuing his walk round the village boundaries, the cat trotting confidently along the dusty lane at his side. When they had completed the circuit of the village and

367

got back to the garage door Giò paused, his thumb resting on the rusty latch. He stood back and looked up at the small rear windows of the *remise* above the garage. Then he went into the building, cobwebbed and dusty with its earth floor and awkward wooden stairs to the floor above. The garage was never used for cars; Domenica and Robert always left theirs by the front gate in the Place de l'Eglise, and visiting family did the same.

'It could be perfect,' he said to the empty space. 'Near to Dad and Ma, but absolutely private.' He climbed the rickety stairs rather cautiously, and looked around the loft that had once been used as an extra holiday bedroom. I could easily put in a shower and a loo, and cupboards and stuff he thought. He crossed the room to the window overlooking the walled courtyard garden, opened the casement and then pushed back the heavy, creaking shutters. Below him, the ancient umbrella-shaped fig-tree spread its protective branches, and Giò recalled the leisurely family meals of so many long hot summers, seated round the battered fruitwood-table in the shade of that beautiful tree. He saw Honorine, his mother's friend and housekeeper for most of Giò's life, her short bent legs supporting her sturdy old body, her grizzled hair pulled back from her crumpled brown face, coming from the kitchen bearing an enormous festive platter, followed by the much younger Olivia, carrying baskets of bread, cheese and figs. He sighed. That was then, he thought. Now is now.

He closed the shutter and went downstairs. I'll have to put in a new stair but otherwise all it needs is a proper floor, maybe a fireplace and a cooking space along the end wall. It could be lovely; I could be rather happy here. From the staircase came a plaintive mew and he turned and saw that his cat had decided to get stuck halfway down, and was crouching against the dusty stone wall, looking helpless. 'Come on, you daft thing,' said Giò, picking him up and carrying him out into the courtyard, closing the faded-blue door behind him.

In the New Year the Turnbulls flew back to London. Eva had already returned from Germany; she had the house warm and welcoming for them, and a chicken casserole simmering in the oven. The children ran down at once to the kitchen to see her, followed by Nelly. Eva had brought a present from her mother, a big spiced apple-cake, and seemed overjoyed to see the girls again, although she could not conceal her shock and concern at Gertrude's worryingly wasted appearance after her illness. Her little legs were like matchsticks and her eyes huge in her thin face.

'We must feed you up, *liebling*,' Eva said, putting her arms round Gertrude and giving her a hug.

Gertrude, who was actually feeling perfectly well now, but was not one to miss an opportunity when it presented itself, looked up at Eva and smiled. 'I wouldn't mind a bit of apple-cake.'

'Why not? You must all be tired, after the journey?' Eva looked at Nelly for confirmation that this was all right, and Nelly smiled at her.

'Good idea. Thank you, Eva; it was very kind of your mother to think of us.'

'Shall I make some coffee for you? It's good with the cake.'

'Lovely, thank you. I'll just pop up and see whether Hugo would like some.'

Hugo was in his room, standing at the French window staring out at the darkening garden.

She went and stood beside him, and he put his arm

369

round her shoulders. 'Is anything the matter?' she asked quietly.

'No. Should it be?'

'I just wondered. You seem so quiet and detached, somehow.'

Hugo looked at her. 'I was thinking of Mum and Dad, and how easily we might have lost Gertie, too.'

'You must try not to dwell on it, darling,' said Nelly gently. 'Start working again; it's the best thing, really.'

'For you too, I expect?'

'Yes, for me too. Back to the hospital tomorrow.'

She left him sorting papers at his desk and returned to the kitchen. 'We won't interrupt Papa, he's busy sorting his mail.'

She sat down at the table with the girls around her. The beautiful apple-cake had been unpacked and now sat on a blue-and-white plate, waiting to be cut. Eva brought the coffee and a jug of milk for the girls, and sat down. She handed a knife to Nelly, to cut the cake. The coffee was strong and good, the cake delicious and Nelly looked at Eva with gratitude.

'Did you have a good Christmas, Eva?'

'I did, it was lovely. I went to ski with my brother; it was fun.'

'Oh, you are lucky,' said Phyllida. 'Could we come and stay with you, Eva, and go skiing?'

'Maybe sometime, if your mother wishes it, Phylly.'

'Sounds wonderful,' said Nelly, doing her best not to feel jealous.

'It is wonderful,' said Eva, looking straight at Nelly, her arm round Sophie, her eyes bright. 'But I am so very happy to be here with all of you again, it is also like home for me.'

'Is it really, Eva? I'm so glad.' Rather touched, Nelly

smiled at her. 'I really don't know what we'd do without you, you're a tremendous comfort to us all.'

'Mummy?' said Gertrude, sensing a good moment.

'Yes, darling?'

'You know that white puppy we saw?'

'Yes,' said Nelly warily, remembering.

'Well, if he's still there, could we have him? Eva would help us look after him, wouldn't you, Eva?'

Poor Eva, caught in a trap, looked helplessly at Nelly, saying nothing. Nelly laughed, and four pairs of eyes looked relieved. 'OK, I give up,' she said. 'If Eva agrees, it's fine with me, too.'

In early March, to his great surprise, Basil was sent to continue his training with the team of correspondents in Moscow. Olivia felt isolated and very lonely living at Pigalle by herself, but did not really want to return to Grands-Augustins, now that she had taken the major step of leaving home. Instead, she went round to see Hester and asked whether she could come and stay in Baz's room while he was away in Russia. Touched by her asking, Hester readily agreed. Like Hugo before her, Olivia was the perfect lodger. She was gone early in the morning, either to the Beaux-Arts or, at weekends, to Pigalle, where she sometimes worked, sometimes did a little cleaning, watering the plants and dreaming of Basil. In the evenings she went shopping with Hester and carried the basket back to the apartment. Usually, Hester cooked the supper with Olivia's help, but quite often Olivia did it alone, particularly when Hester's work was at a critical stage and she needed to carry on a little longer.

Olivia had always enjoyed good food and wine, and now she found herself increasingly interested in its

371

preparation. To her, it became a creative act, the association of colours and textures, the composition of each dish on the plate and the subtle choice of the wine that would enhance the meal. Most of all, she began to feel that the giving and receiving of food was a ritual, an act of love. While she chopped parsley, garlic and lemon-zest to a fine, scented *persillade* to add the finishing touch to her *osso bucco* she thought of Honorine in her grandmother's kitchen in Souliac, performing exactly the same pleasant task, and for the very same reason. She did not make a distinction in her mind, between the skill and concentration she would apply to the making of a drawing, and that given to the successful creation of a meal.

One night after supper Hester and Olivia sat watching the news on television. Suddenly, without warning, a brief item about unrest in Izbekistan appeared on the screen and there was Baz, his hair even wilder than usual, and wearing a flak-jacket. He was standing behind the correspondent who was interviewing a tired-looking elderly man in a grey overcoat. The little piece was over before they could collect their wits, and the anchorman in the studio introduced another story. Olivia felt cold with shock and surprise, and the enormity of Basil's having to wear a flak-jacket filled her with fear. She met Hester's eyes, speechless with the possibility of losing him to a sniper's bullet.

Hester smiled at her, a small tight sympathetic smile. 'Try not to worry,' she said. 'He'll be all right.'

'Dear God, I hope so,' whispered Olivia, twisting the ring on her finger.

That night, before she got into Basil's bed, she stood before his icon and asked the Blessed Virgin to protect him, to bring him back to her, and thus began a nightly habit from which she was to derive strength and comfort all her life.

On the first mild day of spring, when the almond-tree was in tentative bloom, Hugo sat in the garden planning his new book. After some absorbing reading on the subject, and discussion with his publishers he had decided to go ahead with his plan to write a biography of Marguerite de Valois. Beautiful and temperamental, the daughter of Catherine de Medici and with three sex-mad, power-hungry tearaway brothers, she had been manipulated and abused by all of them from an early age, both sexually and psychologically. Precipitated into the everlasting and frequent wars of religion which in the fullness of time culminated in the frightful Massacre of St Bartholomew, and spurred on by the lunatic ambitions of their appalling mother, this wild bunch killed as they fornicated: constantly and without mercy. Ordered by her mother, Marguerite was forced into marriage with Henri de Navarre, himself no mean political manoeuverer. In order to accede to the throne of France as Henri IV, he rapidly abjured his Protestant faith and became a Catholic, remarking casually that Paris was 'worth a Mass'. The new queen became celebrated throughout Paris not only for her many lovers – it was rumoured that her husband was the only man she did *not* sleep with – but for her considerable gifts as a poet. In 1599 she was repudiated by Henri and sent into exile in the Auvergne. Six years later she returned to Paris, built a huge palace on the Left Bank with a vast garden stretching to what is now the Musée d'Orsay, where she held her own court and continued to lead a colourful life in every sense of the word.

Hugo had the satisfying feeling that he had chosen a curiously contemporary subject, full of religious intolerance, incestuous relationships, sexual abuse and manipulation, murder and war. A great stack of history books was piled on the desk in his room and he was working his way through them, making notes as he went.

At eleven o'clock, as she always did, Eva brought him a cup of coffee, with the mail. He drank his coffee, then flicked through the small pile of letters. One of them had a Kenyan stamp and he opened it reluctantly, fearing that it would be yet another try-on from his father's bank, endeavouring to extract money from him. But to his astonishment and delight it was from Gabrieli: he and Margaret had called the bluff of the bank and their offer for the farm had been accepted. Hugo read the letter twice, then went into the house and telephoned Margaret at her office in Nairobi, to tell her how very glad he was to hear the news and wish them both the best of luck.

'Thank you, Hugo. I hope that when you come to see us it will not seem strange or very different to you. You will come, won't you? And Nelly too, of course.'

'Yes, of course we will, sometime. That would be wonderful, thank you. Tell Gabrieli that I will write to him, and give him my love.'

'I will, Hugo. Thank you for ringing. Goodbye.'

Hugo put down the telephone, and sat for a moment savouring a small feeling of triumph, for his father and for himself. That bloody bank, he thought, it's typical that I should hear the good news first from Gabrieli; what a shower they are. He went down to the kitchen where he found Eva slicing leeks and carrots. 'What are we having for supper tonight, Eva?'

'*Baeckeoffe*, is that all right?'

Hugo had no idea how the dish was made or what it contained, but he laughed. 'Sounds terrific. Will there be enough for the girls to stay up?'

'I can easily make it so, just put in more vegetables.'

'Will it be OK with champagne?'

Eva looked at him thoughtfully, her chopping-knife poised. 'Everything is OK with champagne, I think,' she said seriously.

The *Baeckeoffe* simmered away all day in the slow oven and in the evening Hugo and his daughters set the table for a party, decorating it with sprigs of almond-blossom and candles. At half past seven, Nelly arrived home from the hospital and got wearily out of her car. As she usually did, she glanced over the area railing to see what was happening downstairs and was surprised to see the festive table and her children looking pretty, with clean frocks and carefully brushed hair. What's going on? she wondered, as she went up the front steps and let herself into the house. She put her bags on a chair and hung up her jacket. She heard footsteps and Hugo ran up from the kitchen.

'Hi,' she said, smiling at him. 'How was your day?'

'It was wonderful, Nelly. Take a look at this.' He took the letter from his pocket and gave it to her.

She sat down on the stairs, unfolded the letter and read it. Then she looked up at him. 'That's marvellous, I'm so glad,' she said.

Hugo sat down on the stair beside her, and put his arm round her shoulders. 'Are you really?'

'Yes, of course I am. Very glad indeed,' she replied with an effort.

Hugo told her about his call to Margaret and her invitation to them to go out for a visit. 'Would you like that?'

'I'd love it.' She leaned against him and was silent for

a moment. 'You know, Hugo, since we've been back here I keep thinking about Lamu. I keep seeing that wonderful peaceful house; Farah and Mahommed; that beautiful empty beach; the warm clear sea. I really would love to go back there.'

'And so we will, one day, and we'll take the girls with us. On one condition, though.'

'What's that?'

'We'll go when I've made enough money to pay for the trip myself, OK? So don't start plotting.' Nelly laughed and turned her head to kiss him. Then they heard footsteps on the kitchen stairs and Phyllida appeared, looking bossy.

'Are you two coming down?' she asked severely. 'The dinner will be ruined.'

Postlude

Towards the end of March, Olivia contracted flu and had to spend a few days in bed. On the fourth day she was well enough to get up for supper and Hester cooked a comforting little dish of chicken, delicately seasoned with fresh young thyme and lemon juice, and made real English mashed potatoes. She was slightly worried at Olivia's appearance; she had lost weight and seemed listless and out-of-sorts. Obviously, she was at a low ebb, missing Basil badly, even though he was now safely back in Moscow.

'Olivia,' she said, as they sat in the warm kitchen eating their supper, 'I really ought to go to Ramatuelle for a few days, check everything out, make sure the house is ready for the summer tenants. I was thinking of driving down in Baz's car, but I must admit I do feel rather nervous about doing the trip on my own. I was wondering, do you feel like taking a little break and coming with me?'

Olivia raised her pale, unmade-up face and her sad blue eyes met Hester's. She was not fooled by the ploy to give her a little holiday, but very touched by the older woman's concern for her. She stretched out a hand and touched Hester's. 'What a good idea. I'd love to, thank you. And maybe we could make a detour, and stay at my house in Souliac as well? You could meet my grandparents; you'll like them, I know.'

'Why not?' said Hester, 'I'd love it. It'll do us both good to have a treat, and some sunshine. Shall we have a small Armagnac, to celebrate?'

Olivia laughed. 'Do you always have a drink to celebrate?'

'Always,' said Hester. 'But at least I don't smash the glass, as George used to do.'

Robert and Giò had bought a second-hand vineyard tractor, one of the ubiquitous little toy-like machines with flashing orange warning-lights used by all the local farmers, and had spent a week in the spring sunshine, well wrapped-up against the *Mistral* that had swept the sky to a deep intense blue, working their way through Honorine's vineyard, grubbing up the old vines. When two or three rows had been dragged from the hard stony ground, they hitched a trailer to the tractor and tossed the uprooted vines into it. Then they drove back to the Presbytery, unloaded the roots into a wheelbarrow and ferried them through Giò's half-finished *remise* house and stacked them in the log-shed at the back of the Presbytery.

'I reckon these will give us at least a couple of years' free fuel,' said Robert, wearing his complacent expression of self-sufficiency.

Giò smiled. 'Can you spare a few for my fire, Dad?'

'Of course, dear boy,' said Robert, 'why not?' He would have given Giò the sun, the moon and the stars if he had asked for them, and the partnership with his son had brought him not only an absorbing new interest but much unlooked-for happiness.

'Tell you what, Dad,' said Giò, as they chugged back to the vineyard to carry on with the work, 'we're going to have to buy or rent a barn soon. We've got loads more roots to store and we're going to have chemicals, spraying equipment, all sorts of stuff, plus the tractor and trailer. You name it, we need storage space for it.'

'It's true. I'll start asking around. Then we're going to have to decide whether to send our crop to the co-operative or be really ambitious and go for an independent enterprise.'

'What's your feeling, Dad?'

'Sending to the co-op is less hassle and much less work, of course. Maybe it's a bit daft at my age, but I'd really rather grow the very best aromatic vines, make our own wine and market it ourselves, wouldn't you?'

'It's more of a risk, of course, and we'd need a fair bit of financing for all the equipment and so on. I should think it would be wise to get in one of these new young travelling wine-makers. There's an Englishman who's making wonderful wine all over the Languedoc. We should get him involved, or someone like him. It will be money well invested, I'm sure.'

'Sounds like a good plan, Giò. If we're going to do that though, perhaps we should increase our acreage, don't you think? I'll start putting out a few feelers.'

'Yes, you do that. It was good of Olly to sell us Honorine's patch.'

'Well, I don't suppose she found it of any particular interest; just an unnecessary responsibility for her.'

'Still, it was a bargain, none the less. She didn't haggle.'

When all the vines had been grubbed up and the ones they couldn't store had been stacked in a tall heap in one corner of the vineyard, the serious ploughing could begin. For two days Robert drove the tractor up and down the field and Giò followed behind with the small plough, turning the hard, compacted earth. A couple of days later, early in the morning, the planting team arrived: M. Privas the *chef des vignes* and his two men. Robert drove the tractor, while M. Privas ploughed the furrows for the new vines, spaced at the correct intervals. Stakes were driven into the ground at either end of the furrows, and a stout cord was tied firmly between them to keep the planting straight. Then the bundles of new vines were unpacked from the van, and divided between Robert, Giò and one of the helpers. M. Privas took from the van a large wooden triangle, which he used like a wheel, turning it over and over along the line of the cord, the points of the triangle marking the planting hole of each new vine. The second man followed him, plunging a heavy hollow metal rod into each mark. After him came the planting team, slipping new baby vines, the size of a man's finger and tipped with scarlet wax, into the waiting hole and firming the earth solidly round each one.

At noon, they all took a swift lunch-break and the food was dispatched in ten minutes, since half the field remained to be done and dusk still fell at a comparatively early hour. All afternoon they toiled, up and down, with sweating brows and breaking backs. I must be nuts, thought Giò. The sun was setting in a red blaze behind the Cévennes as the team packed its equipment into the van and prepared to depart, refusing Robert's offer of a drink. '*Il est l'heure de manger*,' explained M. Privas as he shook hands, then jumped into his van and drove away.

Robert and Giò stood side by side looking proudly at their new vineyard. It looked beautiful, immaculate, the minute stumps of the baby vines standing up like a small army, the entire field bathed in the rosy light of the setting sun. They drove the tractor back down the lane to the Presbytery and parked it by the garage door, Robert insisting that they walk round the lane and go through the Place de l'Eglise and in at the front entrance, to get out of the habit of going through Giò's new house. They failed to notice the old Riley parked outside Olivia's house, so absorbed were they in congratulating themselves on their enterprise and cleverness and so busy making plans for the future. They pushed open the old green metal gate and entered the front courtyard, scraping their boots beside the wide double doors. Then they went into the kitchen together.

Domenica sat at the table, drinking a glass of wine with Olivia and Hester. 'Look who's here,' she said.

'What a surprise,' said Giò. 'Have you come by yourselves?' He looked at Olivia, his eyes bright, his face flushed.

'Yes,' she replied, 'all by ourselves. Baz is in Moscow.' She got up and gave Giò a kiss, and he hugged her hard, glad not to feel badly towards her any longer.

'Robert, my darling, come and meet Hester,' said Domenica. Robert shook hands, apologizing for their filthy state and poured wine for himself and Giò.

'God, I'm ravenous,' he said, 'what's for supper?'

'*Daube*,' said Domenica without enthusiasm.

'*Comme d'habitude*,' said Giò, laughing and sitting down next to Olivia.

'Why don't we all go to the café?' said Robert. 'After all that hard work I feel like a bit of a celebration, and we can always have the *daube* tomorrow, can't we?'

'Good idea, it's always better on the second day.' Domenica looked around her, entirely unmoved at the unspoken denigration of her culinary efforts, delighted to be once more in the company of those she loved best, her husband, her son and her grand-daughter, and already pretty sure that Hester, like Basil, would prove to be an enrichment to their lives.

Hester and Olivia stayed for two days in Souliac, duly admiring the new vineyard and Giò's conversion of the *remise*. They relaxed, enjoying the sunshine, the smell of the *garrigue* and the slow pace of village life. On the second evening Giò and Olivia walked up the back lane to the vineyard with the cat running along in front of them. At the iron bridge over the little river, overhung by the big old willow-tree they paused and looked down at the stream below. A pair of birds, flashed past them, darting like arrows along the surface of the water.

'Look,' said Olivia, 'the swallows are back.' She turned to Giò, shyly. 'Are you OK, Giò? You look a bit thin.'

'So do you, my love.'

Olivia laughed and put her arm through his in her old affectionate way. 'We make a fine pair, don't we?'

Giò looked at her sadly. 'Is he all right?'

'I don't know, really. He phoned once, but the line was awful. But you know Baz, don't you? When he's here, he's here. When he's there, he's there. One has to learn to live with that, somehow.'

'I'm glad we can be friends again, Olly.'

'So am I, Giò. I've missed you.'

The next day Hester and Olivia drove on to Ramatuelle, arriving in the late afternoon. They left the car in the car park and walked down into the Place de l'Ormeau. They went under the archway into the inner village, buying bread at the *boulangerie* on the way. Olivia was enchanted by the narrow streets twisting around inside the ramparts of the high hill-village, so unlike Souliac in every way. When they turned the corner and she saw Hester's little house crouched so snugly at the end of the cul-de-sac, she could not prevent herself from giving an exclamation of delight.

'Is that it? Really your house?'

'That's it.' As always, Hester was pleased at such a response to her treasured bolt-hole, and led the way to the door in the tower. Louise had been in and the place was aired, though slightly chilly, and she had left a stack of kindling and logs beside the fireplace. She had put milk, butter and eggs in the fridge, and vegetables in the rack.

'She's forgotten coffee,' said Hester, looking in the cupboard. 'Never mind, we'll go out and get some, and a chicken for supper. We'll just take the bags up, shall we?'

She led the way upstairs and showed Olivia the way to Baz's room, up its steep wooden staircase. She went into her own bedroom and put her bag down at the foot of the bed, already made and turned down for her by Louise, a small lump indicating the presence of a hot-water bottle. Hester smiled at this piece of kindness, took off her jacket and went out again to the landing. She went into the studio, closing the door behind her.

There in the fading light of evening, seated on his stool at the easel, his neck brown beneath his greying hair, his shoulders broad in his blue-denim workshirt, brush poised in his freckled hand as he contemplated the next stroke, was George. She crossed the room and put her arms round him, resting her cheek against his warm, strong back, and closed her eyes, full of relief and thanksgiving.

'There you are, my darling,' she said softly, 'I was wondering where you'd got to. I should have known you'd be here.'

THE END